APOCALYPSE

Gary W. Babb

APOCALYPSE

DOUBLE DRAGON

Chapter 1
(Preparing)

"HOLY Crap!" I bellowed, "Thank you Lord ... thank you...thank you!" I suppose this might be a typical shocked response for anyone winning $283,000,000 in the Powerball Lottery. I once checked the odds and discovered it was 173,000,000 to 1. Now I just became the (1) and became extremely wealthy. I had always said it would take Divine Intervention to win, but this was something else. Brin had given me the winning numbers. I played the numbers, even though I considered Brin to be full of shit. I would now have to change my opinion of him and accept that he must be correct in all the other things he had told me.

I met Brin in a Prepper website. I had posted the following:

I am convinced that a catastrophe (from nature or more likely man-made) of some sort will happen in the near future. I believe that the average person is totally unprepared and ignorant in the basic skills of "survival". I'm thinking the flow of events would happen like this:

1. Catastrophe happens – panic, fear, uncertainty, loss of hope
2. Infrastructure collapses – communication, electricity, water stop,... stores stripped clean, looting, law enforcement ceases, and the strong/bully segment emerge.

3. Average person huddles in their home/apartment hoping that everything will somehow come back to normal (or at least for as long as their personal resources last).
4. After about 3 days to a week of no food, the layer of 'civilized man' begins to crack and people begin to do anything necessary to acquire what they feel are the essentials.
5. The initial grouping would be at the church/family/close friends level, because of inherent trust.
6. People begin to carefully group to gain the protection of numbers... Groups will battle each other for available resources or power.
7. Areas more remote and miles from metropolitan cities should be in better shape, because in many cases these are rancher/farmers and as such have a better understanding of living off the land... plus, they stand a much better chance that what they have will not be ravaged by roaming gangs from the city due to the distances.
8. The folks in these remote areas may very well have the opportunity to come together (as neighbors which have helped each other in the past) and form a protective group of their

own which is charged with defending their "homeland".

9. The gangs will grow larger and canvas further out, and no one or group will be safe.

10. As food becomes more scarce, without the existence of law enforcement or organized armies, the gangs will kill to take what they want and become primitive. Civilization ceases to exist.

Brin asked me in an e-mail, *"What are you doing about it?"*

I responded, *"Well, nothing. I have plenty of ideas and plans, but unless I win the lottery I don't have the capital to do them."* I guess this random statement laid the groundwork for everything that followed. We got along well, and his enthusiasm transferred to me. We communicated via e-mails for weeks exchanging ideas, even plans, but it wasn't until last week that he came right out and asked me to partner with him to build an off-grid complex for survival and defense. I told him I would love to, but nothing had changed, and I didn't have the capital.

Brin asked, *"You are still waiting to win the lottery?"*

"Yep, that is the problem."

His next e-mail shocked me to the core. It said play these numbers in the Oklahoma Powerball Lottery on this date. When you win I will assume you

7

will then be my partner and will follow my guidelines.

Can he be for real or is this some kind of sick joke? Of course it's a joke, but the doubt remained. Certainly, I was curious enough to play the numbers, which I did, and incredibly I won! Now what? I'm committed but committed to what? I started to get scared. I better find out just what I have gotten myself into. Obviously Brin has some kind of power, but at least I'm the one with the $ 283,000,000. Maybe I'm the one with the power. Oh well, it's time to find out.

I sent an e-mail to Brin. It simply said, *"I won the lottery. Now what?"*

His response simply replied, *"Now you start building the off-the-grid compound ... quickly. I suggest that you deposit the money in several banks for diversity and protection, set up a $30,000,000 account with a stockbroker, immediately start negotiations with several of the major Muskogee/Tahlequah area contractors capable of building fast and, if necessary, can build night and day. I have developed detailed construction plans for the complex you described, which are attached to this e-mail. I have added and improved your plans to accommodate some of our needs."*

"I have also done some research on you and know you currently live in Muskogee, Oklahoma. This is an acceptable area of your country to base our complex. Through Google Earth I have also located a prime location in your area. As you will see on the attached map, this one hundred acres is on the banks of Lake Tenkiller just east of you. This

acreage also includes an island, two in fact. The big island provides the perfect protection for the main complex. It has water on three sides and access to the island from land will be by bridge, which will be a draw bridge, also for protection."

"You need to find an aggressive real estate agent to purchase this property for you. It could be complicated and difficult, so be ready to pay incentives and bribes. I discovered that you are 50% Cherokee Indian and are a member of the Cherokee Nation. This property is within the boundaries of the Cherokee Nation, so it might be beneficial to seek their help, possibly even partner with them."

"This is a good beginning. Good Luck."

Talk about panic, I have no idea what I have gotten myself into, and I did not respond to his e-mail. I figured I had plenty to do, and I could figure out what to say later. It took all the next day getting the money. I had to take off work to drive to Oklahoma City to claim it, and I remained doubtful until I actually had the certified checks in my hand. The IRS was standing in line to get the government's share, not to mention the State of Oklahoma. Between the two they took over $100,000,000 … unbelievable, but I finally was approved and paid. Like Brin suggested, I had them give me four checks. It was still hard to believe I had won that much money and kept staring at the checks in disbelief. By the time I returned to Muskogee I was a believer, especially when I deposited the checks into the Banks. The bank officials looked at me like I couldn't be for real, and I felt ten-feet tall. Luckily, a branch manager helped me set up the stockbroker account, but that's what Brin asked for. I still didn't know what I was going to do with it.

I was all smiles as I left the last bank. Being a poor man, I was not used to money, but I was learning fast. My wallet was full of $100 bills and blank checks, and the first thing I did was head to the GMC dealer and pick out a new, bright-red GMC 4/4 extended cab pickup. Well, it was the second thing I did. The first thing I did was quit my job. I always wanted to say, "Take this job and shove it." I didn't say it, but it was nice to know I could have. It was fantastic not to have to worry about the price for the pickup, and I didn't even haggle. As a business major in college, this was completely out of character for me. Usually I love to haggle price, but I figured this once I could live with it. When they asked me if I needed financing I of course said no and proceeded to write a check. Being a thirtyish looking Indian male, I'm sure they didn't take me serious at first, but when they called the bank on my check they became serious quickly.

With my scheduled chores done for the day I found the most expensive restaurant I could find. The waitress would be surprised at her tip today.

It was time to consider my situation. I had tried to keep my mind clear today, but it was time to consider some of the red flags waving in my head from the last conversation with Brin. Things just didn't seem to add up. Several times he had mentioned the need for speed on our project. I would have to find out more. Another thing bothering me was an apparent slip in the use of a word. Brin had said, "Your country", like he was not from this country.

Just where the hell was he from? But, I suppose the most troubling thing: Brin had delivered on providing the winning lottery numbers. How the hell did he do that?

My attention was focused inwardly upon my thoughts, but shockingly, it immediately turned to the gorgeous black-haired waitress. Wow, what a beauty. My concerns could wait, it was time to concentrate on some serious flirting. She had long curly black hair that shined in the dim light. Her smiling face lit up her light brown eyes. The tuxedo like white shirt and black skirt were filled out with a stunning figure that totally captured my attention.

Throughout dinner she returned often to check on me, and since the restaurant was slow, she even sat and visited, and I began to learn more about her. Janet Walsh was her name, and she was a senior at NE University in Tahlequah earning a degree in chemistry.

I got brave and asked, "What time do you get off? Maybe we can go get a drink somewhere."

Janet frowned and said, "I'm sorry. I have a boyfriend."

I said, "That's too bad. I would love to know you better."

When she came back to take my bill, I dished out two hundred dollar bills for a bill of $75.00. When she gave me a questioning look, I said, "The rest is for you. Keep the change." I always wanted to say that. When she returned with my receipt she leaned over and said, "My boyfriend is working out of town. Maybe we can go for that drink. I get off in an hour if you like."

"I would like that very much. I'll meet you outside in an hour."

I thought to myself, *"Wow! I can't believe my luck."* I then remembered my small apartment. I couldn't take her there. It was a dump. I took off to get some wine and a room in a nice place. That went quickly, and I was waiting in my new pickup when I saw her come out. I blinked my lights and got out to wait. I opened her door and helped her into the passenger seat, while I continued to appraise her beauty. She was shorter than I had expected, maybe 5' 2", maybe 115 lbs, with a round bubble butt and large breasts. In short, gorgeous. We talked easily as I drove to the hotel room. It didn't seem to upset her as I pulled into the hotel parking lot, seemingly expecting this.

Once we were in my room I popped the cork on a bottle of red and white wines. Janet sat on the bed and took the white, while I took the red. All the signs seemed good that this was going to be a good night. Janet had accepted the fact that I had taken her to a hotel, she accepted the wine and even set on the bed. Things were looking up.

We sipped our wine and talked. I was curious about her boyfriend, but I didn't want to bring up the subject, thinking that I didn't want her thinking about him. She, however, brought up the subject. She mentioned that they had been going out for a few months, but he worked much of the time out of town, and she hadn't seen him in over a month. Yep, this was going to be a good night. I moved from my chair to sit beside her on the bed, and I was

12

ready to make my move. Unfortunately, her cellphone started ringing.

Janet looked at her phone and said, "Shit! It's my boyfriend." It looked like she might just let it ring, but finally she said, "He knows I'm off work. I have to take it."

Graciously, I said, "Go ahead. I'll stay quiet."

She said, "Thank you," then "Hello." She was nervous but continued the pleasantries with her boyfriend. They were obviously catching up and talked about his work and her job, but slowly the conversation got more personal. I could tell when she said, "Yeah, me too. I miss you. Me too." Obviously, he was talking sexual to her and after a while she slowly began to respond. She didn't want it to happen with me there, but there was nothing she could do without him starting to ask where she was and why she couldn't talk. I watched her and slowly began to massage her neck. She stiffened up, but there wasn't much she could do. I felt her slowly begin to relax and gently pushed her back on the bed. She resisted at first, then allowed herself to lay back as she continued to talk softly. I heard her say, "My bra and panties." I knew then that he was undressing her on the phone and allowed my hands to begin undoing the buttons on her white blouse. She immediately grabbed her shirt with her free hand to stop me. She looked into my eyes and I into hers, then she dropped her hand away giving me access. I slowly began to unbutton all the buttons, pull the sides of her blouse back on either side, exposing her black lace bra and soft skin. My hands gently began rubbing and caressing her stomach. As I continued,

13

her breathing became heaver. I'm not sure if it was from me or his phone seduction, probably both. My hands slowly slid over her breasts and began caressing them. Janet was really getting into this now, and when my hands slid under her bra to cup her breasts she moaned loud. I lifted her bra and let her breasts free. Her nipples stood hard, and I rubbed my thumbs over them, then rolled them between my fingers and thumbs. She was breathing heavy and moaning almost continuously. I began kissing and licking all over her beautiful breasts. When I sucked her nipples she screamed.

She said into the phone, "Oh yes, keep talking to me. Keep doing these things to me."

I took this to mean keep doing what I was doing. I kissed down her stomach and wiggled my tongue deep into her navel. Her body began quivering. My hands slipped down and under her skirt and began slowly working her skirt up to her waist. She wore matching black lace bikini panties. Even though her panties were black I could see and smell her juices, and it was intoxicating. She kept moaning and talking, encouraging her boyfriend as I slipped her panties down and off her legs.

Janet said, "Hold on a minute, Danny. I need to remove my bra and panties and get naked for you." She lay the phone down and quickly set up and began removing her blouse, bra and skirt, then her panties. She leaned toward me and kissed me hard on my mouth, then wiggled back up on the bed and propped her head on a pillow. Janet looked at me, smiled and spread her legs. I smiled and dove between her hot thighs. I wrapped my arms under and around her thighs and spread them wide. She had picked her phone back up in time to moan heavily into it as I slid my tongue through her pussy lips. Her thighs quivered, and her pussy generated an abundant flow of sweet nectar. I wanted more, so I slid my hands under her butt cheeks and lifted her butt into the air and propped her up on my elbows. The angle was perfect and my mouth completely covered her bald pussy, as my tongue explored every inch of her center. When my tongue touched her hard clit, her pussy and thighs began to quiver violently. I sucked her button into my mouth, while rubbing it with my tongue. She began screaming and her entire body went into convulsions, her pussy flooded my mouth and face with juice, and her thighs clamped down hard on my head. I would say she had one hell of an orgasm. I heard her say, "Hell yes, I had an orgasm. Thanks."

When she calmed some she released my captured head and twisted off my propped hands to fall face down. Her and her boyfriend were chatting more calmly now, but I was screaming inside for release. I quickly straddled her thighs and began probing my dick between her butt cheeks. She was so wet I had no trouble finding her hot tunnel and sank deep into its depths. Her pussy was still quivering from her strong orgasm, as I began pumping into her. She was shocked but seemed to love it. Her butt cheeks and pussy muscles gripped my dick so hard I almost screamed, but I held it. I heard her say, "I made a mess. I have to go get cleaned up. Yeah, it was great. Talk to you soon. Love you, too."

Janet relaxed and grabbed hold of her pillow and held on screaming, while I pounded into her hot, tight pussy and butt cheeks. I was in such an excited state that it didn't take long before I exploded into her steamy and quivering pussy.

I finally rolled over beside her, and she cuddled up close and said, "What the hell did you say your name was?" We both started laughing hard.

I said, "My name is Mike Brannon."

Well, Mike Brannon, that is the most kinky and erotic thing I have ever experienced, and I'm about to show you how much I appreciated it."

That is exactly what she did for the rest of the night. She rode me like a cowgirl and each time I thought I was finished she always found a way to get me going again. It was unbelievable.

By mid-morning we were both exhausted. We showered together, dressed and said our goodbyes. Janet gave me her number with instructions to call her anytime, and I'm sure I will.

Damn the whole evening had been surreal. Certainly, I had forgotten about Brin, but as I dropped Janet off at her car everything came flooding back.

Sure enough when I returned to my apartment there was another e-mail from Brin. It was simple: *"How are things going?"* A second later e-mail said, *"I have found a real estate agent for you. She actually works for the Cherokee Nation, so she can be double helpful. He gave her name, Nancy Macintosh, and contact information. Please contact her as soon as possible. I have already sent her the*

16

map of the property, and she is already working on it."

This annoyed me. Damn he was pushy. I fired back an e-mail saying, *"Brin, first I have done all you suggested. The money is in four different banks, and I set up the stockbroker account. I hope you know I don't know a damn thing about buying stock. Next, I will go see Nancy Macintosh tomorrow and see what we can work out on the property."*

"Now, for you. You need to provide me more information about where we are going with this and why such a fast rush. You also need to tell me more about you and your group. I have lots of questions which need answering."

There was no immediate response, and he didn't expect a fast one. I would just have to wait, so I would proceed with the meeting with the Realtor. I really hated to be pushed, but actually it was still early in the day and decided to go ahead and take off for Tahlequah and try to make contact with Nancy Macintosh. If he was honest with himself he was actually excited about this project. It offered many challenges, and that intrigued him. He had never been backed with huge capital before, which gave him a tremendous negotiating advantage.

On the relatively short trip to Tahlequah he called Nancy, and she answered after only one ring. Obviously Nancy had already programmed his number into her cell phone and was anxious to talk to him.

Nancy said, "Hello Mr. Brannon. I'm glad you called."

17

"Please, call me Mike. I'm on my way there to see you. Can we meet this afternoon to discuss this project?"

"Of course. Let me suggest we meet at Starbucks just down the street from the Cherokee complex on South Muskogee. My office space at the Cherokee complex is limited. We will have a little more room to spread out there."

"That sounds great. I should be there in about 30 minutes. I'll be the one wearing a red ball hat."

I arrived there a little early, but I immediately saw her standing outside. Wow! what a beauty she was. She looked to be in her late twenties, smallish, dark complexioned with long, dark hair, and as I got closer I saw those big beautiful brown eyes looking and smiling at me. It didn't take long, however, to discover that she was totally focused on business.

We wasted little time and got right to business. I quickly realized that Nancy was quite competent and totally committed and focused to accomplishing this project. I immediately gained confidence in her ability. In fact, she had already made offers on the property that was privately owned. She informed me that Brin had been correct in his analysis on the property owned by the State of Oklahoma. The only option for a deal on this property involved the state selling to the Cherokee Nation, which then could be co-owned with a Cherokee citizen as the majority owner. Precedence exists, because the State of Oklahoma has a history of selling state property to a nationally recognized Indian nation. She said it's a little on the gray side but it could be done with a few carefully selected political contributions. She smiled at this statement and kind of shrugged, as if to say, "It's up to you."

We continued our discussion through a couple more coffees and finally a sandwich. Papers and maps were spread out over the table top, but we didn't seem to have enough room. Finally, Nancy said, "You know, I don't live too far from here. Maybe we should move over there and spread out. I have a conference table that will let us view all the maps and documents."

I said, "Actually that sounds like a good idea, but I wouldn't want to inconvenience your family."

Nancy said, "I'm not married. I do live with my sister, but she is out of town, so there is no inconvenience. Let's do it. We still have a lot to discuss, and we still need to sign some contracts."

We quickly packed up, and I followed her to her home. I was impressed with the decor, and Nancy had certainly been accurate about having a conference table. It was positioned in an oversize dining room, which obviously had been purposely planned for a business office. Apparently, she had used this room for her business many times.

They continued to review maps, documents and contracts for hours. Unfortunately, my busy night with Janet and my lack of sleep began to take its toll on me, and I began to nod off. After jerking awake I said, "Damn, I better head home and get some sleep. Maybe we can continue this tomorrow after I get some sleep."

Nancy said, "I don't think you better try to drive all the way back. You will fall asleep at the wheel, and I don't want you crashing before we get

19

the contract finalized and signed." She smiled really big when she said that. "You can crash instead in one of my bedrooms."

I thought about it for a few seconds and said, "You might be right. I'm really tired. If you don't mind I will accept your offer." Nancy quickly ushered me to a bedroom down the hall. The bedroom was equipped with a full King sized bed, which had an attached private bath. I was very tired, but I hate to go to bed without a shower, so I quickly showered, dried off and slipped my boxer shorts back on. I was asleep almost immediately after falling in bed.

I have no idea how long I had been asleep, but I awoke with a start to the sensation of soft warm flesh straddling my thighs and a wet and extremely hot quivering pussy engulfing my cock. It certainly was not unpleasant. Actually, it felt wonderful. I was extremely hard and deep in this hot, velvet sheath, and she was riding me hard. I could hear her breathing hard, but in the dark I couldn't see a thing. Nancy must have gotten aroused and decided to visit me during the night. I was almost afraid to move, thinking it might end, but I was really aroused. I lost control of myself when she began pounding down hard and grinding on my stiff cock. My hands moved as if on their own to slide up her soft thighs and up to grab her hips. I was building up a massive orgasm and held her hips and began to drive up into this tight pussy gripping my cock. I held her still and began to piston up into her hard and fast, lifting her and bouncing her on my cock. This seemed to surprise her, and her pussy muscles clamped down hard on my cock as she erupted into a massive orgasm. As she did she began to scream through her orgasm. I continued to impale her tight pussy, feeling my own orgasm rushing up.

Suddenly, the lights of the bedroom flashed on, which abruptly ended my pending orgasm. I quickly looked toward the door and saw Nancy standing there in total shock. Almost simultaneously Nancy and I yelled "What the hell?" I then looked up at the naked lady still impaled on my cock.

She was shocked also and said, "You're not Tom."

She was trying to roll off my cock, but I continued to hold her hips. She was petite and I held her easily. Sure, I was shocked, but my cock needed release. I was almost out of control with pent up lust and desire, and after all, she started this, and I intended to finish it.

I said, "You're not going anywhere until I finish." I remained inside her still quivering pussy as I rolled her on her back. My arms slipped under her knees and pulled them high. My hands gripped her upper arms as I began pumping into her. Initially she started to resist, but that only lasted a few strokes. She was still recovering from her massive orgasm and soon began her climb to another. She began moaning that quickly turned into screams, which got louder as I pumped faster and harder. I was pounding hard into her clinching pussy when her second orgasm hit her. Her screech almost deafened me just before she passed out.

Nancy, dressed in a short nighty, had crawled up on the bed at some point and was holding the young lady's hand with one hand and had her other

21

buried between her thighs. Apparently she had become highly aroused watching me bring the lady to orgasm.

Nancy said, "Mike, she passed out."

I smiled at her and said, "You're still awake." She just smiled. I pulled out of the limp woman and moved on top of Nancy. My lust continued to rage and still had not been released. I spread Nancy's willing legs apart and drove my cock deep in her already wet pussy. She moaned and wrapped her beautiful brown legs around me and drove up to meet my thrusts. We fucked like primitive animals and experienced thunderous orgasms together. I felt her vagina muscles spasming and milking me as I filled her with my seed. We eventually relaxed but remained joined.

As we recovered, we lay in a tangle of arms and legs. Nancy finally said, "Sue, are you awake now?"

From behind me I heard, "Yeah, barely, but I'm sure sore."

Nancy said, "Mike, meet my younger sister, Sue. Sue, meet my client, Mike. What are you doing back, Sue? I thought you wouldn't be back till tomorrow."

"Well, I got back early, and I thought I found my friend Tom in my bed, so I took advantage of him. I guess the jokes on me."

I said, "More like in you." We all laughed. "I didn't mind at all. Feel free to do that any time."

We all fell asleep wrapped together, and I really enjoyed all the warm flesh. I was still enjoying the flesh when I awoke in the morning with my morn-

22

ing wood wedged between Nancy's cheeks from behind. I couldn't resist. I tried to get my cock fully embedded in her warm and still slick pussy before it woke her. I almost made it. Maybe I shouldn't have started power driving it in so early, but she didn't seem to mind. She grabbed my hands and pulled them around her to her breasts, while she pushed her butt cheeks back against me. We must have woke Sue with Nancy's screaming and the bed shaking, because Sue spooned to my back and began humping against my butt cheeks, matching my rhythm and increasing speed, helping me drive my cock deep into Nancy. I could feel her little hard nipples pushing into my back, feeding my lust even more. I felt it coming and pushed deep and held her tight. When she went over the edge her pussy clamped down hard on my cock and began quivering, which set me off.

Nancy and I climaxed together in a steaming, explosive orgasm that seemed to last for hours. My cock kept jerking inside her and pumping a copious amount of thick juice deep inside her. Afterwards, we lay cuddled with me sandwiched between these beautiful warm bodies, and It felt wonderful.

Sue said, "Damn, that was so hot." After a pause she continued, "Mike, are you spending the night again tonight?"

We all broke out in hysterical laughter. It was quite obvious she wanted more. After we calmed, I said, "I don't think so. I have some business to do back in Muskogee and after last night's abuse I need some sleep. We all had another laugh. These girls could abuse me any time.

Nancy said, "I also have a lot to get done today. I'm glad in more ways than one that you came home with me for the work we got accomplished. Now I need to act on much of it. But, you are welcome to come back tonight, or any night for that matter. We still have a lot of work to do." This last part was said with a wink and smile.

Sue said, "Well, hell, I guess I will go to work, too."

I showered, found my lost boxers, donned my dirty cloths, and headed back to Muskogee.

***

As I was leaving I noticed a Verizon store. I used a simple Verizon cell phone but decided that since I would be traveling so much, I needed access to the Internet and communications with Brin. There wasn't a Verizon store in Muskogee, so I quickly pulled in. It's satisfying not to worry about spending money. I got the best they had and had them program everything up.

While I was still in the parking lot I accessed my e-mail account, and as expected there was mail from Brin:

"Thanks for the quick action on depositing the funds and making contact with the real estate agent. As you will soon see, it's very important."

"Mike, I understand that you have many questions, but you will have to trust me for a while yet. You will have to admit, though, that I have given you a massive amount of money. It's all in your name, and it's yours; although we are hoping you will use it to further our joint plan. You can't say that I am taking advantage of you. Of course we

chose you and expect you to partner with our group as agreed."

"Additionally, you need to understand that you were chosen by my group for a reason, because of your original posts warning of future chaos and an apocalypse. Your descriptions of the fall of civilization were and are more accurate than you know. The apocalypse is coming and quicker than even you know. I tell you this with certain confidence. So you will believe me I must share one of my secrets with you, which must be held in strict confidence. Our group has the limited ability to look into the future, as evidenced by us giving you the correct lottery numbers. I know you will believe this. How else could we have given you the right numbers? Now you must believe that we have seen the future apocalypse. It is real and WILL occur in the near future."

"We needed an advanced partner to prepare us all for survival, because our arrival time there will be too late to prepare. We needed someone like you and the group you will gather to assure our and your survival. We must be self-sufficient and be able to defend ourselves before civilization collapses. I hope now you understand the need for rapid compliance. There are other secrets I must share with you, but those secrets must wait."

"As to the stockbroker account, I am already working via the Internet with it. Because of the previously disclosed secret I have, in fact, more than doubled this amount in the two days I've had with the account, and it will continue to grow at an accelerated rate."

25

"I hope that you understand better now and will push an accelerated pace, and an important part of that, excluding the physical property and buildings, is the gathering of a vetted group. You will need to advertise for potential members of this group to consist of a hundred members. You will need twenty-five females and seventy-five men, all need to be educated, healthy, unattached and mostly under thirty-five. They will need an incentive to join the team, because they need to commit to be sequestered for two years in a survival study and experiment. I suggest offering them one million at contract end. This will provide the incentive, but the apocalypse will occur within this two year period and money will be worthless afterwards. But, they will survive the destruction of civilization, so it is not like we are tricking them."

"I hope everything is well with you. You are important to all of us. Please let me know if you remain a team player."

Mike's thoughts of Brin's words began churning in his mind, but one thing that was certain was that Brin had him. He was a believer. Things had been so busy since this started, and he hadn't given much thought about the magic behind the winning lottery numbers. It made since though ... the only real, believable explanation was that Brin must have been able to look into the future. Really, nothing else made any since. If that was the case, then the apocalypse must also be real, and that was scary. Yes, he believed and was onboard with the plan, and if he believed this, and he did, then he believed far more than he was being told.

Mike immediately began his response to Brin: *"Yes, Brin I am onboard with this project. What you tell me is believable, and what you are not telling me is also clear. I'm not stupid. I believe you are not from Earth! Earth technology does not exist that can view future time, and there is nowhere on Planet Earth that you couldn't get here within a month. Now, before you panic, I really don't give a shit if you're an alien. I'm in for survival. Still, I would like to know who you are and what to expect."*

I knew he wouldn't respond right away, even if he got the message. I'm sure he would be a little shocked and surprised that I called him out, but I was quite positive I was correct. Instead, I called Nancy. Again she answered me on the first ring. Motivated as I was I simply told her to proceed with great urgency on the purchase of all property and pay whatever was required and pay whatever extra fees were required, but I wanted ownership by next week.

Nancy said, "Damn, this is the easiest negotiation with a buyer I've ever had, but I will get it done."

I said, "Thanks Nancy. You might also pick up any additional land that might be available adjacent to our target plot. Let me know how you do. Oh, by the way, I want to talk to you and Sue about another project I'm working on. Remind me." I think these two girls might be my first recruits.

I went straight home, and even though it was only noon, showered and fell into my bed. Even as I drifted off I couldn't help but smile, remembering

27

my sexual activities over the last two days. Wow, three young and beautiful women. I couldn't believe my luck.

I slept through the afternoon and night, waking mid-morning refreshed, invigorated and horny. I couldn't believe that I could be so randy after the last couple of days, but I was. I called Janet. When she answered I said, "Hello Janet. This is Mike Brannon."

She said, "Yes, I see. How did you know that I've been thinking about you?"

"I've been thinking about you too. Can I come over to your place?"

Janet said, "I would like that, but I only have a couple of hours before I have to go to work.

"That works for me." She gave me her address, and I was dressed and out the door in ten minutes, which was hard to do considering that I was already hard in anticipation. Janet must have been just as randy, because she met me at the door wearing only a long terry-cloth robe, and it was half open exposing her beautiful breasts. As soon as I had the door shut, my fingers were opening her robe. She grabbed my face and kissed me hard, snaking her tongue deep in my hungry mouth. Damn, she was hot. As we kissed I slowly backed her toward her bed. I pushed her back on the bed and dropped to my knees, spreading her soft, warm thighs. My mouth quickly found her steaming pussy as my tongue probed deep. My tongue dragged through her hot puffy folds until I reached her clit. I flicked it with my tongue as she moaned. When I gently bit it and sucked it hard her moans turned to screams.

28

Her thighs squeezed down hard on my head as she began a violent orgasm. I stopped my assault to allow her to calm down. When I felt her still quivering muscles began to relax I gently resumed exploring and probing, and she began building toward another orgasm. This orgasm hit her hard. Her whole body began convulsing and her hands gripped and pulled my head.

Janet said, "I need you inside me ... now!"

This of course was music to my ears, as I too craved her warm depth. No doubt this would be rough sex. We both knew and needed it. I stood, taking her legs in my arms, and walked into her, driving my cock deep and hard into her wet, quivering pussy. We both moaned loud as I began pumping into her. I was pounding into her hard, and she was pulling my back with her hands to make it harder. We were like wild animals. Our orgasms hit us simultaneously, and I felt my cock explode inside her tight pussy, jerking and filling her with spurt after spurt of my seed. Our combined juice gushed out of her stuffed pussy, running down our thighs. I eventually relaxed, laying my weight on her and breathing heavily. Her arms and legs wrapped around me, and she painted my face with kisses.

I was still inside her when she said, "That was the hottest sex I ever had. I wouldn't want to have sex like that all the time, but I'm sure pleased we did this time. You know you're big don't you? I probably won't be able to walk comfortably for a while, but I loved it. Thanks, Mike. See, I remembered your name this time." We laughed. She continued, "I think you can take it out of me now so I can go shower and get to work." Again we laughed.

I started to join her in the shower, but I knew we would start again, so I said, "I'll go ahead and take off. I have work to do also. Can I call you again?"

She yelled from the shower, "You can call me anytime, Mike."

Chapter 2
(Building the Team)

I decided to get out of my apartment and find a new residence in Tahlequah closer to the project. Luckily, I didn't have much to pack, and it didn't take long to get my pick-up loaded. On my way out I stopped to tell management I was leaving. Of course they charged me for leaving early, but so what. As I was leaving, I got a call from Nancy.

Nancy said, "Things are going well, but I need some cash to give out for all the approvals. I'm sure you understand. I need $30,000 in cash to make it all happen."

"I'll stop by the bank and bring it right over. Oh, another thing I want to ask you about. Is there a motel, apartment complex, or cabin complex anywhere near our project? It needs to house around a hundred people for at least several months."

Nancy thought for a few seconds and said, "I can't think of anything close, but there are cabin rentals in Burnt Cabin State Park. The cabins are on the lake not too far from the project, but I don't know how many people they can accommodate, maybe that many if they double up."

"That sounds like a good idea. Please check it out and see if we can buy or lease the cabin rental area for a year. Buy it if that's easier."

By the time I picked up the cash and drove to Nancy's house she had an answer for me.

She said, "Mike, they are crazy. It is much cheaper to buy their franchise than lease it. I did kind of take them by surprise when I quickly accepted their offer. They gave me a price and I said 'Yes'. I've already started putting the paperwork together. To tell you the truth, we got a good deal, far better than having to buy a motel. We won't have a problem with the state either, because the cabin operation is a franchise lease. But, sight unseen, it might be a bad deal."

Well, let's go see it now. I need a new apartment close to work," I said with a smile.

I hadn't even seen the project location Brin had chosen, but Nancy pointed it out en route to the cabins. Sure enough, the cabins were not very far from our project, and when we got there I was impressed. I loved the idea of living on the edge of the lake, and I loved the cabins. Nancy had called ahead and they gave us the royal tour, but I had already decided this would serve our purpose. I told them I wanted to see and claim the best unit for myself. It was rustic but large and clean. I would be comfortable here.

Nancy was doing her job well, asking many questions. The books were kept at the Marina, and there was not a set of books only for the cabin rental operations. I was only interested in the cabins and not at all interested in running a marina. Nancy was not happy about not being able to see the books and said so very forcefully.

The manager asked me if I planned to keep her and the maintenance staff. I immediately said, "Yes, I plan to keep them all." I didn't want any

32

distractions to my main focus. Plus, I knew Nancy would make it all happen. I was getting used to her, and I liked her competence.

We finished our tour, as Nancy continued to outline her requirements for completing the transfer. Once we were alone, Nancy helped me move my things into the deluxe cabin, and it didn't take long to get settled in.

Nancy said, "You don't have any food stocked in the cabin. Too bad, I could have fixed you/us something to eat. We need to go shopping for you. I notice you don't waste a lot of time eating, but I'm getting hungry. Let's go find a restaurant."

I said, "Well, I can tell, with the shape of that beautiful body, that you don't do a lot of eating either."

That professional lady, Nancy, smiled at me and said, "Are you flirting with me?" She didn't wait for an answer. She simply walked up to me and kissed me hard on the lips. When she slipped her tongue deep into my mouth I was instantly on fire with desire.

She slowly pulled back and said, "I can wait to eat. I think we should subject your new King Size bed to an initiation. What do you think?"

I said, "I like the way you think." I resumed our passionate kissing and began walking her backwards toward the bed. The vision of her laying under me our first time, taking my animal thrusts set me on fire yet again. Even the second time when I took her from behind in the morning was rough, but she seemed also to be on fire. She had given as much as she took. I wanted this time to be different.

33

I fought the animal in me to slow down. I wanted this time to be passionate and gentle. I wanted to explore her beauty and arouse her to a higher level.

The professional pants-suit she wore didn't entice me much, but the shapely curves of her body filled it out nicely. I gently lay her back on the bed and kissed her on her beautiful face and neck and those beautiful soft lips. The sparkle in her golden, eyes, shown bright in anticipation of what she now knew to be imminent. I smiled as I helped her set up and took my time undressing her, which seemed to excite and please her greatly. The suit jacket came off first, then the blouse, undoing one button at a time. I admired her soft, smooth skin as I removed her bra. The nipples stood out, deep brown. My hands fondled her breasts and my fingers gently pull and rubbed her nipples. Nancy was trying to remain calm to extend our pleasure of discovery, but she was failing. Her moans erupted loud when I sucked her nipples and gently bit them. My attempt at slowness also failed. I lay her back on the bed and began to undo her pants and slide her zipper open. Her panties were black lace, matching her bra, but I hardly noticed. I slipped her pants down along with those panties to get to the treasure below. I don't know how I missed it before, but her pussy was covered with a sparse and fine layer of black hair. Indian women don't have a lot of body hair, and what there is is very fine and soft. I forced myself to go slow, and began kissing and licking far below her pussy on the inside of her thighs ... ohhh so soft and smooth. Nancy's thighs began to quiver and her moans elevated in pitch. I could see the

34

nectar leaking from her lips, and the aroma pulled at my mind. I continued nibbling and licking my way up, even faster than I wanted to. When I tasted her nectar, I could not resist any longer and plunged my lips and tongue inside. The suddenness of my assault sent her over the edge. Her thighs slammed down on my head and her hands held my head still. Luckily, this blocked her ear piercing scream. I just held still, even my tongue, knowing how sensitive she must be. The sweet nectar flowed over my tongue, as her pussy convulsed and quivered. I waited and soon her thighs began to relax. When they did, I very slowly allowed my tongue to explore her inside again. I began sucking on the puffy lips and running my tongue back and forth over her inner lips. Eventually my tongue touched her clit and her body shuddered and jerked. I began rubbing my face up and down inside her lips and sucked her clit. Her hips hunched at my mouth and her body shuddered. I think she actually blacked out.

I slid up beside her and held her quivering body in my arms. Eventually she responded and began kissing and snuggling me. Her kisses became harder and more intense. I felt her hand slide over my painfully hard cock and began stroking me. This time she became the aggressive animal and rolled her leg over me to straddle my cock. Suddenly, I was impaled deep inside her, as her steamy hot pussy pounded down on my cock. Damn, it felt good, but I think Nancy was in another world by then and wasn't interested in my pleasure, only her own. She rode me like a horse at full gallop, then she picked up the pace and took us to another place. We exploded together in this new world.

We lay joined for a long time before either of us revived. She was the first and said, "I've never had orgasms like that before. Wow! Now I'm hungry. Let's go eat something." We laughed.

I said, "Yeah, I'm hungry too, now, but you still have me captured inside you." We laughed again. "You don't have to hurry, though. It feels incredible."

Nancy said, "Yeah I do, or we will start again. We tried out your bed. Now let's try out your shower and go eat."

After we showered I let Nancy drive my new pick-up. Amazing, but I didn't know the area, and Nancy said she knew a place not too far. She took me a few miles and pulled into the Fin and Feather Resort, and they had an excellent restaurant. I didn't realize I was so hungry. Even better, the coffee was better than good, and I filled up on it.

The conversation was also good, and I learned much more about Nancy. We hadn't discussed it before, but I learned that Nancy was also an attorney. That surprised me, and I looked at her in a new light. She was only 28-years-old but had operated her own law practice. She had worked herself through college by selling real estate. She was so good at it that she eventually took her law experience and applied it to her real estate business. She said in real estate she made far more money than she ever made in her law practice, enough to put both her younger sisters through college. That was easy to believe, because she was good at it. I had been lucky in finding her. Humm, come to think of it, I didn't find her, Brin found her. Did Brin choose her for the team?

Thinking about Brin caused me to wonder if he had responded to my last e-mail. I quickly looked and was a little surprised to see a response on my tablet. I didn't want to read it while I was with Nancy, but as she was busy driving back to the cabin, I opened it.

Brin: *"Well, Mike, it seems that I underestimated you. I was afraid to tell you everything in fear that you might run away screaming or not believe me. We need you to get most of the project completed before we get there, otherwise we will all die. This is a fact."*

"Now, as for us. Our race is from another planet, but we are, in fact, human, at least we came from a common ancestry, human. We are called in English, the Water People. Our evolution developed on a world that is mostly covered in water. We breath air just like you, but live mostly in water in underwater housing. We look like you, with some noticeable differences, which we don't have to go into right now. You may wonder why we are coming to you when your race is also facing extinction. The reason is simple: Our race is ancient and it is almost extinct. We are almost totally unable to procreate. Our males can't produce the sperm to impregnate our females, and we hope our races are close enough to cross breed. Your race is the only other human race we have found in the universe. We need our females to mate with the male members of your team so we can create a mixed in-

37

bread race. It is the only way our race can survive, even if it is in part. Mating with our females will not be an unpleasant experience. I believe your human males will enjoy it."

"As I have mentioned, we bring 25 males and 75 females in our group. We also bring technology that will help us all survive, but the facilities must be complete before we arrive. We are still far out in space and estimate we will arrive within a few months, your time. I will try to answer any other questions you pose. I will hold nothing back. I'm pleased that you accept our partnership."

I typed out a response: *"I understand all that you have said. I will keep everything a secret until much later. Will you need any extra accommodation for your people? Indeed, we will get along well. Oh, I am attaching a copy of the ad I will be posting tomorrow to find and recruit members to my group. Nancy is working out well. Let me know if you find any more potential recruits for my group. We may need to win another lottery to cover the 100 million retainer I will need to recruit these members. All is well Brin."*

Nancy got my attention when she pulled into a grocery store. I had forgotten about the groceries. I don't like to shop, but Nancy took care of everything, and we were back on the road soon. Just as we finished unloading and filling my cabinets, we heard a car pull up in front. Soon Sue was knocking at the door. Oh my. These girls were going to kill me.

I let her in and met her huge smile with one of my own. She said, "I didn't come to seduce you. I

38

came to apply for a job. Nancy left a note telling me what you were buying."

I said, "What kind of job are you applying for?

"Oh, that's right. You have no idea what I do. I have a degree in finance and I'm also a CPA. I want to keep your books."

This also surprised me. Nancy had never said what Sue does, nor had it ever come up in conversation. After all, I only just met her a couple of days ago, and the first I saw her she was riding on my dick. I was not interested in what she did for a living at that time.

I said, "Really, actually I do need someone to keep my books, look after my money, and write checks. Can you do all that?"

"Of course I can. I'm an accountant. Do you control enough money to keep me busy?"

I smiled and said, "To tell you the truth, I don't know how much money I have, but it is somewhere over $100,000,000.00." I'm not sure, but I think I heard both their jaws hit the floor.

Almost in unison they both said. "No Shit! You've got to be kidding."

"No hon. I'm not kidding, and I really do need someone to look after it. Can you handle that much activity? We are going to be building a lot and spending like crazy."

Sue said, "I never ever thought you were THAT wealthy. I just thought you might need a bookkeeper for this project. I've never handled that much, but then few have. But, it's only numbers, and I trained in them. Yes, I can handle it."

39

"Well, OK then. You have it. Actually, I'm very pleased to know this. There is something I want both of you to consider." I went to my computer and printed out two copies of the ad I had written and handed both a copy. I sat down and let them mull over the ad.

The Apocalypse Group is seeking 100 (75 men & 25 females) professional, educated, unattached and healthy individuals to participate in a two-year study group of how to live well off-the-grid. We will literally be writing the how-to book on survival after any future apocalypse. We will be learning the best ways to survive. If you feel you have something to offer toward this project, please forward your resume and contact information along with a cover letter describing how you could contribute. You will be required to remain sequestered and under contract during the study in a remote area near Lake Tenkiller, Oklahoma. If you fulfill your obligation you will be awarded a $1,000,000.00 at the term for your contribution.

Respond to: The Apocalypse Group
P.O. Box XXXX
Tahlequah, OK

I broke the silence and said, "I want both of you to be part of my group. You're a perfect addition for what the group needs."

Nancy said, "Well, the phrasing of your words speaks volumes, specifically, 'unattached', 'seques-

40

tered' and '75 men & 25 women'. That means 3 men for every female. It sounds kind of slutty."

Sue said, "That sounds good to me."

We all laughed, and Nancy said, "Of course it does you little slut!"

Damn, Nancy was quick witted and cut through all the BS and went straight to the bottom line. I said, "It is not as ominous as it appears. I'm merging our group with another group that will come in a few months. They have 75 women and 25 men, which makes it far more even. Still, being sequestered for two years could become a problem initially. I don't want to get any of the men killed for trying to pair too early. That's why everyone will be encouraged not to be exclusive, at least appear so."

Nancy thought about that for a moment then said, "That kind of makes sense, but I think Sue and I both like being with you. I hope we can keep getting together."

"I certainly don't mind that if I can keep up with both of you." We all laughed.

"Now, are you two going to join my team?"

Sue and Nancy looked at each other for a second and both said, "Yes."

"Great, because I really need both of you. This project is far more important than you can imagine, and being a part of it ensures your future survival. This is important to me and all of us." From their expressions I realized that I said too much. I continued, "I can't tell you any more right now. You will have to trust me. OK?" Nancy was really smart. I knew she realized much more was going on.

They both nodded and said, "Yes." Nancy continued, "What do you need us to do."

I said, "Just what you are doing now. We must control the property before we can begin anything else. Afterwards there is much you both can help me with. Speaking of the property," I reached into my satchel and pulled out the $30,000 in cash. I showed it to her, then in second thought, tossed the money back in the satchel and handed it to her. "I'm worried about you carrying that much money around. Maybe you need to get a Cherokee Police Officer to go with you."

She said, "I'll be alright. I have a Concealed Carry Permit, and .380 Browning in my purse, and I know how to use it. Besides, if anyone is with me the people I need to bribe won't take the money. This is all illegal and under the table, but it's what I had to do to expedite the closure. Hopefully, I can finish it all tomorrow. Oh, by the way, we need your signature on the documents and title, or assign me Power of Attorney to do it for you."

I said, "Let's make some coffee get all this done." All three of us worked late into the night, and the Power of Attorney was prepared and signed. Nancy had all she needed. Sue listened and chimed in. She was going to get a P.O. box in Tahlequah in the morning, add the number to my ad, and post the ad on the Internet to reach Oklahoma and other surrounding state universities. I also asked Sue to find us a contractor to start working on the road into the property and set up some appointments here with some general contractors. I figured that Sue would be the one paying them, so why not. We were all

42

set until we realized Nancy didn't have her car. She had come with me.

Sue said, "I can take you back in the morning, but tonight I'm going to stay here and molest Mike. You can help."

Nancy said, "I'm not sure Mike has anything left. I know I don't. We had a fantastic afternoon."

Sue said, "And you called ME a slut!"

I was still laughing when Sue asked, "Well, Mike do you have anything left?"

"I guess we will find out."

Nancy said, "I'll just watch. I'm still recovering."

Sue said, "Get you another cup of coffee and sit back in that lounge rocker. I need a shower. Then, we will find out if there is anything left for me."

Nancy was already taking off her suit. I watched her beautiful nakedness while she rummaged around in my drawers for a T-shirt to wear to bed. It sure looked better on her than on me. I must be the luckiest man on Earth to have two beautiful women joining to please me. Well, I guess it wasn't all one sided. They seemed to be happy and with no jealousy. That in itself seemed amazing. Actually, I was getting attached to both of them. I hope I never have to choose. That would be hard.

Nancy sat Indian style with her legs up and spread on the couch across from me, and it became obvious that she had no panties on. She smiled when I stared and she said, "Don't worry, Mike. I'm still tired." I laughed, but she was definitely arousing me. Damn, she was hot.

43

Sue caught my attention when she said, "If we keep meeting like this we need to bring some clothing to stash here when we stay over."

I had to take a double look. Sue stood in front of me wearing my robe, but her hands were propped on her hips inside the robe, and her legs were slightly spread. Sue could not be more than 5' 1" and 100 lbs, very petite. Her beautiful breasts were not large, but they poked out directly at me. My robe draped over her but covered nothing. It was all beautiful, but the most striking feature was her mound and pussy. Unlike Nancy, Sue's pussy was completely hairless and so smooth and soft. Before I hadn't registered this fact. It was more than just shaved clean. It was smoother than that, like her hair had been removed by a laser. I could see every detail of her small pussy. It was extremely erotic seeing her stand there.

I said, "Damn, you are both hot. I don't have a chance with you two. Do you always gang up on the men in your life?"

Nancy spoke up first, "Actually, Mike, we have never done it before, and the truth is, neither of us has had much experience with men. This is all new to us."

"Really, how do you explain it?"

Sue said, "Well, with me it was the accidental sex we had. You wouldn't let me stop, and I'm so glad you didn't. You took me to places I have never imagined with by far the strongest orgasms I've ever had. It's like being addicted to drugs I imagine. I'm addicted to you already."

44

Nancy said, "I'm kind of like Sue. I got so aroused watching you pound your big dick into Sue and watching her wither in orgasms, I had to join in. I'm certainly glad I did. As far as teaming up on you, it's like we started off as a team with you, and it just seems natural. Do you mind"

"Not one damn bit. It seems right to me also."

Nancy said, "What about Tom?"

Sue said, "Tom who?" We all busted out laughing. "Well, Tom and I have only gone out a few times. We have had sex, but when I thought it was Tom in my bed, I decided to get a little kinky. Wow! What a surprise I got with that."

Sue had moved to the floor and had slipped her hands up my thighs to take hold of my shorts. She began pulling them down slowly, while looking up into my eyes for my reaction. I just moaned, which told her to do whatever she wanted. Once my shorts were off she slipped between my legs and began to stroke my cock, which was quickly growing in her hands. She held it and began licking up and down the sides, then she slipped her hot mouth over the mushroom head. I closed my eyes and relaxed in the chair as she continued to bob her mouth up and down. I guess I did have something left over, because my cock was rock hard.

Sue smiled and climbed up on my lap and began kissing me. Her kisses were loving and gentle. I felt her warm, naked body against me, her little hard nipples pressed into my chest. Her knees slipped around me inside the plush arms of the chair. I felt her body lift up and a hand guide my cock into the depths of her tight pussy, as she

45

pushed herself down on me. It felt like a tight, slick vise was gripping me. Her warmth encased my cock as she slowly pressed down on my cock. As she did that I began to rock in rhythm with her. As we rocked back I would slowly push in deeper, just to feel her slip off as we rocked forward. The slow rhythm was erotic to us both. I had never experienced anything like this before. We continued rocking many minutes and my arousal continued to climb. Sue was wrapped totally around me, holding me tight, as she continuously kissed me all over my face. She then began to push her tongue deep into my mouth in the same rhythm as our rocking. I found myself begin to rock faster as my lust grew. I suddenly rocked forward and slipped my arms under her thighs, grabbed her butt cheeks and stood. I was still impaled deep as I carried her to the bed, her arms wrapped tight around my neck. I rolled her on her side and slipped back inside from behind. We spooned like this, as we continued the slow pumping. I felt her body and thighs begin to quiver and knew she was close. I suddenly began driving hard and deep, and she began screaming as her orgasm hit her. I stopped when her orgasm peaked and left my cock deep in her until her breathing slowly returned to normal. She didn't know there was more to come. Every so often I would stroke into her and feel her pussy muscles quiver. I started stroking again slowly, allowing her climax to build. When I felt her push back on my cock I commenced pounding hard and fast. Again she would scream with a renewed orgasm. I took her to orgasms three more times like this, but at the peak of her last one I rolled her on her stomach and straddled her thighs and relentlessly pounded into her hot, quivering pussy. I even screamed with the intensity of my orgasm and my cock jerked and exploded inside her. I'm not sure if she passed out, but Nancy had joined us on the bed and was stroking her face. I rolled between them and tried to catch my breath.

Nancy hugged and kissed me and said, "That was so hot watching you two rocking then devouring each other here. Yes, she passed out again, but she is all right."

I said, "I think I am done for tonight."

Nancy started laughing hard and snuggling. I rolled on my back and pulled Sue, who was now awake and grinning, and Nancy to me. I remember Nancy covering us all up, and as I went to sleep I felt one of them holding my cock. I also heard the girls saying something about Bess, whoever that is.

I slept hard all night, but for some reason I woke up. It was daylight, but that is not what woke me. I looked down to see Nancy's head on my stomach and felt her slowly sucking me. Yep, I was hard again. Sue was also awake and watching Nancy sucking me.

Sue softly said, "I didn't think you liked oral."

Nancy continued to hold my cock but pulled her mouth off and said, "Well, I never did before, but what Mike did to me yesterday definitely changed my mind, and when I watched you last night I was turned on. I've been practicing on his dick on and off during the night. I love it. I hope he does."

Sue said, "Oh I think he will."

I surprised them both when I said, "I do, but I wish you would get on it. You've got me so aroused."

Nancy jumped when I spoke, like she had been caught, but she quickly smiled and tossed her leg over me and straddled me. She slowly sank down on my hard cock and immediately began moaning. Her hips moved up and down, and I could feel her hot tunnel gripping me hard. She began riding me and I loved it. "Sue, come up here let me explore that hot little pussy with my tongue."

Sue squealed with joy and quickly came to straddle my head. Both my girls were loving me. I loved the smell and taste of that sweet pussy rubbing over my tongue and pressing down, and she obviously loved it too. Nancy was riding my cock and Sue was riding my face, and I was in heaven. Sue got really excited, and I had a hard time breathing but grabbed her clit with my mouth and sucked. She screamed and flooded my face with nectar. I don't think even she knew she was a squirter. I lapped it up, but she couldn't take anymore stimulation and fell off to the side, giving me a clear view of Nancy riding me. We came together. I pulled them close on both sides, and they responded by half rolling on to me. We lay cuddled close. We had only known each other for a few day, but I couldn't imagine life being any better. We were becoming very comfortable together.

After a while we got up and showered together, washing each other, then we dressed for another day. They insisted on making breakfast. They said I needed my strength. They were probably right.

Over our bacon and eggs we talked work. I asked Nancy if she needed any signed checks to close the deals, but she reminded me that I had already signed a check for escrow to cover the whole amount, and if she needed more she had power of attorney and could sign them.

Sue said, "Mike, we need a P.O. Box for business, but if we are in a hurry to get the recruits we should set up an e-mail address for The Apocalypse Group. We will get far quicker responses."

"Excellent! Can you see to it?" She nodded.

Nancy said, "Speaking of recruits, We have a favor to ask."

"Okay."

"We have another sister."

I thought, *"Oh shit."* But I said, "You know the recruits must have something to contribute. What does she do?"

Nancy said, "She is a Marine Biologist."

Sue said, "Botanist."

Nancy said, "Well, yes. She is both, Marine Biologist/Botanist. We want to save her too. Yeah, yeah, we know you didn't say that, but we aren't stupid."

I said, "Well we could use both. Send her the ad and see if she is interested."

Sue said, "I already did. You will love Bess. She will fit right in with us."

"Huh? You want her to move in with us?" When they asked I didn't realize what they were asking, now it dawned on me. "Girls, I can't handle three girls in my bed. You're going to kill me."

49

Nancy said, "It will work out great. Trust us. We will feed you good. She is pretty, too. She was born between me and Sue, but only Sue is a slut. Actually, Bess won't know about this part until she gets here." Nancy and I laughed at her slut comment, while Sue just stuck out her tongue.

Before they left Sue asked me for a couple of signed checks.

Nancy said, "Yeah, Sue wants to buy a new, very plush recliner rocker. It was so hot watching you two last night, and I want a turn at being rocked to sleep."

I laughed and said, "I kind of liked that myself. We can do that often. I'll be happy to give you the checks, but before you go, get all my bank account numbers and take control. Oh, and get a Platinum American Express for our new company. I will probably have to write you a letter, right?"

Sue said, "I have a form letter that you can sign."

"Thanks Sue. Nancy, I will worry about you all day until you complete our business. Call me throughout the day to let me know you're fine.

When all was complete the girls kissed me and left me to myself.

I was waiting on the girls to leave so I could check on a response from Brin, which is what I now did. As expected, Brin had responded:

Hello, Mike.
"The ad you sent us was excellent for our purpose. Please let us know the responses. As to winning another lottery, I'm afraid we will have to wait

50

for a while longer, closer to the end; because an-other win will trigger an investigation. We will wait until it becomes too late to investigate but before they stop awarding the money. I will let you know when and provide the numbers."

"Thank you for considering any special needs for my group. We plan to completely interface with your group in the structure you are building, but, now that you know of our nature, we will require an underwater dome structure to house our ship. We want to be able to hide it from view and protect it. It will be our last line of defense. I have already forwarded the plans of the building and underwater dome to an architect. His name is Jeremy Hodge, and he lives in Tulsa." Brin gave me his contact information. *"We believe he can get the job done in time, and we believe him to be a potential recruit worth considering. Either way will work for us. You might want to give him a copy of your ad and see what he might want to do."*

"Also, since you are going to Tulsa, I suggest that you begin purchasing gold and silver. Eventu-ally, money will be worthless, gold and silver should be reliable in the future."

I responded to his email:

"I will make contact with Jeremy today and at-tempt to see him. BTW, I think you already know Jeremy will work out like Nancy. While you are at it, we will need a doctor and a dentist almost imme-diately to check out and health clear our recruits. You might give me contact information on these people, and any others you might feel necessary."

I called Jeremy, and he picked up on the second ring. I introduced myself, and he immediately knew who I was and what I wanted.

Jeremy said, "Yes, Mr. Brannon. I received the information your partner provided. This is a very interesting project and will require a lot of work to be done in a hurry, but it can be done. It will, however, require a lot of money, because it will require 24-hour work and a lot of overtime. Can you live with that?"

I said, "Well, I'm not giving a blank check, but we can negotiate a deal. Come up with an estimate so we can start on the same line."

"We can do that. Actually, I'm already working on it and do have a rough estimate. When can we get together?"

I said, "Time is short. We can meet today."

Jeremy said, "I'm headed for Muskogee for a meeting, but I can meet you for lunch."

"That sounds great. How about Jimmy's Egg on Shawnee Dr. at 12:00?"

I didn't have time to go after gold and silver, but I had been wondering what the hell I would do with the gold and silver. All I could come up with was to bury it in the yard, but that didn't sound all that safe. So, speaking of safe, I decided to purchase one. I looked around and finally found one at Lowe's. Once it was loaded in the back of my truck I proceeded to Jimmy Egg. It was almost noon, so I got a booth and waited and started on the bottomless cup of coffee. I watched for a single man looking for someone. I noticed a tall, thin man with red hair in a suit. He surprised me somewhat, because he was young, no older than 30. He noticed me at the same time, and I waved him over, and we introduced ourselves.

After we had lunch and coffee we began talking about the project. He was genuinely interested in the project and challenge. We haggled over the price some, because I knew he would have the cost padded, but in all honesty, I knew the project would be uncontrollable. He admitted that his company was small but was confident that he could get it done on time.

I said, "You better be, because getting it done on time is extremely important and would be a contract requirement with severe penalties.

"I understand," he said, "I'll get it done."

I agreed and we shook hands.

He said, "I'll get the contract typed up this evening. I would like to meet you tomorrow morning at the project and go over the details and study the obstacles."

I said, "I'll bring my attorney to review the contract. I'm staying close, so I can be there early. We'll have some fun with this project. Oh, here is the ad that's being posted today. You will get an idea of what we are doing. It's going to be a long term project and will grow."

Jeremy and I were standing by my truck in the parking lot when I got a call from Nancy.

Nancy said, "Everything is fine. I got all the documents signed and the money transferred. The titles will be recorded next week, but I just wanted you to know that you now own the property."

I said, "That's great. I think we will go out to dinner tonight and celebrate."

I didn't want to tell Jeremy that we just negotiated a deal and the land wasn't mine yet.

The next thought was maybe heading over to Janet's apartment and giving her one of the ads, like I had thought about initially. I hesitated, knowing what would happen, and I didn't know what to think. In a practical matter, I couldn't handle more women. On an emotional level I was becoming very attached to Sue and Nancy. I enjoyed being with them. It felt comfortable being with them, maybe too comfortable. I told myself that it was getting late, and I needed to get back to the girls. Oh hell, Janet was probably at work anyway.

Chapter 3
(Another Recruit)

When I pulled up at the cabin I noticed that both Nancy and Sue's cars were already there. I backed up to the porch and strained to unload the safe I had purchased. Oh course, nothing was in it, but at least I would have a place to store the gold and silver when I finally got it. When I finally went in I received a double surprise. There were three beautiful, and I do mean beautiful, ladies already dressed out in party dresses. Nancy and Sue ran to me, hugging and kissing me. I really enjoyed the greeting.

Sue and Nancy stepped back to allow me to see the third lady. She looked very much like them, except she had short hair, and she was very muscularly defined. Being more or less physically equal to the other two, but maybe a little heaver in pure muscles. All and all, she was very pretty, as pretty as the other two but in a different way.

Sue said, "Mike, this is our sister, Bess. Bess, this our Mike."

Bess shyly reached out her hand to shake mine, but Nancy pushed her against me in a hug. I took Nancy's lead and hugged Bess. This lasted only briefly before Bess pulled back.

Sue said, "Hon, you better go shower and change into the clothes Bess and I bought for you today."

I said, "You're dressing me now? What's wrong with the way I dress?"

"We've only seen you ever where cargo shorts and T-shirts. We just want to show you off."

I said, "I'm surprised you remember, since you always take off my clothes." At that everyone laughed, even Bess, but I took off to shower like I was told. Afterwards, I dressed into the clothes Sue left for me in the bathroom: tan Dockers and a brown Polo shirt. She had even bought me new boxers, socks, and shoes. When I came out Sue and Nancy whistled. I must have looked good.

Nancy said, "We can all go in my car. Sue said you have plenty of money, so we are going for steaks in Tahlequah."

It was a really nice place, and the steaks were great. We had a corner booth with no one around so we could talk freely. I asked Bess, "When did you get in?"

Bess said, "Sue picked me up at the Tulsa Airport today."

I asked Sue, "Why didn't you tell me she was coming?"

Sue looked scared and said, "To be honest, we didn't know how you would react, but we really wanted her here as soon as we could get her here. We didn't want her caught out there and stranded. I sent her the first ad."

I looked around to see if anyone was close enough to hear. "What did you tell her?"

Sue said, "We told her what we know and believe is going to happen in the future and asked her

56

to come. She has finished her education now and quickly agreed."

I asked Bess, "What did they tell you, and what do you think about it all?"

"Well, they believe civilization is about to crash, and you are building a survival community. I can certainly see the possibility of that. They also believe you are right and you wouldn't be spending this massive amount of money just for a study and book on survival. I can contribute to the community. They also told me about your relationship, how the three of you live together. They want me to become part of it."

I said, "How do you feel about that?"

"Well, I guess this is as good a time to bring this up as any, and let me just say it. My sisters don't even know this, but I'm lesbian."

This shocked Nancy and Sue, but I held my hand up to request their silence. I said, "You know this could be a deal breaker on joining the community. Even your sisters don't know this, but we are also building a survival community for the future generations, which our society will generate, which means at some point you would have to pair with a man. Of course, Nancy, Sue and I are pretty much joined. I wouldn't want to be without them." At my last comment, Nancy setting beside me, hugged me tightly and kissed me. Sue also leaned over the table and did the same.

Bess said, "Well I do have a solution. Sue and Nancy told me that you are an excellent lover. I want you to make love to me and let's see how this goes. I have never had sex with a man, in fact I'm

57

still virgin. My hymen is still intact. I hear it hurts, and I've been afraid of losing my cherry, as they say. I have been curious, but I haven't done it. I'm also not on the pill. If you will take your time with me, I'm willing to try it."

Boy, this conversation didn't go as I expected. I've never negotiated taking someone's virginity, and in reality I had never actually done it before. I said, "Girls you have a say in this. Is this what you want?"

Nancy said, "Yes Mike, we want her with us, and we are willing to share. It has worked out great with Sue and I, and it can work out with Bess. We're sisters after all." Then to Bess, she said, "Sue and I will be with you and help you. It's nothing to worry about, and with Mike, I promise you will love it."

We all looked at Sue, but she was nodding in agreement with everything Nancy said, and her devilish grin told us much more. Sue pulled Bess into a big hug.

I was already beginning to get excited at the possibilities. I said, "Well let me pay the bill and we can go home and talk about this more or whatever."

As we pulled into the cabin Nancy leaned over to embrace me and whispered in my ear, "Make her love your cock and you, too."

Once in the main room Nancy and Sue began stripping my clothes off. They didn't stop until I was completely naked. It was quite arousing, knowing Bess was intensely watching everything. They then pushed me up on the bed and began tak-

58

ing turns sucking me. After a few moments they got up, took all their clothing off, then turned to Bess and began stripping her. Bess didn't resist. They pulled Bess up on the bed close as they continued to suck me. At one point Sue took Bess' hand and placed it on my cock. She took it tentatively in her hand as Sue showed her how to stroke it.

Bess said, "This huge dick is not going to fit in me. This is a mistake!"

Bess looked panicky, and Nancy motioned for me to get up, which I did. I then watched Nancy and Sue take Bess by the arms and gently lay her down on her back. They caressed her face and gently laid over her arms facing each other. Together they took Bess' nipples into their mouths and began gently sucking. Nancy waved me forward. Bess had relaxed, allowing them to nurse and excite her. I began gently stroking up and down her thighs. Her tight muscles relaxed under my attention. I wasn't going to just jump in and take her. She needed to be far more relaxed. I spread her thighs and began kissing and licking her inner thighs. When I pushed her legs wider I noticed the girls wrapped their legs over Bess'. Bess didn't seem to notice. I began getting closer and closer until my tongue touched her pussy lips. Her thighs began to quiver when my tongue slid inside her folds. She was so wet her juice was dripping out. I dragged my tongue through her inner pussy, at which point she began moaning loudly. I tasted ever inch, but when my lips covered her little hard button she screamed for the first time, and when I sucked it into my mouth and rubbed my tongue over it, she went into convulsions and flooded my face with nectar. It was a good thing the girls had their legs over hers, holding them open. While she slowly relaxed I moved up and rubbed my cock between her wet pussy lips. Ever so slowly I pushed myself into her. It was so very tight, but I pushed harder and deeper. I felt the barrier stop me and knew it was her fully intact hymen. I continued stroking in and out against her barrier. I had to go through it, and I knew there was no easy way, so on the next stroke I pushed hard and felt it tear. Bess let out a scream in pain and jerked, but the girls held her tight. After a few seconds she stopped struggling. All the while I had held still inside her, allowing her to get used to it; but now I began slowly stroking again, slowly going deeper with each stroke. As I bottomed out fully inside her, I felt her cervix. God she was tight, and her muscles within her pussy squeezed me so hard it hurt. I had to wait for her muscles to relax before I could begin stroking again. Finally she began to relax inside, and I began slowly stroking in and out. I went deep and she began to moan loud and begin to meet my strokes. I picked up the pace and she matched me. Soon I was driving hard inside her and she was continually screaming.

Bess yelled, "Let my legs go."

As soon as the girls did, Bess wrapped her legs around me and seem to go crazy driving up against my cock. I was no longer pumping. She was driving on me. Suddenly, she squeezed me tight and her pussy latched down on my cock … hard. She

60

had me captured and I couldn't move. I felt her body quivering and convulsing for many long minutes. Finally, she began to relax and fell to the bed. I gently removed my cock from the relaxing vise, but I was still extremely aroused. Nancy saw my dilemma and rolled on her back and spread her legs. I was in her in seconds, driving in and out. She was very tight, but I was able to pump into her hard. It was incredible. She felt good, and I was rough. Soon Nancy was screaming also in orgasm as I exploded inside her. I was kissing her passionately. I finally rolled over and cuddled her in my arms.

I'm not sure how long Nancy and I lay cuddled, but Bess set up in bed and said, "That was fucking incredible! Just think about what I have missed all these years. Mike, I love you, and I love your cock. Nancy - Sue, thanks for convincing me and helping me to try sex and for sharing Mike with me. I see what you like about him and why you love him. I love him too, now. Just make room for me in this bed, because I want more. I want his cum." Her expression suddenly changed and she said, "I want his cum. I earned it, and I want it. Where is it?"

She looked at me. I just pointed to Nancy's oozing pussy, and Bess dove between her sister's still spread legs and began licking it up. Nancy's eyes bulged in surprised, but she didn't stop her. Bess' tongue was digging deep in Nancy's pussy for my seed. I even saw her push on Nancy's stomach to force more out. I also watched Nancy's initial surprise turn to arousal. I got up and moved behind

Sue and held her close, as we both watched Bess devour Nancy.

Sue said, "I love spooning with you, but I wish you were hard so you could push it inside me from behind. I would love to sleep with it inside me."

It was quite arousing to watch Nancy and Bess, and before long I did have my cock buried in Sue's pussy from behind. My arms were wrapped around her, holding her breasts in my hands, rolling her nipples. I couldn't just leave it still inside her and began to pump. Sue hadn't had an orgasm tonight so she was quickly screaming. I, on the other hand, had been drained, so I was slow to climax. I gave her three more orgasms before I unloaded inside her, and much to her satisfaction I left it inside her as we drifted off to sleep.

The alarm went off far too early, but I forced myself to sit up. My arms were around Sue, but my cock had softened and popped out of Sue during the night. We looked over at Bess and Nancy and chuckled to see them still wrapped together in a lover's embrace. I leaned over and kissed Nancy. She slowly opened her eyes. I said, "Sweetie, we need to go shower. We have work to do today." She kissed me back, but her eyes wouldn't look at me, like she was ashamed of what she had done. I kissed her again and said, "I love you." Her eyes darted to mine to see if I was serious. I was.

I moved to get up and Sue grabbed me and looked into my eyes, waiting. I said, "Yes, you little shit. I love you too."

Sue said, "I'll get Bess up and we will go fix breakfast, while you two mess around in the shower."

I slapped Sue's butt cheek as she got up and took Nancy by the hand and headed for the shower. Once we were in the shower Nancy took my face in her hands, looked hard into my eyes, and said, "Do you really love me?"

I met her stare and said, "First of all, I don't say it often, but, yes, I do. I love you both. I care deeply for both of you. Is that all right?"

She smiled big and said, "Yes." Then she kissed me hard.

We dressed for work and joined Sue and Bess in the kitchen. As we ate, I asked Bess, "What do you know about aquaponics?"

Bess looked excited and said, "Hell, I know everything! I've studied them, built them and maintained them."

"That's great, Bess; because I need you to design a huge aquaponics bed and greenhouse for food production for our community. This will be a major contribution and necessity. Can you do that?"

Bess said, "Oh, hell, yes. I would love to do that. What kind of budget will I have?"

I said, "Well, like I said, it will be a major part of food production for the community of 200 people. You will have whatever funds you need."

Sue said, "Yeah, that reminds me. Mike, I checked out your banking accounts and you are really wealthy. You have over $150,000,000 in banks and almost that much in your stockbroker account.

So, Bess, you have what you need but spend wise-ly."

I was a little surprised to learn that Brin had turned the $30,000,000 into $150,000,000 already. Good for him. I mean good for us.

I said, "I know it is probably too late to ask, but are you girls on the pill?

Nancy and Sue broke out laughing and both said, "Yes."

"Well, Sue you need to get Bess to town and get her on the pill, also. Otherwise Bess is never going to get a load herself. As it is, it's your turn to get Bess' load, and you know how she goes after it." I was rewarded with three blushing girls.

Nancy and I headed to the property. I was sur-prised to see the road graded, then remembered I had asked Sue to hire someone to work on the road. We followed the road in about a half a mile to the turn. We would have to build a new road for anoth-er half of a mile to get to the island. Jeremy was already there, and he had a bulldozer and crew steadily clearing brush and trees. Surprisingly, the bulldozer had already opened up several hundred feet. He smiled as we pulled up and came to meet us. I made the introduction.

Jeremy said, "The road grader did a fair job on the old road, but it will need much more work to handle the heavy equipment and traffic we will have. I just want a passable road around this hill and down to the island. I'm afraid it will take a lit-tle while to clear the main obstacles so we can drive down. It's a long walk."

I asked, "What do you think so far?"

Jeremy said, "I don't think I told you before, but I like the basic design of the building. It's sturdy, almost like a fortress. But, I guess that is what you have in mind."

Nancy and I looked at each other in surprise. Were we that obvious? Apparently so.

He said, "I see the shock on your faces, so I believe I am right. I read your ad, and seeing what you are trying to build, I know what you're really doing. I have been trying to prepare myself. I also see a civilization collapse coming and want to be ready. I was with a large firm in Oklahoma City and quit. Fearing what will happen there, I moved to Tulsa, thinking I could more easily build something there. Unfortunately, I don't have that kind of money. When I saw your plans and your ad I knew I had better throw in with you. I checked you out and you certainly have the money to do it right. I guess what I am saying is that I want in."

"Are you single ... unattached?

He said, "I am, but why does that matter?"

"It has to do with population of the community. We only have room for those that can contribute, and you don't know everything involved with the project yet."

Jeremy laughed and said, "Oh, I understand."

I said, "You are welcome to join. I was kind of hoping you would. But, it's not common knowledge, so keep your beliefs to yourself. OK?"

Jeremy had given this project much thought. He took us along the road and pointed out a flat hilltop location on the main road coming in where he wanted to bring in temporary modular buildings

65

for his office, a construction office, and locations where he assumed I would want a business office, accounting, etc. and medical facilities during construction. We might also want to build a permanent barn for maintenance equipment. It all made sense. He explained how he would bring electrical power and telephone underground into the area, and how it would be safer and easier to protect that way. He informed us that a septic tank and water well would be installed in a few days.

He said, "From other documents I located an existing natural gas well. It's supposed to be out of service but pressurized and capped. Unfortunately, it's just outside the entrance of your property. You might want to purchase that property as well. We could use an unlimited supply of natural gas."

Nancy said, "When we get back to our truck point the gas well location out, and I will make a deal to purchase it."

Jeremy looked at me for conformation, and I said, "Nancy is our real estate agent. She made the deal for all this, and it was quite complicated. She is also my assistant and attorney."

Jeremy looked impressed and said, "That's great. One day you must explain how you got the State of Oklahoma and the federal government to agree to sell you this property. It's a great location."

Nancy laughed and said, "Well, some of it is top secret, but it helped that Mike and I are Cherokee Indians and the Cherokee Nation is a partner in the property ownership; although our group retains total operational control. The property is within the

Cherokee Nation, so you're looking at land of a sovereign Cherokee Nation outside of the federal government's control. It would be hard for anyone to stop us."

Jeremy said, "Very clever indeed."

We had spent several hours surveying the area, so we drove back to the new road activity and were able to get much closer to the island, enough to see and study it. The island was bigger than I had thought. It was quite large, maybe ten acres, and tall with somewhat steep sides. The transition went from a tall hill on the mainland side down to water level then back up on the island. I imagined the cement building sitting atop the island, and it would look very much like a castle or fortress, as Jeremy had said.

Jeremy studied the island for a while and finally said, "Mike, I'm going to suggest that we build a bridge across between the hills at about 75 feet high. I might also suggest a draw bridge. I also think I'm going to suggest a change already. The island's hill is high enough to build the building, complete with the underground storage complex under it, and still be able to do as I'm now suggesting. I'm going to recommend we excavate a large reinforced cave at the end of the bridge. We could drive directly into this cave. The cave could be massive, and we could store far more inside along with much of our vehicles and equipment. We could even build an elevator through the cave roof to connect to the main building."

"How many people do you plan to house in the building?"

67

I said, "The plan is to house about 200 people."

"Oh!" He said, "I wasn't counting on that many. Mike, we may have to go to four floors to ensure enough space to live comfortably."

I said, "We have one shot at this, so let's do it right, but remember the time limit is the limiting factor. We do, however, have enough money, so feel free to improve the plans as you feel necessary within the time restrictions, but do keep me apprised."

"I will definitely do that, and I'll work on the changes tonight. I already have an Oklahoma City engineering firm constructing the underwater dome. When it's complete it will be delivered in pieces to a barge somewhere on the lake. I'm not sure where yet. I will contract them to do the underwater foundation and construct it. Oh, who do I see for money?"

I said, "That would be Sue. She is staying with us. We bought the cabin franchise for Burnt Cabins Park a few miles from here. We will have you over for supper one day soon so you can meet the other community members. Bess will also be anxious to talk to you about her aquaponics and greenhouse project for food production. BTW, there is a cabin there for you and the other recruits as they come aboard."

"Speaking of the dome, We will want a tube or some sort of physical connection between the dome and the building."

Jeremy said, "understood … an escape route."

I just shrugged.

"Jeremy, what do you need us to do to help?"

68

He said, "I have all the contacts and who to call, and I will get the construction started immediately. All I need is for you to pay the bills. I will keep the design ahead of construction and construction on schedule."

I said, "Great. We will get out of your way so you can get to work. We will continue working on getting recruits, and Nancy will purchase the extra land you need. Let us know when the modular buildings are ready to move in. If you need checks before then you will have to get them at the cabin. We'll empty a cabin next to us so we will be close. Welcome aboard, Jeremy."

Jeremy said, "I will head back to Tulsa tonight. I need to close out my office and apartment and pack up some personal items and clothes, but I like the idea of the cabins and living close to the project. I've actually stayed there before and love it. I'll move in late tomorrow."

On the way back to the cabin Nancy and I shared our thoughts about Jeremy. We agreed that he seemed very competent and would be likely to be an excellent addition to the community. I also mentioned that we needed to work up a contract for the new recruits, something that will allow us to expel them if they don't work out. It was a short trip, so the conversation wasn't detailed or long.

Just as we were getting to the cabins we passed an Office Depot truck and a furniture store truck. Nancy and I passed a knowing look at each other, and I said, "Well, Sue has the checkbook. I guess she is using it." We both laughed.

As we entered the cabin we stopped to stare. Sue had removed the kitchen table and replaced it with a large cherrywood conference table and half a dozen office chairs. On the table were computers, printers and other items I could only guess what they were. I looked farther into the room and started smiling. The recliner/rocker had been replaced with a bigger one, one with plush padding and large arms. The covering almost looked like sheepskin, hell, maybe it was. In front of it sat a matching ottoman that also rocked. My kinky mind began to imagine how that could be used.

Nancy, standing beside me, nudged me and said, "It's my turn on the rocker with you tonight."

I laughed, pulled her into an embrace, kissed her, and said, "That sounds good to me."

Sue seemed quite serious and said, "Mike, we are getting many serious responses on our website, I mean a lot. Bess and I have been printing them out and separating them, trying to eliminate as many as we can by an older age, lack of education, or unnecessary occupations." She pointed to an impressive stack.

I said, "I see you and Bess have been busy today."

Sue laughed and said, "Yeah, we got Bess on birth control today and spent some of your money. How do you like the chair and ottoman?"

"I like it a lot, but Nancy already reminded me that it's her turn on the chair tonight."

Sue said, "That little slut!" But we all had a good laugh, even Sue.

I said, "Sue, do we have any electrical engineers, doctors or dentists?"

"Oh, yes"

I sat down at the conference table in one of those fancy chairs, and Sue began putting down in front of me what I had asked for. There were three doctors, two dentists and two electrical engineers, and I began reading through their very impressive resumes. The most impressive and highly educated doctor lived in Oklahoma City. He was 35-years-old and had just finished his internship at Mercy Hospital. Dr. George Groom was considering starting his own practice when he saw our ad. The dentist (Susan Wong), I felt was most qualified, also lived in Oklahoma City. She was 30-years-old. She had also included a picture, and if her picture was correct, she was Asian and quite stunning. The electrical engineer (Al Martinez), with whom I felt most comfortable with, lived in Kansas City. He was 29 and currently working for a large consulting firm there. I sent each an e-mail scheduling interviews for tomorrow afternoon at Starbucks where I had first met Nancy. I figured I would find out how serious they were, at the least. Surprisingly, all three responded within the hour agreeing with times.

While the girls went off to fix something for supper, I took the opportunity to check for messages from Brin:

"Mike, I can't help with other names. We did know about Nancy, because we once saw the two of you together at a glimpse into the future, but we didn't look often. It is quite disturbing, knowing

71

*what is going to happen, so we only sought neces-
sary details. We do have winning lottery numbers
for the future, which we will use when necessary."*

*"Now that detailed planning and construction
is nearing, I wanted to share with you some of the
technology we will be bringing. We will be providing clean power sources capable of providing
enough power to serve a medium size city. They are
relatively small and are fueled by water. Also, since
we are coming from a polluted and dying world, we
have learned and developed a sewage treatment
system capable of treating tons of raw sewage, con-
verting it to clean usable fertilizer for adding nutrients to the fields and pure water. We are bringing
edible plants from our world that will grow underwater. We plan to farm and harvest these plants.
We also hope to stock the lake with fish from our
world. They grow fast to a large size and will provide a stable source of protein to our colony. I'll
provide more information in continued communications."*

I responded:

*"We added Jeremy Hodges to our membership
today, and Nancy and I believe he will be a valuable
addition. He is taking charge and has already broken ground. We are also purchasing another plot of
land that has a natural gas well. It's always nice to
have a permanent source of gas."*

*"I will be interviewing a doctor, dentist and
electrical engineer tomorrow. I hope they work out.
We need to get a doctor on board quickly so we can
health vet all the new recruits. I will let you know
how that works out."*

72

"Let me know the size requirements for your power generator and sewage treatment plant, so we can fit them into the design plans. Oh yes, the dome is already under construction. They are being pushed, so it shouldn't be too long."

"Sue, my accountant, says your stockbroker account has around $150,000,000 in it. You must be doing great with the investments."

"Things are beginning to get busy here, but I will keep you informed."

After I finished the Brin e-mails I took a shower and slipped into my robe. By the time I came out, supper was ready. I have to tell you, there is nothing like setting down to a meal with three beautiful ladies that you love, that also happen to be lovers. I never know just which one will come after me first; although tonight I know. It's still hard to believe that they didn't mind sharing me.

After we had eaten and were chatting I said, "While I think about it, Jeremy will be moving in next door. I plan to ask him to dinner tomorrow evening. Should we go to the Fin and Feather or try to eat something here?"

Bess said, "I'm not really busy yet. I can cook up something."

I said, "Great, we will have more time to discuss work."

"You know there is another thing, and I'm surprised it has never come up from any of you. When you came and the other recruits come aboard as community members you actually have to walk away from your past life. There must be bills, car payments, house payments, etc. How should we

73

handle this? I mean, once we become sequestered, which will happen sooner than later all the needs will need to be taken care of. But, what should we do? Think about it. We can't really tell them up front that all else but us are doomed. Do you have any ideas?

Nancy said, "It doesn't make sense to pay them a salary for the few months during constructions. I guess we could give a small advance on the $1,000,000 scheduled for payment at contract term. They could use that money to settle all their bills. I could tie the advance into the contract I'm writing, making them liable for the advance if they default."

I said, "Actually, that sounds like a workable solution. Sue would just have to write a few more checks."

Sue popped back, "I don't mind writing checks. I have or can get more checks than you have money. Come to think about it, that would be a lot of checks."

Nancy said, "Mike, since you brought the subject up, should Sue and I sell our house and belongings?"

Mike said, "Well, that sounds like a good idea. It won't be worth anything after the economy crashes. I guess it's best to get cash while you can get it and turn it into gold, because putting cash into a bank wouldn't be good either. If there are things you want to try and salvage I suppose we could build a storage facility on the property somewhere. Sue, could you find a contractor to build us a storage facility ... maybe for 50 units? Not everyone will need storage. Check with Jeremy to find out the best location. He'll be here tomorrow evening."

"Sue, I would like for you and Bess to continue going through the resumes and make recommendations. We are going to need a chef, too. I was thinking about putting another ad out to find highly qualified and experienced soldiers for our security force. Nancy has got more property to purchase, and I have the three interviews tomorrow. Bess, you might go over your ideas on the greenhouse and aquaponics with Jeremy when he comes. Anyway, you three are quite competent, so fall in and take charge."

Nancy handed me a full mug of coffee and said, "Here hon, go try out your new chair and relax, while we clean up the dishes and take a shower."

I have to admit, I was eager to try it out. It looked so comfortable, and it was the most comfortable chair I was ever in. The chair must have been built with a layer of gel underneath, because I sank into it, and it conformed completely to my body. I sipped my coffee and slipped off into dream land.

I don't know how long I slept, but I became aware of the girls coming into the big room. I looked up and saw them, all in robes. They were laughing and talking among themselves, like I wasn't there.

Sue said, "Your turn, huh Nancy? I'll get him ready for you."

Sue got down on her knees by my legs and slowly opened my robe. Bess quickly joined her on the other side. Sue began caressing my dick. I continued to pretend to be asleep, but my cock was betraying me and was starting to grow.

Bess said, "It's not so scary when it's soft." They all giggled and Nancy joined them on the floor. Sue began stroking it as it grew and soon had it in her mouth. It was still soft enough that she was able to get it all in her mouth. Damn, it felt good. Nancy took my cock and sucked it into her mouth also. Sue and Nancy began passing my cock back and forth until Bess reached over and captured it in her mouth. She sucked too hard, but I didn't care. They continued to pass my cock from hot mouth to hot mouth. By this time it was fully hard, limiting how much they could take.

Bess said, "How big does this thing get? I can barely get my mouth on it. Is this normal?"

Nancy said, "I read that the average length of a man's penis is 6 inches. I think Mike is much bigger than that."

Sue said, "He's a lot bigger than that. Hey, let's measure it." They all giggled again in unison, and Sue ran off and came back with a ruler. Nancy held my cock up and Sue measured it.

Bess said, "Wow! It's 9 1/2 inches. No wonder it felt like a baseball bat when he fucked me."

Sue said, "Well, I didn't hear you complain about it when he was pumping you and you were screaming and flooding it with juice." Again they giggled

Bess said, "Yeah, and I won't complain next time either. I just don't see how he got it in my small hole."

The girls were almost continually giggling, and I was wishing they would get back to passing my cock around. That's when it got really interesting.

Bess said, "Nancy, I think he is ready. Are you ready? We better check."

I almost missed the next. I heard Nancy moan as Bess's fingers dug into her pussy. Bess helped Nancy up on to the ottoman and pulled her butt back. Bess moved between her thighs and started licking and sucking on her pussy lips. She pushed two finger into her hot, tight love tunnel as she latched onto her clit. After a few minutes she seemed satisfied that Nancy was ready, but Sue had other ideas.

Sue said, "I want to taste her." She pushed Bess out of the way and buried her face in Nancy's pussy. I didn't have to worry about my cock going down from lack of attention. I was rock hard. Nancy moaned really loud, clamped her thighs on Sue's head and flooded her face with fine sweet nectar.

When Nancy released Sue's head, Sue said, "I've been wanting to do that since I watched Bess devour your pussy. I liked it ... a lot. Now Nancy is ready." The giggling started again.

It took a few minutes for Nancy to stop shaking, but Bess and Sue helped her up on the chair above me. Her knees slipped in beside me. I felt a hand on my cock guiding it into Nancy's pussy.

Bess said, "I've got to watch his big dick go inside her."

In it went, tight, hot and slick. Nancy slowly lowered her pussy down. I felt her weight forcing her pussy down over my cock. I didn't pretend to

77

be asleep any longer. I pushed deep. My hands gripped her hips and pulled her down on me all the way. My lips found hers and the passion consumed us both. Our tongues rolled in each other's mouths, and I began the slow rocking. In and out, in and out slow and deep. I'm not sure what was the cause, maybe the orgasm with Bess and Sue, but Nancy seemed on the verge of orgasm the whole time. The slow pace was driving her nuts. I felt her pussy begin to constantly quiver. I changed the pace and pumped three times deep into her depths and she exploded. I felt her pussy clinch my cock, but I continued with the slow rocking through her orgasm, which didn't seem to stop. I found that I could make her orgasm whenever I changed the pace. Nancy floated in and out of orgasms, but the slow pace kept me from climaxing. I wanted to give her as much pleasure as possible, and I lost count of how many orgasms she had. Finally, her breathing became far too labored, so I quit. I lifted her still impaled on my cock and carried her to the bed. She was exhausted, barely able to keep her eyes open. I covered her with the sheet and kissed her goodnight.

I then looked for Bess. She was going to get the action tonight. Bess was laying on her back and saw me crawling toward her, and she knew it was her turn. I crawled between her thighs and drew my tongue through her already wet pussy. Yes, she was wet enough. I moved up and kissed her hard and slowly began pushing my hard cock between her pussy lips. It wasn't quite as tight as the first time, but it was still extremely tight. I began taking short forceful strokes, pushing deeper with each stroke. She was already moaning and screaming by the time I got halfway in. Her arms wrapped around me and her legs shot up to grab on to my hips, but I continued my assault. Her heels began to dig into my butt cheeks, and I increased my pressure and rhythm to match hers. Finally, my cock drove into her steaming hot pussy at full depth. I noticed Sue stroking her face and encouraging her. Bess soon exploded in a mammoth orgasm and her tight pussy clamped down like a vise on my cock, and I couldn't drive it in any longer. All I could do was wait until she released her hold. When the eventual release came I pulled out quickly and grabbed hold of Sue. I moved my lustful assault to Sue, but she was ready and more than willing. Sue was also very tight, but I was finally able to push all my cock deep into Sue. Her screams echoed in the room as I began to drive into her. By this time I was almost out of control with desire. I was bouncing little Sue on the bed, so I grabbed her legs, wrapping my arms around them and pulling them high. Her entire tiny body was quivering and convulsing in orgasm after orgasm, but I continued. When it came it was explosive, and I unloaded inside her. My cock began jerking and pumping my hot juice, and Sue had another orgasm. Her pussy muscles gripping and milking my seed. When I finally relaxed and opened my eyes, Sue was smiling at me and kissed me hard.

Sue said, "I thought I had a strong orgasm the first time, but they keep getting better. You know I love you, Mike."

79

I kissed her passionately and said, "I love you, too sweetie." I rolled off of her and lay cuddled to her.

Bess said, "Damn, Mike I think you spoiled us all tonight, but you gave my load to Sue. I'll have to go after it."

I continued to hold Sue, at least the top part, because Bess had Sue's legs spread and was going after her load. At some point Sue turned around and was doing the same to Bess. At that point I went to the other side of the bed and snuggled up to Nancy. Sue and Bess were still at it when I finally went to sleep.

Chapter 4
(Breaking Ground)

We were all up early working on breakfast. The girls were making sure that I ate well each day. They had gotten to where I was being given meals to have during the day. Nancy worried about my habit of not eating regularly during the day. It must have been her or Sue that ordered Texas Super Food and kept me supplied. It was only a drink, but it was supposedly full of all the healthy stuff I was supposed to have. I mean I am healthy, and if I do say so myself, I'm in good shape inside and out. Still, breakfast was our time to visit and talk about the day's work, and probably most import right now was finding the necessary recruits.

Mike said, "Sue, as you go through the resumes, keep in mind that we need an agriculture expert to oversee the farms, animals, fruit trees we will need to survive. I'm thinking we are also needing someone to oversee a dairy operation, and a security expert. See if we've received anything from a dog trainer.

Nancy said, "I'll let you know what I find out about the property, and I will look around to find out about other property. Talking about farming, we seem to be outgrowing our site."

We said our goodbyes, and I headed to the site. I was shocked when I got there. It looked like a beehive of activity. Now I understood what Nancy meant about outgrowing our site. Off to one side a great hole was being dug for a basement foundation to a metal barn. I could tell, because the material was already stacked up along with lumber for the forming. Men were busy moving all over the site. The land for the modular building was already scraped and leveled and the buildings were parked just offsite. A drilling rig was already busy digging for a water well, and farther downhill they were already lowering a huge cement septic tank in place. These different crews must have worked all night to be this far along.

I continued down an already graveled road toward the island. I had to pull over and let a dump truck pass, but the gravel was being dumped almost to the main side of the future bridge. Between the island and mainland a temporary road was in place, and a bulldozer was scraping a drive up the island side hill. I didn't see Jeremy, but it was apparent that he had been busy.

I was beginning to feel very comfortable about this project. I found myself smiling to myself. I was about to call Jeremy when I suddenly remembered I had left my phone back in the cabin. I would need it, so I went back after it. I'm glad I discovered it early.

I pulled into the cabin and went inside to get the phone. I was surprised that the door was unlocked. I saw Bess still dressed in her robe at the sink cleaning up the dishes.

I said, "Hi Bess. I forgot my phone. Where are the girls?"

She said, "Nancy had an appointment at the County. Sue went to Tahlequah to check the P.O. Box and shop for groceries we need for tonight."

I went in and grabbed my phone and went to stand behind Bess. I had intended to kiss her bye again, but I placed my hands on her shoulders and turned her to face me. My knees went weak looking into her eyes. What a beautiful woman. I placed my hands on her face, holding her still, while I looked deep into her liquid eyes. They were brown with gold streaks and very wide. Was she nervous? I couldn't resist. I placed a gentle kiss on her soft lips that slowly got more passionate. I realized suddenly that although we have had some incredible sex, it had always been in a group. This seemed different, apparently to both of us. Our tongues met and played. My passion and lust grew. I felt it. This was love and not just sex. I was seducing her in love. We were alone together for the first time, and I wanted her, only her right now. This would be our moment together. I picked her up in my arms and held her close, as I carried her to the bed. I lay her down on the bed and could feel her body quivering. I lay beside and over her. We continued to kiss, but my kisses began to move over her face to her nose, her ears and down the sides of her neck. She gave herself to me completely, laying her arms and legs wide. I sat up somewhat and let my finger explore her face. They slipped down her neck to open her robe, exposing her beautiful breasts. Her nipples jutted out, and I suddenly captured them with my lips. She screamed out in an obvious orgasm. Her hands grabbed my head and pulled them against her breasts, and I continued to move from one little, hard nipple to the other until she groaned and gently pushed my face away. I raised up to admire her body. She had a sheen of moisture glistening over her body accenting every curve and crevice. Bess had little body fat to hide the underlying muscles, of which she had many.

I let my fingers slide over her stomach, tracing those six-pac muscles. As my fingers ran over them they quivered under my touch. I slipped my body between her thighs and began sliding my fingers up and down her inner thighs eliciting loud moans. I wanted to taste her, so I slipped my hands under her butt cheeks and lifted her high enough to prop my elbows on the bed under her. The access to her little pussy was perfect, and I covered it with my mouth to feast upon it. Her loud moans turned to screams as my tongue worked its magic in her pussy, and I lapped up her sweet juice. When I sucked on her hard clit the pitch of her screams went up a few notches, and she almost crushed my head with her thighs. I stayed with her, because I had no choice. Eventually, I was able to lay her butt back down, and I kissed my way back up to her face. Her hungry mouth sought my tongue, as I pushed my cock into her. She was so slick I was able to push through her tight squeezing pussy lips to full depth. I was so aroused I immediately began pounding into her hot tunnel for many long minutes. Her legs wrapped around me and again the heels pushed me deeper. I pumped faster and faster and I jarred her hips into the bed. Her screams got louder, but then she suddenly got strangely silent and still. I realized she was frozen in an immense orgasm. Her little pussy clamped down on my cock as her body shook violently. He decided to push through her paralysis. I gritted my teeth and pushed through her hold on my cock. The grip clamped hard, but I didn't care. I continued pounding deep and hard. It felt like my cock was ballooning inside her from the tight grip. Bess had come alive again and was biting my shoulder. The combination of pain and pleasure drove me to a huge climax, and I exploded deep inside her with several hard spurts of my seed. She bit even harder and flooded my cock with her juice. I lay still with my cock jerking within her quivering pussy. Eventually I knew I was crushing her and moved to pull out, but I was stuck deep inside her. I realized I didn't care if I ever pulled my cock out. I just rolled her over with me on the bottom so she could catch her breath. She was like a rag doll and heaving for breath. I knew we would have to wait until my cock went down before we could separate, so we just lay that way, my arms and hands rubbing her back and quivering butt.

We lay together like that until we heard clapping and whistling. I looked toward the door and saw Sue. She stared in awe.

Sue said, "That was the hottest thing I've ever seen. I wish I had been here for the whole thing."

The only thing I could think of to say was, "I forgot my cell phone." Sue started laughing so hard she almost fell over. Bess even chuckled.

Sue said, "Bess, are you going to stay on him?"

I said, "Wait, don't move yet. I think we're stuck together." Sue did fall to her knees this time with huge gut wrenching wails of laughter.

Once she was able to control herself Sue asked, "Am I going to have to turn the hose on you two? At that she started laughing again, and Bess and I joined her.

Bess said, "Let's see if I can get off it now. She raised up slowly and gently lifted off my cock with a slight pop as it came out. When she lifted off, our backed up combined juice flooded out of her all over my crotch. I took a careful look at my cock to make sure it hadn't burst inside her, but I saw no blood.

Sue got on the bed and pushed me down on my back and said, "You're supposed to be at an interview soon. Let me clean you up so you can get dressed and get out of here."

Sue immediately started licking our juice off and sucking my cock clean. It felt nice, but it was dead, and I knew it. So did Sue. Sue finished cleaning me up. I leaned over to her and kissed her then got up.

When Bess started to get up Sue pushed her back down and said, "No, you are a mess. I'm going to have to give you a good licking and then when I'm finished you will probably have to clean me up."

I looked at the clock and realized Sue was right. I would have to hurry to make the appointment. I kissed Sue again and bent over and pressed a passionate kiss on Bess. I said, "See you girls tonight." When I left, taking my cell phone this time, Sue was

86

already between Bess' thighs. I wondered if Bess had another orgasm in her. She already had more intense orgasms today than I have seen her experience, and these were really strong ones.

I made it to Starbucks in Tahlequah right on time. My clothing was a little wrinkled, but oh well, who cares. I smiled to myself at the reason why. I went inside and immediately saw Al Martinez, at least I thought it was him. There was a tall, stocky Mexican looking at me. I waved and walked toward him. We introduced ourselves and took a corner table, somewhat isolated. I went to the counter and ordered coffee for us. Al already had a coffee, but I knew we would talk for a while.

From Al's resume I already knew his expertise was off-the-grid power generation, which is what we needed. Still, I needed to know his personality and how he thought. I asked many questions just to get him talking. Initially, I got the impression that he had a tendency to be a smart ass, but I kind of liked that about him. Finally, I asked, "What attracts you to want to join our survival team?"

Al said, "Well, I have made a lot of money in the last couple of years designing and building wind, solar and stand-alone diesel generators and power plants for rich people. They wouldn't have built them and spent all that money if they didn't firmly believe in a future collapse of civilization. Like I said, many of my customers are very wealthy, and I believe they know things and can foresee things I can't imagine. I didn't spend much time worrying about it, because I don't have the capital to do anything about it. But, when I saw your ad, I saw a way to get involved. If it does happen, it will probably happen during the two years we will be sequestered, and if I'm inside I will survive. If it doesn't happen, I will be a million dollars richer. I can't lose. Plus, you need to know that I'm very good at what I do."

His answer made perfect sense, and I made my decision. I said, "All right, Al, if you want in, you're in. When can you come aboard? We will give you a contract, but it's pretty straight forward. You will also have to pass a medical screening, but as long as you don't do drugs or are diseased you should be fine."

Al said, "I don't do drugs. I like a beer every now and then, but I don't abuse it.

I said, "We also check for STDs, since we will be sequestered for a couple of years."

Al chuckled and said, "Interesting. That's nice to know. I can be available in a week."

"That's great. Our accountant, Sue, will call you and send you a money advance so you can close out your affairs. We will also have a temporary place for you to stay as soon as you get back. You will be sharing a cabin with others, but it is close to the project. The project and construction has already started so make it soon. OK?"

We shook hands, and Al left, and I waited for my next appointment with Dr. George Groom.

I had spaced the interviews out two hours from each other, and I had finished with Al in less than an hour. I took a bathroom break and got another coffee. I love Starbucks coffee, probably too much, but it kept me flushed out.

I had settled back down at the same table and was enjoying my coffee when an average looking but physically fit blond man walked in and ambled up to the counter. As he ordered and was waiting for his coffee he look around and spied me setting in the corner. He added half & half and Splenda and came toward me. He said, "Are you Mr. Brannon?"

"Yes. You are Dr. Groom I presume."

"Yes I am."

He didn't wait for an invitation and set down. I liked his attitude immediately. He seemed serious, confident and comfortable. We began to simply chat, and I felt comfortable with him. It was almost like he was interviewing me and asked many probing questions and began to draw out an understanding of the size and scope of our project. I could tell he was interested.

Dr. Groom said, "It seems you will need a doctor for the project to vet the other members and keep them healthy during the two-year term. I think I would like to be that doctor, assuming I will be allowed to bring in the necessary equipment and supplies to last two years and maybe more."

I said, "You can have anything within reason. I want someone to take charge of medical and do the things you are suggesting, but there is one question I must ask. With your credentials and accolades, why are you interested in joining us?"

He shot me a hard stare and said, "For the same reason you are doing the so-called study. I want to survive! I knew I wanted to join you before I even came. To be honest, I checked out your finances and was shocked to discover the amount of your wealth. I knew I would be funded adequately to support the group. You seem surprised that I know the truth behind this study. I bet I'm not the only one to figure out the truth. If you're in the know, it's easy to see. Yes, I want to survive the coming apocalypse."

I said, "No, evidently there are many to figure it out, and many are trying to join us. But, we must maintain the illusion."

"Yes," He said, "I understand."

It surprised me to find out we had been talking for almost two hours, and our time was almost up. I said, "Well you're in if you want it."

Dr. Groom said, "I thank you. I will take care of the community very well."

I said, "I have another interview due, but since you are now a team player, I would like you to stay. This one is for a dentist."

We continued to chat, and I continued to watch for Susan Wong. I had seen her picture, so it wasn't hard to pick her out when she came in. She looked in my direction, and I waved. She quickly nodded and pointed to the coffee bar. I guess she was telling me she was getting a coffee first. I looked at mine that was still half full and tasted it. I hate cold coffee. I said, "Doc, would you mind getting us another HOT coffee?"

"Not at all."

Susan approached the table, and I stood to introduce myself. I knew she was pretty from her picture but assumed her to be a petite Asian beauty. She was a fair skinned beauty with long black hair and dark eyes but not so petite. She was on the slim side, but she had slightly, larger, muscular arms and stood at least 5' 6", maybe even taller. Her hand-shake was firm, if not hard, and she looked directly into my eyes.

She said, "Mr. Brannon, my name is Doctor Susan Wong, and I'm pleased to meet you."

Dr. Groom returned, and I introduced them. I said, "Let's sit and talk a while. Susan, Dr. Groom just joined the project, as I hope you will also. He lives in Oklahoma City also. Too bad I didn't think to introduce you two before. Maybe you could have traveled together."

Doc said, "Maybe next time."

I said, "Susan, do you have a dental practice now?"

"I am a junior partner in a dental practice, but it's just started. Your ad is more appealing, and I would rather be part of your project. There's many valuable things to be learned here."

I held my hand up to stop her and said, "Okay, don't give me your practiced answers. Why do you really want to be part of our community?"

For the first time during the interview she laughed and said, "Would you believe I like the idea of being sequestered with seventy-five men for two years? I think I can work my way through all of them during that time."

I choked and almost spit out the coffee I was sipping, and Doc and I both burst out laughing … hard. I had to hold my stomach from the ache of laughing. Everyone in Starbucks turned to flash us a stern look.

Susan grinned and said, "I thought a little levity might work here, but the truth be told, I am a sexually aggressive woman, and the situation does conjure up a cartoon picture in my mind of me riding seventy-five men as I work on their teeth."

Doc and I had just barely gotten control of ourselves when she said that, and we lost it again. We were beginning to get some grim glares from the patrons, but there was nothing we could do.

Susan said, "Gentlemen, there is some semblance of the truth in what I said, but honestly, I do want to learn how to survive in an apocalyptic world, which is a conceivable threat. Besides, not only am I am a good dentist, but I worked my way through college as a masseuse. I worked through a chiropractor's office and learned much of that practice I could also use in our closed community. I don't have a degree in chiropractics, but I am quite functional in the practice. I will take care of the community's dental needs." She grinned really mischievously and followed up with, "Among other needs."

That last comment set us off again. I liked this woman, but I couldn't tell if she was serious or pulling our legs. I don't guess it mattered. She would make a good addition, and I don't think we would have to encourage her to mingle around the men.

I said, "Well, Susan, I guess you're in if you want it."

"I do."

I told them both about the status of the project so far, about the temporary modular buildings being brought in for medical, about the cabin living space, advance to clear up their affairs, etc. I added, "We have a limited number of cabins available, so you two will have to share the medical cabin, along with a shared nurse."

Susan said, "Do we share a bed as well?"

I laughed and looked at a blushing Doc and said, "There are several bedrooms, and if you want to share a bed, well, that's up to the two of you. Two years is a long time after all."

They both agreed to be back in one week. I assured them that the modular building would be in place by then. I told them to start ordering equipment and to call Sue for the details, credit applications, checks, etc.

We said our goodbyes and I headed back to the property. En route I considered all that occurred today and felt very good about the interviews and new recruits. These three would make excellent additions. I also thought about Bess and smiled.

The beehive was still active when I got there. A busy trencher worked from what must have been the gas well location. We didn't own the property yet, but no one was going to stop us. The trench would also be bringing electric and telephone cables to the first stop: modular buildings and barn. At the building location modular building already rested in place. I had no idea which building was assigned to what purpose. The water well driller team was gone, evidently finished. There was no activity on the metal barn, but the cement had been poured for the underground basement/storage. It would take a few day to cure.

I drove down a very functional gravel road to the island, and I was surprised to see heavy equipment already working the roads and mountain top on the island. The foundation for the bridge had been poured on both sides, and steel "I" beams for the bridge itself were stacked to the side. Dirt had been pushed into the water between the island and mainland to make the temporary road. The dirt would evidently be back-hoed out again once the bridge was in. Off to the side sat a huge portable generator and large lights. Obviously they would be working through the night.

I called Jeremy to find out where he was. He was on the other side of the island, and I soon saw him driving around the edge headed toward my location. He was all smiles when he got out. I can't blame him, since things seemed to be going well.

Jeremy said, "I guess you have already seen the activity up the road. The modular buildings should be in place and ready for occupancy within a couple of days. I've got to get Sue operational so she can start paying some bills stacking up. I'm spending a lot of your money you know."

I said, "That's what it's for. Oh, by the way, you're invited for dinner tonight. I assume you will be moving into your cabin tonight."

"Yeah, I've got my personal items and clothes, but I seriously doubt I will be spending much time at the cabin. We're in 24-hour construction mode. Have you given much thought about security? As long as we're working around the clock it won't be a major problem, but it's something to worry about.

I can hire a security firm to start, but I'm thinking you may want our own people for that eventually."

"Actually, that's a good idea. I'll work on it." I told him about the recruits I signed up today.

He said, "That's great. I thought finding a doctor might be difficult, but I'll have his temporary clinic ready by the time he gets here."

"Yeah, well, he kind of sees the truth like you did."

Jeremy said, "It's easy to see. Agriculture considerations should come next. We need a Master Farmer to lay out the land and crops."

"Yeah, I was thinking the same thing. What do you think we need for fencing and security?"

Jeremy said, "I'm keeping the large bulldozer busy, but I will hire another small crew and dozer to clear the property lines all around the property for a fence. I'm thinking an 8' chain link fence."

I said, "I'm going to head to the cabin. We have more applicant resumes to go over, so come on over. If you like, you can bring the bills you want paid and go over them with Sue. Bess has some plans for the greenhouse she wants to go over with you. We should know also, if Nancy completed the purchase of the property you asked about. You will see my truck there, so just come on in."

Jeremy gave me a strange look and said, "All three girls live there with you?"

"Yeah, we're close. Nancy and Sue were my first recruits and Bess came shortly thereafter." I know that I didn't really give him a straight answer, but I figured he got the point.

Jeremy smiled big and said, "Hurry up and get me some recruits for my cabin."

We laughed and I took off toward the cabin. It's such a short distance I didn't have much time to consider much, but my mine was replaying the sex Nancy and I had in the chair and the morning sex with Bess. Both had been fantastic, but I realized I had never been alone with Sue. I would have to make that happen. Damn, I really loved these girls. I hoped I could keep them.

When I reached the cabin I noticed the cars and knew the girls were there. When Bess saw me she squealed and ran to me, leaping on me. Her arms and legs wrapped around me and she gave me the biggest kiss. Sue gave me a knowing smile, but Nancy looked at Sue as if to say, "What's going on?"

Sue shrugged and said, "Mike left his cell phone." She immediately broke out laughing then said, "Mike left his cell phone this morning and came back to get it. Mike and Bess must have had marathon sex. By the time I came in they were stuck together like a couple of mating dogs. I thought I was going to have to hose them down to separate them."

From the mental picture Sue provided, Nancy broke out laughing, joined by Sue and even Bess and me. Nancy and Sue joined Bess and I in a common embrace, and they added their kisses. I really felt loved and appreciated.

Nancy said, "Stuck? Really?"

I said, "Well, it's kind of hard to explain. You kind of had to be here."

Nancy said, "I'm sorry I missed it."

Bess disentangled herself, gave me a final kiss, and said, "Dinner is ready. Where is Jeremy? I thought he was coming."

From just inside the open door Jeremy said, "I'm here."

Dead silence fell on the room. None of us had seen him come in, and he had remained quiet. Finally, I said, "How long have you been there?"

Jeremy grinned and said, "I came in right behind you, but you were already tangled up with Bess. I assume this is Bess. Mike said you cooked dinner tonight, and I'm sure ready for food that doesn't come out of a paper bag."

Jeremy, in essence, notified us that he witnessed and heard the whole episode, but he also quickly passed over any necessary explanations by moving the conversation to dinner. That was a smooth move on his part and welcomed. Still, there were four blushing faces.

"Yes, I'm Bess, and I hope you like pork chops, black-eyed peas and fried potatoes. I have some cherry cobbler for dessert."

Jeremy said, "You bet I do. Yummy."

During dinner we chatted about different aspects of work. I told them about the three new recruits, and I even told them about what Susan had said about working herself through all 75 males and her comment about riding the men as she worked on their teeth. The girls giggled at that.

Jeremy said, "I hope they get back soon. I feel a toothache coming on." The latter was said with a huge grin.

The giggles increased along with various other humorous comments.

I said, "Sue, how is the recruit research going? I think we are going to need, as Jeremy calls it, a Master Farmer, someone for sanitation/water treatment, dog trainer, soldier/security chief. We will also need one, maybe more, nurses for the doctors." I looked around the table for comments and said. "What else?"

Jeremy said, "We will need a head chef to oversee the planning, cooking, food preservation and storage, and you might want to kick that phase off early to take care of all the recruits, maybe even some of the contract workers. I'm thinking military training would be best. We need nutrition, not fancy meals."

Sue said, "We are still getting tons of applicants, and I already have them separated out for you. I think we have applicants for all those categories. I'll give them to you, but I better go get the key for Jeremy's cabin before it gets too late."

Sue dropped a stack of applications on the table before she took off, while Nancy and Bess cleared the now conference table. I let the three of them pour through the stack, while I excused myself. I went to the upstairs balcony to check my e-mails for one from Brin. I'm not sure why I don't spend more time up there. It's peaceful and beautiful with an unobstructed view of the lake.

As expected there was one waiting:

"Mike, I'm happy to hear things are going well there. Things are going well for us here, also; which is my focus with this e-mail. We estimate that

our arrival will be sooner than we projected, and I must speed you up on the underwater dome. We must be able to hide our ship when we get there. Even if the building is not done, we can continue to live aboard as long as our ship is hidden. The early arrival also works out well, because we plan to launch a few satellites. This way we can keep up with the progression of the collapse of civilization after communications fails, plus be able to monitor our facility for security. As a reminder, be sure and stock up gold and silver. We will need it later during the recovery. Keep up the good work and progress"

I typed my response.

"Brin, thanks for the information. I will speed up the work on the dome. I gained three more recruits today, the ones I mentioned and the property looks like a beehive. If you don't know what a beehive looks like ... well, let's just say there is a lot of activity going on. I will make it a point to go get my first load of gold and silver tomorrow. I already have a safe. I like the idea of having observation satellites. What type of weapons will you be bringing?"

Sue came stomping back in when I came down, and she obviously fuming.

I said, "What's wrong, Sue?"

Sue said, "I screwed up. I didn't tell the manager we would need the cabin for tonight and she already rented it out tonight. I blew up at her and told her to stop all rentals, but we don't have a cabin for Jeremy tonight."

99

I said, "No big deal. We have plenty of rooms. Jeremy can stay in one of our bedrooms tonight." Sue looked relieved that I wasn't upset. "Jeremy, I guess you will be our guest tonight."

Jeremy said, "That's fine by me. I never get tired of looking at these beautiful women." Then after a few moment he said, "Bess, can we go over your ideas for your greenhouse?"

They went to the end of the table and started going over her drawing, talking dimensions, depths, lighting, and on and on. Nancy, Sue and I started going over the applications. They already had them narrowed down to only a few for each category, except for security. There was quite a large stack, but Nancy tossed one down for me to look at.

Nancy said, "I have some thoughts on this guy, Robert Arrowhead. I actually know him. He is Cherokee Indian and a Captain in the Cherokee Police, but more important, he was a Major in the Army Special Forces. From what I have seen, he is a serious man and is not being properly utilized currently. I think he might be an excellent candidate for our security force. My other thought, since we are actually part of the Cherokee Nation, we could call our security force part or a branch of the Cherokee Nation Marshal Service. Anyway, that's my thought. We also have others in the Marshal Service with applications in."

I said, "I like that very much, hon. Set up an interview with him for tomorrow afternoon. If we like him we can let him pick his officers. What else do you have?"

Sue said, "I think we have an applicant like Jeremy suggested for chef. His name is Bob Patterson, and he has a degree in Culinary Arts from The Culinary Institute of America in San Antonio. That's reputed to be one of the top schools in Culinary Arts, but Bob's best experience for what we need is that he was a major in the Marines and served three tours in the Middle-East establishing food distribution centers and cafeterias for our troops. He's done what we need in a much larger scale. I really like him on paper, and if his personality is a fit, I vote for him."

"Thank you, Sue. Let's interview him. Who else do you have?"

Sue said, "There is only one applicant that claims to know sanitation and water treatment." She put the application down, and I took a look. I couldn't believe the name, Janet Walsh.

I said, "You can't be serious? I know her."

Nancy looked at Sue with a smile and said, "You mean you KNOW her as in you've been between her thighs breathing heavy?" They both laughed, and I blushed. Even Bess and Jeremy laughed at my reaction.

Nancy said, "Well, she is qualified … the only one, and she certainly has the education for it. I'd sure like to be at that interview. That could get interesting."

"Well, set it up, and you will be at the interview; because I need to go to Tulsa to get some gold, and I need your gun to protect me."

Sue said, "You need to take Bess with you too. She's a martial arts expert." When I looked sur-

101

prised, Sue continued, "Where do you think she got all those muscles?"

"No shit? Really?"

Sue said, "Why do you think Nancy and I held her when you ...." She came short of saying 'when you took her cherry.'

I said, "Well, that settles it. Nancy and Bess are going with me. That works out well, because Jeremy needs to go over some accounts payable with you."

"Oh, that reminds me. Jeremy, we need to put a rush on the dome construction, and Bess, we need to buy diving tanks and equipment to survey the lake foundation for the dome. Do you dive, Jeremy?"

"I never have, but I'm comfortable swimming, and I do need to see underneath the water. I assume you or Bess can teach me?"

Bess said, "Yeah, I can show you around the equipment and teach you how to use it."

I said, "What applications do we have for a Master Farmer?

Sue said, "Oh, we have several good ones, but I think this one is probably the best. This is James Baker. He has several degrees in the Agriculture field: Plant and Soil Science, Animal Science, Poultry Science, plus he has quite a few courses as a veterinarian. Best of all, however, is that he is from a long line of farmers here in Oklahoma on a large ranch and farm. According to his resume his parents died in a car wreck while he was still in school, and he lost the farm due to exorbitant inheritance tax. I think this is right up his alley."

"Great." I said, "Please set up all those inter-views. Nancy, I forgot to ask you about the proper-ty. How did you do?"

Nancy said, "I made an offer, but they are thinking about it. I'll give them tomorrow to get back to me. If not, I will increase the offer. I will try the easy way before I get tough. We will get it, however."

"Thanks, hon."

We all started cycling through the shower, and I showed Jeremy the bedroom he would be sleeping in. The girls and I looked longingly at the rocker, but we knew that would have to wait for another day. We all snuggled into the king size bed. Even so, with four, it was snug, but we didn't mind cud-dling. I lay between Bess and Nancy, but I figured Bess might still be tired from our morning episode, so I turned my total attention to Nancy. Boy was she randy and ready. In fact she rolled to me and yanked my shorts off, grabbed my dick and gobbled it down. Wow. She was obviously getting into oral, and it sure felt great.

Little Mike swelled hard almost instantly. My fingers slipped into her hair and I began to caress her head as it bobbed up and down. I think I was the first to moan, and I think it was loud. When Nancy began to moan around my hard cock, the wonderful feeling intensified. Nancy tossed her leg over me and guided my cock into her steamy hot tunnel. Her hands pushed down on my chest as she began to push herself down on me, gripping my cock in her velvet sheath. Soon she was bouncing up and down and riding me hard. Sue cuddled to my side and began covering my face with kisses. All three of us were moaning by then. Sue swung her leg over my face and pressed her hot pussy down on my mouth and nose. I began licking and sucking on her sweet lips as she rubbed her pussy over my tongue. I began rubbing her clit with my tongue and soon was sucking it hard. When I gently bit it, Sue screamed and flooded my mouth with her fruit, sweet nectar. I tried to continue licking, but she must have been very sensitive and quickly dismounted my face and pressed her small body against me, watching Nancy riding me. Once Sue was no longer blocking my view I immediately saw Jeremy standing by the side of the bed by Bess. He was completely naked.

Jeremy said, "You guys are driving me crazy. Can I join you?"

When he spoke Nancy froze impaled on me, and silence fell on the group. No one spoke for a while, but Bess eventually raised her arms, beckoning him to her with her fingers. Jeremy fell between her thighs, wrapped his arms around her upper thighs and buried his face in her pussy. Bess immediate began moaning. Nancy watched Jeremy feasting on her sister, which must have excited her, because she began riding me hard and fast. Nancy suddenly leaned over me and kissed me hard. It felt like her tongue was searching for my tonsils, but I loved it. Her hips continued to pound her pussy down on my cock. I don't know how she was doing it, but I didn't really care as long as she continued. Eventually she screamed and stopped, and her quivering pussy muscles clamped down on my cock causing me to go over the edge and unleash a torrent of cum inside her. We both remained still for a long time, calming. I looked at Sue and she was staring across us at something that had her rapt attention. I followed her stare and saw Jeremy pounding into Bess. Her legs were high in the air and she was screaming. I don't know why I didn't hear it before. Nancy rolled over on her side beside me, and we continued to kiss. Actually I was switching between Sue and Nancy. Sue began caressing my cock and started gently cleaning my cock with her mouth. I heard Bess let out a blood curdling scream and fall limp, and Jeremy rolled off of her between her and Nancy. Jeremy was obviously laying against Nancy's back and spooned with her. I looked into her somewhat shocked eyes, but she didn't move. After a while I saw Jeremy's hand sliding over Nancy's butt cheek, thigh and side. Nancy's eyes bulged from what I imagine feeling his cock push into her. She looked at me strangely. I looked back and kissed her. I continued to kiss her even when I felt through her body the impact of Jeremy driving into her from behind. Nancy's kisses became more intense and she began to moan, then she no longer seemed to know I was there. Jeremy rolled her over and crawled between her thighs and continued his assault on her pussy. I rolled over Sue and spooned with her as we watched Nancy and Jeremy. It was hot watching them, and I soon was able to slip my cock into Sue from behind. I took it slow and continued to pump into her slow and deep. She loved this position, and so did I. Nancy screamed in orgasm and so did Jeremy, but I continued to enjoy Sue. My arms wrapped around Sue caressing her breasts and kissed her neck. Each time she moaned. I was in no hurry and just continued to slide in and out of her.

At some point Nancy fell asleep and Bess woke up. I saw Jeremy take Bess by the hand and lead her off toward his bed. I think this was going to be a long night for them. I think Jeremy would have liked to try out Sue, but I had been keeping her busy.

Sue suddenly screamed and pushed her butt cheeks and pussy back on my cock. I met her action with a series of violent and quick thrusts into her that took her into a major orgasm. I held still to allow her to calm, but as soon as I dared I began the assault again. I loved doing this and taking her to orgasm after orgasm, which I did many times. Finally she turned her head and kissed me and said, "Mike, I love you so much, but I can't take any more."

I said, "Sorry babe, but I need to get off. Can you hold on for one more orgasm?"

Sue said, "I'm really exhausted and sore. Give it to Nancy. I think she needs your attention after what just happened. She needs to know you still love her."

"OK, babe. I do you know. I love you all."

Sue was right. I needed to show Nancy that nothing was wrong. Still, I had been holding off my orgasm, and I needed a release. I kissed Sue a final time and rolled over and snuggled up to Nancy. I pulled her into my arms and kissed her. She kissed me back … hard. I said, "Everything is fine, I love you." The look of relief on her face spoke volumes. My body was still in control of me, and I moved between her thighs. We kissed hard as I drove my throbbing cock deep into her. Nancy groaned and wrapped her legs around me and tried to pull my cock as deep into her as possible. We pounded into each other. We were like animals driven insane with lust. Nancy began to scream at the same time I reached my peak. Both our bodies convulsed at the same time, and I filled her with my seed. She continued to kiss me through our orgasms, but I finally fell to the side between her and Sue. Both girls cuddled and held me, and my arms wrapped underneath them to pull us even tighter. I never felt such love before.

After a few moments of basking in their love I said, "You know what? The situation we find ourselves in with the pending apocalypse and our absolute need to survive as a close knit community, what happened tonight with Jeremy will probably happen again and with others, possibly even often. Still, I want you to know that I love all three of you, and nothing will change that." I chuckled when we heard a scream from Bess in the back bedroom, "I guess you will have to explain to Bess what I'm telling you. I want you to know that I want to be with you all always, no matter what happens with anyone else. If you want the same we will make it happen. The time is not right for a while, because we will go through times we will have to fight to survive, but when it comes time to pair up to have children in a new world, I want the three of you to have my children."

I think I could have given a great motivational speech and not gotten a reaction like I got from Nancy and Sue. I guess I said the right thing, because they were all over me kissing me and crying and thanking me for those words. The thing is, I meant every word.

Chapter 5
(Building the Team)

We all jumped up with the alarm. Bess, Nancy and I immediately hit the shower, with very little messing around. We knew we had a busy day ahead and had even decided to skip breakfast in lieu of a quick pass through McDonalds' drive through. After all, I have to have my coffee in the morning.

Before we left I helped Jeremy load our safe into his pick-up. Since we were going after gold and silver, he was going to get it installed in my trailer before we got back.

On the way to Tahlequah I had a brain flash and said, "Nancy, why don't we call Robert Arrowhead and ask him to meet us somewhere and go with us. It would be nice to have a decked out and armed law officer with us when we pick up the gold."

Nancy said, "Good idea. You can interview him as we drive."

As it turned out, Starbucks was close to him, and I got more coffee. He *was* in fact decked out in an impressive uniform, armed and more than willing to go with us. I already knew much about him from his impressive resume and from what Nancy knew about him. He stood 6' tall, slightly shorter than me, with a stocky Indian build. I just asked straight out, "Why do you want to join our project?"

Robert said, "I have thought much about it. First, I want to know about survival in an off-grid situation. Secondly, If I hadn't seen your ad about your project I would still be trying to find a way to do it myself. Almost anyone in law enforcement or in the know can see it coming. It's inevitable. The world is in the process of imploding. You say your project is for a book. No matter the reason, you are doing it, and I want to be inside the project when the collapse comes. You say two years. Well, two years is a long time and a lot can happen and probably will in that time, and I think you already know that. I'm thinking what you should be worrying about is if I can help. I can assure you I know what I'm doing. I have the experience in actual battle, which we are likely to see if civilization falls. I can obtain weapons, armaments, ammunition, and even others in my organization that would come aboard."

I said, "Could you fight and kill our military if necessary?"

He said, "If you mean when they come for our food stores, the answer is yes. When they try to take ours, they will no longer be an official army. They would just be a marauding gang in uniform trying to look like an army. I see you have given this some thought, too. Those that know what we have will try to take it when they get hungry, but most would be smaller gangs ... I hope. Our plan should be to try to remain secret and isolated and not let anyone in that doesn't belong to tell the outside world. I can do that, too."

I said, "Nancy has suggested that since our property is considered part of the Cherokee Nation, we can claim sovereignty from the US, at least legally for as long as the federal government is active and concerned. Also that our security force can remain a legal branch of the Cherokee Marshal Service. What do you think about that?"

"That is an excellent idea. Actually, that is a much better plan than what I was considering. May I ask, how many members will there be sequestered?"

I said, "Initially, one hundred but a second group of a hundred will join us."

Robert said, "How large are you thinking for the security force?"

"I'm thinking twenty-five of your choice, comprised of men and women. Once we are forced to sequester there will be no going to town for companionship, if you get my meaning. It could be more, but we must keep the numbers for all departments within the hundred limit, and we have many. I do, however, envision all residents trained and capable of fighting if necessary." I waited in silence then asked, "Are you in?"

Robert said, "Yes Sir, I'm in."

I said, "Welcome aboard our project and family. Nancy is my assistant, well sometimes my boss, real estate agent and attorney. She will get you squared away."

We turned off of the Creek Turnpike on 41st Street to look for the dive shop. I couldn't remember the name, but I figured I would be able to see a red dive sign. I heard Nancy telling Robert about the advance, the cabins, etc. as we drove down 41st. Sure enough I saw the dive sign and pulled in. I wanted to get the dive equipment before we picked up the gold, so we could head directly back.

The four of us went in and started looking through the display equipment. I was somewhat familiar with what everything was, but Bess was an expert. She got their attention immediately when she told them we wanted four complete sets. The owner came out to personally take care of us. Bess picked out two BCs (Buoyancy Compensators) for males and two for females, four tanks and a spare. Bess was going down the displays pointing, and the smiling owner was filling up carts with equipment. She picked out various sizes of fins, gages and adapters, a depth finder, dive computer, watches, face masks, underwater flashlights and cameras, knives, and wet suit tops and bottoms, boots. Bess didn't go the cheap route, picking from the best and most expensive. There wasn't much she left out. Just when I thought she was finished she asked for a tank compressor. Now, I hadn't thought of that. After everything was checked out and totaled, which came to a sizable amount, I demanded a discount, which I got. I then presented him with my American Express Platinum Card. I thought his eyes were going to pop out. He started looking around for something else to sell us, and he finally found something. We had forgotten to buy a diving flag for the boat. I was beginning to wonder if Bess was going to buy a boat, which was probably a good idea. We could store it at the marina by our cabin. I decided against it, since we were running out of time, and we would have a small fortune in gold and silver in my truck, but at least I had a lockable cover on the back.

During the shopping I sided up to Bess and quietly ask, "Bess, you ever have sex underwater?"

She blushed heavily and said, "Hush. You know I haven't."

I winked at her and walked on, but I think I planted the idea in her mind.

We stored all the equipment my truck and headed on down 41st a few blocks to Tulsa Gold and Silver. The four of us went in, but the guard stopped Robert, telling him he couldn't come in with a gun.

We stayed by the door, but I said, "Get me the owner or manager."

He was there shortly and introduced himself, and I said, "Sir, I intend to spend one million dollars in here today. This officer is here to protect me and my purchase. He is also deputized with the Tulsa Police Department and many others municipalities. I want him with me and armed. Now, do we do business?" I spoke low, because I didn't really want any others to know.

The manager dismissed the guard and escorted us into a private conference room where we could discuss business without being overheard. Understandably, he chose to handle this transaction himself.

I said, "I'm looking to purchase gold, silver and platinum 1oz coins. I believe we are talking in the neighborhood of 30 lbs of each or some combination."

His eyes bulged somewhat and punched out some numbers then said, "You realize we are talking a little over a million? Do you have the money with you?

"Yes, I realize the amount, and no, I don't have cash on me, but here is my ID and bank account number. While we are taking care of business please have your accountant check me out. I'm sure the bank can wire transfer what is required."

He called someone and handed her my information and give her instructions. It didn't take long before his phone buzzed. When he answered I saw his eyes go wide and he said, "Really?" After that he was all business and very friendly. He excused himself for a while to check his inventory. When he returned he said, "This is quite a large order, and I'm afraid I will have to give some of it to you in larger bars. I just don't have that much in 1oz coins."

We finally agreed on a combination of coins and bars, but we haggled with the price. I got my Gold Eagle coins without paying a surcharge, because I promised to come back and buy another 30 lbs. The transaction concluded and as inconspicuous as possible carried the bags out to my truck and locked them in the back. To avoid being followed we left as quickly as possible and sped back to Tahlequah and Starbucks for the other three interviews.

We had missed lunch and weren't about to stop anywhere, so I shared some of my Texas Super Food drinks. Robert and I set up front and Nancy and Bess rode in the less roomy back seat. Nancy leaned over my shoulder and kissed my cheek, much to Robert's surprise.

Nancy whispered in my ear, "What's the plan? You aren't going to leave the truck in the parking lot during the interviews are you?"

"Yeah, I was just thinking about the problem. I'm thinking maybe Bess can drive my pickup and you and Robert can lead and run interference in his cruiser. I really don't see or expect anyone is following, but I'm still a little paranoid. This will give Robert a chance to see where and what we are doing out there. It will also give you two a chance to figure out how to effectively transfer a branch of the Marshal service here. I know you probably already have it figured out."

"Damn, I hope Jeremy has the safe secured. Hell, I don't know what to do with the gold if he hasn't."

Robert said, "We could use the safe at my office if we have to."

I said, "I guess we could, but Jeremy knew we would be bringing back a load, and he is very good at getting things done. You will like him. He is a go-getter."

Nancy nibbled my ear and said, "I want to be there for your interview with Janet, so I will come back and get you early."

I laughed and said, "I figured you would. She is the last interview. Introduce Robert to Jeremy and let him get a good look around the property before you come back. And Robert, we are happy to have you with us. You are welcome to move in any time you're ready. The sooner the better. Oh, Nancy, put Robert in the large trailer at the cabin complex. That way he can move many of his recruits in

115

there with him, and also ask that complex manager to stock food for all the cabins and anything else you can think of. She doesn't have anything else to do with no customers. I just don't want the new people having to scramble to eat."

Nancy said, "Yeah, that's a good idea. I'll take care of it."

We were a little early when we reached Starbucks, but we split up according to my plan, and I was left alone. I managed to find a bagel and egg sandwich and settled in my normal spot in the corner. I had just finish my bagel when I saw James Baker enter and look around, at least I thought it was him. I waved and pointed to the baristas, indicating that he should get some coffee. He nodded and proceeded to do so. He was of medium build and somewhat muscular. James looked to be in his late twenties or early thirties with fairly long brown hair. He seemed to have a perpetual smile on his tanned face.

We introduced ourselves and started chatting. All the remaining candidates I already knew I wanted from reading their resumes. All I really needed to determine was attitude and personality and if they would fit into the group. Well, job performance was a major factor, of course. I said, "I assume you know what we are doing. What I need for you to tell me is what can you do for our community?"

James said, "I am a graduate of Oklahoma State University with various degrees. I excelled in college, but my real experience is actual farming. I have been a rancher and farmer all my life. I grew up on a wheat farm, but we also raised cattle, both

116

for food and dairy. We sold milk and chickens for a cash source. In college I learned how to improve and maximize those commodities. I am educated in soil enrichment for growing more and better crops of all kinds."

"How many people will be sequestered and how many acres will you have available for farming? I assume we plan to produce our own food and not depend on outside supplies."

I said, "You are correct. We will have 200 people sequestered and at last count we have close to 200 acres for food production, but we can purchase more if we have to. We will also have a large greenhouse and aquaponics system."

James said, "200 people is a lot to feed on 200 acres. Aquaponics can produce a larger amount of food for the space, but not nearly enough. We lose some acres to fruit trees and poultry and cattle. More acres would be better. I assume I would have the money to invest in designing soil supplement and fertilizer to condition the soil and the equipment necessary to do it?"

I said, "Food production is key to our survival, so you will have anything you need."

He said, "That's great. I would like to take on this project. This project would give me the opportunity to use my expertise and education."

"Very well", I said, "Where are you living now?"

"I just graduated from OSU in Stillwater. I believe you know that I lost my ranch, so I am living in a small apartment in Stillwater until I find a way to buy a farm. With this project I think I will be better off and have a better opportunity for growth."

James seemed totally focused on farming and didn't seem to have a clue about any potential civilization collapse. No need for him to know now. We needed each other, and hopefully we will all survive.

I said, "Well, you're in, and if you aren't in a hurry you might stick around and wait for my assistant and attorney to return. I have two more interviews to do."

"I'll be happy to stick around, and thank you."

We continued to chat until I saw the chef come in. I was pretty sure it was Bob Patterson. He stood tall but slightly pudgy, like I envisioned a cook would be. He was more muscular than I expected. That must be the military influence. I waved and he came straight to me and shook my hand quite firmly, again the army training … assertive.

I said, "Would you like some coffee"

Bob said, "No, thank you. I only drink coffee I make myself. I make the best you know."

"I'm sure you do." We both laughed. "I've read your resume, quite impressive. Why do you want to get involved with my group?" I was getting tired and just wanted to get right into it.

Bob said, "Well, I finished my third hitch in the army. I have been debating re-enlisting, but the current attitude of our leaders in the military is not to win our wars. Fighting a politically correct war is suicide to the troops, and I'm not that stupid. I have been floating, doing nothing for the last few months, just living off my savings. When I saw your ad I knew this is something I can do well and want to do. You already know, I'm sure, of my culinary training and military experience. I'm thinking both areas of expertise appeal to your plan, or I wouldn't be here now. This very fact tells me that you do foresee armed conflict in your future. Now, from this, the next reasonable assumption is that this group is in reality an *actual* survival group and not just a study. I don't expect you to confirm or deny this. I just want in."

Damn, this guy is smart. I liked his assertiveness.

I said, "Consider yourself in." I introduced Bob to James and suggested he wait with James for Nancy to return. They began chatting just as Nancy … and Sue came in. I wasn't expecting that, but, Oh Well. I asked them to get Bob and James indoctrinated. I took the opportunity to go to the restroom and pick up another coffee. On my way back to my table I felt a hand on my shoulder and turned to see Janet standing there.

Janet said, "Hello Mike. What are you doing here?"

I said, "I'm here for an interview."

She said, "Really? So am I."

"Yeah, I know. Your interview is with me."

She looked confused, then shocked as reality set in.

Janet said, "My interview is with you?"

"Yeah, myself and my attorney and bookkeeper." Then she got nervous, but she had her coffee already, so I led her to my table. Bob and James

119

had already left so it was only Nancy and Sue, and they stood. I introduced them, and we all began to talk. At first I was a little bit nervous, because I had no idea what game Nancy and Sue were up to. They, however, seemed friendly, very friendly. I started the interview.

I said, "Janet, I thought you were graduating with a chemistry degree."

She laughed and said, "Well calling oneself a sanitation engineer doesn't sound glamorous, but it involves a lot of chemistry, and I chose the field because it pays well. Water treatment doesn't sound very glamorous either, but both fields are degreed under the chemistry heading. If your ad is for real, I would love the opportunity to be involved and join the project."

Nancy said, "Is there anything else in the ad that makes you uncomfortable?"

"Well, actually the ad is very clear if you give it some thought. Being sequestered with 75 men it's understandable why you request unattached members. With 3:1 odds of men to women, the females are obviously expected to do double duty, or in this case, triple duty. I can live with that, but I hope this project is not just about orgy sex. Like I said, I can live with that, but I want to be productive in something real."

I said, "This is real, Janet. It is also very important, and you would be productive, and I might add, necessary. You mentioned being unattached, but I seem to remember that you had a boyfriend."

She laughed and said, "He was gone too much. I dumped him. Maybe if I can join this project I can replace him with three others." We all laughed.

Sue said, "So having sex with multiple partners and not being able to partner with someone special doesn't bother you?"

Janet said, "Does it bother you?"

Nancy said, "We have had to learn about sharing. We have learned that we can love and still share."

Janet shot a quick glance at both girls and said, "Oh. I see. You two are with Mike?"

Nancy said, "We three. We have a sister, too."

Janet laughed and said, "Mike, no wonder I haven't seen you lately, but isn't that a reversal of the odds?"

I'm sure I was blushing, because all three started laughing.

Nancy looked at Sue then me and said, "Janet, I guess you're in." She then looked directly at me and said, "Mike, Sue and I are going to ride back to the project with Janet and get her all indoctrinated. I know you are anxious to get to the project. We'll see you later for dinner. Bring Jeremy and Robert."

They didn't wait for me to respond, and all three left me sitting there wondering what the hell was going on and what they were planning. I thought I was in charge!

I was still wondering about it as I pulled up at the project. Was I ever surprised? I was met at a new heavy duty gate with a uniformed security guard, complete with his own guard shack, and an 8' chain-link fencing for as far as I could see. He

121

must have known who I was, because the automatic gate opened to let me pass. I waved as I passed and saw in my mirror the gate close behind me. Things were certainly improving.

I had to stop in the road when I came to the temporary complex. It was shocking to see all the modular building sitting in place, apparently operational. The barn across the road was even up. Impressive. I saw Jeremy's pickup next to one of the buildings and pulled in next to it. There were no signs, but I remembered this was my office complex. Jeremy saw me pull in and came out to greet me.

Jeremy looked serious and solemn and said, "Mike, I want to apologize to you. I'm sorry, but I didn't fully understand." He sort of hung his head in shame.

I said, "For Pete sakes, Jeremy. What did you do? Spit it out."

"After everyone left this morning I tried to get Sue to go to bed with me. She stopped me cold and told me in no uncertain terms that it wasn't going to happen. She told me she loved you and would consider it cheating to go behind your back for sex. She said it could happen, but only as a group with you being there. I just didn't understand your relationship with the girls, and I had no intentions of offending you. Can you forgive me?"

I chuckled and said, "No offense taken, Jeremy. Our relationship, the girls and I, within the community must be somewhat open. All the women must be open, because there will be far less women than men. The girls and I do love each other and at some point will be a family, but for now we share. So, Jeremy, you are fine, and I have no resentment. Actually, I don't blame you. The girls are some of the most beautiful women I have ever seen. I'm the lucky one. I do love all three, but there are three of them and only one of me. Sometimes a little help is beneficial. Oh, by the way, you are supposed to come to dinner again tonight. Maybe you will get your chance after all." I smiled, and he smiled back in understanding.

I said, "Have you met Robert Arrowhead yet?"

"Yes, Nancy introduced him, and he has already taken charge of the security firm I hired. I guess you saw the gate and guard. He agrees with me that no outsiders should be admitted. We have a phone installed already at the shack. I knew you were coming, because he called me. I think Robert is driving around the project taking a look. We should do that also. I think you will be surprised. First, however, let me show you your office. Believe it or not, it is furnished and totally operational."

We went inside, and I truly was surprised. There was a reception counter up front with two offices to either side, one for accounting, another for Nancy. My office was in the back adjacent to a large conference area, with a single bathroom and small kitchen area. The building looked totally functional. There was a closet in my office, which he opened to show my safe.

Jeremy said, "I helped Nancy, Sue, and Robert load it. The contents are safe."

123

I didn't remember the combination, so I couldn't take a look. God, I hope Nancy has it. Duh, of course she has it. She had to have it to load the gold. I said, "What else is ready here?"

Jeremy said, "My office is also operational, and the medical clinic is ready. Equipment has been coming in for two days. We were letting the deliveries come and be stored in the barn, but I hired a moving crew to come in and set up our offices and the clinic. I'm setting up the security building over next to the barn, since we will be storing supplies in the large basement that need protection. I'm sure you saw it when it was being built. The basement is the size of the entire bottom floor of the barn, which looked massive. Also, the farming office is the partial second floor of the barn. There are additional office spaces there for other functions. I also ordered a large modular building for the cafeteria, but I'm waiting for the chef to tell me how he wants it. I'm setting it up just down from our offices."

I said, "I recruited the chef today. He's military trained and somewhat assertive, so I'm sure he will have his own ideas. Still, I like that about him. We won't have to worry too much about his department."

Jeremy said, "Let me show you the other end of the project. You're really going to like the progress there."

We got in my truck and headed for the island. The road was finished, and bulldozers were busy clearing land for farming. I noticed that many of the trees had been cut up in stacks of firewood, and the brush and waste of the trees were burning in

124

pits. Firetrucks stood by to contain the fire. Jeremy had obviously been working with authorities to keep the fire concern down, although they had little control over us. Not only were the trees being systematically removed, but the land was being leveled for crops. I was amazed at the acreage already completed. Where the grade didn't allow total leveling, sections were established in tiers. James Baker would be pleased.

The first thing I noticed as we approached the island was a completed bridge. It was large enough for two trucks to pass abreast. Vehicles, heavy equipment and dump trucks were coming and going. Roads already existed passing around the island to the top. I could see heavy equipment working on the top. Along the island's edge were vertical cement walls in places anchored into the bedrock of the mountain. I could see the final goal. The walls would be built and filled in to level the terrain, making dumping sites for dirt and rock being excavated from an already huge hole in the mountain. The wall would, obviously, also serve as a defensive barrier for the higher structure. Even before we crossed the bridge I could see an "I" beam structure being constructed inside to ensure the cave ceiling would be abundantly reinforced. I had seen Jeremy's sketches and plans and knew the cave would be very large, huge actually. Inside the cave would be an elevator that would go up through the small mountain into the octagon structure, some called it a fortress. I hoped it would never come to that, but Brin had cautioned me to plan accordingly, and Jeremy seemed to agree with the concept.

Jeremy directed me to the top of the island. The road to the top was wide, and once there he pointed out the basic layout of the structure. The entire hilltop had already been leveled, and stakes driven to mark the eight sides of the structure. It looked much bigger than I had envisioned from the drawings Brin provided, and Jeremy had already indicated that we needed a fourth floor to get everything inside. It would be a huge structure, and I dare say, expensive. I was beginning to wonder if I had enough money. I would have to remember to ask Sue.

Robert pulled up beside us and walked over. He said, "This project is very impressive. The members I've met so far are also impressive. Jeremy and I are getting along great, and he is accomplishing much."

I said, "Before I forget, Robert, you are invited to dinner tonight at my cabin. I think Nancy wants to go over plans on dealing with the Cherokee Nation about your transfer."

Jeremy kind of shot me a surprised but knowing grin, but Robert missed the exchange and said, "That's good. I'll follow you when you leave."

Me, however, had no idea about what the girls were planning. One thing for sure, I would find out at some point. These girls are good at surprising me.

I turned back to Robert and said, "What are your security concerns for the property?

Robert thought for a few seconds and said, "The castle will be easy to defend unless we have to consider air strikes. The thick walls being constructed make it easier to defend. That was a good

126

move on Jeremy's part. The fact that it is surrounded by water adds to the defense capabilities. Jeremy told me about the underwater dome and the interconnecting hidden tunnel from the cave. That too is a good move. Of course the drawbridge prevents any large assaults. Our major defenses will be mounted on the roof. The height gives us a major advantage. Unfortunately, there is not a lot we can do about an armed assault on the fields and crops. There is too much area to protect."

"With the security fence, surveillance cameras and motion sensors, we can detect small breaches and dispatch security officers to run them off, but it would be a losing battle to try and go one on one against an armed assault. The best defense in this situation is to have an abundant supply of food stock (at least 2 yrs.) stored in the cave, which I believe you are already planning to do. That's a smart move and something we can defend."

"Thanks, Robert. Not a bad analysis for only being on the job for a few hours. I know you are already making plans, but expedite your arms and ammunition order ASAP. We can store them in the barn basement until this structure is ready. And Robert, think of this as Christmas. Order all the guns, ammunitions, and other toys you might want. Remember, bullets could become as good a trading commodity as gold in the future."

I turned to Jeremy and said, "Jeremy, clear your schedule for tomorrow morning. We picked up the scuba gear, and we need to take a look at the dome foundation. We picked up cameras, depth finders and a distance measuring laser. We can rent a boat at the marina down from our cabins."

Jeremy said, "Sure. I just need to let my foremen know."

It was getting late, so we headed to the cabin, and we were there in a short time. As we entered my cabin I was met by three beautiful ladies and three sweet kisses, which raised Robert's eyebrows. It was then that I realized the girls and I always acted professional during the day and only let our hair down, so to speak, at our cabin.

Nancy said, "We picked up some fast food on the way back, so we can eat now."

When I looked around I was surprised to see Janet standing behind me smiling. I wondered what she was doing here, but I knew I better not ask. I'm sure a perplexed look shown on my face, because Sue leaned in to my ear and whispered, "Janet is here because Nancy wants to watch you have sex with her, and so do Bess and I." Huh? I knew I would find out what they were up to, but this is crazy. I just stood there until Nancy called us all to eat.

While we ate we talked business. I said, "Nancy and Sue, our office is ready for occupancy. You can move in tomorrow, and I get the impression that you will need a receptionist, so look through the applicants and pick one. Make sure she or he has another trade or profession that will benefit the community."

"Nancy, have you heard anything from the offer on the property?"

She said, "Oh yes, they accepted the offer. So, we now own 80 more acres as soon as we send them a check. Sue and I can do that in the morning before Robert and I go to the Cherokee Nation. I may have to bribe someone, but no big deal."

Robert said, "I want to pick up some Cherokee Nation signs. They will give us an identity, no matter if it's true or not."

I said, "Bess, Jeremy and I are going diving tomorrow to check out the dome anchors."

The conversation finally reverted to normal chat over coffee.

Bess stood up and took charge. She said, "You all are spending the night. I have robes for everyone but not enough hot water for everyone's showers, so some of us will have to double up. Mike, Nancy and Sue will have to shower together. Janet and I will share the first shower. Robert and Jeremy will be on your own. Good luck."

Janet's eyes went wide and round, but when Bess took her hand, Janet followed her.

Chapter 6
(The Mission Begins)

We, the remainder of us, sat at the table looking at each other, wondering what just happened, except for Nancy and Sue. They seemed to be into a conversation about absolutely nothing. Since we all had our instructions from Bess, we poured another round of coffee and waited our turn in the shower. After a while Bess and Janet came out of the bathroom dressed in robes. Bess looked pleased, and Janet was quiet and breathing heavy.

Bess said, "Mike it's your and the girls' turn. We'll see you soon."

Nancy and Sue led me toward the bathroom. The girls had us naked before the water even came on. They washed me down and each other in short order. I could get used to this kind of treatment. We finished, slipped into our robes and they led me to our bedroom.

On the way, Sue said, "When you guys finish your showers come join us."

Jeremy, after last night had a pretty good idea what was coming, sprinted to the bathroom to be next.

I froze mid-stride when we entered our room at the scene before us. Janet was naked and laying sideways across the bed. Her eyes were closed and her knees were spread wide displaying her beautiful, bald pussy, but the vision of erotic beauty didn't stop there. Bess was totally naked on her knees on the floor with her face buried in Janet's crotch. Bess' legs were slightly spread displaying her beauty. I didn't know where to look. Both visions were erotic. Nancy and Sue jumped up on the bed and got on their knees and let their mouths devour Janet's breasts and nipples, and Janet moaned louder. I dropped to my knees behind Bess and lay my face on Bess's back. I was incredibly aroused and began probing my cock inside her pussy lips. She was wet and slick from her juice, and I pushed inside. Bess began to moan as I went deeper with each stroke. My hands grabbed her hips and pulled her onto my cock. She was so hot, but she never stopped devouring Janet's pussy, in fact she licked faster. Bess was moaning on her pussy and Janet was moaning from Bess' assault. I began slamming into Bess' cheeks fast, driving her face into Janet's pussy. Janet screamed in orgasm, which set Bess off into her own. Bess clamped down on my cock hard. I saw Nancy and Sue continue to assault Janet's breasts. I wasn't about to try again to push through her tight internal muscles clamped on my cock and risk being stuck again. I waited for Bess to relax.

Sue said, "Come on Jeremy. Here is your chance to have me."

I had been unaware of Robert and Jeremy coming into the room, but I now saw Jeremy up on the bed behind Sue pushing his cock inside her. Robert caught on fast and wasn't waiting on a special invitation. He was rubbing Nancy's butt cheeks, then spreading them. I heard him say, "OMG" as he buried his cock into Nancy.

131

Bess finally relaxed enough for me to pull out. Bess collapsed on the floor and rolled to the side to make room for me. I stared at Janet's quivering pussy and walked toward it. Nancy and Sue watched with interest as I pushed my cock into Janet's pussy. Janet moaned as I began to pump into her, stretching her and going deeper. She never opened her eyes. I grabbed Janet's legs and pulled her closer to the edge of the bed and began driving into her very hot pussy. All four girls were screaming. Grunts and squeals echoed in the room and the smell of raw sex filled my nostrils. Jeremy bellowed and almost pushed Sue down on Janet from his thrusts. Janet was going into one orgasm after another as I continued to fill her pussy. I saw Sue and Jeremy fall over on their sides heaving air. Nancy and Robert quickly climaxed in what must have been a common enormous orgasm. I felt my own orgasm raging in my balls and felt my cock erupt with stream after stream of hot liquid inside Janet. She screamed again as I filled her with steamy cum. I just held my jerking cock deep in her hot, quivering pussy until we both came down. My knees threatened to buckle, so I slowly pulled out of Janet and stepped back. As I did I saw Nancy and Sue fill the void I left. They both got on their knees between Janet's legs and spread Janet's thighs even wider.

Sue said to Nancy, "Well, like Bess said before. Janet has got our load. Let's go get it."

They giggled and dove in. They began devouring her pussy, and Janet didn't know who was doing what to her, nor do I think she cared at the moment.

132

I just stood there admiring Nancy and Sue's beautiful backside. They were so erotic I couldn't move. I was standing there holding my cock in my hand and noticed it was still hard. I didn't know if I had another one in me so quick, but I wasn't going to miss this opportunity. I dropped to my knees behind Nancy and pushed inside. I heard her moan and saw her look back and smile. That set me off again and I began pounding into her cheeks. As I was doing that my hand pulled Sue's butt closer and began fondling her. I quickly moved behind her and drove my now extremely hard cock deep into her hot tunnel. I began taking turns on them, several hard strokes in one then the other. Both had orgasms, and I was just about to lose my nut when I heard Robert.

He had been watching intently as I switched back and forth and said, "Damn, look at that horse cock. I think I'm going to start calling him Trigger." When the girls looked puzzled Robert said, "Trigger is the name of the cowboy Roy Rogers's horse." They understood.

When he said that I and everyone else started laughing. I got to laughing so hard I lost my lust, plus I was now self-conscious. When I got up both Nancy and Sue got up also.

Jeremy recovered the quickest from his orgasm and laughing. He was staring at Janet who remained spread. It certainly was arousing to see, and it must have been so for Jeremy.

Jeremy got between her open thighs and pushed inside Janet and began pounding like a mad man. Janet began moaning again, and Bess moved up to

133

Janet's face and was kissing her wildly. I lay beside Sue and pulled her to me and watched. Jeremy looked like he was trying to drive his cock completely through Janet, who was continuing to scream. He suddenly held still as he poured his juice into Janet. Jeremy finally pulled out and went to the bathroom. Janet lay still with her knees held wide, still locked into a kiss with Bess. Robert had been watching and moved between Janet's thighs and plunged into her. Janet screamed and began her orgasms again, but went silent about halfway through Robert's assault.

Bess said, "Robert, she passed out. Come up here and finish in my pussy. I have room for another cock."

Robert grinned and came around and slid between Bess' thighs and started pumping into her. Bess squealed in delight.

Nancy said, "Jeremy, can you carry Janet to your bed. I think she's done for the night."

Robert and Bess finished with another loud orgasms. After a few minutes a grinning Bess said, "I will go with you, Jeremy. Janet needs to be cleaned up."

Nancy, Sue and I began laughing.

Bess said, "Just because I now like fucking doesn't mean I lost my taste for pussy."

Robert helped Jeremy take the sleeping Janet to Jeremy's bed followed closely by Bess. Nancy, Sue and I cuddled up together in the now mostly empty king-sized bed. We had plenty of room but were drawn to each other. The girls were both on their sides with their heads resting on my arms. I loved

134

these times. As we lay there I had to ask, "Did you three plan this all out?" They gave me those giggles I so loved.

Nancy said, "Well, you know Sue. She wanted to know from Janet all about her sexual experience with you. We told her about our relationship with you and that we knew about her. We finally convinced her that we bore her no harm or jealousy and she finally began to talk. She told us about your first time when she was on the phone talking to her boyfriend. We laughed so hard, but it aroused us too, and we decided we wanted to watch you pound into her like in her story. Once Bess saw her and we told her what we planned, Bess got excited and said she would take the lead. We knew she was hot for Janet from the first, but I'm not sure Janet realized what she was getting into, but she seemed to enjoy it. So, we can blame Bess."

Sue said, "Yeah, it's all Bess' fault."

As we lay together Robert, still naked, came back into the room. He said, "Thank you, all of you, for tonight. Joining this team is so right, and I'm thankful for your acceptance. I also want to thank you for a dream come true. This has been the best sexual experience of my life. I have been inside three of the four most beautiful women I have ever seen, and I realize what happened tonight may never happen again. The only thing that could possibly make this night better would be if I could be inside the fourth beauty."

Sue realized Robert was talking about her and said, "Well, slip back in bed behind me and let's spoon, while you tell me how beautiful I am."

I stifled a laugh, because I knew Robert was serious. Hell, I also believe these women were among the most beautiful and sexy women alive. Robert didn't take time to consider the invitation and slipped in behind Sue. I saw his arm slip around her to cup her breasts. Sue was looking into my eyes, so I kissed her lips to let her know I loved her. She kept her head on my arm, but I felt her shift her hips. Soon I felt her hips move in rhythm to Robert's thrusts, which were slow but solid, just the way she loved it. Sue began to moan. Nancy slipped her arm over me and let her hand slip down to hold my cock. She stroked me as we watched Sue and Robert. As Sue's moans increased, Nancy slipped her head down my chest and took my cock into her mouth. Nancy seems to really enjoy sucking my cock, and I certainly didn't mind it. She was becoming addicted. We suddenly heard Sue scream in orgasm.

After a few seconds we heard Sue say, "Leave it inside until it slips out, Robert."

Sue's orgasm excited Nancy and she brought her leg over me and slipped down on my cock. After my foiled previous orgasm I was ready, and so was Nancy. She began riding me with power drives up and down on me. I felt her thighs begin to quiver and her pussy gripped my cock, which set my orgasm off. I filled her pulsating pussy with my juice. Nancy stayed on me as she fell forward and begin kissing me. We continued to lay like that, but we began hearing a sound coming out of Sue we had never heard before. It sounded like a loud squeal and hiss. We both looked and saw a look of pure pleasure on Sue's face. Her body was shaking and quivering in a tremendous orgasm.

Nancy said, "Robert, what are you doing to her?"

He said, "Well, it never slipped out so I started pumping into her again, and I pushed a finger into her anus as well. She went wild and had a massive orgasm."

Nancy said, "Ewww."

Robert said, "You have never tried anal? Some women like it and some don't. I think Sue likes it. If you girls ever want to try anal I would be happy to teach you, but don't try it with Trigger. He is far too big."

Nancy laughed and said, "Oh I like Trigger just the way he is and where he is."

Robert kissed Sue on the head, said his 'good nights' to all of us and headed to his bed. Nancy rolled off me back to her side and Sue cuddled up to me. We didn't talk about what happened, but one thing for sure, Sue had sure liked whatever Robert did to her.

As always the alarm went off far too soon for my liking, but we all got up. Nancy, Sue and I hit the shower very quickly, and we were dressed and ready early. The others cycled their way through the shower and joined us at the conference table. We had decided not to try and cook but find breakfast outside. Jeremy, Bess and I decided we would get something after the dive. The others could do what they wanted, restaurant or cook here. I ask Nancy to get Robert the key to his unit, the larger trailer.

I said, "Nancy, you are in charge at the property. I expect some of the new member will start
showing up. Don't let them stand around. Get
them what they need and put them to work. Janet
doesn't have anything to do yet, well maybe she
does, but let her take over the receptionist desk for
now. I trust your judgment. Sue, I know you have
bills to pay and things to order."

Janet burst into the conversation and said, "Are
you always so business-like in the morning? Can I
ask at least one question about last night?"

I said, "Work is work and play is play. We
have a big job to get done in a hurry, so yes we are
usually serious in the morning, but you can ask your
question."

I just wanted to find out if everyone fucked me
last night. I feel like my pussy was pounded up to
my throat."

We all looked around at each other and burst
out laughing. I said, "Well, yes, I think everyone
did fuck you last night, but you seemed to enjoy it."

She said, "I didn't say I didn't enjoy it. I just
wanted to know for sure. It felt like everyone did.
Do we do this often?"

I said, "Not often and never at work and only
on special occasions. Last night was to welcome
you to the community."

She laughed and said, "I certainly feel welcomed, but please don't welcome me anymore until
I recover from last night."

We laughed again at her comment but turned
serious again.

I said, "Robert I know you and Nancy have to get some things accomplished at the Cherokee Nation. As soon as you can, start bringing in your team, you know the requirements, and let Sue know about your needs in vehicles, equipment and the like. She likes to spend my money and is pretty good at it."

Bess, Jeremy and I headed down the road to the marina to find a boat. Once we got to the marina and found the manager, it didn't take long to find a boat. He equipped us with a nice sized, open boat designed for diving. We loaded up our equipment and idled out of the marina before we sped off. It didn't take us long to get there and get anchored, but we had to pull closer to land to find the bottom with our anchor, since there seemed to be a deep hole below the center. This was exactly what we were looking for. Bess had already gone through the equipment and set everything up. We had already put on our short wet suits back at the cabin, so it was just a matter of strapping everything on. Bess checked us out to make sure all worked well, and since Jeremy didn't have much experience with scuba gear, Bess instructed him in the safety and operation. Since she was the one responsible for the safety, she had a second regulator on her tank ... just in case. We were ready, but just before Bess rolled back into the water she shocked us by pushing her diving bottom off and sat there naked below the waist.

Bess said, "Mike, you got me thinking about sex underwater, so come and get me." She smiled then disappeared under the water.

139

Jeremy and I looked at each other and quickly jumped into the frigid water. Bess was already swimming fast down to the bottom. She was a vision of beauty with the light shimmering off her bare butt cheeks, but she was a fast swimmer. No way were we going to catch her. Once she reached the bottom she waited for us to catch up. I think she stopped not so much to let us catch her but to ensure we were breathing well in the gear.

The thought of sex underwater, especially in cold water, made me wonder how that would work or if it could. I grabbed Bess by the hips and pulled her toward me. Her pussy lips were closed tight in the water, but I could tell she was already aroused at the thought. I didn't see any way for kissing or foreplay, so I pulled her legs around me and pushed my diving shorts down. Wow! The diving shorts had been keeping my personal equipment warm, but the cold water made me gasp in my mask. I could see her eyes smiling within her mask, but she reached for my shrunken cock and began rolling it in her hands. Surprisingly I felt it begin to stir, then leap to life. I held her hips and pulled her close as she guided my cock to her pussy. As I slowly began to enter that slick tunnel, the heat, in comparison to the water temperature, engulfed my cock, which incredibly stimulated my cock. It was impossible to describe the feeling, but let's just say, the extreme heat of her pussy set me on fire. I began to pound into her burning pussy. Her body floated, while I held her hips. It felt so great that I knew my climax would come quickly. I was like a wild man driving into her and didn't stop until I exploded inside her. I reached my climax first, but that set her's in motion, and she clamped down on me, which felt wonderful and milked me dry. I was pulling hard on my regulator for air, and the bubbles from Bess' and my regulators seemed to be continuous. I vaguely wondered how much air in the tank we used. I slowly pulled out of Sue and the frigid water immediately took me back to my little boy size penis. I laughed in my throat. I moved to Bess' side and held her hand to let her know I was concerned. Her eyes smiled at me to let me know she was fine.

Jeremy didn't seem to have much of a problem with the cold water, because as soon as I was out of the way he plunged in like a jackrabbit. He began pumping fast, and the look on Bess' face told me she was indeed enjoying her sex underwater. They both climaxed, and we all slowly recovered.

We all got back to business, especially Jeremy. He began swimming all over the cove taking pictures, measuring water depths and distances. He found three spots for the anchor locations along the underwater canyon walls and took many closeup pictures. At one point we went down to the very bottom, or tried to. It was much deeper than I had thought and wondered how Brin knew the depth was sufficient for the dome and space below it to park their spaceship. Bess stopped us, motioning 'NO'. She pointed to her air gauge then pointed up, but she insisted we go up slow. I didn't mind being behind her with her glistening butt displayed.

We returned the boat to the marina, unloaded our equipment back into the truck, decided to get something to eat at the marina cafe, then headed back to the cabin to get dressed for work. It was early afternoon by the time we made it to the property. Jeremy immediately took off to his office to check in with his foremen and their progress and get to work on the data we collected for the dome foundation. Sue met me when I entered my office.

Sue said, "Nancy had to take off to close the deal on the additional property, but she wanted me to let you know that Dr. Groom and Dr. Wong reported in and are already set up in their cabin and now busy setting up their clinic. I think there are a couple of more, but I'm not sure who or where."

I said, "Thank you, Sue. Can you make a few calls to determine what is everyone's status?" She nodded confirmations.

For the first time I actually went into my new office and set in my chair. I must admit, it felt comfortable. As I began just thinking about the overall situation I suddenly remembered that I hadn't checked my e-mails for a couple of days. Sure enough there were two e-mails from Brin. I closed my door to read and respond in private.

"We are now actually in your solar system. Yes, we are ahead of schedule and should arrive in approximately one month, but will spend a few days launching satellites in orbit around your planet and trying to stay hidden from Earth's radar. It's not too difficult to stay hidden, but it is risky. I'm not sure I told you before, but most of my crew are in cryogenics. Only myself, Meg and Peg remain awake. We are anxious to know the status of construction and organization of the community, espe-

142

cially the dome. Although we may arrive early, we can hide our ship in the dome, and I can keep my crew in cryogenics until our teams becomes sequestered. It would not be good for any of us if our existence becomes known to the outside world before your civilization totally collapses. Your government may try to get involved, and that wouldn't help our situation."

I immediately went to the second e-mail and read:

"I hope everything is well with you. I'm concerned with your lack of response to my e-mail, but I am assuming you are just busy with all the activities at your end. Please, however, try to keep me informed. Also, let me know if I can provide any information or assist you in any way. I advise you to buy as much supplies and equipment as you can, while money is still good. I'm assuming you still have plenty of funds remaining, but, just in case, please note the lottery date and numbers provided. The end is close enough to risk another lottery win, and the high dollar amount on this lottery makes it worth the risk ($320,000,000)."

Both e-mails were enough to almost panic me. Am I going too slow? Is Brin expecting us to be much further along? Are we running out of time? I remember that Brin had said not to win another lottery, because it would trigger an investigation. The economic collapse must be imminent, and we are far from ready. I called Sue on the phone and ask her to bring the books to my office.

She could tell immediately from the look on my face that something was wrong and became very

143

serious and totally attentive. I said, "Sue, how much money have we spent so far?"

Sue looked at the checkbook and ledger and said, "We still have plenty of money in the bank, and the stock market account is growing greatly. It's over $300,000,000. Actually, Mike, we have only spent a few million."

I said, "Crap! I want you to get on the phone to those we have recruited so far, well, the main ones anyway and get them in here for a meeting. If they haven't reported in yet, find out when they will be here and speed them up. For those available, try to make it for 6:00 pm this evening."

"Oh, have you found a receptionist?"

Sue said, "No, we haven't done that yet."

I said, "Well, get Janet in here to help you. I need you to review the applicants and organize them for our meeting this evening." She nodded and rushed to comply.

I was still in a panic and knew it would be a long afternoon. Before I got started I decided to make some coffee and try to relax. Relaxing and coffee didn't seem to go together, but then I have always been unconventional.

After my second cup I stated working on my list of one hundred community members. This proved more than just making a list. I had to establish department heads and find organizational slots for all of them. I also had to try and identify our potential needs for the open slots. It took me several hours, but I finally finished the list... almost.

Apocalypse Survivor Members

144

Name	Position
Mike Brannon	Chairman

Nancy McIntosh	Real Estate/Attorney/Property Mgr./Assist

Receptionist

Castle Manager
Laundry
Laundry
Laundry
Janitor

Janitor
Seamstress
Seamstress
Weaver

Chaplin

Sue McIntosh	Accountant

Warehouse
Warehouse

Bess McIntosh	Marine Biology/Botanist

Greenhouse/Botanist
Greenhouse/Botanist

Bob Patterson	Chief Chef

Cook/Food Preservation
Butcher
Cook
Cook
Cook
Miller
Canner

Dr. George Groom	Doctor

Nurse

Susan Wong — Dentist

Nurse/Dental

Veterinarian

Veterinarian Asst.

Jeremy Hodge	Architect

Al Martinez — Electrical Engineer

Electrician
Electrician

Construction Supervisor
Carpenter
Blacksmith/welder
Plumber
Geothermal Engineer
I T/Communication Engineer
AutoCad Designer
Maintenance
Maintenance
Maintenance

Janet Walsh   Sanitation   Eng.   &   Water
Treatment Specialist

                                     Sanitation/Water Eng.
                                     Sanitation/Water Eng.

James Baker   **Master Farmer**
                             Dairy
                             Poultry
                             Farmer
                             Farmer
                             Farmer
                             Farmer
                             Mechanic
                             Cattle
                             Cattle
                             Horses
                             Tanner/leather Craftsman

Robert Arrowhead   **Chief of Security/Militia**
                                     Surveillance/Communications
                                     Surveillance/Communications
                                     Heavy Armament Specialist
                                     K-9
                                     K-9
                                     K-9
                                     K-9
                                     Security Officer

                                     Security Officer
                                     Security Officer
                                     Security Officer
                                     SWAT Officer
                                     SWAT Officer
                                     SWAT Officer
                                     SWAT Officer
                                     SWAT Officer
                                     Sniper
                                     Sniper

Combat Officer
Combat Officer
Combat Officer
Water Security Officer/Boat
Water Security Officer/Boat

I was finally pleased with the list and left my office for more coffee. I noticed Janet setting at the reception desk and asked her to make copies of my list for those coming to the meeting. Nancy came in the door as I was headed to the coffee pot.

Nancy said, "Mike, I picked you up a coffee from Starbucks, but we need to put it in the microwave to heat it up. Sue said we were having a meeting, so I also picked us up something to eat."

Sure enough she was carrying a bucket of KFC and several sacks. I didn't realize how hungry I was. I detoured by the microwave with my coffee then followed Sue and Nancy into the conference room. I tore into the food as soon as Nancy put it in front of me. I said, "Oh, Nancy, thanks so much for the coffee and food. I had no idea I was this hungry."

Nancy said, "Well, you did go diving this morning. That will sap your energy."

I laughed out loud and said, "Yeah, and Bess forced me to have sex with her underwater this morning. That will also sap energy."

They also laughed and Sue said, "I didn't realize our sister was such a slut." I joined them in the laughter again.

Nancy said, "Sue told me you seemed stressed about something. Anything we can do to help?"

147

I said, "Yes, there is something everyone can do to help, but let's wait until the meeting."

Nancy said, "That won't be long. You know it's almost 6:00 don't you?"

"No shit?" I didn't realize I had spent that many hours working on the list, but obviously I had. They would be showing up any time now, so I hurriedly finished my food.

Soon the members began to file in, and I was pleased to see the addition of Bob Patterson (Head Chef) and James Baker (Master Farmer) arrive. Many of them got coffee on their way in and grabbed a piece of chicken as they took a seat around the conference table. Janet was the last to come in, and she closed the door behind her.

I said, "Welcome everyone. Hello Bob and James. I hadn't heard you arrived, but I'm pleased to see you. This is important. Hello Doc and Doc." They all acknowledged with a wave or nod. "You can all introduce yourselves to each other a little later when we have more time, but I must cover a few items that require immediate attention. You all know that we are building a survival team, but none of you know the real reason. Well, many of you have guessed. This team has been brought together not for a study. It is the real thing! We ARE a survival team. Within a few short months, maybe even weeks, the world as we know it will cease to exist. The economy will collapse first, taking everything else with it. What we build here will be the basis of the new civilization. It grows from here and us or it will fail. I was going to wait to tell you this, but it is happening faster than I had hoped, and there is still far too much to get done before then. Any questions before we go on?" I looked around the table, and all had sober looks.

James, the Master Farmer raised his hand and said, "This is for real? How do you know? I mean the economy might improve or not fall as fast as you think."

The question coming from him was not surprising. During the interview he was the only one that didn't seem to have a clue about the world around him. He knew farming and knew it well, and that's what we needed.

I said, "James, yes, this is all real, and no, it will fall. It has been foreseen in the future and will happen. Before you start to believe I'm some kind of nut, I must explain more. Now, no one here knows what I am about to tell you, not even Nancy and Sue, and no one outside this room must ever know any time soon and certainly not outside the community." They were all silent and extremely attentive. "Before I go on, Sue, how much am I worth?"

Sue said, "You have about $200,000,000 spread out in several banks and another $300,000,000 in a separate bank and growing."

"I'm sure many of you have checked me out, but does anyone know how I got so wealthy? I'll tell you. I have a partner coming with the other half of our team and community. My partner gave me the winning lottery ticket numbers and I won this money. Why and how was he able to do that? That group wanted me to build this survival facility for both groups and they looked into the future to get

149

the winning numbers. This is also how I know the collapse is imminent. They saw it, and I tell you all this now so you will believe me. The proof is that I now have the money, and I have access to unlimited additional funds if necessary, as long as it comes before the economic collapse. The real problem is that when the collapse comes all this money will do us no good. Money will be useless. Our immediate job is to spend this money and get this facility built and stocked. We must convert this money to THINGS ... equipment and inventory. We must buy everything we need to survive, and that includes equipment, fuel, tanks to store it, immense food stocks, arms and ammunition to defend it, anything you can imagine. That is why you and the rest of the team are here ... to survive. If we need cattle, horses, goats, chickens to survive, get them, and we must build the barns, stock the hay, feed, medical supplies. I need you to use your imagination and spend money like crazy. Like I said, we have the money and can get more, but we must hurry. If we have to build more barns to store things in, so be it. Think of what you might want to buy now, because later will be too late."

"Janet will pass out the survivor list if you haven't already got one. I developed it this afternoon. It's malleable, but take a look at it. I have established department heads and assigned other members to most of you. We must find member to fill these slots quickly, because they too will need to order for their needs. Sue has a voluminous list to pick from, so please see her and value her opinion.

150

This is extremely important, and keep in mind the gender mix of members."

"Jeremy, other than Robert with security, you probably have the biggest responsibility, because you have the biggest demand on you. We must complete the Castle before the fall. This will be our new home and defense. Hire as many contractors as possible to get it done and work them around the clock. That goes for all of you. Hire it done and get it done, and that includes the underwater dome. Our friends need it for their survival."

"Nancy, you closed the deal on the additional property?"

Nancy said, "Yes, it is done. We own an additional 150 acres."

"Great, we now have a natural gas well. I guess we need to fence this new property in, too. James, you now have more fields to farm. I suggest you fill your member slots quickly. At best, your growing season for this year will be short, maybe plant for a fall harvest. At least we should be prepared for next year."

"Robert is head of security. This will be a tough job, especially after the fall. The world will turn hostile and dangerous. The world outside our gates will get very hungry and violent, and they will come for what we have. We don't plan to let them take it from us. We will defend what's ours. We must be ready to kill to save ourselves. Robert, order your vehicles and build your army and gather a more than abundant supply of arms and munitions. I mean hoard them."

151

"Robert can you make another run to Tulsa and pick up another supply of gold and silver. I'm thinking twice the amount as last time."

Robert said, "Sure, Sue, can you give me a check? I'll go tomorrow. I have already recruited several officers, and I'll have a couple go with me."

"Bob, we haven't heard anything from you. Do you have any questions?"

Bob said, "Sir, no Sir. I had pretty much figured out the truth of what is happening. You already told me what I need to know. I will be ordering plenty of food stock and spending lots of money on walk-in freezers and the lot. I know what to do, Sir."

"Thank you, Bob. You can call me Mike. I figured you knew what to do. That's why you are here."

"What about you, James?"

"Well, let's just say I'm thinking a lot different leaving this meeting than I was coming in. My dedication to the project, knowing this is survival for real, has greatly improved. Besides, I like the challenge."

I said, "Anyone else have anything to say or additional questions?"

Dr. Groom said, "Since I am charged with keeping everyone healthy, I want all of you to file through my office when you leave here. I will be taking your blood samples for analysis, and I must insist that all new recruits are subject to my final medical approval. I want to screen for any infectious diseases, especially STDs and HIV. These would be disastrous in a closed community and easily preventable. Sue, do you have any nurses in that stack of applicants?"

Sue said, "Oh yes, I have a stack of them and every other category as well. To all of you, please take a look."

Nancy was the one that just came out with it and said, "Tell us more about your friends, the other group coming. How are they able to see into the future? Why aren't they here helping us? Besides money, which is very important, what are they bringing to the table, so to speak?"

All at the table were milling around, but at Nancy's questions, they all became totally silent and sat back down ... attentive. It was like Nancy asked the very questions they had all been thinking about but was afraid to ask. I thought, "Oh Crap!" I didn't want to have to tell everything. I wasn't sure they were ready, but now I didn't have much of a choice.

I said, "Well, errr awww. Well, I didn't want to go into this right now. We have so many other things to consider, plan, and get done; but oh, well. I'll just come right out with it. Those I have been dealing with are aliens, and I don't mean Mexicans." I let that settle into their reluctant brains then continued, "Their leader, Brin, and I have only communicated via e-mail. Brin tells me that, although from a different and distant world, they share a common ancestry with humans of Earth. Brin says they are humanoid and share a common DNA, that at some point in both our pasts both races share a common forefather. The reason they aren't here to help us is because they are still en route to Earth,

153

but they are getting close now. They intend to hide their spaceship in the dome we are building."

Nancy continued to press me and said, "If Earth is falling into ruin, why do they want to come here now?"

I was beginning to wonder if I talk in my sleep. It was like she knew the answers already and was intentionally dragging the answers out of me. Certainly the group was hanging on my every word.

I continued, "According to Brin, Earth is the only other known source of lifeforms with a possible DNA match to their race, and their race is far more advanced than ours, thus their greater technical capabilities. It seems their race is dying. They hope to mix with us in an effort to partially save their race from total extinction, and in order to do that they must save us. This is how we gained the funds to finance this survival group. As you can see, we need each other to survive."

James said, "How do they intend to, as you say mix, with humans?"

I had to laugh at the naivety of the question and said, "I believe they intend to mix in the same manner humans have mixed for generations. Their females want to have sex with human males in hopes our DNA will allow them to reproduce. I don't really know what they look like, but I must assume, with common DNA, they look much like we do. Brin says their females are pleasant looking, but then he is probably a little biased."

Jeremy said, "What technology are they bringing?"

I said, "Brin mentioned an advanced waste management system, a high power output source that runs on water, and he also mentioned weaponry. The Castle was originally my concept, but Brin designed it. In fact, I believe he is the one that sent it to you, so you have his e-mail address if you want to contact him directly."

Jeremy said, "I would like that very much."

I said, "Nancy, have I answered your questions to your satisfaction?"

She grinned and said, "You have indeed my love."

As a final thought I said, "The department heads should try to meet each morning so we are all dancing to the same tune."

Jeremy said, "Mike, let me take you on a tour, so you can feel better about our progress."

"Right after we go give blood."

Chapter 7
(Progress)

Jeremy, Nancy, and I went to Dr. Groom's temporary clinic. Doc seemed pleased to be among our group and was even humming as he took our blood.

Doc said, "I will need to do a more extensive physical evaluation and take other samples for testing, but that can be scheduled."

I noticed Dr. Wong grin at him as he mentioned the other samples, but it was quick. I had no idea what was passing between them, but I was sure I would find out in time.

On the way back to my office Nancy slipped her arm around me and asked, "Are you mad at me for pushing you?"

I said, "How could I ever be mad at you, I kind of expected to be pushed but not by you. Why did you?"

"No one else pushed, and I know they wanted to. So, I pushed, but not for the obvious reason of your answers. I couldn't care less. I did it for you. I wanted you to get it all out, so you would feel better about your secrets. You're carrying enough pressure. I wanted you to share it."

Nancy kissed me and went back to the office, and I jumped into Jeremy's pickup for the tour. I had noticed a steady stream of cement trucks going in and coming out all afternoon, but I had no idea where they were going. As we left the complex and turned on to the island access road the landscape totally changed from what I remembered. I noticed three new barns. I looked at Jeremy for an answer.

Jeremy smiled and said, "I wanted these barns within sight and firing range of the Castle. Two of these barns are for poultry. The first one is an incubator for hatching eggs and raising the young chickens. The second is for raising the older chickens. It has slaughter and dressing tables in the end. A third one will be erected for egg laying hens. It will have a fenced yard for them to run free, up to a point. Now, the third existing barn is for dairy cows. The milking machines have already been delivered. As you can see, the barn and equipment will be able to handle quite a few dairy cows, but we hope to start small. That decision will be made by the dairy farmer we bring in. We haven't decided what field the dairy cows will graze on, but we will have an abundant supply of hay to last for a while. It will be stored in a large pole barn soon to be constructed behind this barn. Off to the other side of the road two more barns will be constructed for beef cows, horses, pigs, goats, sheep or whatever James wants. These two barns will have storage basements for feed and supplies. Along the road there will be a line of those silver, round Butler grain storage bins for feed, grain and farming seeds."

"Very impressive," I said.

As we moved on toward the Castle I noticed large backhoes opening up a large deep trench. To the side were sections of prefabricated cement ducts big enough for a large man to stand upright inside. "What's that for?" I asked.

157

"That's for utilities to and from the Castle/Cave, but it can also function to move security personnel unseen from the Castle to points out here in the field. We will bring it up first in the horse barn. Hopefully, it will never be necessary, but we never know."

I noticed that the digging was in the direction away from the Castle. I said, "Am I to assume you started from the Cave and it's already installed to this point?"

Jeremy smiled and said, "Yes. The hardest part was the section underwater below the bridge. I ordered that entire, curved section out of steel and coated with waterproof epoxy. It came in one piece and was delivered and installed last night while we slept."

As Jeremy was explaining this, we came to the bridge and nothing could be seen of the underground installation. This time we drove directly into the Cave over a cement floor and parked well into the cave. Jeremy wanted me to see the progress inside, and there was indeed progress. The damn Cave was huge. We could park dozens of semi-trailers packed full of supplies in here. We walked around inside and I saw the marvel of engineering. The ceiling was at least twenty feet high. Much of the ceiling and most of the floor was finished, but in other sections cement hadn't been poured, and I could see the engineering. The basic roof of the Cave was a solid slab of rock and the floor was also solid rock. I remember Jeremy had mentioned that the Cave would be built by removing packed dirt sandwiched between layers of rock. The main trick would be preventing the top layer of rock from falling when the supporting dirt was removed. They had built an elaborate steel structure of columns, "I" beams and crisscrossed rebars and poured concrete between them. This Cave wasn't going to collapse.

I saw light coming in from above and walked over to look. I was shocked. There was a large open shaft going straight up. I walked under it and looked up. There was the basement of the Castle about a hundred feet above! It had to be the Castle and this had to be the elevator shaft. I was very pleased with the progress.

Jeremy said, "I knew you were panicked, so I wanted you to see the progress. I told you days ago that I would be working crews around the clock, and I hired many different crews." Jeremy took me by the arm and led me over to a corner and pointed down. "This is the completed tunnel going down to the Dome. The special duct will be delivered and installed tomorrow. It starts here and ends 75 feet underwater. We drilled the tunnel smooth. Now we have to push the duct through it and seal it. Contractors have done this, and the same contractors will begin on the anchors for the Dome as soon as the forms are delivered, which should also be tomorrow. Barges are standing by to transport fast-curing cement trucks to the site. I forwarded the measurements and pictures to the firm as soon as we got back, and they are building the forms. Divers and equipment are currently en route from Houston."

"Now off to the left is a horizontal tunnel that goes to the outside. Steps will lead down to the

159

dock. Don't worry. There will be a strong gate at the end to seal off the tunnel and another one on this end."

He then led me to the Cave's doorway and pointed to the side. "This is the other end of the duct construction you saw on the road." He then pointed to the "I" beams surrounding the opening. "I'm having the door built, and it will be delivered and installed in a couple of days. I talked to the Electrical Engineer, Al, and ordered the power generators he wanted. They will be installed in the back. I ordered three 1000kw diesel generators. They are coming a long ways, so we are looking at next week for installation. I have a contractor installing a large diesel tank outside but underground. We already installed the diesel exhaust to exit out of the mountain and the fuel feed. I have also contracted for three wind turbines to be installed on the mountain top. They should be here tomorrow to start construction. We could go topside, but the cement trucks will make it difficult to get up there, and we could get stuck up there."

By this time I was grinning broadly. Brin certainly chose well when he sent me to Jeremy. I really didn't need to see topside. I wanted to save that for another day. Yes, I was happy, and I could give Brin a good report.

I said, "Jeremy, I am really pleased you took me on this tour. I do feel much better. You are doing an exceptional job, and Brin will be pleased to hear the progress. I know I certainly am."

I was a different man when we reached the office. Nancy noticed the difference right away and came to give me a hug.

Nancy said, "Are you about ready to go to the cabin?"

"Not just yet. I need to send Brin an e-mail on our progress here, then we can go."

Sue brought me a cup of coffee and said, "I ordered more checks. We are going to need plenty after your speech today. I've been on the phone establishing credit with vendors all over, but once they check you out they are all smiles and giggles. Everyone is taking your request to heart and are ordering like crazy. Hell, I even ordered three forklifts, and by the way, I have two warehouse people coming in tomorrow. Call me biased, but they are also accountants with muscles ... I hope. We are going to have a large inventory to track. I also have a crew coming in tomorrow to build storage shelves in the Cave and the Farm Barn, and we should be able to start warehousing soon."

I said, "Thanks Sue. Have others sought your applicant records?"

"Oh, yes. They all have been pouring over the files. I think many new recruits will be coming onboard soon."

As I enjoyed the coffee I put together an e-mail to Brin:

"I just took a tour of the facility and it is progressing very nicely. A great deal has already been built at an extremely fast pace. Crews are working around the clock. You would be impressed. I know you are most concerned with the Dome. It will be

161

ready for you when you get here, as long as you don't arrive this week. It will take longer for the Castle, that is what everyone calls it here, but it too is also coming along at a fast pace. I think we will be ready before the fall if we maintain the pace we have set. While I think about it, Jeremy will be contacting you for the specifications on the waste processor and power generator you talked about. Yes, I told the key players here about you and your group, but then I don't really know a lot about you. I think it went well."

As I finished and was preparing to leave, Nancy said, "Mike, Dr. Wong wants to see you before you leave."

"OK, I'll go over there now."

When I went into the dental office Dr. Wong, dressed in her white smock, directed me to the hydraulic dental chair. After I was seated she leaned me back and said, "I need to get a sperm sample from you for Dr. Groom."

I said, "Huh?"

Dr. Wong said, "Oh stop being a baby. I'm a doctor. Just relax. It won't take long."

Dr. Wong had a serious doctor look on her face and proceeded to undo my shorts and pull them off. I kept telling myself ... "*She is a doctor.*" Of course I was flaccid and still shocked. One of her hands cupped my testicles and began rolling them in her hand, while the other began pulling the skin back on my penis. The combination stirred excitement throughout my body. She then took her palms and began rolling my penis between her palms like a piece of clay. Needless to say I began to get hard.

162

She then put KY Jelly on her finger and slipped it up my anus, saying she needed to massage my prostate. Well, she's the doctor, besides all the stuff she was doing was making me very hard. After a minute or two she tore open a condom and began to roll it down over my hard cock. I assumed it would collect the sample. Then everything changed. It was no longer professional. She lifted her smock and straddled me. She wasn't wearing panties and slowly slipped her hot pussy down over my throbbing cock. If she wanted a sperm sample she was certainly going to get it. Once she was fully impaled with her warm thighs pressing on mine, she began riding my cock … fast and hard. I didn't know her hips could move that fast. With all the previous stimulation I came fast, filling the condom.

Dr. Wong smiled hugely and said, "See, that wasn't so bad was it? Ever since our interview I promised myself I would do this the first time I got you in my dental chair. Still, I almost backed out until I saw your cock. You have a nice cock. I'm going to look forward to working on your teeth."

She slipped off of me and pulled the condom off to process the sample, then began licking and sucking my shrinking cock clean. "Wow!" I said, "Are you going to collect sperm samples this way on all the men?"

Dr. Wong smiled and said, "Maybe. Do you think I will get any complaints?"

I laughed out loud and said, "I seriously doubt it."

When I got back to the office Nancy was ready. She said, "Bess went back to the cabin to prepare

163

something for us to eat. If you are ready, I'll get Sue. I think we have all had a long day."

"Yeah, I'm ready and hungry, too."

Jeremy and Janet pulled in right behind us just as the sun was setting. Yep, it had been a long day. Bess met us at the door and kissed everyone, and I do mean everyone. She was definitely feeling amorous for some reason.

Bess said, "I just opened some cans and fried some chicken. Nothing fancy.

It may not have been fancy, but it sure was good. I stuffed myself on creamed corn, green beans and chicken. And, as was our custom, we sat around the large table chatting. I told the table how pleased I was with the progress.

When it was Bess' turn to talk she shocked us all. She said, "I think I was fucked today."

I almost choked on my coffee, while the entire group burst out laughing. I quickly joined them.

Jeremy said, "Well of course you did at 75 feet underwater. Mike and I were with you. Did you forget?"

Jeremy just admitted to having sex with Bess, but all at the table looked to me for conformation."

I again choked on my coffee and sputter out, "Well, she made me."

Sue said, "How did she make you? She had her mouth covered up with a breathing mask and couldn't talk."

I laughed and said, "Bess only had her face lips covered. She was diving without her suit bottom, and her lower lips kept blowing kisses at me."

164

Bess' face turned beet red, attesting to the fact that my statement was true. The room reverberated with explosive laughter. Nancy and Sue were laughing so hard tears were rolling down their cheeks.

Nancy finally was able to say, "That's our Bess. She has always been the wild sister."

Bess finally calmed enough to say, "I wasn't talking about this morning. I was talking about my physical exam at the doctor's office. I think I was fucked there."

Nancy said, "What do you mean 'You think'. You either were or you weren't"

Bess said, "You know when you see a doctor they put your legs over these cradles and slide a curtain across your tummy so you can't see what they are doing? Well, he did that and felt around inside me for a long time. He put several things deep inside me and one of them was hot. When I say he put it inside me I mean a lot and for a long time. I felt his hands holding my hips as he kept pumping it inside me, and then I heard him groaning. Still, I can't be completely sure it was his cock. That's why I only think I was fucked, but I'm not sure."

We all looked around the table at each other, then we broke out laughing at the same time.

Sue said, "I think we all agree that you WERE fucked."

After the laughter died down I said, "Well, I know for sure I was fucked today and not underwater, but I was also tricked by a doctor. Do you remember when I interviewed Susan Wong, the dentist, and she told me she wanted to do all 75 men during the sequester?" My girls remembered. "Well, she started with me ... maybe I was first." I told them the whole story of how professional she was right up to the point she jumped up on me and personally milked my sperm sample. We broke down in laughter several times as I was relating the story, especially when she told me to stop being a baby, that she was a doctor.

Janet said, "Does that really work, massaging the prostate?"

I said, "I can't say I enjoyed it, but it did make me hard. I guess she knew, since she is the doctor." That brought a few more chuckles.

Janet said, "Bess, it sounds like you have received several loads today. Maybe after coffee I should go get them. Why should you have all the fun."

Bess stood and did an animated stretch and said, "I'm getting sleepy. Maybe I should go lay down for a while. Come on Jeremy. I'm sure you can be useful."

Jeremy grinned and gave his animated stretch and the three of them headed off to his bedroom.

I really was tired, so Nancy, Sue and I headed for the shower. I do love seeing my girls naked, but after a hot shower all I felt was tired and sleepy. We went directly to bed, and I pulled my girls tight to me in a blanket of warmth and love. I kissed them and almost immediately went to sleep cuddled on both sides by the loves of my life.

I'm not sure how long I slept. It must have been a while, because I felt refreshed and quite aroused. After blinking a few times I realized why.

I looked down to see Nancy sucking my now very hard cock. She was laying between my spread legs and bouncing her head up and down. Her eyes smiled into mine, and I lay back to enjoy it. When I began moaning Sue was instantly awake and kissing me.

Sue said, "I see my slut sister is abusing you again."

I chuckled and pulled Sue toward me. She understood and immediately tossed her leg over my head facing Nancy. Sue slowly lowered her hot, sweet pussy down on my mouth, and I wiggled my tongue and began to feast on it. Her moans replaced mine and she began sliding her slick pussy back and forth over my probing tongue. Nancy gave up her oral attack and moved up to straddle my thighs and slide her flaming hot pussy down over my cock. The heat of her pussy engulfed my cock and set me on fire. I doubled my efforts on Sue. My hands gripped her hips as I pulled her down tight on my mouth to probe deep for her nectar. Sue's moans turned to screams. I could not see what was happening, but the screams became muffled, and I felt the girls lean toward each other. I could envision in my mind them embracing and kissing each other. Just the thought of it inflamed me. I felt Sue's hard nub on my tongue and I latched on to it with my mouth and sucked. My hands held her from lifting away, and her thighs began to buck, followed by a loud and continuous muffled scream. Her nectar flooded my face, as she succeeded in finally rolling off my face. Sue collapsed onto the bed beside me, allowing me to see the raw lust on Nancy's face. I turned my total attention to Nancy and grabbed her hips and began driving up into Nancy's already quivering pussy and thighs. I was driving hard, lifting her with my thrusts. She bounced and screamed as I assaulted her pussy. Nancy's orgasm triggered my own, and I filled her. Nancy collapsed on my chest heaving for breath. I tenderly stroked her back and butt cheeks as we calmed, and I whispered in her ear, "I love you."

Nancy was beyond being able to talk and slowly rolled to my side, and once she did, I saw Jeremy, Bess and Janet standing naked beside the bed, just watching in awe.

Bess said, "That was awesome. We heard the screaming and knew something incredible was happening." She then proceeded to spread Nancy's legs and lay between them staring at her oozing pussy for a few seconds before she began licking her clean. This quickly elevated to dragging her tongue through it. Nancy began moaning again and they were off again.

Janet was far less aggressive than Bess, but she was obviously attracted to Sue's leaking pussy and lay over my legs to tentatively taste it. It was like her first time tasting a female and maybe it was. If it was her first time she must have liked it, because after a few licks she dove right in. Jeremy moved behind Sue and spooned her. Sue was laying partially on her side, and he lifted Sue's leg to give Janet easier access. After a few moments of Janet's attention Jeremy pushed himself into Sue. The double attention excited Sue and she began moaning, but Janet couldn't reach where she wanted and

168

pulled back, laying her head on my thigh. We watched Jeremy and Sue. He was going faster and harder.

Between her moans Sue said, "Do what Robert did the other night."

Jeremy said, "What did he do?"

"The butt." She said.

Jeremy said, "I don't understand what you want."

Frustrated, Sue bellowed, "Dammit, Jeremy. Fuck me in the ass!"

I think it shocked us all, especially me, because Sue never used that kind of language. Bess was the potty mouth, but Jeremy understood then what Sue wanted and began exploring. He took his time, but apparently found a way to enter her anus. Sue started again with the squeals we heard when Robert said he had a finger in her anus. He must have had much more than his finger in there. Sue's excitement was obvious from the high pitched squeals, a completely different sound from her normal virginal sex. I was a little envious of Jeremy, since he was experiencing something I would probably never be able to experience. I knew I was bigger than most, but that night when Robert was here he nicknamed me Trigger. Everyone laughed, but I knew it would be painful for a woman if I tried. Still, Sue seemed to like it very much from the squeals she was emitting. Jeremy seemed to like it too. He was bucking into her now with renewed vigor, and they both seemed to explode at the same time. It was exciting to watch, but I had just had a massive orgasm with Nancy. I knew I was dead for a while, but Janet seemed to have other ideas. As Janet lay over my legs she began playing with my cock, but nothing was happening.

I said, "Janet, I think you are wasting your time."

Janet said, "Well, maybe if I act like a doctor and treat you like a patient I can get a sperm sample."

I laughed and heard Nancy and Bess laugh as well.

Janet said, "Humm, let me see. You told us she rolled your dick between her palms like this." Janet proceeded to take my cock and roll it like I had described at dinner. "Maybe if I warm it up like this." As she was rolling it she sucked on the mushroom head. She stopped long enough to say, "Oh, and the doctor massaged your prostate like this." She began rubbing my anus and slowly pushed her finger inside and found my prostate and began rubbing it.

By this time all of them were watching and listening, as Janet continued her personal administration to me. I didn't realize that it had worked until I felt Janet's hand squeeze my now painfully hard cock. I also realized I was also extremely horny. I assertively guided Janet face down on the bed and straddled her hips. She was going to get sex now whether she wanted it or not, but I suspected she wanted it. I spread her butt cheeks and pushed inside her. I held her shoulders and began driving into her hot tunnel from behind. I was not gentle, but she didn't seem to mind it. Janet started having orgasms almost immediately, but I continued pounding into her. Her screams eventually came in short bursts and matched her clamping pussy muscles, which drove me faster and harder. Her butt cheeks quivered as I drove into her, and I squeezed them. Her arms flayed out, slapping and griping the sheets, and her lower legs started kicking, but I had her pinned down. She caused my excitement. Now she was getting her reward ... or maybe punishment. My jerking cock gushed deep inside her over and over. Janet's body slowly relaxed but didn't stop quivering. I remained inside to absorb and enjoy the quivering. I was still deep inside her and said, "Did you get enough sperm sample?" Everyone laughed, including Janet.

Bess said, "Come on Janet. Let's go back to Jeremy's bed, so I can clean the sample off." This set our laughing off again. Bess continued, "And, little sis, you can forget about me cleaning up that hole." That set us off again, including a blushing Sue.

Our room settled back down to just the three of us, all exhausted. We cuddled, kissed and were soon sound asleep again.

When my alarm went off I was up immediately. Nancy, Sue and I hit the shower together, but once we were dressed, all the others were already gone. We found a note on the table that said, Bob called to let me know he would have a breakfast buffet for the existing members in his temporary kitchen. He said it is just him so far, but our membership is still low and he can handle it. So, we will see you in Bob's Kitchen.

As we approached the property we noticed a fence already being installed on the new additional

171

property, and bulldozers were hard at work clearing trees, building terraces and leveling ground. When we got to the Farm Barn two new John Deere tractors were parked outside, along with numerous plows, harrows, seeders, cutters and bailers and others I didn't recognize, parked in a row along the back. Yep, James had been busy. It also looked like James was also taking care of seed storage in addition to what Jeremy planned for on down the road. Several circular cement foundations were curing, and the first shiny, silver grain bin was being erected. These looked to be about 30 feet wide, kind of big I thought, but what do I know. One would hold a lot of wheat.

Bob's Kitchen was operational when we went in, well somewhat for a few. He smiled hugely when we came in and pointed toward a buffet counter full of eggs, bacon, waffles, grits, everything I like, especially coffee.

We filled our trays and joined Jeremy, Janet, Bess and James at their table. Actually, there were only three tables in the room, but that was enough for the current community members, most of which weren't present. Robert and a tall, muscular black woman sat down across from me.

Robert said, "Let me introduce you to Jane Johnson, JJ for short. JJ is one of my lieutenants in our security force. Like me, she is an ex-Marine officer and will make a great addition."

All around the table introduced themselves and welcomed JJ to the group.

Robert continued, "Mike, have you been listening to the news lately?"

I said, "No, not really. Am I missing something?"

Robert said, "Well, yes. Riots have been breaking out in almost every major city across the country. Many of the anarchist blacks are protesting against police. In a few large cities they have openly declared war on the police and have been ambushing and killing them. It's not a major race war, but the anarchist and criminal elements are making it so. It's fueled by no jobs and drugs, but they want to neutralize the police so they can loot and plunder. In some cases it has gotten so bad that in a few cities the mayors have authorized the police to shoot looters on sight and fire on crowds, and aggressively shut down any protests. It could easily explode into an all-out war between the police and the thug gangs. This has only happened in the very big cities so far, mostly on the East coast, but it's spreading. I think there was a policeman shot in Oklahoma City last night and some minor riots it Tulsa. Things are getting very unstable. It's getting so bad that I want our members armed if they leave the complex. I'm serious, Mike. I want you armed especially. Better yet, you should have an armed guard with you."

I said, "I do have a concealed carry permit, and so does Nancy, but I don't usually carry a weapon. I also have Bess to protect me. She is a martial arts expert." At that last comment several faces turned to her in shock.

Robert said, "That's all good, but if you don't have a weapon on you, and Nancy has to search in her purse for her pistol, you're going to wind up

173

dead. Remember also, you are worth a lot of money. That in itself makes you a major target. I will get you both some better weapons that are easily accessible."

"Oh, while I think about it, JJ and I picked up the inventory yesterday you requested, and Sue opened the safe for us. The shipment is safely locked away."

I had no idea things were getting that bad so soon. It was disturbing. I also had to think for a moment to place just what shipment he was talking about before I remembered the gold. Robert was just being careful with his language.

I said, "Thanks for telling me, and thanks for picking up that shipment. How do you stand with your shipments?

Robert said, "Oh, quite well. Sue purchased two trucks and had them delivered yesterday. I have already recruited ten officers, five of which are from the Cherokee Nation Marshal Service. Four officers are off picking up a shipment of AR-15 and a shit pot of munitions. They will make several more runs in the next few days. We emptied one supplier warehouse already and will be working on several more. We also ordered a major shipment of munitions of various caliber. It should be delivered in a few days. We will also make a run to the Cherokee Nations marshal's office for much of theirs. I won't clean them out. They would probably stop me if I tried. I can only get by with so much. Besides, they will need some also for as long as they survive, which probably won't be long if a war starts."

"Sue has contractors building shelving in the cave, and a high fence around the arms area. The shelving will be stocked quickly."

The others around the table were listening to Robert's report, so it wouldn't be necessary to repeat it. It probably wouldn't even be necessary to go to the conference room.

I said, "James, I see some new equipment at your barn. Are you getting squared away?"

James swallowed a mouth full of food and said, "Yes, I'm getting some of the equipment, and much more is en route. I talked to Jeremy and we decided to have a large tank installed underground for storing the diesel, maybe in additional locations as well. The barn location is convenient for all, though."

I said, "Have you recruited anyone yet?

"Not really, but I have several interviews today. There are some great looking applicants, well educated in multiple fields, but the main ones I want to find quickly are poultry and dairy ... well, beef cattle too. I'm working on the land management myself. In fact, I have a firm coming today to treat and fertilize the fields prepared already. I want to get a late crop planted, even if it's alfalfa for hay."

I said, "Very good."

Nancy said, "If we are having our morning meeting now, I'll let you know that I have some interviews scheduled for today. One is for the Castle Manager position, and she looks good on paper. She was a Naval officer from the Academy and was in charge of quarters and housing in Mayport, FL. I'll let you know how that goes. I also have interviews scheduled for a Chaplin and Receptionist."

175

Sue said, "I recruited one of my Warehouse Accountants yesterday. He was what I was looking for … an accountant with muscles. I'm interviewing another this afternoon. Mike, I think I might need more warehouse personnel than the two allotted. We will have a lot of inventory to handle. Do we have extra slots?"

I said, "We do have extra slots. I think about thirteen additional, mainly because I knew I didn't cover all the functions necessary in my original list, and I knew someone might need extra workers. Sue, take another slot for yourself. Also, everyone, keep in mind that all departments are expected to help each other out in times of need and learn other's jobs as well. As an example: I want Robert to train all members in gun training and community defense. Everyone here has a vested interest in protecting and defending our community, and have no doubt, it will be required. In times of emergency everyone becomes a soldier."

"Bob, thanks for breakfast. How are you doing so far?"

Bob had been standing close, listening. He said, "It's still just me so far, but I went through Sue's applicants and found many I would be happy with. I've already talked to some, and I will fill my slots quickly with great and useful members. I will also have several trailers full of storable food delivered tomorrow, and I have much more coming. Jeremy said I could park them in the cave until Sue gets shelving up for storage."

I said, "Very good, Bob."

I said, "It looks like the docs are the only ones missing. So, I don't really see a need to have a meeting in the conference room. Jeremy, if you like we can finish the tour."

Jeremy said, "I have contractors I need to get started. Can we meet in a couple of hours?"

"Sure. Nancy, I know you will be busy with your interviews. Sue, are you free for a couple of hours? I need to run into Tahlequah on an errand."

Sue said, "Yeah, that will work out fine. I'll just go check out my voice mail and meet you outside the office."

Robert said, "Wait until I get back before you leave, OK?"

I nodded and got another cup of coffee. I was just finishing it when he got back. He was carrying a black holster and attached clip holder. He handed me a Ruger .380 pistol and two loaded clips. He then handed me a flip leather wallet with a badge and ID identifying me as a Cherokee Marshal. I have no idea how he got my picture, but it looked official.

Robert said, "I'm serious about you not leaving the complex without being armed. I'll get you a bigger one later, but I just picked this one up. The ID is fake, but no one will question it."

I said, "Thanks." I strapped it on.

I met Sue outside and we took off. She looked funny at the gun but didn't say a word. With all the unrest around the country I wanted to get my lottery ticket a little early. The drawing would be next week anyway. After I purchased the ticket I looked at the estimated amount and saw $333,000,000.

Wow! I already knew I would win. This would certainly give us enough money, even after the IRS and State of Oklahoma took their cut. I told Sue we would need to put it into different banks than the ones we were already using, solid banks.

Sue said, "I'll check around with some other CPAs to see if there is a safer way to store and protect the money. There must be a way. Maybe the best way is, as you said, buy things. We are certainly doing that for sure."

While we were in town I stopped by Starbucks for a coffee. I had to have my coffee. Thankfully, Robert was wrong, and no one tried to kill or capture me. I guess that wasn't so strange for a small town like Tahlequah, but Tulsa might be a different story. Certainly, I would be armed when I went to pick up my lottery winnings in Oklahoma City. In fact, I would take a whole squad of security when I went for the money. It would be a little difficult to hide from that kind of attention.

Wow! As we reached the property a guard waved us through a very new and substantial main gate. I noticed the road had been blacktopped. There were even cement curbs being poured. I drove over the new blacktop all the way to my office. I didn't see Jeremy's pickup, so I let Sue out and headed toward the Castle. The blacktop crew was working on the Castle road, which I had to detour around. After crossing the bridge I saw Jeremy's pickup inside the Cave and parked beside him. He was nowhere to be seen, but one of the workers pointed toward the tunnel going down to the docks. The tunnel wasn't long, maybe a hundred feet before it opened up outside on a stairway going down to some floating docks. I noticed two new boats moored on the docks, both carrying Cherokee Marshal Patrol emblems. Out in the water were several barges with equipment and divers working on them. Off in the distance I could see several other barges coming with cement trucks on them. The barges were being pulled by small tugboats. I have no idea where they came from. I have never seen anything like them on the lake before. I realized that I was watching the Houston crew installing the anchor forms and preparing to pour cement. I finally noticed Jeremy on one of the anchor barge, and he noticed me about the same time. Jeremy waved at me and indicated that I should stay put. He called one of the boat security to come get him. I walked on down to the docks and waited for him.

When he arrived he jumped on the dock and said, "Do you still have the diving gear in your truck and are the tanks filled?"

I remember Bess and I unloaded the tanks on the porch of the cabin, and she had filled them. So the answer to the second question was, yes, but I didn't recall loading them in the truck. Bess might have, since I don't remember seeing them laying around the porch.

I said, "They could be in the truck. Do you need them?"

Jeremy said, "I could sure use them. I would love to see the anchors and if they anchored them properly before the cement is poured."

I said, "Let's go check. My truck is in the cave, but I don't want you diving alone. I'll go down with you, and I'll call Bess; she's the expert."

I called Bess from the dock and learned that she had in fact filled the tanks and reloaded them in the truck. I asked if she could come go down with us. She seemed eager to dive again and was in the Cave by the time Jeremy and I got back up. I'm not sure if it was the excitement of diving or having the opportunity to be useful, since her greenhouse wasn't yet ready.

We got the gear and went back down to the dock. Bess checked out our gear and made sure everything was working well before she allowed us to get into the water, but we were soon swimming along. Once underwater Jeremy took the lead. He knew what he needed to see. Bess and I just followed and enjoyed the dive. Jeremy went to all three locations and inspected the forms and anchor rods that had been drilled unto the bedrock. Each time he gave thumbs up to the divers. Jeremy took pictures of each locations and upon completions we went to the bottom. He seemed interested in the depth below the dome. Actually, it was deeper than I thought it was, so deep that Bess slowed our accent to adjust from the pressure. That's why she was absolutely necessary. Once we were back on the dock, workers on one of the barges began pointing toward us and directing a boat toward us. The boat was marked with Oklahoma Parks and Wildlife insignias. Oh crap! We didn't need officials nosing around. They would only slow us down.

Chapter 8
(First Obstacle)

I called Nancy and said, "A Parks and Wildlife boat is here. I'm sure they will be looking for permits from the Army Corp of Engineers. Can you bring Robert in full uniform and come to the docks. We're going to have to work a number on them and run them off. We can't handle the bureaucracy delays of federal or state interference."

Nancy quickly said, "We'll be right there."

I stood waiting the approach of the boat and even took the tossed rope and hooked it over the dock cleat. Two uniformed officers exited the boat. Neither looked friendly.

I offered them my handshake, which neither took, and said, "May I help you?"

The federal officer said, "You may. For one, we would like to know just what the fuck you think you are doing here? You have no permit or authorization to construct here. Hell, you don't even have a permit for this damn dock we're standing on much less whatever you're doing underwater." He stuck out his chest to clearly show us his badge and gently tapped his pistol. "We are here to shut this crap down."

Before I could even respond I heard a somewhat out of breath Nancy say, "Excuse me officers. My name is Nancy McIntosh, and I am the attorney of record for the Cherokee Nation, and you are trespassing on the Cherokee Nation, a sovereign country unto itself. We purchased this property and the adjacent peninsula from the state and federal governments, and you no longer have authority here."

I turned as Nancy spoke, and she looked firm and resolved...stolid. There was no perceived weakness in her, and with a uniformed and armed Cherokee Marshal standing beside her, she looked quite intimidating. As I watched I noticed several other uniformed and armed guards approaching, not to mention the two armed boat officers. I saw the recognition dawn on them as they looked around. They noticed for the first time that I was carrying a holstered pistol as well. The federal and state officers lost their imposing stances and doubt flooded their faces.

The federal officer said, "We weren't aware of the change of ownership, but we are still charged with compliance of federal and state laws governing construction on the shores and water of this lake. And, the law states that any construction on a shoreline or in the water must be approved by the Army Corp of Engineer and permits issued."

Nancy smiled and said, "Let me ask you a question. On lakes you share with Mexico, would you try to impose US laws on the Mexican side of the lake?"

The officers looked at each other and the federal officer said, "Of course not. We have no authority on the Mexican side."

Nancy said, "Exactly! And, you have no authority on Cherokee land, this land in particular, since it is registered as a high security area. Our authority extends 500 feet into the water, and you

182

are trespassing. I suggest you honor our borders in the future, because once we are operational we will shoot any trespassers on sight. We will soon install warning flags in the lake to mark our perimeter."

The federal officer said, "What do you mean, high security area?" Then after a moment of thought, continued. "Are you threatening us?"

Nancy said, "High security is exactly what it means. It could be that we are working on a Top Secret US Government project that they would not like outsiders to know about. Were I you I wouldn't ask too many questions of your government. As far as threatening, not at all; we are simply warning you and others. Please pass the word along. Now, I'm asking you politely to honor our sovereignty. And, unless you wish us to file charges against you personally, I suggest you leave and cause us no further problems."

The officers simply looked at each other and turned and left.

I said, "Damn, Nancy that was fantastic. You did great."

Nancy's stolid facial expression broke into a huge grin and she said, "Mike, It was all bullshit. None of it was true, but by the time they pass the information upstairs, worry about stepping into a secret government project, let their lawyers study it, and file court papers, a lot of time will go by. I don't think we will hear from them again. If they finally do decide to take it to court it will probably be too late to accomplish anything. In the meantime they will leave us alone. Even if they finally file with the courts I can stall them off and drag it out so long it won't matter anymore."

I said, "I'm glad you are on our side. I sure hope you never get mad at me." We all laughed.

Jeremy said, "If they stay away for the next few days it won't matter. We will have all the cement poured, it will be set up and the dome installed. It's already at the docking area and as soon as the barges are free from hauling cement trucks, I will have the Dome loaded and brought here. I'm keeping the trailers covered and guarded to keep noisy people from snooping. I bet our recent visiting officers have been trying to figure it out, but there isn't much to see and the Houston crew knows it's a secret and where their pay is coming from. They won't say anything."

With the potential immediate crisis averted, Nancy and Robert returned to the office, and Jeremy and I continued the tour. I thought Jeremy would lead me back to the pickup, but instead he led me passed the elevator shaft toward a stairway I had not seen before. It's no wonder I hadn't seen it with so many workers inside the Cave. Toward the back of the Cave in generated light I could see the power generators being installed and set up, and I saw Al Martinez hovering over the installation. He must have come directly here when he arrived. I would bet by tomorrow they would be running, assuming the diesel tank had been filled.

We started up the sawtooth stairway for what must have been six or more floors, where it opened up in the basement of the Castle. Portable lighting illuminated the octagon shaped basement, which was huge. It was not as enormous as the Cave, but it was very substantial. Jeremy had told me before that the Castle was 240 feet across, and there were eight sides on an octagon. There was already an existing, 20 foot high basement ceiling or main floor, and I could see through the elevator shaft that the second level floor was going in. They had really been busy. Sue's shelving crew was also busy placing shelves. They would be ready when Bob had his food stores delivered.

Jeremy said, "The contractors have set a fast pace, at my insistence, and I am pleased with their progress. You can see more from outside. We can go out through the loading docks on the back side. As you can see, Bob is getting his massive, walk-in freezer installed just inside the unloading dock and close to the elevator. His kitchen will be located right above us on the main floor. This basement will mostly be food storage."

I was shocked as we exited the basement. The basement opened directly under a cement overhang over the unloading dock. Thick steel doors swung to each side, providing for a total and secure access closure of the dock. The backside was excavated level to allow trucks to back up under the overhang to the dock, very efficient. The road circled up and around each side of the Castle, but the roadway directly in front of the dock extended level to the edge. There was a retainer wall with water drains to keep the area clear of any standing water. We walked up the road to get a better view of the outside of the Castle. A cement pump truck was stationed at the top of the hill to pump cement to the upper levels, which it was in the process of doing as we watched. I could see a line of cement trucks waiting to dump their loads into the second level wall forms. The main level had already been cured and the forms removed. Surprisingly, the form texture made the wall look like stacked blocks. Even more surprising was the walls were easily two feet thick. I could also see that Jeremy had used "I" beams liberally throughout the structure. In fact, the third floor "I" beams, rebar and conduits were already erected, and crews were busy on the fourth deck. I was impressed. We walked around to the front where another crew was working on the third and fourth decks, but on this side there was a large double door opening on the main floor. Portable lights were on this deck and crews were busy inside doing numerous things from painting to running electric lines. I was surprised that the height of this level was at least 20', at least on the sides. The center open octagon section of 100 feet was open to the second floor reaching a height of about 35 feet. The surrounding lower structure was supported at each corner of the octagon by Roman style columns and rails around the entire structure. I could see the columns continuing upward to the base of the third floor.

Jeremy saw my questioning look and said, "This is the main big room. In here will be the kitchen, mess hall, entertainment and recreation area. This main area has no windows for security reasons. The front doors will be made of heavy steal like the basement back doors. All the offices and medical facilities will be on the second floor. There will be glass doors and balconies on that floor and on the third and fourth floors, which will be used for housing. Each balcony exit access door will have an automatic security steal door for protection. The roof will have a balcony style, cement, walkway wall around it with firing slots. The building will actually look very much like a Castle, and we are promoting that look. Janet wants a fair size water tank up there as well to maintain water pressure, and, of course, the elevator equipment room will be up there. We'll probably make the roof of the elevator equipment room a firing post for heaver equipment."

"I'm keeping Sue busy paying bills, but the contractors love us for quick payments, and I'm not having a shortage of willing contractors. I am, however, spending a great deal of money."

I said, "I don't care. Spend as much as it takes but get-her-done."

Building something this complex in the short time we have taken has to be some kind of record.

I said, "Jeremy, keep up the good work. I think I will drop by and say 'Hi' to Al then run by Bob's kitchen before I go back to the office.

I retraced my steps returning to the Cave. I said, "Hey Al. When did you get in?"

Al said, "Oh, Hi Mike. I got in last night and came looking around and found these." He pointed to the generators."

"Is this what you ordered? Does it look good?"

Al said, "Oh, yeah, even better. These are bigger units and Jeremy ordered three, and I was asking for two. This is better. I haven't seen Jeremy,

187

but I hear that he ordered three wind generators. This is also good. They will generate a lot of power, but we will have to build a huge battery bank here in the Cave to store it."

I said, "Have you eaten anything today, Al?

He said, "No, and I am getting hungry, sleepy, too."

I said, "Well, Jeremy is around here somewhere, but I was headed to Bob's kitchen to get something to eat. Why don't you follow me? We need to get you settled in anyway."

"That sounds like a great idea."

I had actually totally lost track of time and took a look at my watch. I was surprised to see that it was after 8:00 pm. If Bob was closed down we might have to scrounge around in the kitchen for something. Luckily, when we got there I saw most of the others already there and joined Nancy, Sue, Bess, and there was another lady there. She was hard to miss. She had long, fiery, red hair and a slim freckled face that seemed to always be smiling.

Nancy saw me looking at her and said, "Mike, meet Mary O'Shay. She is our new Castle Manager."

Mary stood to shake my hand, and I looked down only slightly to look into her bright green eyes. That would put her at about 6 feet tall. I said, "I'm pleased to meet you. Let me introduce you all to our Master Electrician, Al Martinez. I found him up at the Castle."

Bob came over and said, "Hey, I still have some warm roast beef, mashed potatoes, green beans. Anyone want some?"

Al beat me and said, "I would love some food. I haven't eaten all day"

Bob said, "Well, I'll get you a double helping. You should have come by today. I most always have some food here."

"I'll take some, too," I said. "Bob, did you recruit any help today?"

Bob smiled and said, "Yes, I brought three onboard and talked to three more. Two will be here in the morning."

"Great!"

Al started fading after he ate. I decided to take him to our cabin and put him to sleep in the loft bedroom. I didn't think it would matter to him, since he was so damn tired. Nancy volunteered to put Mary up also. I'm not sure where she was going to put her up, but I figured she would work it out. I mean we did have a foldout in the couch. When we reached the cabin I tossed Al a robe and pointed him to the shower and showed him his bed. It didn't take long before we heard him gently snoring upstairs.

Jeremy came in and joined the rest of us at the table for coffee. Nancy was talking a lot to Mary. They must have hit it off well. I could see why. Mary was friendly and outgoing, but when asked a serious question she could switch to a professional demeanor. Just as quickly she could switch back. I liked her and felt that she was the right person for the job.

Suddenly, we were interrupted by a knock on our door. Sue was closer and jumped up to open the door. Robert came in with JJ, and JJ was visibly, terribly upset. As she tried to voice her problem she broke down in sobs, more in frustration than fear. Sue, being the mother hen, sat her down in her chair and put her arm around her in support.

I said, "Robert, what's wrong? What happened?"

He said, "I'm not really sure. She just said she wanted to come talk to you."

JJ finally said, "I know that all the women here are expected to have multiple sex partners. I mean it's easy to figure out. There will be 75 men and only 25 women. I understand the situation, but in our trailer there are 9 men and only me. I'm willing to do my part, but I'm not ready for a 9-man "gang bang", "train" or "chain", whatever it's called. I've got 9 men staring hungry at me. I am afraid to undress just to take a shower. I'm just not ready for that. I want to stay here tonight, and if you want to kick me out in the morning, I'll go."

I said, "Damn, Robert. You're not thinking. I don't blame her for being upset."

Robert said, "Well, put that way, I don't blame her either. I have three more females coming, but they won't be here for a couple of days. I just wasn't thinking. I'm sorry JJ. It's my fault."

I said, "Nancy, we will have to explain the situation a little better. I don't want the women members thinking that they have to sex everyone else. I just assumed sex would just happen naturally in time. The only thing I worried about was exclusive pairing. Over time that would cause resentment. It just never occurred to me that the females might feel required. It was Brin's idea for our numbers,

190

because he is bringing 75 females and only 25 males. Once they are here we will have even numbers. Hell, I don't know what to do."

Sue spoke, "Well, JJ. You poor thing. I know what to do. Let's go get you a shower and cleaned up. We need to get you calmed down, and of course you can stay here." Still hugging her, Sue led JJ off toward the shower.

We all sat around staring at each other at this latest development wondering what to do, but it was Janet that came up with the solution.

Janet said, "I think we can all prevent this "Gang Bang" idea from surfacing again with just a little better planning ... Robert. But, why don't us girls go over and take care of this problem this time?"

It was Nancy's turn to give an intelligent answer, "Huh?"

Janet said, "I'm serious. Think about it. It's the perfect solution...this time anyway. Everyone knows the three sisters, who happen to mostly be at the top of the chain of command, are with Mike. The rules appear to be completely reversed for him. I obviously know that is not the case, but it probably appears that way with all the others. I know you girls have been with others. Hell, we have been with everyone here, with the exception of Al and Mary, but they are new." We all laughed. She continued, "You have all heard the old adage, 'Don't ask anyone to do anything you aren't willing to do yourself.' The word will get out, and it will go a long ways in establishing respect. Think about it. Sue can stay here with Robert and Jeremy, JJ can

191

stay here with Mike, and we all know he is compassionate, not to mention a good instructor. There are only eight men left over there now, and there are four women here. That's only two each, and we would probably have sex with two tonight anyway."

We all sat in silence pondering what Janet had said. It really made sense, but I was not going to be the one that said it.

Mary broke the silence and said, "I suppose from now on this type of problem will fall under my authority. I had hoped to slip into this position more smoothly. As Mike said earlier, 'Sex just happens over time.' I really didn't think I would have to step into this job pussy first, but, under the circumstances, I agree with Janet, and I'm willing if you girls are."

Nancy looked at me for a comment, but I just shrugged. It did make sense, but it was her body and her decision. Still, I knew I had to say something, "I love you girls no matter what."

Nancy smiled, kissed me, and said, "Well, I feel kind of slutty saying this, but let's go service security." Bess giggled her agreement, and we all laughed at her.

Janet said, "Being slutty is kind of exciting."

Sue and JJ came out of the shower in their robes, both looking calmer. I doubt if Sue took advantage of JJ under her condition. Bess might have, so I was happy Sue had taken her under her wing. They had obviously showered together and bonded. When they came out I saw Nancy giving them instructions as the team left for the security trailer. I, however, headed for the shower.

When I returned to the kitchen for my final cup of coffee for the night, they were gathered around the table.

When Sue saw me she asked, "Mike, what is double penetration?"

I had just taken my first sip when she asked that question. I quickly raised my robe sleeve to keep from spraying them all and said, "What did you just ask me?"

She said it again, "What is double penetration? Jeremy and Robert want to do that to me, but I've never even heard of it."

When I looked at Robert and Jeremy they both were blushing. I laughed and said, "Well, double penetration is when two men put their dicks into a woman in two separate holes at the same time. Knowing you, you would probably like it."

Sue smiled hugely and said, "Yeah, I probably would. OK guys let's do it."

When they left for Jeremy's bedroom JJ and I were left alone. I said, "It's just you and me now. You can sleep with me or we can fold out the couch for you. If you want to sleep with me you don't have to do anything you don't want to. OK?"

JJ said, I would like to sleep with you. I don't like to sleep alone, and I love to cuddle. Is that OK?"

"I like that too." I took her hand and led her toward my bedroom. When we got there I said, "I do love to cuddle, but we need to get rid of this robe." I slowly pulled her robe open and slid it off of her shoulders. I was amazed at her beauty. Her hips were narrow and her legs were long and muscular. Her breast were firm and pointed straight out. The hard nipples were black as midnight and pointed like fingers. I also noticed a bush of curled hair covering her pussy. All this was new to me, as I had never been with a black lady before. As I said, she was beautiful all over, but the most attractive feature was her full facial lips. I stared at everything, but I kept coming back to those luscious lips.

I slipped my robe off and slipped into bed and held the sheet open as an invitation. JJ paused only slightly before slipping into bed beside me. She continued sliding right up to my body and cuddled snugly. She placed her head on my arm and looked directly into my eyes.

JJ sort of looked away and said, "Thank you, Mike, for what all of you did tonight. I'm really NOT a cry-baby, but I was just frustrated with the unfair position I was placed in. I know it really wasn't anyone fault. It just happened. I have another confession to make. I'm really not all that experience with sex. I mean I am prepared to do what is necessary to survive and live here among the group, but I have never experience a "Gang Bang", and I was not prepared to go that far tonight. I hope you understand how I feel. To be honest, I'm more experienced with females than males."

I said, "Of course I understand. You bear none of the fault tonight. And, as far as liking women, well, let me just say, you will get along great with Bess."

JJ looked surprised and said, "Really? I will look forward to it. All your girls are so beautiful,

194

and I really appreciate what they did for me tonight; I really do."

As JJ had been talking I kept staring at her beautiful lips moving. I couldn't resist and leaned in and kissed those enticing lips. They were soft and warm, and she kissed me back. We continued to kiss, getting more heated as we progressed. I'm definitely a sucker for tongue action, and when she slipped her tongue into my mouth I went crazy. We pressed against each other. Suddenly, she jerked back and pushed her hand down between us and grabbed my very hard cock.

JJ said, "Oh my God. Mike your dick is so big. I definitely want it in me, but I don't think it will fit."

I chuckled and said, "It will fit. We will just have to go slow."

She didn't respond, and she never let go of my cock. Her fingers explored me, touching, caressing, stroking, and our kisses got more passionate. I began to explore her body also. The skin was smooth and soft, but I could feel hard muscles underneath. Her nipples were like nubs of hard candy and just as sweet. My hands slid everywhere. It was like magic; wherever my hands slid her skin began to quiver. JJ began moaning when I moved between her thighs. I began kissing her inner thighs, and as my mouth and tongue found her mound I became completely fascinated with her hair. It was soft but springy when I pressed my lips into it. I let my tongue play in the hair until I found her slit. My tongue slipped inside and JJ grabbed my head and pulled it against her pussy, all the while moaning

195

louder and louder. She suddenly climaxed, locked her strong thighs around my head and flooded my face with the sweetest honey. I had to eventually force her thighs apart just to breathe. That is when I noticed how small her pussy was; it was tiny. She may have been right. I might not be able to fit inside, but I was sure going to try. I moved up her body and began kissing her again as I probed my cock against her hot pussy. I slowly pushed against her, but my pressure resulted in pushing her body up the bed. She wanted it and held her legs wide, but my effort was getting us nowhere. I decided to take a different tact. I raised her arms and placed her hands against the headboard so she could push. She caught on quickly and began pushing against my cock. I then held her hips so I could pull her against me. Very very slowly I felt my cock begin to slip inside. As soon at the mushroom head was inside it got easier but not much. I was finally able to get a couple of inches inside and began stroking. She was so tight, but she remained relaxed and wasn't resisting at all. I would never have got it in if she tightened her internal muscles like Bess. I began to worry what would happen if she did, but I didn't let it stop me. A few more inches penetrated as she pushed. I kept going until I felt her springy pubic hair against my balls. I was having to stroke slowly because her tightness prevented me from building any speed, but my lust and her ability to accept me increased. Finally I was able to thrust hard into that velvet pussy, and JJ was in apparent heaven. Her moans were loud, and she began meeting my now hard thrusts into her. Her long legs wrapped around me and her heels dug into my butt cheeks driving me harder. I felt her fingernails clawing my back and teeth biting my shoulder. Soon we were pounding against each other in perfect rhythm, which JJ now controlled with her heels. We peaked our orgasms at the same time, and when they came it was an eruption. I unleashed a torrent of cum from my jerking cock deep in her fluttering pussy. It felt like my cock was a firehose trying to put out a never-ending fire. Afterwards I could not move, because JJ, during her orgasm, clamped her pussy muscles down on my cock. It hurt, but I didn't care. Eventually I rolled with her to my back. She remained on me with me still deep inside her and started kissing me.

JJ said, "That was the most incredible sex I have ever had. You must promise me that I can come back and we can do this again sometimes."

"I'm sure it will happen again. Right now, however, you are going to have to really relax so I can get my cock out." We laughed

She said, "Maybe I'll just keep it inside."

JJ tried several time to lift off before she finally began to slowly slip off. When she did our combined juice flooded out. We lay together and talked and finally got up and took a shower together. We had finished and were having a cup of coffee at the table when the girls came back. I knew something was wrong immediately by the looks on their faces, especially Bess. Plus, they came in cussing someone.

I said, "What's wrong?"

Nancy said, "Oh, one of the Marines thought it was ok to slap women!"

"What? I said, "Who did he slap? Who was it? ROBERT!" I was already headed to put my clothes on. I was going over there.

Nancy said, "There is no need. Bess took care of it already."

I turned as Robert was coming out slipping on his robe. I'm sure he picked up on some of what was said.

Robert said, "Who was it? What did he do?"

Bess said, "We really didn't introduce ourselves over there, so I have no idea who. I can tell you that it is the one with a broken arm and missing teeth. Once I heard the slaps and Janet scream in pain I was in there almost immediately and threw him against the wall. The stupid bastard then tried to slap me around, and I beat the crap out of him."

Mary was laughing and said, "You should have seen Bess flying all over him, and she was as naked as the day she was born."

Robert said, "I'll run him off tomorrow. We can't have male members treating women that way. It won't be tolerated."

Nancy jumped in and said, "Wait. I'll bet he never tries to hit another woman ever again and walking around with an arm cast and missing teeth will make a great example for other would be woman beaters. Besides, he probably knows too much about us. We need to maintain our secrets. Actually, he is damn lucky Bess didn't kill him outright. She is quite lethal you know."

Robert said, "Where is he now?"

Nancy said, "Some of your guys took him to Dr. Groom's cabin. I would imagine the doctor, and probably the dentist, have him at the clinic."

I said, "That sounds like a good plan, Nancy. Other than the beating, how did it go?"

That's when the girls started laughing, and Nancy said, "Well our little slut, Janet, just announced that we came over there to fuck everyone. That kind of eliminated the foreplay and got us down to business. The eight guys paired up on each of us and took us to the bedrooms, undressed us and started having sex with us. It was just about that quick, but they tricked us. They started switching rooms trying to get all of us. When my second guy finished and pulled out, number three pushed right in, then four. I'm pretty sure I was with the sixth guy when the ruckus started. By the time we figured out what they were doing it was too late, or we didn't care by then. I'll tell you; I never felt more slutty in all my life, but like Janet said, slutty can be exciting. I have to admit, it was."

"I am so full of cream. I need to go take a shower."

Sue and Bess went with her. Robert took off to chew ass and check on his guy. Jeremy, Janet, Mary, JJ and I had another cup of coffee.

Mary said, "JJ how are you doing now."

"I'm great. I just had the fucking of my life, and I loved it."

Janet said, "Mike? Yeah, he is fantastic and big too.

"OMG ... huge!"

199

I saw Mary staring at me during this last exchange. I thought, *"Yeah, your turn is coming."*

Bess, Sue and Nancy were returning to the gathering, and Bess said, "Did I just hear that JJ fucked Mike?

The look on JJ's face spoke volumes. She didn't know what to say, because she, like everyone else, knew I was with the sisters. She didn't know if she was in trouble, even though it seemed that she had the blessings to do so.

JJ simply said, "Yes. I hope that was all right."

I knew what was coming, and I had even warned JJ, but she wasn't thinking about that with the apparent challenge Bess had thrown out.

Bess said, "Yeah, it's OK, but usually when someone takes Mike's load. I go after it."

A relieved JJ smiled and said, "You are welcome to it. I would actually like that. But, you should know that I've had a shower since I took his load, but I would welcome the opportunity to take another for you."

Bess laughed and said, "Oh, I'm sure there is still enough in you, besides, I'm more interested in your juice anyway." Bess took JJ by the hand and led her off toward the bedroom.

What surprised me most was when Nancy said, "I want a taste of that, too."

Nancy took off after them, with a smiling Sue right after her. My girls were evolving I guess. Janet and Mary chuckled and took off toward the shower, leaving me alone with Jeremy.

Jeremy said, "Mike, I love being here. The construction challenges and opportunity to express

200

my dreams is beyond belief." In a lower voice he said, "I've also had more sex since I've been here than in my entire life before. Did I say I love it here?"

We laughed together, and I whispered, "Me too." We were still laughing when I heard my name being called from the bedroom. When I went in I saw JJ's legs spread wide, Bess laying between them feasting on JJ's pussy and Nancy and Sue on either side of Bess taking turns nibbling on her hair and pussy lips. JJ was moaning with a huge smile on her face. Bess looked up, got up and turned around and pressed her pussy down over JJ's mouth. JJ grabbed Bess' hips and pulled her down on her mouth. It was very arousing to watch.

Sue said, "You got your cock in this small hole?"

I said, "Yes, but it took a long time."

Nancy said, "I've got to see that."

Laughing, Sue said, "Me too.

JJ pushed Sue over and said, "Yes, please. Again."

At that outburst we all laughed, and I liked the idea of getting back inside that hot velvet tunnel. In fact, I was already hard with the thought. I didn't wait for a second invitation and positioned myself between JJ's thighs, but Nancy stopped me. She grabbed my cock, stroked it a few times and sucked it right in her mouth. She made sure it was good and wet, then positioned it at JJ's tunnel. Like before, she was very tight, but not entirely like before. I held her hips and pushed so hard it hurt, but the head slowly stretched her lips and began to slowly slip inside her.

Nancy said, "Oh my, it's going in. Come see, Bess."

Bess scrambled down to watch. Sue already had her head next to Nancy, watching. Knowing that we were being watched excited me more. Bess wiggled around until she could see my cock stretching those pussy lips. I must not have been going fast enough for Bess, and she began pushing on my butt cheeks. It didn't help, because my progress was depending on JJ's pussy stretching to accept me. Still, I was entering faster than the first time. JJ was moaning loud now, and her legs began flapping against my sides, which seemed to be helping. I could tell JJ sure wanted it inside. I tried to pull back out so I could start a rhythm, but she was so tight on my cock it wouldn't let go. All It did was pull on my cock. I pushed back in hard and sudden and felt my cock slip deeper. I did it again and finally slipped all the way in. When I did JJ had a major orgasm and clamped down on my cock, stopping all my progress.

Nancy said, "Wow! look at that. He is all the way in.

I heard Mary from behind me say, "That is incredible, and she already had an orgasm."

I was almost out of control with lust and couldn't stroke into JJ. I said, "Dammit, I didn't. Who wants it?"

Mary yelled, "I do. Do me."

I took hold of my cock with my hand and forcefully pulled it out of JJ's clamping pussy. I grabbed

202

Mary by the arm and pulled her down beside JJ and jumped between her thighs. I guided my cock into her steamy hot, slick pussy and drove it home hard. Mary screamed ... another screamer. I immediately built up a fast and hard pace, roughly pounding into her. Mary was definitely an active participant. Her arms and legs were flailing and her hips met my every thrust with as much force as I was driving into her. We climaxed together. I couldn't even remember much about the sex. It was animal, hard and fast. I lay between her quivering thighs breathing heavy.

I noticed that everyone was still watching us, all but Jeremy. I watched him climb between JJ's still spread thighs. He pushed inside her hard and sank deep in her stretched pussy. He screamed and JJ screamed. Jeremy went to work on her pussy, driving hard and fast. JJ opened her eyes and saw Jeremy, then smiled and wrapped her arms and legs around him. I knew Jeremy wasn't going to get away from her anytime soon. I also knew he was probably doing more for JJ than I had, because he could slide his cock in and out. I kissed Mary and moved toward Nancy's embrace, and we watched Jeremy and JJ. They were driving against each other fast when I heard JJ scream then Jeremy scream. I knew JJ had clamped down on him. I knew Jeremy had climaxed also, because of the two-tones of his scream: orgasm and the pain of being gripped.

After a while they came apart. Jeremy didn't seem to have a problem getting out. JJ set up and smiled, and said, "I want to thank everyone for my introduction into the membership. I honestly feel

203

much better, and I will be able to do what is necessary after tonight. I think I might even look forward to it. Robert will be my first tomorrow night, then I will see. Right now, however, I think I will go grab a shower, and I guess I will slip in bed with Al. Won't he be surprised in the morning. Mary, would you like to join me in the shower and sharing Al's bed?"

Mary said, "Yeah, I think I would. If you hear Al screaming in the night, well don't worry about it." At that we all laughed.

When she mentioned Al, I was wondering how he had slept through it all tonight. He was tired, though. It would be fun to see the look on his face in the morning, however.

Bess said, "Mary, usually I would be going after Mike's load in you, but I'm tired after all that has happened. Can I have a rain check?"

Mary laughed and said, "Any time, Bess. Any time."

Jeremy took Janet by the hand and headed off to bed. Bess stayed with her sisters and I, and I finally had them all to myself. I loved it, and gave them lots of hugs and kisses. As usual I had Nancy cuddled on one side and Sue on the other, but Bess wanted in and climbed up on my chest. She was so light I hardly felt her. We finally went to sleep wrapped all together, and it felt great.

I had a very restful night, but I woke up even before the alarm went off. It took me a moment to realize why, then I heard it again. Mary was screaming from an orgasm, at least it sounded like one. There was no mistaking Mary's high pitched orgasm scream. I set up and chuckled. Yep, I guess Al woke up sandwiched between two naked women and responded like any other healthy man would do. Somehow Bess had slipped between Nancy and I and was snoring lightly. She was laying on my upper arm with drool on my bicep. She was so cute. Very carefully I slipped my arm out and gently worked myself out of bed. I decided to leave the girls alone for the remaining thirty minutes and let the alarm get them up. I proceeded to the bathroom then made a pot of coffee. I looked upstairs on the way and saw a lot of movement, so I knew they were awake.

While I was alone I decided to shoot an e-mail to Brin.:

"Brin, today I took a tour of the Castle and was extremely pleased with our progress. We are progressing at an amazing pace. I think you would be pleased. We have stored over $3,000,000 in gold and silver and will increase this amount once we install our vault in the Castle. We should have our internal power plants operational today. The anchors for the underwater dome were poured yesterday with fast curing cement, and the Dome parts should be on a barge on site. This place is really taking shape. Do you have an estimated time for your arrival on site?"

I should have checked first for a message from Brin. Oh well, there was one.

"Mike, we are close, close enough to view the property through our onboard telescope. We can see the progress. Your team is preforming well. We can see that you have expanded the property beyond

our original plan. This is great. If you have the opportunity to purchase more, please do so. Buy ... buy lots of food, stores, machinery, parts, medicines, anything you can't produce later. Please hurry. Collect your lottery winnings quickly, and take plenty of security with you when you go. The US dollar will collapse soon, which will start the decline. After that, start your perimeter security. The fall will start in the major cities, but eventually spread to smaller cities as the food is used up. I caution you again to store up plenty of food. I'll let you know when we place the satellites. Keep up the good work.

Brin

Chapter 9
(Second Obstacle)

By the time I finished with my e-mail to Brin the alarm was going off. It was loud enough for the entire cabin, and everyone began getting up. I was enjoying my second cup of coffee when Al joined me at the table.

Al said, "I guess you know I was one surprised dude when I woke up with two naked women snuggling me. Was that your idea? If it was, thanks."

I said, "No. Actually it was JJ and Mary's idea. Plus, they needed a place to sleep, and your bed was the only space available. Mary is new also. She doesn't have a permanent bed yet; you might want to invite her to bunk with you, since it looks like you will be occupying the loft. JJ will be going back to the security trailer. She was just here for the night."

"I will definitely invite her. I like the way she introduces herself."

I liked Mary. She jumped in like a trooper, and I knew she would make a strong mother hen for all the members in her new position, especially with the women.

The others were coming out of the bedrooms, most of them dressed for work already. I was the only one still in my robe, so I left them to their morning coffee and went to get dressed. Being summer, my dress usually consisted of no more than shorts, T-shirt. slip-on shoes and now my sidearm.

207

It didn't take me long, and we were ready to head to Bob's Cafe, the kitchen trailer's new name.

Bob had his standard buffet ready, and we dug in. As I was getting my food I noticed three new workers, probably cooks he recruited, all females. I guess he had been busy. I also saw many other new faces as well.

I said to those assembled, "We won't talk business here. The department heads will meet in the conference room today. Bob, I need you there for a while, also." He nodded.

Nancy and I finished up quickly and went to our office. She sensed that I was in a hurry for something. As we left, Nancy leaned over Mary's shoulder and spoke into her ear.

Once in the truck Nancy said, "You know you need to spend some quality time with Mary tonight. A quickie hump doesn't count as quality time. I'll make sure that happens tonight. I want her to know she is appreciated and needed for her abilities and not just for her body. She is important to the community, and I like her."

I said, "Yeah, I understand. I felt bad about that later, but it was you'll's fault I was all worked up at the time. But, when I asked for a volunteer she jumped right in. What was I supposed to do?"

Nancy laughed and said, "I guess you are right. She did volunteer quick enough. She beat me anyway. No big deal I guess, but at least kiss her tonight before you pound her into the floor." We both laughed.

By the time I had the coffee perking the others were on their way into the conference room. I sat at the head of the table, Sue and Nancy in the first seats on either side. Bess sat by Sue. Sue was already writing checks, and there were a lot of them. I was thankful I didn't have to sign them all. The doctors took seats together. Robert and JJ came in together, and James followed. Janet stayed out front to answer any calls or walk-ins. Bob and Jeremy were the last to arrive.

Robert jumped in and said, "Anyone hear the news this morning?" When no one said anything he continued. "The riots hit Tulsa and Oklahoma City last night, and looters were shooting at the city electric crews to keep them from getting the lights back on. Five police officers were shot, but they took out about ten looters. Gun battles were going all over both cities. Things are getting worse. But, that's not all. China and Russia started dumping dollars. That set off a stock market crash. They say the worst one ever. I'm not sure how much time we have left."

I said, "I know we are running out of time, but as long as we can continue to pay real money we should still be able to get what we want and keep contractors working, even if we have to pay them in gold. Speaking of gold, we need to buy up as much as we can store. Jeremy, when will the vault be completed in the Castle basement?"

Jeremy had sat at the other end of the table. He stood and said, "It was delivered and installed last night. They are just doing cosmetics on it now. It's big. I just came from there. It looks like a vault in a damn bank. I guess that is what we need, huh?"

I said, "Robert, Sue help him, call around the gold dealers and buy as much as you can find. Don't cause a panic. Just purchase what you can without alarming them. Do wire transfers, but get guaranteed delivery. Let them worry about an armored truck delivery. I don't want you having to haul gold around. Sue, I guess we still have plenty of money?"

Sue said, "I'll call the bank and get them to set up the armored transfer and guarantee. They'll probably charge for the service, but I agree. It's best that way. On your second question, We have probably spent $40,000,000, but we have lots of outstanding bills still, and we are ordering more each day. It's moving so fast I can't give you an exact account. But, we still have plenty of money in the bank. By the way, the stock market crash didn't hurt us. All the stocks were unloaded yesterday morning before the crash. I got a text from the bank to let me know the new stock market account balance is at $500,250,000. Brin did good, huh? With the new deposit tomorrow you will have very close to a billion in all the banks, but taxes have to be paid. The government will take the taxes on your new deposit, but the taxes on the investment earnings won't be due until after the collapse, therefore ... never."

I said, "Thanks Sue. I forgot about the Oklahoma City trip tomorrow. Robert, I need you and a couple of your people to escort me. Sue, maybe you should go too and wire transfer the money instead of having to deal with certified checks. Maybe we should use other banks also."

"Everyone, keep buying, keep ordering and keep thinking about anything we might need.

I pulled out a Google Earth map showing our property and slid it over to Nancy. I said, "Nancy, I think we should buy all the land on our side of these roads. More land can't hurt, and I don't want anyone traveling through our property to reach theirs. It's easier to just buy the land. James will just have to farm more land."

"Bob, food. Where do we stand on food?

Bob said, "We are doing good, actually, but we can never have enough, and I keep thinking of new things. So, it's on-going. Still, we received ten semitrailers stacked full of canned food. I have some contractors filling the shelves Sue had installed." Bob chuckled, "It could go faster if her bean counters got out of the way, but I understand that the inventory is necessary. We have a whole section in the storeroom for canning jars, lids, seals and canning and preserving supplies. We may even start trying to do some canning when crops are ready in the outside markets. The basement freezer, I'm told, will come online today. It's big and will hold a lot of beef I have already contracted for, but I can't order it delivered until the freezer is operational. Our mill, two actually, are installed in the back of the Castle kitchen, our storage tanks are full of wheat, and yes, I have recruited a miller. I also have some excellent and educated cooks, and they all have other abilities, such as canning and preservation, butcher, distilling; and some are ex-military. My staff is coming together. Jeremy had a temporary housing trailer like Robert's brought in for my

211

staff, and we have moved in already. You can reassign our cabin. Oh, and as extra back-up I ordered several years' worth of MREs for 200 people. They store well, 25 years, but we can last for two years without even dipping into the MREs. By then, worst case, we should be able to start producing some of our own food."

I said, "Excellent! But, remember we have plenty of additional storage in the Cave, so keep ordering food stores. Like you said, 'We can't have too much food, and we have the money.'"

"James, I guess it's your turn in the spotlight. Give us a status update from the Master Farmer." I kind of wanted to put pressure on James. I still had my doubts about his ability to build and run a crew, and it's not too late to make a change.

James said, "Well, I came away from our last meeting with a better understanding of what's at stake here. To say my attitude has changed is a gross understatement. I picked all my staff yesterday, some sight unseen, but my phone interviews and reviewing resumes identified some really good talent. Like Bob's people, mine have multiple talents, like for example, one of my farmers is also an experienced beekeeper. Bees are very important to pollinate our crops, and everyone likes honey. Honey is far more healthy than sugar, especially when you can't grow sugar cane. By the way, Nancy, we want Bob's cabin if that's all right. Right now we have cots in the Farm Barn."

Nancy said, "Absolutely, James, but I think we can do better. This is a good time to introduce Mary O'Shey. Mary is our new Castle Manager, and among many other things, she is responsible for billeting, which includes temporary housing. Mary, Sue and I will go over the billeting arrangements with you after the meeting, but for right now I will make the decision to order in another temporary housing trailer for you, James. Can you handle that, Jeremy?" Jeremy nodded.

James said, "Thank you. Now, to continue my status report to the assembly, I have two poultry experts checking in today. I know these ladies and was thankful to find them as applicants. I met them through the attorneys fighting probate from my parents deaths. Like me, inheritance taxes bankrupted them." They ran a successful family poultry house for their parents until they died. They are hardworking sisters, identical twins actually, and they will be able to jump right into this operation. In fact, they are out purchasing equipment, feeds, stock, and incubators as we speak. Sue, I gave them your number to call to set up accounts. I also interviewed with a dairy farmer yesterday, and he is reporting in today, along with two misplaced cattle ranchers. The cattle ranchers are very experienced, one even experienced in dairy operations. Both are recently out of the Marines and back from the Middle-East. I haven't found my horse rancher, but I'm interviewing one today. The mechanic is already at work setting up his shop. I'm saving the land farmers for last, because I have contractors working on the fields. Most of the fields are cleared, but the native soil itself is not great. I'm having tons of topsoil trucked in and spread, along with sprayers pumping nutrients into the soil. Soon our fields will

213

be able to grow anything we want. I also have depleted most of the stock of trees of several large nurseries in the area. We have every kind of tree you can imagine, but we are heavy on pecan, apple, peach ... well, most fruit trees and bushes. They are setting in the field behind the Farm Barn. They're in containers, so I'm not in a hurry to plant them yet. The pole barn is up and already full of hay. I bought up all the available hay to be had in the area, much of which is not in the barn, but it will be all right. In some of the unleveled areas between fields we will plant grape vineyards for fruit and wine. I'm looking for someone knowledgeable in vineyards and wine making. I also have contractors currently installing an irrigation system for the growing areas. We are pumping water up from the lake finger between the islands. Just let me know where the land is you are buying so I can get started on it. Everything is beginning to look good for my department."

"Bess, I took a look at your greenhouse yesterday. That is an incredible design. I like the way you think. I know you are a botanist. I could certainly use your help and ideas with my department if you have the time."

Bess said, "Of course. I'd be happy to help in any way I can."

I said, "Very good report, James. Thank you." I no longer doubted James. He had been very busy. But, now I was curious about the Greenhouse. I hadn't seen one anywhere. "Bess, I haven't seen the Greenhouse. Where is it?"

Bess smiled and said, "If you were on the docks you must have walked right passed it. Want me to give you a tour?"

"Yeah, I would. Right after this meeting."

James said, "Do you mind if I come, too?"

Bess quickly said, "Not at all."

Bess was obviously proud of her project, and sadly I hadn't probed into it. She was obviously happy to be praised for it, even if it was from James and not me. I would correct that I'm sure, judging from what James had said.

Jeremy said, "Now, as far as the Castle, Al Martinez here is our Master Electrician and will be supervising the activation of our Castle power generators as soon as we leave here. Janet Walsh is in charge of our sanitation and water treatment. She has elected on a Hydrotron system of water filtration. It's a more advanced state-of-the-art system that uses high frequencies and energy pulses to kill any bacteria and separate any sediment in the water. We don't need a lot, since the water is already relatively clean, but what little bacteria and sediment there is will be eliminated by this system. The unit is already installed in the Cave close to the electrical generators. But, the water tank for the water storage and pressure can't be installed until we finish the fourth floor of the Castle. The sewage treatment will … I should let Janet describe that, since it's complicated, besides, this is her area of expertise. Janet?"

Janet did like the others and stood and said, "Jeremy, you were doing a good job of explaining how the system works, but I would be happy to con-

215

tinue. I understand our friends will be bringing a sewage treatment plant, but without knowing anything about it I felt we should do the best we can, just in case our systems don't match. The sewage treatment presented a particular challenge, because we are on an island and don't have large fields to build a treatment plant on. With the unit I have settled on this is all done electronically. All water and waste products are sanitized through electrolysis, everything that flows into the unit is zapped to kill all germs and bacteria. This process also causes the solids to separate and settle, leaving only clean water to pass through and flow back into the lake. The sanitized sediments are processed out as fertilizer, which is hauled off and deposited in the growing areas. It sounds simple, and actually it is; but the unit is about the size of a large shipping container, still much smaller than building a plant. We ordered two, which is overkill, but hey, we don't do anything small. Jeremy prepared a level spot just downhill and to the north of the Cave entrance. As you know, 'Crap doesn't flow uphill.', so it had to be lower than the Cave with easy access to the lake."

We all laughed at her joke, even though it made sense. I said, "Dr. Groom, how are things going in your area?"

Doc said, "Well, other than a broken arm and a few teeth knocked out, we are doing good." When he said that he stared directly at Bess, but I'm sure he was wondering what Bess might have done to him if she knew he took advantage of her on the examining table. "We have recruited our veterinarian,

216

her assistant and two nurses. We have a major stockpile of medicines and supplies, an X-Ray, Cat Scan, and various blood analyzing units. Dr. Betty Jones, our new veterinarian, just came aboard today and is preparing her order for equipment, supplies and medicines as we speak. I've seen Jeremy's plans for our medical clinic, and we love it. We can't wait to move in. We still need blood samples from most of the recruits to match their provided doctor's health certificates. We will also need to schedule physical examinations for all members. It would help if we had volunteers, so we can more easily fit into your schedule."

Before we could continue Robert received a phone call. He listened for a few seconds and said, "We'll be right there. Do not admit them! Mike, there are some FEMA officials and a couple of US Marshals at the front gate demanding access."

I said, "Here we go again. Nancy, go do your thing. Robert, send security to the front gate ... armed." Robert and JJ took off and Nancy and I were right behind them. I turned around and Bess was following close.

Bess said, "I'm going too."

It only took us a few minutes to get to the front gate. As we pulled up the guard had his pistol pulled and aimed at the marshal and was ordering him and the others off our property. The federal agents, all four of them were armed and waving their badges at the guard. Robert took over. Robert and JJ had their pistols pulled and aimed.

Robert said, "You gentlemen have been told to leave our property. I suggest you do so, and do so immediately."

The spokesman for the FEMA agents was hollering, "We are federal agents backed up by the full force of the government. We demand access."

I was pretty sure Nancy's bluster wouldn't work this time. I'm sure they had been briefed by the Fish and Game officer, and I'm sure Nancy knew it also.

Still, Nancy went into her spiel, "I'm Nancy McIntosh, attorney of record for the Cherokee Nation. As you know the Cherokee Nation is a sovereign country unto itself and the US government has NO authority on our property. You can demand nothing here. As you can clearly see, we have posted our Cherokee Nation identification signs and 'No Trespassing' notifications. Maybe if you would have been more respectful for our sovereignty we might be interested in knowing your business, but you tried to force your will upon us beyond any authority you might perceive to have. Please vacate our Nation immediately."

The FEMA officer stood his ground and said, "I too am an attorney of record for the US government. By order of the president, FEMA may confiscate food stores in time of emergency, and the US government wants to inventory your stores. We are here to do that now."

Nancy said, "Are you stating that a 'State of Emergency' has been declared?"

"No, I'm not stating that, but we are preparing for such an emergency."

Nancy said, "Well, when a 'State of Emergency' exists feel free to come back and see us in a respectful manor. The results will be the same, however, since we are not part of the US."

The officer said, "You don't seem to understand. We are under orders, and you cannot refuse us."

Nancy stood like a stone and looked directly into his eyes and said, "You have been warned. Chief Marshal Arrowhead, if these gentlemen are still on our property in 30 seconds order your officers to shoot them for trespassing. You will note the trespassing signs states violators will be shot. You will also notice that we have backhoes to bury the bodies."

The officers' eyes shot open and quickly looked again at the sign, which in fine print did in fact state 'Violators will be shot.' As if for the first time they noticed ten officers with drawn guns staring at them.

Nancy said, "You now have 20 seconds."

The officers turned in unison and bolted back through the gate. The spokesman said, "You have not heard the last of this."

Nancy calmly said, "We also bought the 80 acre plot you are standing on. You're still on our property."

The officers quickly got in their trucks and sped off. I said, "Damn, Nancy. Remind me never to play poker with you. You can sure bluff."

Nancy didn't smile and said, "Who said I was bluffing? No one is going to take our food! That would destroy what we are trying to do... survive.

He is right about one thing, though. We haven't heard the last from them, and they have considerable reach. We had better get delivered everything we need quickly. If we own this property, they own everything outside of us, and they will use that fact. They can stop our deliveries. Think about that."

Oh shit. They could, and that is exactly what they will do. I said, "let's identify what they might do, and let's identify what we can do."

Robert said, "They can blockade our incoming traffic, and that cuts off our cement trucks for one thing. That would be devastating."

I said, "Oh crap! Wait. Let's go back to the office. We need Jeremy in this conversation, hell we might as well pick everyone's brain. Bess, can you call him and the others while we drive back?"

Again, it was a short trip, and luckily some were still there. We went back into the conference room. I grabbed another coffee while Robert was detailing our confrontation at the gate to the others.

I said, "Correct me if I'm wrong, but we already have arms and munitions, food, fuel, grains. What will hurt us most is the cement, especially since we are using high volumes. What would happen if that flow stops?"

Jeremy said, "It would be disastrous! Maybe … yes, we could try to get a massive shipment of bags of concentrated cement in, and we could mix our own. We have the sand and gravel. It would take a lot longer, but it might work. I'll make a call and order in a huge shipment of Portland cement. I can even order several tons of gravel and sand, too.

We can use the cement trucks to mix it, just like they do. I'll call them now and get them en route."

I said, "How much time do you think we have?"

Robert said, "Probably no more than two days, but for sure on the third day. The feds don't really have troops for blockades. They would call on local or state police agencies, but I doubt the Highway Patrol would get involved. If they used the National Guard or Highway Patrol the governor would have to approve it."

Nancy said, "I think I can stop that, but Mike, you will have to make some additional campaign contributions." I just nodded. "I'll also call an influential legal firm in the city and file a Cease and Desist Order. It will take them a few more days to work their way through the legal quagmire, assuming they can. In the meantime, Robert, do you have any influence with the Sheriff's Department? If not we will have to make another campaign donation. There is always a chance the US Marshals could try a blockade themselves. I doubt it, but if they do we will need the Sheriff to serve them papers and run interference. I think we can stall this off until they get smart and bring in the Army or FBI, calling us a terrorist group. By then I hope we have it all done, because when that happens we will be at war."

Robert said, I know the Sheriff well. I also know that money talks with him, but I know him well enough to talk, and he trusts me enough for me to pass off some money."

I said, "This all sounds great. Let's do it. Sue, give Robert some cash for his meeting. Nancy, take whatever cash you may need, but I want someone with a gun going with you. JJ, can you back Nancy up? Robert, I hope you are at full staff and they are committed.

"I'm close enough, plus we have other combat veterans in our group. Hopefully, it won't come to that, with the shootings and all to investigate. I'll talk to the Sheriff. At least he will be able to give us some warning, anyway.

I said, "Jeremy, you might want to consider the barges for bringing shipments in. We can probably get a few of those in if we need to. And, how about those huge helicopters that haul shipping containers? We might want to line up a few of those. James, get all those cows, horses goats and chickens in here quickly."

Dr. Groom said, "Are we really going to fight the government and shoot it out?"

It was silent in the room for a while, and I said, "Well, it has always been inevitable. It is just earlier than we had hoped. But, ask yourself why we are here? We're here to survive, and survive we must. Nancy was right. We can't let them in. Once they see what we have they will have a better idea how to attack us later, and they will when food runs out for the population if they know we have any. Let's just hope we can stall this off for a while. The government won't last long after the collapse. Do you have any other suggestions?"

Doc said, "No, not really. I'm just clarifying it to my mind."

We broke up the meeting and James, Bess and I headed to the Greenhouse. I needed the diversion.

As we drove into the Cave I noticed the steal door was now installed. It would definitely seal off the Cave. I drove toward the dock tunnel and pulled over to another tunnel Bess pointed out. I hadn't noticed this one before. Bess was excited and steered us down the tunnel for about 75 feet where it opened into a large room about a hundred feet wide by a hundred and fifty feet deep. The entire room was sunken about 15 feet and the roof at the entrance elevated to about 30 feet. From there the glass or plastic, I couldn't tell which, pitched down toward the far end, where the ceiling was about 20 feet off the floor. The whole upper structure consisted of beams and cross beams housing the glass. It was bright inside and easy to see the impressive engineering of the design. It was very majestic and extremely functional, but what caught my attention was a lattice of metal strips on the outside attached to the beams by adjustable gears. I could tell they moved like venation blinds to adjust and direct the volume of light entering. I had never seen anything like it before...ingenious.

Bess said, "I see you looking at the adjustable light, but I bet the significance of it hasn't dawned on you yet. Jeremy helped me design that. As the sun moves in the sky with season change, the blinds can regulate the amount of light taken into the Greenhouse. Summer requires less light, which reduces the heat inside. We are sunken to take advantage of the geothermal temperature of the earth, which is about 55 degrees year-round. So, no freezing in the winter or burning up in the summer inside, but one of the best features of the blinds is that the panels are made of 1/4 in. stainless steel and can be completely closed as an extra security feature. This is assuming the clear panels might be subject to damage, which they are not. They are made of double panels of 1/2 in. polycarbonate panels, which are virtually indestructible. The two panels are spaced apart to provide an incredible insulation temperature barrier. Between this insulation and earth geothermal we don't even need any heaters or air conditioning. As you can see, however, we do have fans to keep the air moving through the vegetation. We have rows of 4 ft. deep water ponds running under these raised tanks and connected at each end. Each of the 16 tanks per row is 4' X 8' and they are placed end to end for the length of the greenhouse in 17 rows."

"As you have probably already figured out, this will not be a standard greenhouse. This will be a habitat for a year-round aquaponics operation in which we can grow at least four times as many vegetables and also supply a steady flow of fish for food. The basic principle of aquaponics: plants grow in a flowing waterbed full of ceramic balls about the size of marbles. The ceramic balls grow the bacteria cultures and hold the root systems of the plants. The plants produce oxygen to nourish fish in the ponds, while the fish provides carbon dioxide and waste to nourish the plants. The two ecosystems together provide a very efficient operation to supply us with an abundant supply of food, well not all we need but plenty. James has persuaded me to forfeit some space up front for tropical plants and trees like banana, coffee, orange, lemon and the like. There is enough height at that end for full sized trees."

I was truly astonished with her design. I had no idea Bess was getting all this done. I remember her sitting with Jeremy at the cabin going over plans. I knew Bess was educated and smart, but I was honestly surprised. I said, "Bess, you are incredible. You have done a fantastic job here."

Bess jumped into my arms and gave me a huge hug and big wet kisses. I hugged her back, and she felt good...real good.

James couldn't resist and said, "Bess, you really are incredible. Can I have a hug, too?"

Bess and I both laughed, and Bess jumped on him and began applying warm kisses. I knew Bess loved me, but it was obvious she liked James, too. I knew we would have to invite him over to the cabin soon. Maybe he could bring the twins along.

A thought crossed my mind and I said, "Bess, your electricity should be on soon. Do you have your plants and fish yet? If not you better get them coming soon. Oh, please order some more scuba gear too, before the roads close."

Bess came back to my side and slipped her arm around me and said, "I have all the seeds, some of the plants and the tilapia (fish) and water plants are down at the dock in floating pens. And, the extra scuba gear is already stored back in the Cave, enough for five more divers. I don't know if you have noticed yet, but I had the gear in your truck unloaded and stored with the others. I even bought some underwater scooters. I'm not sure why we

225

would need that many divers or even the scooters, but we have them if we do. I've been busy, huh?"

"You sure have sweetie, and I'm very proud of you." That was not just platitudes, I really was proud of her. I also realized I was taking my girls for granted. The sisters were all doing exceptionally well, and I was expecting it. I guess there is nothing wrong with that. They were, after all, smart, talented and beautiful. My problem was not letting them know how much I appreciated them. I promised myself that would change.

As we were about to leave we heard a diesel generator fire off. We walked over to see Al smiling. He saw us walking up and said, "Everything checks out. We will be online in here shortly. I just have a few more details to finalize."

I said, "Great news, Al. Oh, by the way, you're in the loft again tonight."

When we reached the office Bess and James left for his Farm Barn to go over some of his issues, and I returned to my office. Nancy quickly came into my office. She looked pleased but still very stressed. I can't imagine how stressful today had been on her. She walked around to me and leaned back against my desk.

Nancy said, "I've got some pretty good news. I made contact with my friend in the Oklahoma City law firm. I used them before to purchase the property. They have ins in the governor's office. They are working up the Cease and Desist order against FEMA and the US Marshal's office. It will be presented to the governor soon. They have also agreed to present a cash campaign donation on our behalf.

Of course, they will cover that expense in their invoice, but I won't even have to go there. They agree with us about our legal rights and don't believe they will have a problem. They will also fax a copy of it to the Cherokee County Sheriff's office. I still plan to go see the Cherokee Chief, however. I want to ensure an end run through them can't be structured. We would be up shit's creek if the Cherokees disavow our rights under the treaty with the US government. That won't happen, though. Still, another campaign donation will provide that insurance. I've already called for an appointment in a couple of hours."

I said, "Nancy, I really appreciate you. No one could have done what you have done. You make an excellent Secretary of State." I chuckled at my own joke, but Nancy almost collapsed in my arms sobbing. I meant it, but apparently she needed to hear it from me. It was like her stress had built to a breaking point and my words provided a partial release. I held her tight and kissed her passionately. I really love this girl...my girl. She shot her hot tongue in my mouth and our passion grew. There was only one way to get any closer than we were at that moment. I slipped my hands under her loose pleated skirt and began to rub her butt cheeks, then I started slipping her panties down her thighs. She began pushing my shorts down until my cock sprang out. I lifted her butt up on my desk and pulled her to the edge, as she leaned back on her hands extended behind her. I lifted her legs over my arms and began to inch closer. I guided my cock into her hot, wet pussy and began pushing in and out. I went deeper and deeper into that ecstasy. We fit together perfectly, and it felt wonderful. I was soon deep into her, and her moans became louder. I detected movement and saw JJ standing in the doorway. We hadn't even bothered to close the door, but JJ instinctively knew we needed this alone moment and closed the door. She was probably standing guard outside. Nothing would have stopped me anyway. I was driving into Nancy like a wild man. Nancy's head was thrown back, and her eyes were shut tight, and she began to scream. We climaxed in powerful orgasms together. My cock continued to jerk and her pussy continued to spasm. Slowly we calmed. When our eyes finally met we burst out laughing at ourselves, how reckless and overpowering our emotions had developed. She leaned forward and wrapped her arms around me and gave me a tender kiss.

Nancy said, "Thanks Mike. I really needed those words and this stress release. I feel much better and calmer now my love." She slipped her panties back on and left my office smiling. Luckily, only a smiling JJ was in the outside office, but I'm sure others heard. But, I didn't care.

After a while, Robert came into my office. He was smiling, so I knew it was good news. Robert said, "We anticipated correctly, and our timing was perfect. I called the Sheriff after our meeting this morning, and we met at a coffee shop. I told him what had happened and what we suspected they might do. I told him what we hoped he might NOT do to help them. He mentioned his upcoming election, which I knew wasn't true, since he was re-

228

elected only last year. But, following that train of thought, I offered him a large envelope full of hundred dollar bills, fifty of them to be exact. He took a secret look and slipped the envelope into his boot under the table. He then agreed that we were right and he wouldn't help them. The truth be known, I had another envelope in case it took that, too. Anyway, he called me a little while ago to tell me they came crying to him and wanted to press charges against us and set up a blockade, like we thought, he just laughed at them and told them they had no authority on the Cherokee Nation. He said he told them they were lucky we didn't shoot them, that others have gone missing before. He laughed and said they didn't even offer to pay any expenses for the blockade. We both laughed.

I said, "It might have been another story if they had offered to pay."

Robert laughed and said, "I doubt it. They pay by check and late."

I said, "Did you have any more security check in? Another question I've been wondering about. Are they willing to fight?"

"Yes, I'm fully staffed, and I even have some women, too. Will they fight? Once I know I want them I tell them the truth. They all know what is at stake, what they now have and what they stand to lose. Yes, they will fight."

After Robert left I was surprised to discover that it was past 4:00 pm, and I was hungry. I walked over to Bob's Cafe to see if he had any food. Hell, I would be pleased with a good cup of coffee. Bob saw me coming and waved me over to a table. Apparently, he was going to wait on me personally. I had just got my coffee and sat down when he brought me a plate of baked pork chops, potatoes, red beans and cornbread. Damn it smelled good, and I dug in after thanking him. I had just started on my second pork chop when Mary came over and sat down across from me.

Mary said, "Are things always this busy around here?

I laughed and said, "Well, not usually like to-day."

Mary continued, "Nancy called me and told me to go home with you when you left. I think she is kind of pushing us together for some reason. I don't mind, but I know you Nancy, Sue and Bess are in a relationship. I don't want to interfere. You are all apparently somewhat open in the relationship, which seems to work for you. I like Nancy, but I do feel a little awkward. Do you know why Nancy is pushing us together?"

I said, "Well, Nancy got a little perturbed at me. To put it bluntly she thought I shouldn't have just tossed you down and jumped in like I did. It seems to her that I neglected the respect, foreplay and getting to know you. To be honest, I did. I'm sorry, but you saw how aroused I was at the time. I wasn't thinking clearly. Nancy respects you, and you can be a huge help to her. I think she just wants us all to work smoothly together."

Mary said, "I did not take any offense at all. Actually, I was equally aroused watching, and I liked what you did to me. We can always do the get

230

to know you bit and foreplay. We can do that tonight if you like."

I smiled and said, "I like."

Chapter 10
(I Win Again!)

After we finished eating we went to my office. I wanted to see if Sue needed a ride to the cabin. I saw her nose deep in her books, and her hand busily running over the keys of her adding machine, a long roll of receipt paper curled over her desk and across the floor. I didn't want to interrupt her, so I stood by the door until she looked up. I said, "I can see that you are busy, but I wanted to see if you needed a ride back to the cabin."

Sue said, "I need some more time to finish this up. I'll call Jeremy and catch a ride with him or Al."

I said, "Sue, I'm not big on giving compliments, as you have probably noticed. But, I want you to know that you are doing a fantastic job. You're very smart and you get things done without being asked. I know I can rely on you and your sisters, and you are appreciated. I just wanted you to know that."

Sue said, "Awww, Mike, that is so sweet of you to say. Thanks love. I really mean that, but I'm so busy right now, so give me a kiss and get out of here so I can work."

I happily gave her a kiss, pinched her butt and ran out. I still heard her squealing as I closed the door behind me. When Mary and I reached the cabin no one else was there. Mary grabbed my hand and led me to the shower and started removing my

clothing. I returned the favor, and we were soon
standing naked in the shower. I took a close look at
her, seemingly for the first time. I had ravaged her
body before, but I was getting a real look at her for
the first time. I have always known that my preference in women was toward small, petite women
with darker completions, but as I looked at Mary I
saw something completely different and very beautiful. She wasn't quite as tall as me, but she was tall
for a woman. Her long, alabaster legs were tapered
right up to her fiery, red hair on her pink pussy.
Mary was certainly a true redhead. The hair on her
pussy was long but trimmed to accent it. The long
pink nipples on her "C" sized breasts protruded like
fingers, and they were pointing directly at me. My
eyes traveled up to her face, which was smiling.
The bright green eyes were staring back. Her long
red hair hung below her shoulder blades and tended
to accent the freckles on her nose and cheeks. She
was truly a beautiful woman, and it amazed me that
I hadn't noticed before. We began enjoying washing and exploring each other. Her skin was soft. It
felt like sliding my fingers over silk. Mary began
rubbing her thumbs over my nipples, but I began to
lose it and devoured her hard, pink nipples in return.
I really lost it when she began stroking my cock, but
before I could react, she dropped to her knees and
took me into her mouth. When I say took me into
her mouth, I mean all the way. Due to my size I had
never been deep-throated before, but she took it all,
pushing it down her throat. Her hands and fingers
pulled my butt toward her as she drove her mouth
on my cock. It was an amazing feeling. I'm sur-

prised I didn't explode in her mouth. It must have been the shock of the experience. I couldn't wait and pulled her up and turned her around. She instinctively grabbed the handicap-bar and leaned over. I found her hot tunnel from behind and began stroking into her. Soon I was balls deep in her hot pussy and pounding hard. It was a good thing the shower was equipped with the handicap shower bar, because she was having to hold on tight. I knew she was climaxing when the screams started, and they lasted for several long minutes as I unloaded deep inside her.

After a few quivering moments Mary said, "Damn, that was good."

I said, "Oh my, yes. It was very good."

We dried each other off, donned our robes and went into the main room. When we did we heard moans coming from Jeremy's room. Curiosity got the best of me, and we took a look. James and Bess were going at it. Mary and I chuckled and went to my room where we shed or robes and snuggled into bed. We continued to explore each other while Bess' screaming ran its course. The echoes had hardly stopped when Bess and James came into our room.

Bess said, "Mary, we heard your screaming when we came in and decided to join in the chorus. Now I came to get my load." I had to laugh.

Mary just shrugged and spread her thighs. Bess went directly for the fiery red hair and began her assault, which Mary seemed to thoroughly enjoy, judging by her moans. James just sat on the edge of the bed and watched. Mary's moans grew louder and her hands pulled Bess' head into her tighter. Soon Mary's thighs clamped on Bess' head and Mary flooded her face. Even with Mary's thighs clamped, Bess continued to lap it up. After some time Bess moved and Mary's thighs fell back open. She lay totally relaxed with her eyes closed, recovering. Bess tapped James' arm and pointed him toward Mary's pussy. He didn't wait to be asked twice. He was already aroused watching Bess and Mary, and he positioned himself between Mary's thighs and pushed right in. After a few strokes, Mary moaned and wrapped her long legs around James and joined in the effort. I'm not sure she even knew who it was that was in her, nor do I think she cared. I hugged Bess and we watched them slap together into a mutual orgasm.

From the doorway we heard Nancy say, "That was hot. Mike, did you get some quality time with Mary before my slut sister got involved?"

I said, "Yes we did. In the shower, but it was quality time."

Nancy smiled and said, "Good. Did she deep-throat you?"

I didn't quite know how to answer that, but tentatively said, "Yeah."

"Was she able to take you all? Did you like it?"

"Every inch. And, I loved it."

Nancy grinned and said, "Mary told me she could deep-throat, but I didn't believe it possible with you. That's why I wanted you to spend some time with her. I wanted to see if she could do it. She said she can teach me, and I want to learn. OK,

235

Bess, you and James go back in there. School starts in here now. Mike, would you like me to learn how to do that?" I was nodding animatedly.

They didn't argue and left us. Nancy started stripping off her clothes and joined us. She immediately went for my cock. It was still flaccid, but that didn't discourage her. She began rolling it between palms like she had seen Janet do, but she did it better. Nancy took the head into her hot mouth as she rolled my cock. Damn it felt good, and I knew it was working. Nancy spread my thighs and lay between them, as she began sucking my now hard cock. She began trying to take it all in, but would gag and have to back off. I slipped my hands behind my head, closed my eyes and lay back. I thought, "Take all the time you need; I'll be right here."

Nancy said, "Show me how, Mary."

Mary lay across my thigh and took my cock from Nancy. As before, she simply pushed her mouth down on me in one thrust, taking it all in and down her throat. I groaned. She did that a few times then pushed my cock toward Nancy, who tried to do the same. She was having trouble getting past her gag reflex. I heard Mary talking to her, giving her instruction. I heard her say swallow when you get it back to your throat. On Nancy's next try I felt her swallow my cock and it slipped into her throat. Oh my. She did it. Once she did it, she kept doing it. I felt her throat swallowing on my cock. I could tell she was proud of herself, and I could tell she loved doing it. She always loved sucking me. Every women is different in some way

236

sexually. Some like anal like Sue, some like women also like Bess, but Nancy loved giving oral, at least to me. I certainly liked it, and I didn't know how much more I could take.

Mary saw that I was nearing climax and said, "You better mount him now if you don't want him to cum in your throat." When Nancy continued driving down on my cock, I knew she wasn't going to stop. I felt her body quivering and heard her moans and knew she was going to have an orgasm sucking me. She was that aroused. I know I certainly was going to climax, and soon. When it came I pushed up into her throat and released a torrent of semen. Nancy took every drop and sucked even more out. It felt like she was going to suck my balls right up my cock. It was almost more than I could stand ... almost. My orgasm was so intense, but it felt so damn good I couldn't end it. Eventually, as my cock slowly deflated, Nancy reluctantly relinquished it.

Nancy said, "I loved that, and I could tell you did also. Thanks Mary for teaching me."

I said, "Hell, yeah, thanks Mary." I pulled Nancy up and kissed her and said, "And, thank you, baby."

Nancy smiled big and said, "It was my pleasure." We all three laughed.

Mary said, "I told you you could do it. You just have to figure it out." After a few moments relaxing Mary continued, "I think I will go take a quick nap in Al's bed and wait for him."

Nancy and I must have dozed off. When we got up to get something to drink we saw that James

237

had left and Jeremy was now sandwiched between Mary's thighs pumping away, while a naked Sue watched. We knew what Sue wanted from Jeremy. We must have slept through how this all happened, and it must have been interesting. We didn't see Bess or Janet, but we heard moans coming down from the loft, so they must be up there with Al.

I checked the Internet to see if my lottery numbers won. After I entered the numbers I was actually surprised, not that I won but the amount. "I won!" I said, "I wasn't expecting this much, however. $487,000,000. Can you believe it? That's almost a half a billion dollars going into our account. That's billion with a capital 'B'. Well, it would be if taxes didn't take almost half of it."

I yelled, "Hey, Sue. We won, again. $487,000,000. Is there any way to get out of paying taxes on it?" I sent Robert a quick text telling him that we won the lottery and to pick me up in the am to go to Oklahoma City.

Sue came running out of the bedroom naked and leaned over my shoulder to look at the winning total. I could feel her breasts against my back, which was distracting. "Wow! said Sue, "That's a lot of money. Let me think. I wonder if we can pull a Nancy on them by claiming Cherokee citizenship and living on a Cherokee reservation. Maybe it's possible with the state, but federal taxes might be another story. We can try, though."

Robert and JJ were there early in his official looking and armed GMC Yukon. It was black as midnight with racks of emergency lights on the top. The large, white Cherokee Nation Martial Service

238

signs stood out against the black truck, somewhat resembling an Oklahoma Highway Patrol vehicle. Sue and I scrambled to get dressed, which didn't take long. On the way out I told Nancy, "You're in charge, hon. We should be back by mid-afternoon."

I noticed that both Robert and JJ were in full uniform with multiple arms belted on. They even had two shotguns in holders between the seats. Sue and I settled into the backseat for the long trip. Sue, the little shit, had brought her pillow, obviously intending to sleep on the way. Actually, that wasn't a bad idea, and I was considering it when Robert said, "I want to get up there as quickly as we can. There are gun battles raging in Oklahoma City. Looters are running ramped and fighting the police, but it's still not as bad as some cities around the country. It is so bad in Detroit the Michigan governor has declared Martial Law and called out the National Guard. Several other large cities are nearing that crisis level, namely Chicago, Baltimore and New Orleans to name a few. People in the larger cities are afraid to go out. They have begun runs on the grocery stores and some banks."

"Geeze," I said, "Why is all this happening, and how do you know so much about it?"

Robert laughed and said, "It's not like I listen to the radio all day, but I do have one of my Surveillance Officers listening and monitoring the news agencies. She gives me a texted report every morning. I was reading it while I waited for you guys. As to 'Why', this all started with the Black Lives Matter protests. I guess it started off as black protests, but the movement got hijacked by thugs and

239

the criminal elements in our society. They saw that the elected officials were afraid of the black protests and treating their violence in a politically correct way. That's like waving a red flag in front of a bull. The thugs realized they could get by with it and took over and started shooting cops and looting. It's mushroomed from there. Now it is out of control. If the economy folds, like it is beginning to look, it will only get worse. Just think what will happen if the welfare and Social Security checks stop coming."

"I don't even want to think about that," I said, "Sue, maybe we better call Bob and get in one final shipment of food, if it is not already too late." I noticed Sue writing up a text message. Yeah, that is probably better.

Robert was not all that happy with the location of the lottery redemption center. It was right downtown in the middle of the Oklahoma City. He turned his police scanner on to monitor police activity. Hearing nothing major he cautiously made it there. I decided to go in with just Sue, thinking we would be less intimidation to them. Come to find out nothing intimidated them.

What happened at the Oklahoma Lottery Redemption Center was really not all that surprising. They verified my winning ticket, and I had to present my ID. I used my Cherokee Nation ID, and Sue argued strongly about my tax exempt status, but it all fell on deaf, bureaucratic ears. The bureaucrat only knew one way to process the disbursement of money, and that was taking out the taxes. The official gave the canned spiel, telling us that we could file our arguments with the commission and IRS, and if they agreed, they would send me another check. Of course, that would never happen, and we knew it. So, after taxes we wound up with just over $300,000,000, still a sizable amount. Sue was successful, however, in getting the bureaucrat to wire transfer this amount to several of my banks and a couple of new ones. I guess we were successful, since we got the money.

I was pleased to have the money in my bank accounts, so I was in a joyful mood. Robert, however, was not. He informed us that there were a couple of gun battles going on in the city and wanted to get the hell out as soon as possible. The farther we got from downtown the more relaxed he became. He was almost jovial by the time we reached the outskirts.

I saw a Jack in the Box sign and said, "Robert, let's pull in the Jack in the Box up ahead. I love those cheap tacos they sell. Let's get a few dozen of them for the ride back."

I guess he thought it was a good idea, also. I did, however, note that he pulled in away from all other cars, and he backed in on the back row. I took note that he was positioned for a fast getaway if necessary. He was being really careful, and I liked that about him. We ordered our tacos and were waiting when we heard the siren. We watched cautiously as a police cruiser sped in and two officers jumped out. They were immediately fired upon by a man coming out of the restaurant's main door. The man ran around the other side of the building and fired again at the officers. The officers, a male

241

and female, ran forward taking cover behind a car and returned fire at the man. As we sat watching, two more men jumped out of a parked car and ran behind the crouching officers. The officers were totally unaware of the men coming up behind them.

"It's an ambush," Robert said, "Use the shotgun, JJ." Both Robert and JJ grabbed their shotguns and jumped out. Just as the men were taking positions and aiming, Robert and JJ fired at them. One of the men's head exploded and the legs were shot from under the other. The officers spun around in time to see the men fall, and the female officer finished off the fallen attacker as he was attempting to raise his gun. Had Robert and JJ not fired, the officers would be dead, and they knew it. Robert and JJ were in uniform, so the police saw them as friendlies, plus Robert and JJ held their guns high, just in case. The officers nodded their appreciation and turned back to the other shooter. Robert indicated that JJ should stay and watch the officers' backs, and he turned and ran around the back of the building. As we watched, we heard another shotgun blast and saw the third man blown back around the corner from where he was hiding, dead as hell.

Robert came back around the back side of the building. He wasn't about to come around that corner. Him and JJ talked to the officers for a short while. I saw Robert hand the officers a card before they came back to the Yukon. They got in and was about to drive away when the manager came running out with a large sack. He said, "You forgot your food. Thanks for what you did. The food is free." Robert nodded and sped away and got back

242

on I-40 as quickly as possible. He turned his flashing lights and siren on and sped down the highway. He kept them on until we were well out of Oklahoma City limits.

"I didn't want to stick around for the paperwork," he said, "It would take forever. Besides, I'm sure the officers will protect us, since we saved their asses. If not, they'll play hell getting us back in Oklahoma City, even if we have to hide out on the Cherokee Nation. Now, pass out those tacos."

When Robert said that, I jerked out of my shock and realized that I hadn't done a damn thing through the whole episode. I even had a gun, but I froze. One thing for sure: I was going to learn to use it. There would be more of what just happened, and I better not freeze again. I looked at Sue and her eyes were still wide, maybe even in shock a little. I hugged her to me, which seemed to snap her out of her funk. The only thing I could think of to do was hand out the tacos. I began eating one, even though I didn't taste it.

After a while I asked Robert, "I saw you give the officers your card. What was that all about if you didn't want them to know who helped them?"

"I asked them to call me tomorrow." Robert said, "If they are single I will recruit them for our complex. Why? Well, warriors that you happen to save their lives make very loyal officers. I also asked them not to remember who we were, but unfortunately, there were many witnesses and our vehicle is well marked."

"That makes sense," I said.

I noticed that Robert continued to monitor the police scanner, and at one point the shootings were reported with no mention of us. I guess Robert was correct in assuming the officers would protect them, for a while anyway. By then we would be back on our reservation and relatively safe ... hopefully. We did hear more about the incident on the police scanner, but there was still no mention of us. They only talked about an officer involved shooting with three perpetrators down. You bet your ass three perps were down.

We made it back home without incident and breathed a sigh of relief. Still, Robert intended to stay within the property for a while, and so did I. We split up to check in as soon as we got back. Sue had called Nancy and told her about our scary adventure, and she was waiting on us when we went in the office. Nancy could tell that we really didn't want to talk about it, so she began an update of what we had missed last night and today.

"I think you will be happy with the progress," Nancy said, "I think the most important news is that the Dome is finished, but it cost us far more than we expected."

"No shit!" I said, "We got plenty more money today, so we don't care about the cost. I would really like to see it, and Brin will be anxious to know this. Do you want to go diving?"

Nancy laughed and said, "That won't be necessary. There is a pressurized walkway tunnel going down from the Cave and into the Dome. Jeremy took me to see it so I would sign off on it, and it is quite impressive. But, wait. There is more. The

244

Cave and first floor are also done, and most of the second floor. Of course, the elevator is not in, since they are still working on the top floor. Bob immediately filled that huge walk-in freezer with beef, chickens and everything else you can imagine. He was also able to get some more shipments of canned food stores, of course it cost us double. There was another major shipment of weapons and munitions, which Sue's crews have already inventoried and stored in the armament area in the Cave. Oh, and we moved all the contents of our office safe into the vault along with an armored car delivery of $20,000,000 of gold, silver and platinum. We also have several million in paper cash for day-to-day operations. Oh, yeah, we also have a poultry barn full of baby chickens. They are so cute. I was over earlier playing with them. The twins are doing a fantastic job. They've gotten delivery of all their equipment, a warehouse full of feed and supplies. They are in full operation. You have to see those baby chickens, the twins, too. They are all so cute."

"Does Jeremy want to go with us to the Dome?" I asked, "Please call him and ask. I'm going to grab a cup of coffee and go to my office and e-mail Brin." I handed Nancy the Jack in the Box sack and said, "We saved you some tacos."

Chapter 11
(Nearing Completion)

Brin had definitely left a message for me.

"Mike, we definitely see progress on the Castle. We are very pleased with this progress. We are also progressing faster than we anticipated. I'm happy to report that we are here, currently orbiting Earth, and we have deployed the geostationary satellites. Let us know when the Dome is ready, and we can land. We aren't in much danger of being seen. We have a radar masking transmission to hide us, but we can be seen visually if they happen to accidentally see us. Hopefully, we will not be seen visually. If so, we will hide behind the moon until you are ready. We will come in at night, and I suggest you have a landing area where we can lower the sewage treatment unit and power generators before we go underwater. Should we wait until there are no workers available to see us?

I fired back an immediate response:

"Hey, Brin, I am happy to report that the Dome is complete and filled with air. I am about to give it a final inspection, but it is ready for you. We will have an unloading area ready for you, but we still have outside workers going 24-hours a day. We probably need a few more days of this before we let them go. You could, however, park in the dome, and we can wait until later to unload the equipment, since we have both needs under control."

246

"One thing I need to know, however. Obvious-ly, there is no way to hide a spaceship from being seen, but I'm wondering about you and your people. What do you look like? You've said that you are humanoid, but to a casual observer would it be obvious that you are alien? Can your identity be masked from the outside workers?"

When I finished with the e-mail Nancy and I took off toward the Cave. It seems that every time I make this trip things have changed. This time we traveled on a fully blacktopped road, complete with curbs and fully landscaped. Large trees lined the road, and they looked to be all fruit bearing trees. I have no idea what kind, but knowing James they would fit into his food crops. Nancy had me turn in toward the line of barns and into a finished parking lot. I knew she was leading me toward the Poultry Barn.

When we entered the heat caught me by surprise. I saw hundreds, maybe thousands, of small chickens running loose everywhere, but mostly gathered around the feeding trays, water troughs and low hung infrared warming lights. Nancy was right. The baby chickens were cute and ran all over our feet. When we came in two identical looking women came to meet us. These were obviously the twins. Nancy was right about them being cute, also. They were tall, maybe 5' 9" and 130 lbs. They looked to be in their mid-twenties with long blonde hair and crystal blue eyes, and they were beautiful. I didn't know which one to stare at. I don't guess it matters, since they were identical, but it was a little unnerving seeing four "D" sized breasts jiggling toward me. Because of the heat they were wearing loose shorts and what looked like reinforced halter tops, but they did little to prevent the swaying and jiggling. It didn't look like they were trying to show off their assets, but that wasn't something easy to do. They introduced themselves as Ella and Ebba Johansson. Actually, each introduced the other, and like many twins tend to do, they finished each other's sentences. It was cute listening to them.

Ella/Ebba said in partial sentences, "You must be Mike. Thank you for this opportunity. Nancy mentioned you often. This barn is for raising the young chicks. It's the only one we have operational so far. As these chicks mature we will transfer many to the laying hen barn, but that will take a while. Initially, most of the eggs will go into the incubators we purchased, but once the cycle is started we should have many eggs and hens for eating."

"I'm glad you are operational," I said, "You are welcome in our community. Have you got everything you need?"

"Yes, thanks," Ella/Ebba said, "James told us to go out and buy everything we needed, and we did. We have been in the poultry business all our lives and love it. Don't worry about this portion, we have it handled."

"That's good," I said, "Just let us know if you need anything."

As we were leaving Nancy said, "We'll see you later tonight."

"We're looking forward to it," Ella said.

When we got back in the pickup I said, "What was that all about ... later tonight?"

Nancy laughed and said, "Oh I invited them over to the cabin tonight, since they don't know anyone yet. We'll find someone to do them ... I mean something to do. Actually, Mary asked some of us to go with her over to the security barracks again. She said that we need to jump start action over there. The girls there are being stingy, and Mary wants to break the ice, so to speak. I invited the twins over to keep you company tonight."

I laughed and said, "You are getting into it, huh, pimping me out and participating in multiple players. By the way, do the twins have any idea what you're pushing them into?"

Nancy flashed a wicked grin and said, "Well, I did kind of enjoy my visit to security last time. It made me feel slutty in a good kind of exciting way. As for the twins, not really, but we talked about some of the activities that occur in our cabin, and they mentioned that they haven't dated in a while. Oh, and let me warn you. The twins do everything together, so don't try to separate them. I know from experience that you can handle two women quite well."

That last was said with a large smile, and I had to laugh, too. Nancy was always a surprise, but the thought of being with the twins was also intriguing. Okay, I guess it was all right for Nancy to pimp me out, but I wondered how the twins would take it.

Jeremy was waiting when we pulled into the Cave. He was smiling. Of course he was. He loved to show off his construction. He led us toward the tunnel running down to the dock. Just before we got to the opening he stopped before a circular door with a large wheel.

Jeremy said, "We added this branch tunnel after you were here before. As you can see, the entrance is sealed. The physics of an air-filled Dome posed a special problem. An opened ended tunnel would expunge all the air in the tunnel due to the physics (air pressure vs water pressure). We solved that problem by installing pressure doors on each end of the tunnel. We installed safety measures to allow only one door at a time to be opened. When we open this door the door in the Dome is closed. We must close this door behind us before we can open the one at the other end, and to keep pressure in the tunnel and reduce the time to re-pressure, we installed a third door in the middle. A second air pipe continuously pumps air through a check-valve for circulation and pressure. The return air flows through this tunnel with pressure adjustments in the doors. When the doors are opened this return air flow rebuilds the tunnel pressure. This way the built up air pressure is not allowed to escape. Ingenious ... huh?"

Jeremy didn't expect an answer, since he knew his engineering was ingenious. After we closed the exit door I felt the pressure change, the same with the other doors. Soon we were standing inside the Dome. It wasn't what I expected, it was better. The door opened directly on a walkway circling around the outer edge of the Dome, leaving an open center section of about 100 feet in the middle, the requirement Brin needed for the spaceship. The entire

Dome was about 300 feet across and 50 feet in height in the center. I was expecting the Dome to be completely made of metal, but only the curved "I" beams were metal. Between these beams were filled with curved pie-shaped clear glass. It probably wasn't glass. It was probably formed polycarbonate. It was extremely majestic in appearance. I watched the surface sunlight flickering and filtering through the water and was amazed at the abundance of fish life. They must have been attracted to the light within. I tried to remember just how deep we were. I seem to remember around 100 feet deep. When we dove here I remember the crater was deep here between two sharp underwater mountains. Brin had chosen this location for this express purpose. I think he will like it. I know I did.

All the while we were in the Dome no one said a word, like it was a sacred place, but once we were back in the Cave Jeremy started catching me up on the Castle.

"Mike, I want to thank you for giving me the idea of using heavy duty helicopters." Said Jeremy, "I hadn't even considered them. I hired one to bring Janet's sewage treatment units in. It worked great and was much faster. They are now operational. I also used it to set her water tank on the roof. Yes, the cement is all poured. You will be pleased."

"Fantastic. I'm anxious to see it, but I'm getting hungry," I said, "Let's go see Bob."

Bob was happy to see us and rushed over to see what we wanted to eat. I'm quite sure he didn't give this kind of service to everyone, but I was happy to get it. I was also happy to get a medium-well

T-bone steak, potatoes, green beans and the fixings. Bob was tapping into his meat stores for this. Damn, it was good. I even ate two steaks. Bob also brought me a tall, cold glass of milk. He said it was from our own milk cows. That surprised me, since I didn't even know that operation was operational yet. The community was coming together.

While I was working on the second steak the twins came in and joined us. They had apparently showered and changed cloths. They still filled out their shirts but were dressed more modestly. Nancy and the twins struck up a conversation and were chatting and laughing when Sue came in. Sue was grinning ear to ear.

"What's with you? Nancy asked.

Sue just grinned and said, "I just had my physical from Dr. Groom. You know what, Bess was right ... she got fucked."

I choked on my milk, and Nancy and Sue burst out laughing. The twins just stared, not understanding the joke but registering the words. In between burst of laughter Nancy tried to explain about Bess and what she had told us about her physical. They finally got most of the story and joined in the laughter.

"Where is Bess?" I asked,

Sue said, "I think she is hibernated down in her Green House. It's operational now, and she recruited her assistances, and we got them lodged in a cabin. They have been busting their asses down there ever since. I'll give her a call and let her know we are at Bob's Cafe."

252

After a while Bess, Jeremy, Al and Janet, followed by Mary and four other women I didn't know, came in. Bess sat next to me, and the others sat at an adjacent table. Mary came over to speak to Nancy and said, "Janet, Sue, you and I will have to go from here to the Security Barracks, since Robert and his group all moved out of the cabin trailer to their new barracks. I moved my recruits and myself in Robert's trailer. I've already talked to Jeremy and Al. I've asked them to go over there tonight and socialize with them and make them feel comfortable. I only have one man on my team you know. The other seven are women. I'm hoping Jeremy and Al can break the ice and remove some inhibition. I don't think it will be too hard, since some of them were complaining about the lack of men there. Bess, do you want to go with us?"

Bess said, "I don't think so. I think I scare the security guys after the last trip. Besides, I hear that the twins are coming over to keep Mike company, and you know how shy he is. I think I need to be there to instigate trouble. Besides, this is my chance to get Mike in the rocker. My slut sisters keep dominating his rocker time. Now it's my turn." Everyone laughed at her comments, including me.

Bess had been staring at the twins almost from the moment she came in. She was very attracted to them, and I knew what she had in mind. It also made some sense. Both Bess and I knew I would have a difficult time having a climax with her. I loved being inside her, but she was so tight that it remained difficult to build any rhythm to stimulate an orgasm. She knew she would not drain my lust by riding me in the rocker, only build my desire. She knew I would be greatly stimulated to ravage the twins, and she wanted to be there to take advantage of the twins. Bess had a good plan, and I kind of liked it too.

Ebba/Ella said in their seesaw speech, "We can come visit another night if that would be better."

"Oh, no." Nancy said, "Tonight is fine. Bess and Mike will be there, and Mike makes excellent coffee. We want you to visit with Mike and get to know him better. In fact, Bess can drive you guys over."

The twins looked a little wide-eyed but they nodded agreement. I thank they were beginning to get the idea and couldn't quite figure out if they liked it or not. If they didn't like how it could go at the cabin, I would never push the issue. But, I hoped they would warm up to the idea.

Nancy and Sue got up and hugged and kissed me goodbye then left with Janet and Mary. I thanked Bob for the steaks and left everyone else there and took off for the cabin. Nancy had bragged about my coffee, so I put a pot on before jumping into the shower. I had just finished and slipped into my robe when I heard Bess and the twins giggling outside like only girls can sometimes do. I got my coffee and sat down in my comfortable rocker and was enjoying it when they came in. I was looking at the large screen TV on the wall and was thinking how strange that we had never even turned the damn thing on before. Bess showed them around the cabin and got the twins coffee. They came into the big room and sat on the couch facing me.

"I see you showered without me," Bess said, "Entertain the twins while I get a quick shower."

I don't know what they talked about in the car coming over, but the twins looked much more relaxed. Still, I had no idea how to entertain them, so I reverted back to being the Chairman, asking them about their operation, needs, experience, etc.. They seem very comfortable talking about those subjects and were still talking when Bess came back in wearing her robe.

Bess was right. She was an instigator. Bess said, "Girls, come here, I want to show you something." Bess dropped to her knees in front of me when the twins came close, and she suddenly opened my robe. Of course I was naked underneath. I didn't know what to do, so I did nothing. Bess grabbed my hard cock and waved it at them. They didn't run off like I thought they might. They simply stared at it.

"Have you ever seen one as nice and big as this one?" she asked. They didn't say a word, they just got on their knees also and stared. Bess crawled up in my lap and straddled me. She pushed down on my cock and very slowly started to stretch that tight pussy down over me. It was going in too slowly for her and she said, "Pull me down on it, Mike." I reached up and grabbed her shoulders and began pulling her down. The twins had their faces within a foot on either side, watching my cock slowly sink deeper and deeper. They were totally focused on the sight before them, and I soon forgot them in my building passion. I felt Bess settle down on my lap, and I tried my best to pump up

255

into her, but she was so damn tight. I just started rocking back and forth and began to feel her pussy start to slide as she relaxed. After a while I wrapped my arms around Bess and began pulling her down as I rocked back. We started building a rhythm. My lust was peaking when I felt her body quivering. She warned me with a scream just before her pussy latched down on my cock, squeezing off my climax. I knew this was going to happen. That's why I was happy that the twins were here. I looked to see the twins still focused on where we were joined. I let Bess' orgasm pass and after a few moments I felt her quivering stop. I said to the twins, "Help Bess off of me." They both jumped when I spoke but stood and began lifting Bess off my cock. It was slow, but I felt her slipping off. Bess was smiling hugely when the twins helped her stand. I was still hugely aroused. I stood and took the hands of the twins and led them toward my bedroom. They followed automatically, somewhat still in shock. I kissed both of them and started undressing one of them. Bess had followed us in and began undressing the other. The twins simply allowed us to do anything we wanted. I lay both down on the bed on their backs and spread the legs of the closest one. I moved between her thighs and began stroking into her extremely wet and hot pussy. Once I had worked about half of my cock into her she came alive. Her body went into convulsions. Her arms wrapped around me and pulled. Her legs gripped me and she began thrusting up to meet me, and she was beating her head into my chest. By the time I sank all my cock into her she was riding me from underneath. She was moving so fast I stopped trying to watch her moves. Her reactions shocked me and slowed my climax, but just as I felt my orgasm building, she froze stiff. I looked into her eyes and they were rolled back in her head, and she had a silent frozen scream on her face. It was then that I felt the quiver in her pussy and flood of hot liquid squirt on me. It was enough to make me stop and enjoy her intense orgasm. Slowly she relaxed and fell back to the bed slipping off my cock. I moved to the other twin, who had been watching. She had her thighs spread and urging me toward her. I moved between her thighs and began to push into her hot pussy. This girl was very aroused, and like her sister, took over. I figured if she wanted to be in charge I would just let her. I rolled over with her on top and drove up into her. Her moans told me she loved it, and her actions showed me. She kept bouncing on my cock until she got it all inside her, then she rode me hard. Her large breast were bouncing and swaying, teasing me further. Her clawed fingers dug into my chest as she pounded down. My climax came quickly. I lifted her on my cock and pumped my seed deep into her pussy. She also froze and did the same silent scream and flooded her juice on my stomach. She fell down on top of me quivering.

As I revived somewhat I looked over at the other twin. I heard moans and saw Bess devouring her pussy and nectar. That twin had definitely revived and was enjoying it. As I watched, I saw the revived twin push her passed out sister off of me and reach for my deflating cock. She kept her thighs spread wide for Bess, but leaned over to take my cock into her mouth. I didn't mind, because it felt good. She had a very talented mouth. Bess, however, saw the incapacitated and freshly flooded other twin and moved between her thighs. This allowed the revived twin more access to me, which she took advantage of. Her oral attention increased, and surprisingly, I felt my cock growing. She began rolling my balls in her hand as her suction increased. Once I was hard again she mounted me like a horse and rode me like she was in a race. This girl really got into her sex and loved being in control. I liked it too. Having just had an orgasm, I knew I would last much longer, and I wanted to enjoy this as long as I could. She rotated between grinding up and back, bouncing up and down, side to side and varied speeds. The way she was moving I knew I was touching all her hot spots, and she was definitely multi-orgasmic. I felt at least two orgasms before she froze again in a strong quivering orgasm and collapsed on my chest. I hugged her and caressed her back as she lay there, that is until the other twin pushed her off me. She had fully revived and Bess' administration to her had kept her arousal peaked. She quickly mounted me but in a reverse position. It turned me on greatly to see her white butt cheeks. Her hand guided my cock to her pussy as she pushed herself down on it. I watched my cock sliding in and out of her pussy as she bounced herself on it and moaned. Bess rejoined the first twin to continue her feast. The twin leaned forward on my legs and somehow continued to slam her pussy down on me. I watched and enjoyed.

Moans were coming from everyone. I felt the reverse cowgirl reach another strong orgasm, and I saw her squirt her nectar. I had never been with a heavy squirter before, and it was quite exciting. She fell off me on the bed this time, and no one took her place. The twins might be finished, but I was still hard and very excited.

I said, "You girls need to keep going until you get me off."

They both giggled and set up. What happened then completely amazed me. They began double teaming me, taking turns on me. They had apparently done this before. One would ride me hard and fast to orgasm, then they would switch. They kept it going like that until I almost went crazy with lust. I exploded in one of them, and I mean exploded. I held her hips and gushed into her over and over. I thought I would drain my whole body into her. Somewhere during my orgasm she froze again. I looked up to see that silent scream and white eyes before she fell on me, smothering me with those huge breasts.

We were all exhausted but managed to all cuddle together. I think Bess was laying on me, but I was so tired I can't be sure. When I awoke to go to the bathroom we were still intertwined, but at some point someone had covered us up. I extracted myself and went to the bathroom, then noticed that I was covered in mine and the twins' sticky, love nectar and decided to take a shower. On the way back I noticed Nancy and Sue sleeping on the couch. They must have covered us up, and not finding room in the bed crashed on the couch. I snuggled in be-

259

tween them and pulled them into an embrace and went back to sleep.

The alarm was unwelcome, but I mechanically nudged the girls awake. Both were happy to see me in bed with them and gave me some warm kisses. I made the rounds waking everyone up. Last night must have been hard on all, because few wanted to get up, but, hey, work comes first. I saw the twins run for the shower through the main room naked and had to laugh. Wow! What a night.

Once I was sure everyone was up and getting dressed, Nancy, Sue and I headed to Bob's Cafe. Bess said she would bring the twins. We had barely driven off when Nancy burst out crying. I quickly pulled over, hugged her and asked, "What's wrong baby?"

Nancy continued to sob but finally said, "Mike, you know I love you don't you?" I nodded and she continued, "I feel so damn guilty for enjoying being used by those men over and over. I love feeling so slutty, but afterwards I feel bad, like I'm cheating on you."

I didn't know what to say, because I also felt guilty after having sex with others. But, Sue knew what to say. Sue started laughing and said, "I always told you you were a slut. Now you even admit it. I've always known I was a slut at heart. Guess what, Mike is a male slut also. We are all sluts, especially Bess." We laughed at that last part, even Nancy. "But, you know what, having fantasies is healthy and living them out is even better. It keeps us from wondering what it would be like. It allows us to love each other better and deeper. I know Mike loves us, because he keeps coming back to us. Just like this morning, we found him between us. So get over it."

Nancy kissed me hard, and I pulled both girls into my arms. Nancy seemed to feel better, and I know I did. We started again toward the property. That is when Sue set us off laughing again.

Sue said, "So, Nancy, how many men DID you fuck last night?" We all burst out laughing.

Nancy was laughing hard, but managed to say, "It had to be at least eight. I just closed my eyes and lay back and let them use me. One would finish and get off me and another would mount me. All the time this was going on someone was sucking on both nipples. It seemed to go on forever, and I loved it. I had so many orgasms last night I lost count. I don't even know who did me. How about you, you slut?"

Sue said, "Well, since we are telling all, I have no idea how many. They were doing me two at a time and sometimes three, if you know what I mean. Robert was teaching some how to double penetrate me in various positions. Often I had three dicks in me at the same time. I know Janet and Mary were also busy, even JJ, but at some point Mary began bringing in some of the new female security and getting them involved. Yep, I think we broke the ice."

"What about the officer that slapped Janet?" I asked, "Did you see him?"

Sue said, "Oh yeah, the guy in the arm cast. He did me and was a perfect gentleman. Robert was

261

there, so I didn't expect any trouble. Now what about you and the twins?"

"Oh shit," I said, "They almost killed me, but Bess helped." They laughed.

Nancy said, "We figured she would. She had that hungry look on her face when she first saw them. When she stayed, we knew what was going to happen."

I told them about all that happened and how Bess and I doubled teamed them. They thought that was funny, but the girls became excited at my description of the action and kept asking questions, especially about them double teaming me at the end. They looked at each other with a knowing look passing between them.

Bob had the standard breakfast buffet ready when we entered, and I filled my tray completely up with scrambled eggs, bacon, grits, biscuits and gravy and a couple of waffles, plus a big glass of cold milk. For some reason I was very hungry today. Some of the others began filing in as we ate. I saw Robert enter with JJ and a couple of other officers. They looked familiar, but I couldn't place them. They walked toward us.

Robert asked, "Do these two look familiar to you, like from the Jack in the Box?"

"Awww, yes, The Oklahoma City officers." I said.

Robert said, "They are Cherokee Marshals now. They called me yesterday."

I said, "Well, welcome aboard."

Robert said, "Things have gotten worse in the city. Marshal Law has been declared, and I don't think we will hear from them. They have their hands full there. I'm getting them settled in after we get something to eat."

Bess and the twins came in, and the twins came directly to me and gave me a hug. Ebba/Ella said, "Nancy, if you need us to babysit Mike again don't hesitate to call us."

Nancy and Sue broke out laughing and said in unison, "We will definitely call."

We finished eating and headed to my office and conference room. By the time I finished making coffee everyone came filtering in. Mostly only the department heads made this meeting, due to the workload ongoing, but that was fine. Like last time, Robert led off.

Robert announced, "I have a full complement of officers, plus two. The two officers we saved came aboard almost immediately. It's getting really dangerous out there for police officers. Like I said earlier, the officers kept our involvement secret. They claimed the shootings themselves, which is good for us. With the chaos going on in the city, like most of the other major cities, they probably won't do much of an investigation, but they followed protocol for officer involved shootings and put the officers on administrative leave. After we talked they turned in their notice and came immediately. I don't know if you noticed the kennels built behind the Security Office, but we also have a full complement of four K-9 officers and quite a few German Shepherds. The dogs and officers are trained. In fact most of the K-9 officers brought their own dogs and are skilled in training dogs. We bought six four-wheeler for the property for officer quick response. We didn't need anything bigger to patrol our property. We established a gun range, which is now finished and ready for use. JJ will be running a training session for all community members. I want them trained in handling AR-15s and .45 cal. automatics in case of emergencies. After gun training I am issuing all members with sidearms and will insist they be worn. I also want to start a class in hand-to-hand combat for my officers and any other member desiring to learn. I'm hoping to convince Bess into teaching it. I and many of my officers have military combat training, but I believe Bess can teach us more. We have already seen how ineffective this military training is against someone with her skills."

I assumed the Marine with the broken arm and missing teeth represented this military training. I also noticed several awed looks at Bess from the others. Some knew Bess trained in Martial Arts most of her life, and others had heard what she did to that Marine. Still others were hearing this for the first time. Bess blushed at the compliments but nodded her agreement.

Jeremy took the floor next and said, "We are getting there. The Cave is done, the Green House is done, the docks and Dome are done and the basement and the first and second floors are done. This means most of you can move your offices to the Castle. Bob, you can move into your new commissary anytime you like. Dr. Groom, your clinic and offices are ready for your final touches. I'm sure you have all noticed that the cement trucks have

264

stopped coming. It's all poured now and the crews are busy finishing off the insides of floors three and four. The elevator and equipment is on site but not installed. That will be the last thing to become operational. Al has brought his wind generators online and they are tied into our grid. Two more days and we can move everyone in.

Dr. Groom stood and said, "That sounds great, Jeremy. We will come over today and check out the clinic. I have little else to report. No injuries, and all here in the community appear healthy. Everyone is clean and disease free, and I have a twenty-year supply of birth control pills and Viagra. So, have fun." He chuckled at his own joke, but many joined in.

James took his turn and said, "As many of you know, we now have an operational poultry farm, at least the first phase. If you haven't seen the hundreds of baby chicks in the Poultry Barn, I invite you to go take a look. Our dairy farm is also in full operation. Many of you are enjoying milk produced from it. What is not consumed at Bob's Cafe goes toward butter and cheese production. We have planted our first field in corn, and we have fields prepared for winter wheat, and vegetables. The additional land Nancy purchased is currently being cleared. We have horses and even a blacksmith and forging operation. I invite you to ride, just pick out a horse, saddle and gear, and if you don't know how to ride, ask the cowboy in charge. Our beef cattle are roaming the range, and we have some sheep and goats. Our fruit and nut trees, berry bushes, and

265

vineyards are planted. In short, we are mostly operational."

Sue took her turn and said, "After today I will have all outstanding invoices paid, and we still have an abundant supply of money left. I want you to re-evaluate all your operations for improvements and additions. Remember, you can't buy anything after the crash. We will be sequestered and on our own. So, buy anything you can imagine we might ever need. Also remember that the rebuild of the country must be done by us, so get the supplies now while money is still good."

I said, "Thanks Sue, that is right on. Spend the money. I want all of you to try hard to find anything we may have missed. Also think about a possible EMP attack. That stands for Electro Magnetic Pulse. It fry's electronics, killing almost everything electronic. Think about recovery if that happens. That means we need plenty of spare electronic parts for everything from vehicles, to computers. These parts need to be stored within a Faraday Shield area. Jeremy, ask Al about what is needed for that. I reinforce Sue's suggestion to buy, Buy, B U Y." There is one thing I believe we must do. I suggest we build solid walls, at least firing walls at our entrance gate. We shouldn't have to stand in the open to challenge people demanding access. We can't fight a war of attrition. Any casualties need to be on the other side." Jeremy nodded.

Nancy stood and reported, "I didn't have time to personally negotiate to purchase the additional property out to the existing roads, but I hired a good firm I know. They have successfully negotiated for

266

the property you wanted, and I closed the deal yesterday. We now own the peninsula south and a major land mass adjacent and leading to it. We now own all the land to the two major roads and beyond, which kills access for one of the roads. Previously we bought the property north of our access road. Now we can move our boundaries all the way back to the beginning of our access road. We also bought a big chunk of land north and west to the finger off the lake. We can close off all access on this road now and fence it. I guess the other end will be our back gate. James, there are several hundred more acres to clear and farm. You just thought you were about done." James laughed and we joined him. Nancy continued, "Mike, we may have to add a few more working members."

I said, "We still have a few open personnel slots we haven't allocated. If anyone feels they need more personnel, make your requests. Oh, speaking of personnel, Nancy have you recruited a Chaplin yet?"

"No I haven't, but I do have a few good candidates I need to talk to. I want to get several opinions before I choose."

I asked, "Does anyone have anything else to report?"

Mary said, "I haven't started billeting yet, so I can wait."

"Okay, let's get to work." I said.

Chapter 12
(The Ribbon Cutting)

Nancy said, "I need to go to the clinic. I have an appointment for my physical."

I broke out in a grin and said, "Enjoy your physical, hon."

Nancy said, "Shut up!" But she was grinning, too.

When we broke up I went to my office to read my Brin emails. There were two.

"Mike, we are pleased to hear that the Dome is ready for us. We will land in two nights. We will lower the units and supplies at the cleared location behind the Castle before we submerge. We are looking forward to finally meeting you. In answer to your question about our appearance, yes, I'm afraid we will appear alien to humans, but not from our shape or any major abnormal physical appearance. Remember that we evolved on a water world. We differ physically in appearance from humans in that our fingers and toes have a partial web for swimming, but that is not the outstanding difference. Humans have white, black, brown, even somewhat yellow and red skins, where our race will look blue or aqua. We believe our appearance is more pleasing than humans, but of course, that is a matter of belief. Our eyes have a blue pupil, and our body hair is sparse, except for our heads, which is long and mostly black or orange in color. We will stand out among humans, but no more than a

black human would stand out among white humans. The difference is there are no aqua people on Earth. You will get used to us. I hope this answers your question."

The second e-mail was short.

"Mike, we must hurry with the closing off of the complex. Your world seems to be collapsing faster than we anticipated. Already battles are raging in your major cities, especially in your larger ones. law and order has disappeared. Looting and fires are epidemic, even in Tulsa and Ft. Smith. The food has been stripped from most grocery stores in the big cities. Chaos is prevalent and beginning to spill out to the smaller communities. You still have a little time but not many days, a week at most. We should be there by the time we are needed for defense, and we also bring weapons."

I fired a short e-mail back. I didn't really have much more to report.

"Brin, thanks for the warnings. We are almost totally complete with our construction. We also look forward to meeting you. I guess we will meet you in the Dome tomorrow night."

I was thinking about going with Jeremy to tour the Castle, but I decided to go see James. I hadn't reviewed his operation yet, so I was long overdue. When I walked into his Farm Barn he was very happy to see me and came quickly to meet me. I said, "I wanted to see how you are doing and what else you might need. I know we kind of took you by surprise this morning with the addition of so much additional land. How can I help?"

269

James said, "Well, I was feeling pretty good with our farming progress, and I was surprised. But, It's just more of the same. We clear it, build up the fertility and plant. I have already called my clearing crew back, along with the fencing contractor. Nancy e-mailed me the plat maps, so they can get started as soon as they get here. And, just in case, I ordered our own caterpillar. I don't know if you noticed when you came in, but I purchased a combine and spare parts and a firetruck. I haven't told you yet, but I also had several large underground storage tanks for additional diesel fuel installed and filled. I've got one of my people working on another nursery order for more trees. We will have to reevaluate our irrigation system and extend it, but we have the supplies stored. I was going to go out and take a look at our new property. Would you like to go with me?"

"Sure." I said.

James said, "I'll get another horse saddled up for you. It's pretty rough ground."

I thought to myself, "SHIT!" I had to volunteer to ride a horse. I think I rode a horse when I was about ten, and to be honest, it scared the crap out of me. I must be the only Okie that didn't grow up on a horse, and I'm Indian at that.

James must have seen the panic on my face. He said, "Don't worry. I'll get Joan, our cowboy, to go with us. She is an expert at handling horses."

I guess I was stuck, so we went to the Horse Barn. There were about ten horses stalled there. Two were already saddled, and the cowboy, as he called her, was working on the third. He must have

270

texted her on the way. The cowboy was a looker. She was short and stocky with wide hips, slightly bowed legs and large breasts, but she looked like a cowboy, complete with western boots, Levi's and western hat. As she led the horse over she removed her hat and blonde hair fell out on her shoulders. Smiling, she said, "This is Daisy and she is gentle and used to virgin riders."

I'm sure I blushed from embarrassment and a little aggravation. James tossed me a John Deere hat, and I watched as they mounted. I wasn't about to do it wrong. I could just see myself setting in the saddle backwards. I said, "Good Daisy," patted her neck and mounted. I was setting straight, so I must have done it right. They were also armed like me, and I wondered if maybe we shouldn't be wearing western six-shooters.

It seemed like we rode for hours through trees and brush, but finally James said we were at the outside edge of the new property. He pointed out the property lines and we turned west. This was far more acres than I thought we purchased, and he said we had more than what we had seen on the other side. There was no way he could get this all fenced, much less cleared in weeks. I began altering our plan. We would just have to pull back and dig in, take the easy reach land and spread out later. I was glad I took this tour to adjust my perspective.

I said, "James, I don't see a problem bulldozing our property line and fencing it to claim it, but we probably should establish a secondary fence line we can defend and reasonably work."

"Yep, I think you are right." He said, this is a lot of land. Maybe we can run cattle on some of it, but I will lay out that secondary fence line much closer in and get the contractors working on it first and keep them working as long as they keep coming to work. We can always work on it with in-house labor. It will just be slower."

I was happy to be going back. My butt hurt, and I was getting a killer headache, but I tried to act like I was not in a hurry. I was last in line behind Joan, and I kept noticing how smooth and fluid she looked sitting the saddle. She must have been riding horses all her life. James apparently was also comfortable in the saddle. Maybe in fifty years I would be too, if I lived that long. I knew I was lying to myself, because I had no intention of ever riding again.

We went back a different way and eventually hit the access road going into the complex, which made the ride much easier and shorter. Once we came in sight of the Farm Barn I wanted to gallop there so I could get my ass off the saddle. When we finally reached the barn I had to fight to keep from jumping off and kissing the ground, but I managed. I even patted Daisy's neck and thanked her for the ride. Joan unsaddled the horses and began rubbing them down. I thanked James and Joan for the tour and dismissed myself.

We had missed lunch, which was no big deal for me. I usually forgot to eat lunch anyway, but after today's romp, I was famished. I decided to get an early dinner and go soak my aching butt in a hot shower. I dropped by my office and picked up

Nancy. Sue still had some checks to write and some bookkeeping to do, so she declined. We went directly to Bob's Cafe. As always, he was ready for us with a standing buffet. Hamburgers and french fries only, but I didn't care. I was hungry, and started off with my standard, big glass of cold milk. I drank half of the glass on the first drink. It was very good, but the cold set my headache throbbing. I asked, "Nancy, do you have any aspirin?"

Nancy was still working herself down the buffet line and said, "Yeah, I have some Aleve in my purse."

Oh Great, I opened her purse and found a vial. It only had three in it, so I took them all. Maybe that would get rid of my headache. I told Nancy about my horse riding experience today and how I got my headache and sore butt. She laughed at me and suggested I take a hot shower when we got to the cabin, even hinting at a good massage. With that thought in mind, we finished our meal, said our goodbyes and headed out. As soon as we got to the cabin I was stripping off and headed toward the shower, and I was helping Nancy strip. We had managed to strip completely before we reached the shower. I was incredibly aroused, and I was all over Nancy. She reached for my cock and seemed startled.

Nancy said, "Oh my God, Mike. Look at your dick. It's huge and so hard."

I knew I was hard, but when I looked I too was startled. I had never seen my cock that big and hard, and I had never needed sex so much as I did this very moment. I hugged her and kissed her with

273

all my passion. I lifted her and slipped between her thighs and pressed her against the shower wall. I was already pumping when I felt it enter her. She groaned loud as I let her slip down on my probing and pumping rod. She felt wonderful. I couldn't get enough. My cock attacked her hot pussy and drove into her like a steam engine. She had her arms around my neck and her legs over my arms. Her orgasms were many, which drove me to a huge orgasm. My cock unloaded inside her, but I was not sated and never skipped a thrust. I continued pumping into her.

Nancy fell limp in my arms and weakly said, "Take me to our bed."

It was then that I realized we hadn't even bothered to turn the water on in the shower. I walked with her impaled on my cock to our bed and fell with her into the bed, where I continued to pound into her.

Nancy orgasmed again and screamed but breathlessly said, "Mike, did you take something?"

In between thrusts I managed to say, "Only those three Aleve you had in the vial."

"Oh my God, Mike." She said, "Those weren't Aleve in the vial, they were Viagra. You have to stop for a minute and get me my phone."

I was almost crazy with lust and desire. My body was quivering all over, but I registered what she said and pulled out of her and ran to get her phone. I had no idea why, nor did I care, but she wanted it. I handed her the phone and plunged back into her, pumping like a manic. I vaguely remember hearing her saying something to Sue, including

274

the word "Hurry". I don't know how I knew it was Sue. I just remember hearing Nancy trying to talk through another huge orgasm. I continued to drive into her over and over. I did have another orgasm, but again, I continued pumping through it. At some point someone forcibly rolled me off of Nancy and told me to lay on my back. I looked around and saw Dr. Groom, Dr. Wong, Janet and three other females I did not know. No, wait, I also saw the cowboy, Joan Better. I saw Dr. Groom holding my cock. He asked if I was normally this big and hard. Sue told him they had measured me before at a little over 9.5 inches, but I appeared much bigger than normal. The Dr. marveled that I was at least 11 inches.

Dr. Groom said, "He's overdosed with Viagra. He has Priapism and is greatly overstimulated and aroused. His dick is engorged with blood and stretched out, some of which might be permanent. We can't let him fuck like he was. He could burst his heart, but he has to work himself through this. Girls, you need to take over and be on tops. You will have to tag-team him until we can release enough stimulant energy for his dick to go down and get his mind relaxed. Okay, who is first. Hurry before he tries to get up."

I heard Janet say, "I will go first. I love his dick anyway." I felt her naked thighs wrap around me, her hand on my cock, then I felt her push down on me. Yes, warmth again surrounded my aching cock. I wasn't in all the way and reached up and grabbed her hips and pulled her down hard. Janet screamed, but I didn't let go and started driving up

275

into her. Her next scream was a huge orgasm, but I didn't stop. Dr. Groom lifted her off of me, and my dick didn't like it, but immediately she was replaced by another. This one was a beautiful Japanese lady, and I pulled her down on me and the rhythm started again. I looked up into her face, but I had no idea who she was. I just kept fucking her, well her fucking me. I looked around the room and saw that everyone was now naked, including Dr. Groom. He was telling them that I was too big, so he needed to lube them up so it wouldn't hurt so bad, and that is exactly what he was doing. He got behind all the waiting women and began pumping his cock in each one of them. I was not so out of it not to appreciate how he was taking advantage of the situation for himself. I know I was. I had another orgasm with this Japanese lady and watched as she was lifted off me, just to have another I didn't know mount me. No, I did know this one. It was Dr. Wong. They were all fucking me hard and fast, keeping up with my desires and my needs ... all but Sue. I heard Dr. Groom tell Sue not to try and ride me, because she was too small, and me, in my driving passion and increased size, could hurt her. He convinced her to stay with him, as he continued to pound into her from behind. I orgasmed again in Dr Wong, setting off her screaming orgasm. She was replaced by Joan. I knew it was her from her big breasts and wide hips, even before I saw her smiling face. She was definitely enjoying her turn. I began pumping up into her tight pussy. I felt her cervix, and I believe I forced myself inside it. She screamed when I did and flooded me with juice. It was beginning to

276

take me longer to orgasm, and my mind was clearing somewhat. I was also starting to really enjoy it. When they lifted Joan off of me I was still extremely hard, but the crazy, driving lust had lessoned. The lady that mounted me now was one of those I didn't know. I said, "Who are you?" We both laughed.

As she rode me hard she said, "I am Dr. Betty Jones, our new veterinarian."

I smiled and said, "I'm happy to MEAT you." We laughed again, and I drove up into her. While she was riding my cock I turned my head to see Nancy beside me. She smiled and kissed me. I said, "I'm sorry if I hurt you. I really am."

"It's fine," She said, "That was the best sex I ever had, but I am glad I called for reinforcements. I wouldn't have been able to take much more. I managed to tell Sue what had happened and was happening. I asked her to get Dr. Groom and bring over more women."

It seemed strange carrying on a conversation while my cock was plunging in and out of another pussy, but at least I knew I was getting better. Well I better, since it had been hours of steady fucking, and it was still going on. I heard Jeremy grunt and looked around to see him behind the other girls helping Dr. Groom lube them up, which was kind of crazy, since I had had them all already. I had to chuckle. Leave it to Jeremy to get involved too.

I was building up for another orgasm when Dr. Jones froze on my cock, quivering. She was done, and there was no one to lift her off, so I rolled her off. I looked at my cock and it was still hard, but I felt maybe one more orgasm and I might be done. I looked around to see who I might have missed. I had missed Sue, but she was getting hammered by Dr. Groom. I noticed the Japanese lady and motioned for her. She giggled and straddled me. I had stretched her before, so she was able to slip down over my cock all the way to my balls. In my mania before I hadn't noticed how hot her pussy was. It was steamy hot and gripped me tight. She leaned over and kissed me and rubbed her breast and nipples over my chest, which set me on fire. I began bouncing her on my cock, and each time she squealed in pleasure. I held her hips and ground my cock into her. We both drove against each other hard, and she rode me fast. I felt her thighs begin to quiver and her hot pussy grip my cock. I had her balanced on my cock with my back arched when we discharged together. It was a final release of pressure, and I knew I was almost normal again. I settled back down with my cock still deep inside her, while she collapsed across my chest. No one lifted her off, and I was glad. Thankfully, I felt my cock slowly deflating within her.

She eventually sat up and said, "Thanks. I'm JoAnn Ikiko, actually Dr. Ikiko. I'm Dr. Wong's assistant, and I'm looking forward to getting you in our dental chair. Next time you get a toothache come see us, but obviously we also make house calls."

JoAnn was still laying on me, but my cock had slipped out, and she had spread her legs back. Suddenly, her eyes shot open, and we looked back to see Bess wiggling her face between JoAnn's butt cheeks. JoAnn moaned and closed her eyes in ecstasy. I scooted over and rolled JoAnn over on her back. Bess took over from there.

I said to Nancy, "You know we never did get that shower. Hell, we didn't even turn on the water." We both broke out in laughter and headed to the shower, leaving our bed to the churning bodies. As we left we looked back to see Jeremy riding the cowboy, Dr. Groom still pounding Sue and what was going to be a chain of women for Bess. We also passed a smiling and stripping Al, rushing to join the melee.

Nancy and I finally got our hot shower, and I got another erection. I said, "Damn, Nancy, why do you have to be so sexy and beautiful?"

She laughed and said, "Any other time I would be very pleased to have that effect on you, but it's probably the lingering effect of the Viagra. But, it's going to take several days for me to recover from our last sex. I'm going to have to take you back to the room again."

That's exactly what she did. Nancy grabbed me by my very hard cock and led me back into the churning room. The bed was too crowded, so she led me back to the rocker and pushed me down in it. She went back into the room and came back leading a naked "cowboy" Joan by the hand. Joan looked confused until she saw me in the rocker sporting a huge erection. She grinned and climbed up on my lap facing me. Her hand wrapped about halfway around my cock, but she managed to guide it into her. Even after being inside her she was still tight. I had to pull her down by her shoulders to impale

279

her, but even then I wasn't completely inside her. Joan groaned loud as my cock slipped deep inside her.

Breathlessly, Joan said, "Pull me harder. I want it all inside like before."

Joan didn't have to ask me twice. I pulled her down hard and pushed up into her. I felt my cock slip deeper, and I was all the way in. Joan moaned and seemed to purr like a cat. Her large alabaster, white breasts and big, pink nipples danced before my eyes. My hands led them to my mouth, and I nuzzled my face between them, sucking those beautiful nipples one after the other. I had also begun rocking us in time with my thrusts. She loved it, but it seemed too slow for her, because she began riding my cock, grinding and bouncing. Her orgasm came quick, but she only slowed down before she started again. Her speed increased as did mine, and I climaxed with her. We both stopped and just rested against each other.

Joan raised up and smiled, saying over her shoulder, "Nancy, you can call me for help anytime."

Nancy said, "Well, I do appreciate you girls coming over. He was a little out of control. Hell, you should have seen him before you got here."

My cock was deflating, so I figured my crisis was over. I said, "How is it that you came here?"

Joan chuckled and said, "I was visiting with Dr. Jones, the veterinarian, in the cafe when Sue got Nancy's panic call. Sue told Dr. Groom what was happening and he volunteered the other doctors, and since I was there, he volunteered me too."

"I'm glad he did." I said, "By the way, Nancy, why were there Viagra in your purse?"

Nancy laughed and said, "Dr. Groom had mentioned Viagra at our meeting this morning, and I had my physical there today, so I ask him for some. I thought you might want to try one on a busy night, but I never expected you to take three of them at one time."

"I never will again." I said, "That's for sure. Hey, you know what? They did cure my headache, though." We had a good laugh at that. "So you had your physical, huh? Can you verify that Bess was in fact fucked at hers?

Nancy burst out laughing and said, "Yes, she was."

Joan decided to go take a shower and then hunt through the pile of clothing in my room for hers. I kissed her and Nancy and I found an empty bed upstairs in the loft. We fell asleep almost immediately but woke later when Sue snuggled in on my other side. Everything seemed back to normal.

When the alarm went off I was the one that didn't want to get up, but I made myself. After all, I was the leader. I had to. I roused everyone, even the doctors, who had spent the night. My bed was full of people all tangled together, and they finally got up and started cycling through the shower, usually by twos and sometimes threes. I looked at my bed and thought, "These sheets will definitely have to be changed." The cleaning lady probably wouldn't be happy though. I found a new set of clothes and dressed. Soon Nancy, Sue and I were turning into Bob's Cafe. I knew Bess would want to bring her car and hibernate again in the Green House.

As soon as we walked in Bob said, "We are closing down after breakfast and moving to the Castle. Eat hardy, because there won't be a lunch today. We will, however, have a dinner in the Castle tonight, the new Bob's Cafe."

"Thanks for letting us know," I said, "Nancy, I guess we should move, too, don't you think?"

Nancy smiled and said, "Already done. I had it scheduled for last night and today. Jeremy's group moved also and even the clinic. Some of the security moved, but many are staying in the old building, especially the patrolling police."

"Oh, cool," I said, "I'm anxious to see it." I followed Bob's suggestion and dished out a double helping of eggs and bacon. As the rest came in from last night's cabin group, they seemed strangely tired and quiet also.

When we left Bob's Cafe we drove to the Castle. I parked in an assigned spot labeled Chairman just outside the main entrance. I must admit, I was duly impressed as we entered. Just inside the main double doors stood a security counter with two officers monitoring those coming in. They obviously knew the three of us and smiled. We waved back and passed into the main open area of what everyone was calling the "Great Room", and it was truly great. I couldn't help but notice the polished marble on the floor, accented by channeled outside, natural light radiating from glass bubbles positioned in the open area of the second floor and bubbles positioned just under the balcony edges. I remember

Jeremy describing how this was done. There were light concentrators on the roof that focused the sunlight through large fiber optic tubes down to the reverse concentrators (spreaders) to distribute outside light within the Great Room and walkway balconies of the second floor. There was lighting, but it was totally unnecessary in the daylight, obviously. Around the perimeter of the Great Room could be seen Bob's Cafe toward the back. I saw a small theater, a card and game room, a gym and others not yet named or assigned, although pool tables lined the back wall. The elevator was installed but apparently not operational, so we headed toward the double-wide stairway running up to the second floor balcony. On the back side of the elevator was a massive stone fireplace facing out toward the center of the Great Room. We exited the staircase onto a marble balcony circling the inside octagon opening. The balcony had a glass railing, which added to the openness of the first and second floors. We entered our office space through glass doors set into glass walls to reach the reception desk. There was so much glass and light that curtains were everywhere but pulled open for effect. Behind the reception desk I could see my office, with adjacent offices on either side for Nancy and Sue. On the back side was a 6', sliding, thick-glass door that opened out onto an outside balcony. Knowing Jeremy, I knew the glass was unbreakable. It was more likely polycarbonate and expensive. On closer inspection I noticed a roll of stainless steel interlocking slats, that I assumed were emergency automatic security door covers and bulletproof. The balcony had a

283

fairly high (5') and thick outside solid cement railing. I walked out on the balcony and the view was breathtaking. I looked out on the lake from a high vantage point and could see for miles. I also noticed that the balcony stretched across the entire octagon wall section and angled into identical balconies on either side. I assumed a person could walk this balcony all the way around the Castle and on all floors. The solid railing had firing slots in it about every five feet, which added to the defense of the Castle.

I scanned the entire second floor inside and noticed similar offices circling this level, with the exception of the far side. The medical and dental clinic encompassed almost three wall sections of the octagon building on this level. It too consisted of mostly glass walls. Here too, the curtains were open and I could see into it. At two opposite ends of the floor, north & south, were bathrooms strategically placed. I guess that meant there was no bathroom in my office area. Well, I better have a coffee pot. I wasn't going to run down to the cafe every time I wanted a cup of coffee. I noticed the others slowly making their way up the stairs, so I turned to continue toward the conference room. The entrance was stationed within my reception area, allowing for an extra level of security access. As I entered I sighed in relief to see a large coffee pot already brewed. I smiled, poured a cup and headed toward the back of this huge room. The conference table was a massive slab of glass or whatever, and we had at least twenty executive chairs positioned around it. Nice, really nice. Even before I sat I noticed it was far too bright inside and drew the shades. Everyone else was marveling at the design also, which seemed to please Jeremy greatly.

Jeremy continued to stand, while everyone was getting seated. He obviously wanted to go first. He proudly said, "Well, except for some final cleanup and activating the elevator, the Castle is finished." All of us cheered. Jeremy continued, "I'm officially cutting the ribbon and turning over control of the Castle to Mary O'Shay now." At that statement we all stood and clapped at Mary's assignment, "But, before I give her the floor, I need to report that our dam engineer, Mark, will be leading our Houston crew to the dam today to make some modifications required to keep it safe. We'll have it done before anyone finds out, and the paperwork will all be in order. Since they aren't paying anything, I can't imagine them spending money to change it back. Another project done, or will be."

Most around the table weren't privy to the conversation Jeremy spoke of, nor did they know who the dam engineer, Mark, was; so I spent a few moments to bring them all up to speed. Mark Spencer was recruited from the Corp of Engineers to help with a necessary improvement on the Lake Tinkiller damn. Once they understood, they too cheered the project. Afterwards, I motioned for Mary to take over.

Mary stood and said, "Thank you Jeremy. Thank you for turning over such an incredible and beautiful project. I won't let you guys down. I will start assigning billeting locations today. I will have available a form for most everyone. Some I already know to group together. The form will request information so I can assign locations. I will be mixing men and women together in a housing unit, but each unit has four individual attached bedrooms to a central common area. This will provide a basic level of privacy, although you will discover there won't be much privacy. When you go to the bathrooms you will quickly discover there is no men or women's separate rooms. They are a common facility (men & women). There are individual enclosed stalls for some limited privacy. There are two main bathroom/shower facilities for housing, one on each end on levels floors 3 and 4. It's mostly open showers, but I've initially assigned separate shower times for men, women and mixed for those requiring a little more time to adjust to a genderless facility. Our new society does not allow for politically correct rules. We are all in the same boat, so to speak. I need to let all know that we do not have any maid service. We have several people assigned to do the laundry, general maintenance, janitors, and the like; but keep in mind all our members are highly educated, even those assigned to menial tasks. We do not have any common labor here. Everyone must take care of themselves. Keep your rooms clean, change your own sheets, carry out your own garbage, etc. Once we sequester, it will be necessary to have work parties for special needs such as cleaning, harvesting, and anything else that may come up. All who are not a department head could find themselves rotated on a work party. I hope this sounds fair, because this is the way it will be."

I liked this lady. She could be tough if she had to be, and she is doing exactly what needs to be done. I can see why Nancy wanted her, she can get the tough jobs done. I already knew James' situation, and Bob already told us his. I said, "Robert, do you have anything to add today?"

Robert stood and said, "Well, food riots are going on in every major city. Trucks are afraid to drive into the bigger cities. Every state but Alaska and Montana has declared Martial Law, and the president plans to announce Martial Law for the whole country today. That means that FEMA will be coming back with the law on their side this time...they believe. They will probably bring the Army with them this time, but they won't be able to call in reinforcements. The military will have their hands full with the riots. Lots are dying already. Let see, Al is finishing up with antennas on the roof for our radios. That will be our form of communications once the cell towers go dark. Oh, Bess starts her hand to hand combat class today at the Security Barn, and JJ is teaching classes in firearms. Mike, and the rest of you, I would like to see you check in with JJ. We may all need some training soon."

I said, "I will try and do that later today. Now, I have something to share with all of you. Our alien friends will arrive tonight!" I let that settle in. I hadn't even told Nancy, so this was surprising news to everyone, especially those that didn't even know about them being aliens. I read my and Brin's last e-mails and saw shock and a little fear around the table. I continued, "Don't worry. They are our friends, and they funded this whole project. They will help us defend it."

The only comment that came from the table was from Dr. Wong. All she said was, "Blue?" I broke out laughing and was joined from around the table.

We broke up to take care of business and prepare from Brin's arrival, but Dr. Groom waited.

After all but Nancy and I left he said, "Mike, I need you and Nancy to come over to the clinic. What happened to both of you last night could be serious. I need to check both of you out."

Chapter 13
(The Arrival)

When Dr. Groom asked Nancy and I to come to the clinic I got worried, so we followed Dr. Groom around to his clinic. He led us into an examining room and had us undress and put on those gowns with the open backs. He placed me on a flat table, while he had Nancy get on one of those tables with stirrups for women.

Dr. Groom said to Nancy, but really both of us, "I am concerned that Mike may have injured you inside. Hopefully not, but we better be safe. I noticed he didn't close the privacy curtain, but he did slide a privacy curtain around their area. After a while he said, "You have some tearing inside, but nothing requiring any stitches. Get dressed and meet me at the front counter. I will get you some antibiotics to help the healing." He then came in my side and said, "Mike, being overdosed with Viagra can be serious. From what I saw last night you may have some damage from excessive stretching. At the very least you probably have some permanent increase in size and thickness, but we won't know until we take you through a complete cycle of arousal and climax now that the Viagra is out of your system. Dr. Norcross will come in to assist you and observe your reactions and get some new measurements. Hopefully, everything will check out, but we better make sure now, so we can fix it."

After Dr. Groom left I was thinking about what he said. I sure didn't want there to be a problem with my sex life, but Dr. Groom had mentioned that I needed to be aroused and climax, and Dr. Norcross was going to help me. I was very pleased with the other doctors, but I haven't met this one. My mind was building a sexy image of what she might look like when the curtain pulled back and this man walked in. He looked just like Johnny Depp.

Dr. Johnny, my new name for him, said, "I'm Joe Norcross, Dr. Groom's assistant or nurse, whatever you want to call me. We need to get you aroused so I can measure you."

Dr. Johnny shocked the hell out of me when he lifted my gown and began to fondle my flaccid dick. My eyes must have shown my shock, because he chuckled and said, "Don't worry, Mike, I'm a doctor, I know how to get you going."

With that comment one of his hands started massaging my balls, while the other continued to try to stroke my limp dick. After a few futile moments of doing that he said, "Okay, we will try something different. He then leaned over and took my limp dick in his mouth. I almost jumped off the table in shock, but he leaned on my stomach to hold me still and continued to roll my dick in his mouth and suck it hard. I had never had a man suck me before. It was just too strange for me. I started to force myself up and off the table. I mean Dr. Johnny was not a big man. I could have easily pushed him away, but I forced myself to remember that he was a doctor, and he was doing his doctor thing, at least I think he was. After a little while I realized that

290

whatever he was doing seemed to be working, and it was beginning to feel pretty good. Okay, I would let him do his doctor thing. I looked down and noticed that he was able to take less and less of my cock as it grew in his mouth. At some point he began stroking my cock as he sucked. Yep, it was working, and I was enjoying his expert medical attention. As I felt my orgasm building, he stopped. I thought, "Why stop now? I'm about to cum." Dr. Johnny held my cock in one hand and placed a cloth ruler and wrapped it around my cock. He wrote down his measurement then held it against my cock to measure its length. He wrote that down and came back to put a really hard suction on my cock. His head was pumping up and down and the suction when he pulled up had an amazing effect on me. When he began caressing my balls again, I blew a heavy load in his mouth. Actually, it was almost like he pulled it out of me, every drop, and he kept milking me like that until it began to deflate. Hell, I didn't know what to do once it was over. I certainly didn't have an urge to kiss him, and I would really feel awkward saying, "Thanks." I did have to admit to myself, though, that it had felt pretty damn good. I had no reason to worry, however. Dr. Johnny simply lay my gown back over me and left the room.

Dr. Groom came back in few moments looking at the report. He said, "Mike, sorry I didn't treat you personally, but I'm really not into men. Luckily, Dr. Norcross is."

I said, "Yeah, I noticed." He chuckled.

291

Dr. Groom continued, "At any rate, you are very lucky. There seems to be no permanent damage other than having a larger penis. Some might even consider that a positive thing, but then you were already big enough. Sue told us they once measured you at 9 1/2 inches. Well, you now measure almost 10 1/2 inches long and 6 1/2 inches around. That is certainly much larger than average, and I'm almost positive that the additional size will remain permanent.

Nancy was somewhat injured inside from the rough sex, and she experienced some tearing. I want her to have no sex from you for a few days. Give her time to heal, and try not to be rough with any woman. Remember, you're even bigger now and can hurt them. Oh, and if you take Viagra again, only take one."

"Don't worry, Doc." I said, "It was an accident; I thought it was Aleve. I didn't mean to. Is Nancy alright?"

"Yeah, she will be fine."

I said, "Thanks Doc."

Once I was dressed I met Nancy in the waiting room. I was still somewhat embarrassed and couldn't look her in the eyes, but when I did she was grinning ... the little shit. We headed over to Robert's training area. I wanted to see Bess teaching her hand-to-hand combat training class. They were just getting started when we arrived. Bess had about twenty security personnel, including Robert, and a few others from other departments gathered. She was giving them verbal instructions when we arrived. What really got my attention was the way

Bess was dressed, or almost dressed. She wore skimpy spandex shorts and top. I could, hell everyone could, see her taunt muscles all over her body, especially her thighs and stomach. I was not thinking hand-to-hand, I was thinking hand to butt.

As we approached I heard her say, "Would anyone like to try and put me on my ass?" After a few moments of silence she continued, "Okay, let's make this interesting. If anyone, male or female, can pin me or put me down they can have me right here in front of everyone."

That got a reaction from many, but only one large man stepped forward and said, "I would like to try." Bess just motioned him forward. He came forward cautiously and began circling Bess. She just waited. When he sprang at her, Bess became a blur of movement, and before I could even follow what was happening, the man was face down with Bess sitting on his back. She had a hand wrapped around his throat, and he was in total submission. I had never seen anyone move so fast and efficiently.

Bess said to the crowd, "As you can see, size doesn't matter. It is all about using your opponent's own size, weight and strength against him/her. I can teach you these things. Now let's analyze the movements you just witnessed in slow motion." She then reached down and assisted the large man up to continue with her instruction.

I looked at Nancy and asked, "How did she get so good at that?"

Nancy said, "Our parents started all of us at a very young age. It just clicked with Bess. She has a natural talent and stuck with it. Sue and I moved on to other interest. That's one of the reasons Bess was living in California. She exhausted all her instructors skill level in this part of the country and had to move out there to continue to learn. She eventually started her own academy. That's how she worked her way through college. Mike, you have no idea how capable and lethal she is. She is considered by many as a Master of several martial arts disciplines and had a big future in California."

"Wow!" I said, I had no idea. Why in the world would she give that all up?"

Nancy turned toward me grinning and said, "Duh! Mike, she wants to be a survivor, just like us. Sue and I believe in you, and we persuaded Bess to join us. She did. She will make an excellent instructor."

"Duh is right,' I said. I watched with renewed interest for a while as she continued with her instructions. She was very good at it and very beautiful doing it.

We finally left and went to the firing range. We could hear the shooting before we got there. There was a similar gathering of the community at the firing range. Most, evidently, had already received instructions from JJ and were firing at targets. When she saw us she smiled and came over. She gave me a friendly kiss, and we exchanged greeting. JJ took her position seriously and handed Nancy and I an AR-15 and went through the operating instructions and safety features of the gun, which consisted mainly of don't shoot anyone and aim downrange. She then put us to shooting, which we did for a couple of hours, then she had me firing my own new .45 and Nancy her .380. By the time I finished I had a good understanding and feel for the guns. I was far more comfortable about shooting.

We went back to our new office in the Castle. Again, we parked in my designated parking slot, and I felt very special. When we entered through the main front door, we were greeted by smiling security guards. Of course, they waved us through. We witnessed a beehive of activity in Bob's Cafe, but the most surprising thing we observed was an operational elevator, two in fact. We took one up to the mezzanine floor, and it opened up almost directly across the wide passageway from our offices. As we went in I noticed a medium sized black man setting at the reception desk.

Nancy noticed my focus and said, "Mike, meet our receptionist, Agent Tom Brackett, late of the US Secret Service. He will be directing access to us and obviously protecting us. We just don't get that many calls from outside, hell, we didn't even give out the number. So, I didn't see any real need for a phone operator. Most of the contractors call the cell phone of whoever hired them or, of course, Sue who pays them."

I said, "Pleased to meet you, and I hope you do a good job of protecting us. Secret Service huh?"

"Yeah," He said, "I was working out of the Oklahoma City office. Thanks for allowing me to join the team. I will do whatever is necessary to contribute, and I will also watch over you and the girls."

Sue came busting in with some coffee for me, obviously excited, and we went into my office. She said, "You should see our quarters. Wow! I took a look. It's amazing. I had my warehouse guys already move our stuff from the cabin, so we are already moved in. Want to go see?"

"Sure." I said, "But let me drink this coffee first and read my Brin e-mail." We continued into my plush office, to sit at my executive desk. The others took seats in equally comfortable looking chairs. I pulled out my tablet and there was an e-mail from Brin like I expected.

Mike, we will arrive above the Castle at 2:00 am. There should be no moon tonight, which will help us hide. We have lights to illuminate the offload of our equipment, but please have a crew to take control of the equipment. We will suspend a ramp, but we don't have personnel to move it. Afterwards, we will move our ship under the Dome. I'm looking forward to meeting you."

I responded:

"We will have forklifts to move the equipment off and store it. We will also have plenty of manpower to help, also. We, too, are eager to meet you."

I read the e-mail to Nancy and Sue. I also copied the e-mails to Jeremy. I said, "Let's go look at the upper levels and our new quarters. Maybe we can get in a nap and have a late dinner before Brin arrives. By the way, where is our Secret Service Agent staying?"

Sue said, "We have a four bedroom/quarters in our apartment. We figured he could stay in one. That way he would be close if he was ever needed,

296

otherwise he would have no way of knowing if we needed him." I nodded.

On the way out I said, "Tom, you might go with us and pick your bedroom. You aren't really needed here much of the time, unless Nancy needs something done. We headed toward the elevator. I pushed the 3rd floor button. The hallways followed the octagon shape of the building but not nearly as wide as the walkway on the mezzanine. I wanted to see the entire floor before we went to our apartment. We followed the main hallway all the way around. Entrance doors were staggered on both walls leading into numerous apartments. There was a center hallway running north and south through the center section. There were fewer doors, I counted four, in this hallway. Sue said these center apartments were larger than the others, luxury apartments, and one of them is ours. The only downside was these had no outside balcony.

Sue led us to one and opened the door. Wow! It led into a large plush lounge area with four doors leading into individual bedrooms. The floor was covered in thick carpet, the walls were marble, everything looked expensive. I suppose it was. Right in the middle was my big rocker and ottoman, and they did not look out of place at all. Point of fact, the couch and other recliners matched my chair. Sue showed us a large glass shower area, saying only the luxury apartment had bathrooms, showers and kitchenettes. All the other housing units have to use the common bathrooms stationed at each end of our hallway. The kitchenette was small with little more than a small refrigerator, sink and coffee pot, but we would be cooking no meals here, not with Bob's Cafe downstairs. When we entered our bedroom I was surprised at the large size. It was so big we had two king-sized beds across one wall and a large walk-in closet on the opposite side. I thought that might be overkill, but then I remembered times we could have used two beds.

I said, "What is the fourth floor like?"

Sue said, "It's identical to this level, just higher. Truth is, we haven't filled out occupancy on this floor, much less the fourth. Everyone has a bedroom, although they are smaller in the other units. As you know, many will be doubling up, and in some cases, tripling up or more up, like us."

Nancy said, "I sent out a message to all department heads letting them know the time of arrival. Actually, I think everyone here is anxious to see Brin and his group arrive and meet them, and Bob will be ready. Bess should be joining us shortly, also."

"Good," I said, "She can join us in that huge shower before we take a nap."

I have to admit, I loved our shower with its multiple shower heads. We had plenty of room for all of us, including Bess, who soon joined us. I had all my girls together at one time and place ... and naked. I personally made sure they were all clean ... everywhere, and they did the same to me. Still, I was outnumbered and got the better part of that deal. This was the first time in a long time it had just been the four of us, and I had missed that. I loved my girls so much. I think we mutually agreed to hurry up and finish the shower and adjourn to our new bed. We dried each other off and did just that. I lay on my back and pulled Nancy and Sue close to me, and we joined in a three-way kiss until Bess lay on top of me and joined in. I loved being encompassed in warm bodies and was so damn hard. I felt Bess tighten her thighs around my cock. I moaned. Bess giggled and set up and raised up over my cock to guide it into her hot pussy. I didn't think Bess would be able to mount me, but she let her own weight slowly force her pussy down over me, well, up to a point. There she was resting half impaled on my cock and not sinking any lower.

Bess said, "Sisters, I need your help pull me down."

Nancy and Sue stopped kissing me and looked up to see what Bess needed. They immediately started laughing, but they grabbed Bess' arms and began slowly pulling her down. I saw a combination of pain and ecstasy as I felt her slipping down over my throbbing cock. I felt my cock pushing against her cervix then slipping deeper. Bess screamed and her body started having convulsions. She had barely settled on me when the most powerful orgasm I had ever seen rocked her body. I hadn't even begun stroking. Her thighs quivered and her strong pussy muscles clamped down on my cock so hard. I knew it would take some time for Bess to be able to relax. I didn't move inside her, hell, I couldn't move inside her. I just lay there and enjoyed the quivering, like a vibrator. Nancy and Sue seemed stunned at the ferocity of Bess' orgasm and stared in amazement. I was also amazed that she had taken all my cock inside her, and somewhat fearful that she could pinch it off if she had another orgasm. Still, it felt good, and I was highly aroused.

It was then I became aware of others in the room. In fact, Dr. Wong and Dr. Ikiko were up on the bed trying to slowly lift Bess off my cock. I have no idea where they came from. We must have left the door open and they heard Bess' ferocious scream. Slowly she came off and the doctors gently lay Bess in the other bed. Bess was passed out cold from her massive orgasm. The doctors came back and started inspecting my cock for damage or maybe just for the fun of it, because Dr. Ikiko was already naked and climbed up over me and lowered herself down on my hard cock. I looked at Nancy and Sue, and they were smiling at me. Dr. Ikiko impaled herself on me, moaned and rode me hard and fast, like the other night. I remembered how hot her pussy was. She was pounding down on me and grinding. Fast, she went too fast, and I was feeling my climax starting to build, but she beat me. She squealed, her thighs gripped my sides and her fingers clawed my chest. I was still feeling her quiver inside as she was helped off and replaced by Dr. Wong. Every time they had me from on top, but I wasn't complaining. Dr. Wong rode me like before, just like Dr. Ikiko, hard and fast, but this time I was ready. My orgasm was building fast, and I started driving up into her slick pussy, lifting her with each thrust. When it came I arched my back and drove my cock deep into her, setting her off as well. She too screamed and began quivering all over. I loved to feel her pussy quaking and gripping my jerking cock. Her body fell over me and her

300

breasts crushed my face. I started sucking her little nipples, but she didn't respond. She was out of it. It was then that I noticed Dr. Norcross. He was lifting Dr. Wong off of me, and I watched him gently lay her down next to the Japanese beauty. He spread her thighs and began lapping up our combined cream. Nancy set up and watched him in amazement. Sue snuggled up to me and kissed me. I kissed her back and hugged her close. I wanted her tonight, but my body wasn't responding, so we just snuggled.

Dr. Norcross had cleaned Dr. Wong up. I'm not even sure she was awake. He said to Sue, "They kind of cut in line, huh? Maybe I can get him up for you."

Before I knew what was happening Dr. Norcross grabbed my weathered dick and started licking it clean and sucked it into his mouth. I was shocked, so I let it happen. I noticed Nancy's close attention. I continued to kiss and rub Sue, as he sucked me. Maybe he knew something, being trained as a doctor, because my dick was responding and growing in his mouth. Nancy continued to watch in rapt attention and had even moved to watch closer, as he bobbed his head up and down.

Nancy said to Dr. Norcross, "I take it you like men?"

Dr. Norcross said, "I'm bi, I like women too."

Nancy said, "Can't you deep deep-throat?"

He lifted off my now hard cock and said, "I never learned. I can handle most men this way."

Nancy giggled and said, "Here, let me show you how."

301

I can tell you, she really knows how. She took me down her throat and began thrusting down. I could feel her tongue reach out and lick my balls as she went down. She would lift off from time to time, and I could hear her instructing him, but my mind was spinning. When I felt whisker stubble against my stomach I knew he had learned.

Nancy said, "That's enough. It's time for Sue to get her turn. If you like women come on up here with me."

I was not completely out of it and said, "Hon, the doctor told you not to have sex for a few days. I don't want you to be hurt."

Nancy laughed and said, "No. He told me not to have sex with you for a few days. Dr. Norcross isn't as big as you."

Dr. Norcross said, "Hell, 95% of all men are smaller than Mike, especially now."

I laughed at both comments. "Okay, okay." I gently rolled Sue's back to me and spooned to her. My cock was getting cold, and I began probing between Sue's butt cheeks. She helped me find the warmth to slip into. My arms wrapped around her and pulled her tight to me, as I began driving deep into her velvet tunnel. I think she was pounding back as hard as I was driving forward. We built a rhythm of long deep strokes. My moans and nibbles on her neck were rewarded with bites on my arm, bites that hurt but slowed my climax. I could hear moans from both girls. Sue and I continued our love making, but I noticed both oriental girls also staring at me with a hungry look. No, not again. I yelled out, "Tom! I need you."

302

"I'm here." Tom said, "What do you need?"

I said, "I need you to take care of those two Asian girls. I hope you have a big dick." I immediately started laughing when I saw a smiling Tom jump naked between them on the other bed. He was already hard, and he did indeed have a large dick, which the girls were already reaching for. Tom must have been watching the activities and hoping for the opportunity to get involved. Well, he got his chance. While Tom was getting involved I never missed a stroke into Sue, and she seemed to be able to take all of my cock without much difficulty. So much for Dr. Grooms concern about Sue not being hurt by me. Doc just wanted Sue to himself. I can't say I blamed him, though. Sue is an incredibly sexy woman. I could feel her quivering then convulsing inside. I wasn't there yet and continued to drive deep, setting Sue off in a continuous orgasm. I grabbed her hips and pulled her tight to me as I too flooded out inside her. Through her tight squeezing pussy I felt my jerking cock gushing out spurt after spurt of cum deep inside her. We lay together for quite a while as we calmed. Eventually, my deflating cock slipped out of her tight pussy, and I turned her to me. Our kisses were hot and passionate.

Sue kissed me tenderly and said, "You know I love you don't you? Nancy and Bess do also. But, take a look at my slut sister."

I turned around to watch Nancy and Dr. Norcross. He was between her thighs pounding into her. She was moaning loudly and had her legs wrapped around him. Her heels driving against his butt cheeks, setting his fast pace and forcing him

303

deeper into her. Sue and I watched Nancy reaching her climax and heard her screams of ecstasy, driving him to explode inside her. We continued to watch as she calmed and looked over at us and smiled really big and mischievous. Dr. Norcross rolled off of her and took off to the bathroom.

Nancy said, "Sue, I heard you call me a slut right after you screamed like a whore." We all laughed. Bess had recovered and crawled up on the bed with us and lay on top of me. We started the hugging and kissing again.

Bess said, "Damn, Mike, you gave me the strongest orgasm I've ever had. Can you do it again?"

I said, "I hope so. You know I just got my cock in when you powered off. I wanted to do you good tonight. If the little fella grows again I would be happy to do you again. Girls, I might need your help. I want to power through her clamping pussy and orgasm in her, but I'm sure I will get stuck in her again." Sue and Nancy giggled at that, remembering last time that happened.

Even though she was so tight, I knew I had stretched her out, and hopefully it might be easier. Still, I would have to wait to see if my erection returned. I was pretty sure it would eventually come back, since my body was wrapped in warmth of three beautiful and sexy women that I loved. As we lay together we heard heavy moans and looked over to see Tom pounding into both Asians. He would drive hard into one for several strokes, then move to the other and pound into her. He kept going back and forth. Even as we watched both girls had orgasms, but Tom seemed to have plenty of energy and kept going. Finally, he bellowed out and shot cream all over both of them, which they seemed to enjoy.

I said, "Hey Tom. If you guys are going to keep going, move them to your room. We're going to get some sleep." He grinned and took the smiling girls by the hands and led them off toward his room. I still don't know how they happened to be here, but I wasn't going to complain. Dr. Norcross didn't come back in, so he must have gone back to his room, and we were finally alone again. The girls started on me then with kisses, licks and nibbles. Bess slipped down my body and started nursing my nipples. Ohhh, that felt strange, and it made my entire body quiver, which made the girls giggle. I didn't know my nipples were that sensitive. When Bess started nipping and pulling on them with her teeth my whole body jerked and quivered. Not only did my body quiver, but my cock jerked against her warm stomach. Nancy began probing my mouth with her tongue, and Sue nibbled my earlobe. The combination was driving me crazy. Yep, I was hard as a post again. I guided Bess up and lay her on her back between Nancy and Sue. I wanted to go slow so she wouldn't orgasm so fast. I spread her knees apart and wiggled between them. She was already dripping wet as I guided my cock into her burning depth and slowly began to push. Once the head was inside I began to slowly stroke into her. She remained very tight, but I kept applying more and more pressure and felt it slowly slipping deeper. Nancy and Sue lay on her arms and nursed her nipples. It was a beautiful sight to behold. The stroking began in earnest as I slipped deeper. Almost baby, almost. The last three inches were the hardest. My cock hit her cervix and Bess began to quiver. One more push and I was all the way inside. She stiffened, but I waited then pulled out and pushed back inside. She took it all and wrapped her legs tight around my waist. God she was tight, but I continued to stroke in and out, slowly getting faster and harder. Soon we were pounding against each other, and she certainly knew how to drive those hips. Faster and harder we went until she froze in mid movement. Her pussy clamped down on my cock so hard it hurt, but I wanted this, to lose my load inside her. I pulled back to drive more, but all I did was pull her with my cock. I said, "Hold her hips down." When they did I was able to pull my cock out and push it back in. It hurt, but I was crazy with lust and fought through it. I kept driving into her. I felt my cock balloon inside her, but I was almost there. I held her shoulders and drove hard one last time and felt my dam burst. She had been screaming all the while, and I joined her.

It took a few minutes to calm before I tried to pull my cock out. No way. I was anchored firmly. We were stuck. I didn't break anything last time, so I wasn't too worried. My weight was resting on her little body, so I wrapped my arms around her and rolled us over with me on bottom. I knew I wasn't coming out until I deflated some, so I just started rubbing her back and giving her sweet kisses. After about ten minutes I asked Nancy and Sue to try and help her off. She was still tight, but I slowly slipped out, followed by a torrent of cream spilling out on my stomach.

Bess said, "Oh Mike, I love you so much."

I said, "I love you, too, all three of my girls." I was rewarded by a multitude of kisses.

Nancy said, "That was so hot, but I thought we might have to pour cold water on them. Sue, when you said before that they were stuck, I thought you were kidding."

I said, "Let's take another shower and try to get a few hours' sleep before meeting Brin."

We managed to get in a few hours' sleep before Nancy shook me awake. Jeremy had his own luxury apartment, so all we had to worry about was Tom, but he actually beat us up. Sue made me dress in my best cloths, which consisted of one of the polo shirts the girls bought me, new cargo shorts and socks with my loafers. I felt overdressed, but the girls were pleased. I noticed that they too were dressed up, but they would look good in anything or without anything.

The elevator opened into an active cafe. I guess few intended to miss this historic meeting, because many were here at 12:30 am. Bob anticipated correctly and his buffet was ready. We hurried through the line and found an empty table. I had noticed that most of the community members tended to avoid us, I'm assuming due to the perceived hierarchy. I mean they were friendly enough, but a little standoffish. Jeremy, however, wasn't one of them. He, Janet, Mary, James and Robert joined us. I hadn't realized just how hungry I was. We had missed dinner, so I guess it was to be expected. We chatted about small things. I didn't want to mention our showers and extra conveniences, since most everyone else didn't have them. One thing they did have that we didn't was the balcony, but if I had to choose between them I would take the shower and bathroom every time. Still, a balcony and fresh air would be nice.

After we had eaten I said, "Well, kids, it's time. Jeremy, are you all ready for the unloading?"

He grinned and said, "Yep, and I better go now to the unloading area. My crew is just waiting for me to get up."

"Do you need us for anything?" I asked.

"No. Probably the roof is the best place for you to observe."

"Well, girls, let's head for the roof." I said.

We took the elevator up to the fourth deck and the stairs the final level. I loved it the moment we opened the door to the roof. From this height we could see for many miles and all of our property. I guess that is why Robert had sentries posted. I even saw some heavy armament permanently mounted, especially on the elevator roof, which was even higher. The meaning of Castle began taking on a new definition.

It was a beautiful night, but there was no moon present tonight. Brin had chosen the time of arrival well. I think we all became aware at the same time that a sudden cloud bank was forming. We could see the lightening flashing across the horizon, lighting up the sky. Somehow this was different. The thick clouds came toward us, almost against the wind. It quickly dawned on me that this was Brin's arrival. This was camouflage to prevent their arrival from being seen. I hadn't noticed before, but the lightening seemed to be originating from the center of the cloud bank and was likely static energy generated from his ship interacting with the atmosphere. Once the cloud was high over us I could see the bottom of the cloud begin to flare out and open a large hole in the cloud underneath. The cloud underneath began to dissipate, and we got our first glimpse of the ship. It was far bigger than I expected, and I panicked, thinking it would never fit under the Dome. Maybe a foot for Brin was much larger than we measure a foot. The spacecraft glowed but was dimming as it lowered toward us. It continued to lower until it was about ten feet above the lighted ground area. We heard a hum, then a gush of air as a round area of the bottom opened up. A large ramp extended from the bottom to settle down to the ground. The ship continued to hover, but the ramp seemed stable. Lights came on inside the craft and Jeremy's forklifts started up and disappeared inside. We didn't have to wait long to see the forklifts bringing crates and supplies down the ramps and deposit them in the ready area. A small mountain of supplies grew before they finally stopped. We could see Jeremy running around giving orders. It looked like they were altering the plans. He waved a large front end loader over and up the ramp. Soon the loader could be seen backing out, pulling a large container down the ramp and on to level ground. It pulled three more containers down, and they seemed to be satisfied. The ramp retracted back into the ship, and the ship slowly lifted to about fifty feet and again hovered. After a few moments something big, almost as big as the opening, began descending. Once enough was showing I was amazed to recognize what was a miniature of the larger craft. It was a flying saucer. Oh my. It was lowered to the ground by a cable, which detached. A second one was soon lowered. The entire process took around one hour from start to finish, afterwards the bottom closed up again and the craft began to slide through the air toward the open lake side of the Dome. It began sinking into the water.

I said, "I guess that is our cue to go to the Dome and greet them." After all this time, finally meeting them had me a little nervous. The girls, Tom and I, joined by Robert and JJ took the elevator down to the Cave and proceeded to the interlocks connecting to the Dome. Once we passed the third interlock and actually entered the Dome, I was pleased to see the spacecraft had successfully entered under the Dome and was rising. The top bubble on the craft was slowly emerging out of the water. The bubble stabilized and struts extended to clamp on to the prepared "I" beams for docking. The humming and churning in the water ceased, and apparently docking was complete. After a few moments an iris door approximately six feet in diameter opened in the top of the bubble. We waited anxiously.

A man's head emerged from the opening, looked around and continued up a ladder. The man looked totally human in every way, except his skin color. He was aqua, well blue, like he had said. He had long black hair braided down the back and sky-blue eyes. He looked to be about my age and height, around 6' 2" but he was lean, with a swimmer's build. The clothing was sparse, a form fitting, rubber/metallic appearing shirt and shorts and simple slippers. The clothing was the same color as his natural skin color. He smiled directly at me and came toward me with his arms stretched out for a hug.

As he approached he said, "I am Brin."

That gesture jarred me out of my stupor, and I smiled hugely as I met his embrace. I said, "I'm Mike. I'm glad you finally made it. Welcome my friend." After all this time I truly felt he was a friend. While I was hugging Brin I noticed two others emerge from the ship. They were both female and lean, quite stunning in appearance and very identical ... also very blue. They were dressed in the same manner as Brin, with the obvious modifications for breasts, which they certainly had. One striking feature on the alien girls were temple streaks of orange in their otherwise black hair, also long and braided. One other feature I noticed in all three was their tendency to frequently pinch their nose closed, almost like eyes blinking. It seemed to happen without their knowing it, like our noses can flare as a reflex. It wasn't in any way annoying, it is what it is.

Brin put his hands on the two ladies and said, "These are my mates, Peg and Meg."

I introduced Nancy, Sue, Bess, Robert, Tom and JJ., and hugs were exchanged all around, this apparently being their standard form of greeting.

I said, "Can we help you do anything? Do you have gear you need to unload? Maybe you are hungry? Do you have any immediate needs? We have quarters for your crew if they are ready to unload." Hell, I didn't even give Brin time to answer. I realized I was just rambling, so I shut up.

Brin said, "Our crew is still in cryogenics. The three of us remained awake for the whole trip. We will start bringing them out tomorrow, and they will need some medical attention when we do. Can we notify your doctor to prepare for them? As far as eating, I think we could use food. I think we can eat anything you can, although we prefer fish. But, we are eager to expand our taste to Earth food. The one thing we have missed during the long trip is swimming. I think we would like to go for a swim then eat something. We will only need room for the three of us to sleep tonight, although we can sleep in our ship if necessary."

I said, "We will call Bob, our cook, to get something ready for you. Hell, I could eat again myself. The food should be ready when your swim is over. As far as quarters, we have a room in our quarters. That way you won't be on your own until you get familiar with the colony and are ready." When I said this I saw Nancy making the call.

When I finished talking, Brin nodded to me, looked at Peg and Meg and the three of them dove into the water. We watched them swim out of sight, but we quickly picked them up by viewing through the Dome wall. Wow, they were fast and shot toward the surface. Soon they were back, darting back and forth. They swam using both legs and feet

312

together, like a porpoise. I suddenly realized that their ability to clamp their nostrils closed also simulated the air-hole on a porpoise. I guess that is a reasonable evolution modification on a water world. After about twenty minutes they startled us by shooting out of the water to land on their feet standing upright on the Dome deck. That took much strength to do that I realized. They then seemed to shake the water off their bodies, almost like a dog would. The shaking wave seemed to quiver upward through their bodies and quite efficiently shed the water. They laughed and seemed very happy. It almost made me jealous to witness their swimming talent.

When they were ready, we started out and instructed them in the operation of the air-seals in the connecting tunnels as we went. They seemed quite impressed. Brin seemed very interested in the Cave and spent some time looking around, but there would be plenty of time for that, so I steered us toward the elevator.

Before we got in the elevator Brin said to Peg and Meg, "After we eat we need to bring the saucers in here and park them out of sight. Satellites can pick them up and also any military overflight. If we were seen coming in tonight they might just do that." The girls nodded.

I pushed the button for the ground level. I could tell Brin was checking out the facility, construction and overall operation, but when the doors opened on the main floor and we walked out, Brin's eyes flared in amazement at the layout and sheer beauty of the main floor. He looked up, side to

313

side, then all around. Brin's huge smile stretched his face. I also noticed all those around had stopped and were staring at the aliens.

I said, "Attention everyone." My announcement seemed to break the self-imposed freeze of activity. "Let me introduce Brin, Peg and Meg. Introduce yourself as time permits." Most went on about their business, but some came to introduce themselves. I stopped the full introduction by leading them toward Bob's Cafe, and Bob was waiting and introduced himself. He too received embraces from the aliens. Bob led us toward our standard table, at least it must now be standard, since it is where we ate earlier.

Bob said, "Since our new friends come from a water world, I made the assumption that they like fish. I prepared tilapia fillets for them. These are baked with asparagus. In the future you can share your eating preference, and I will try to comply."

Brin said, "I'm sure we will enjoy them. Thanks. I have a few culinary members of my crew I can assign to you when they become available."

Bob waved over a few of his staff to place full plates on our table. We all dug in, but the aliens waited to see us using our forks, which they mimicked. After their first bite, which they must have liked very much, they dropped their forks and any pretense at manners and proceeded to use their fingers to fill their mouths. I have to admit, not being a major fish eater, I was taken by surprise by the fantastic flavor. Even so, I continued to use my fork. Bob smiled at our reaction and, noticing how fast the fish was being devoured, brought more to the table. The aliens were not bashful or very hungry. They continued to feast. They must have eaten three fillets each before they slowed.

Bob asked, "Can I assume you like the fish?"

Brin spoke in a sing-song language to Peg and Meg, which was returned. He answered, "We liked it very much. None of us has ever tasted anything like it. We look forward to many other dishes."

Chapter 14
(The Interfacing)

Hearing the aliens speak to each other in their own language made me realize that I hadn't heard Meg or Peg speak English and wondered if they could understand and speak English. I said, "Are all females of your race identical?" I figured that would get some kind of reaction.

They looked at each other and laughed and one of them said, "No. We are like you humans. We all look different, but we grew from a single egg. I think you call them identical twins, something extremely rare on our planet. We believe we are the only set born in many generations."

"We have a set of identical twins among our group." I said. This seemed to shock them.

They spoke together saying, "We want to meet them."

Nancy said, "Let me check to see where they are. They could be sleeping."

I noticed that Brin was in deep conversation with Robert, JJ, Tom and Bob, and they weren't following our conversation. When I saw Nancy calling them on the phone my attention was drawn to a ringing phone somewhere in the "Great Room". I followed the sound and saw Ella and Ebba sitting at a far table. One of them was on her phone and looked toward us. I waved them over. Even before they got here the two sets of twins saw each other and began staring at each other. Peg and Meg stood and went forward to embrace Elle and Ebba. It was like they had known each other all their lives, a special connection an individual person could never understand. I noticed that no two of them spoke one-on-one but instead as a group, totally inclusive of the others. Soon they were laughing and talking as only old friends could do. I knew I was not relevant to their conversation anymore and joined Brin's conversation, although Nancy, Sue and Bess remained. Since the three of them were so close they could somewhat relate. Robert was going over security measures and weaponry, and Brin was listening intently. I'm assuming Brin must have asked.

In a lull in the conversation Brin said, "I will wake up the security team first. We will need them within the next few days, and we need to mount some weapons on the roof. We have been monitoring the activities in the area, and the food has all been stripped from the stores. Gangs are taking over, but the National Guard will try to prevent the killing...unsuccessfully. They, however, will see the inevitable end and become their own gang. These government forces have numbers and weapons and present the greatest threats. They will eventually no longer represent the government, only themselves. They will keep the food for themselves and not distribute it. And, don't kid yourself, our secrete existence is no secret at all. They will all come for our food, and we must be ready."

"Meg and Peg are my communication experts and pilots. They will set up our satellite monitoring equipment tomorrow, well today, so we can readily identify these threats."

Robert asked, "What weapons are you talking about?"

Brin said, "We have some focused EMP (Electro Magnetic Pulse) guns that will disable electronics in vehicles, planes, helicopters, and the like. We would use these for non-lethal defense. We also have what Earth would call a form of Rail Gun that shoot projectiles at super-fast velocity, so fast it is considered instantaneous and totally destroys what it hits. These would definitely be considered lethal weapons. Plus we have lasers, both large and small."

I asked, "Do you want to get some sleep before we start? If you do we can take you to my quarters."

Brin said, "Yes, we have been without sleep for a while. Sleep would be good before we start."

The two sets of twins said their good-byes, reluctantly, and I thanked Bob and steered the group to the elevator and up to the third level. We quickly made it to our quarters. After showing them their bedroom, I made a pot of coffee and relaxed into my rocker while the rest cycled through the shower. Bess showed them how everything worked so they could shower first. I would go with the girls later. I must have dozed off and realized Nancy was shaking me. I jumped awake and quickly followed the girls to the shower. When we came out Brin and the twins were sitting in the common area very naked. They were not a bit embarrassed, so this must be normal for them. It wasn't so normal for me and

318

the girls, as we had expected to go straight to bed and were also naked. We acted as normal as possible and sat down. They had coffee they were sipping on, which they seemed to enjoy.

Brin said, "We were going to bed, but Meg and Peg were eager to milk your seed. The other girls they were talking to told them that you shared your seed with them and many others. Meg and Peg want your seed, also."

I almost spit my coffee out but said, "What do you mean by milk my seed?" As I said that I noticed my girls giggling. I also wondered what was said in their conversation.

Brin said, "As I have told you, our race is dying since we have difficulty in procreating. This is the reason we came here: we hope your human sperm can fertilize our female's eggs and continue our species...in part at least. Our females have the ability to milk it from you. Over the generations they have developed extreme muscle control allowing them to do this. Let us show you. Insert a finger inside her." Pointing at one of the twins.

One of the twins spread her legs exposing her pussy and waited. I looked at my girls and they were still grinning and just shrugged. Well, if no one was shy about this why should I. I got down on my knees and slipped a finger inside her pussy. It startled me when her internal muscles gripped my finger and yanked it inside. If my other fingers hadn't been spread, the pull might have yanked my whole hand inside her. Her internal muscle control provided a hard undulating pull, almost a suction. When she stopped I was able to remove my finger.

When I did, Bess jumped down and pushed a couple of small fingers inside her, and cooed at the action. I laughed.

I was beginning to understand a lot about them and asked, "How long does this milking take?"

Peg or Meg said, "Just a few seconds."

I bluntly said, "You don't have sex for pleasure do you? Never mind. It is impossible to take pleasure in sex if you bypass a climax or orgasms in both male and female. I bet you don't even get hard. No wonder your race is dying. Maybe living in a water world has trained you away from nature's way. We are going to have to teach you how to fuck again and experience the pleasure of it. Girls, we have a tough job." My girls smiled. I continued, "No, you're not going to clamp that thing down on my cock and milk out my sperm, but I can give you all the sperm you want, my way. It's also going to take a lot longer than a few seconds. Do you want my sperm my way? I bet you will like my way better." I don't think they had the slightest idea what I was talking about, but they were about to find out.

Brin, Peg and Meg looked at each other, then Brin said, "Yes, they want your sperm your way."

I said, "Nancy, you may have to give Brin one of those Viagra. I doubt that he has ever really had a decent erection. I bet you got more, huh?" She just grinned.

I took Meg and Peg by the hands and led them to my bed, grabbing Bess on the way. Nancy and Sue took Brin's hands and led him to the other bed, and I saw her giving Brin a tablet to swallow before

320

I turned back. I knew it would take a while to re-kindle the dormant feelings in the twins, since they probably never experienced them. I hoped those feeling were just dormant and not nonexistent. I hoped their race had not evolved them away. Oh well, we would find out soon enough.

I only knew one way to try to stimulate the twins, and that was to treat them like any other fe-male. I placed both of them on their backs side by side. Bess helped me and started rubbing her hands over one of them, exploring and touching. I began by nibbling kisses on the other's lips and spreading over her face. She looked a little shocked and shy. My kisses moved down her neck, and I heard her catch a breath in reaction. Awww, this was good. I nibbled her neck, but kept moving back to her lips. After a while she kissed me back. I let my hand begin to slide over and caress her arms and body. When my fingers touched her nipples she caught another breath and kissed me a little harder. I let my fingers caress her breasts and roll her little, pur-ple nipples, which immediately swelled into hard nubs. I moved my kisses down her neck and slowly over to her nipples. Her body stiffened, and when I sucked one into my mouth, I heard her moan and felt her body quiver. Those feeling weren't buried so deep after all. Both hands continued to caress her breasts as I moved between her nipples. A gen-tle bite and pull on her nipples generated a groan. It was time, and I moved my kisses and nibbles down her stomach. Already her stomach was quivering. She didn't know what I was doing or what was hap-pening, but she seemed to like it. My hand slid over

321

her quivering hips and down over her thigh. I spread her thighs and moved between them and began kissing and licking up her inner thighs. When I slid my tongue over her pussy slit she moaned loud. My tongue slipped inside and spread her lips. She was wet, so wet. Her body was remembering nature's training. She tasted sweet, and I feasted on her pussy, pressing my tongue deep into her tunnel. I could feel her inner thighs tremble, and when my tongue rubbed over her small nub, she squealed out, clamped her thighs shut on my head and flooded my face with nectar. Her legs finally shot straight out with a shudder. I looked to her face and it was rolling from side to side and obviously continuing in an orgasm, probably the first one she ever had. Her twin was doing exactly the same, but Bess had not relented. Bess had her face buried in her pussy and was taking her into a continuous orgasm. As my twin slowly settled, I moved up between her soft, warm thighs and probed my raging cock into her still spasming, wet pussy and began stroking it into her. She was tight but not so tight it prevented me from pushing into her. Her body awoke and began meeting my thrusts. The moans and squeals increased in number and volume as I got deep inside. She took all of my cock, and her arms pulled me, and her legs wrapped around me. We were locked together and she was moving as much as I was. It was then that I felt the undulation start within her pussy, not strong like before. It was more like a controlled quiver but simulated what I had felt before. I'm not even sure she knew it was happening. I certainly did, and it felt fantastic. As I stroked, her pussy was massaging my cock. Her pussy continued to gently milk me as I pumped into her. The stimulation set me on fire, and I drove into her like a savage. We climaxed together and both of us froze in a locked orgasm, but her pussy continued to gently milk me. It felt so good I didn't go down. I left it in her until I felt Bess pull at my arm. I looked over and she was motioning me to do the other one. I reluctantly pulled my cock out and moved to the other twin. As I began pushing into the second hot pussy, I noticed Bess burying her face in the pussy I just left. I chuckled, but I was intent on feeling that controlled quiver massage again. I pushed in and the squealing began again. My rhythm built and the quiver began again. Bess certainly had her ready. Maybe they had been watching, because this twin knew what to expect and wanted it. We pounded together so hard I was afraid I might hurt her, but obviously not, as she pounded equally as hard back. We exploded together. I almost thought "again", but I realized this was the other twin. Still, it was like this one knew everything the other twin experienced. Maybe that is how it is to be an identical twin, but I didn't complain, because her pussy was massaging my cock, and I loved it. Eventually, I pulled out of her and nuzzled in between them. They both snuggled and kissed me. These girls learned fast, and the urges weren't so dormant.

One of the twins said, "That was incredible. We never knew it could be so great. You were right, your way is more fun. Can we do it again?"

I started laughing and said, "Not from me. I'm done for a while, but I could probably find another man for you." The twins looked at each other and nodded.

I yelled, "Hey, Tom. Are you busy?" I knew he was constantly observant and had heard our previous conversation. He would know how to go slow with the twins ... maybe.

Tom was there quickly and said, "I'm here."

I said, "Would you want to take care of Meg and Peg?" He grinned and took their hands and led them back to his bedroom. I hadn't seen what happened with Nancy, Sue and Brin, but they were all cuddled up together sound asleep, so Bess and I cuddled up together in my bed. Hell, it was already daylight. We would all be sleeping late today.

Unfortunately, sleeping in was not in the cards. Jeremy and Robert came bursting in our door yelling an alarm, which matched the clanging alarm now sounding throughout the Castle.

Robert announced, "Armed forces and heavy equipment breached our secondary outer gate and are moving toward our main gate. I have already dispatched our security guards, but we need to meet them at the gate."

We were all up instantly slipping into whatever clothing we could quickly find and strapping on our pistols. Brin seemed to know what was happening, maybe from looking into the future. He barked orders to Meg and Peg, telling them to retrieve their weapons from the Cave, where they had been stored, and mount them on the roof and be ready.

324

He told them he would activate the satellite equipment.

Before they left Jeremy said, "I've already built the mounts and installed some of your weapons. I didn't know about the other equipment, so I will help you and show you the communication room." The blue group nodded and followed Jeremy out.

The rest of us followed Robert, but Tom blocked our way, holding up his hands. Tom said, "Wait. Never put all your eggs in one basket, and never put all the generals together going into a potential battle. Some of you have to stay behind."

Tom was right. Nancy had to go to talk legal stuff if that possibility existed, and I was going if she was. I said, "Sue, you and Bess stay here. No! Don't give me an argument. If something happens to us you will have to carry on the community." They reluctantly remained behind, while we raced toward our vehicles.

The small army of US Marshals, FEMA Officers and, surprisingly, some Army soldiers were piling out of various vehicles as we screeched to a halt behind the new barriers Jeremy had built. In the rear there were five trucks, and their obvious intent was to haul off our stores. There were at least thirty armed men approaching the gate, which still remained closed. We had about twenty armed guards holding position behind the covering wall. The FEMA forces were trying to intimidate us into letting them in, because their planned confrontation put them in the open. It was not going to play out like they wanted.

Nancy said, "Stop! This is as far as you go."

The same FEMA Officer as before, the attorney, said, "We are under Martial Law. You cannot stop us. We have the authority now. Stand aside."

Nancy said, "You feel that you now have authority over a foreign government?"

The Officer said, "Yes we do. Now stand aside."

Nancy actually laughed at him and said, "Well, this foreign government doesn't agree with you, but I would be happy to review your federal orders and any legal release from the State of Oklahoma, from which issued you a standing order to Cease and Desist. I also note that you do not have any National Guard with you, so apparently the State of Oklahoma has not approved of your action."

The Officer was taken aback somewhat but continued, "Our federal orders are verbal, and we do not need anything from the state courts, as federal orders supersede them."

Nancy said, "That's what I thought. You are NOT a legal organization anymore. The federal government has no idea what you are trying to do, and they certainly would NOT order you to invade another country. You are acting on your own, and, I might add, you are acting very stupidly to position your forces in the open against armed forces behind barricades. As I told you before, the Cherokee Nation owns the property all the way back to the gate you apparently crashed through. So, you have already invaded our land and are subject to our laws, and we find you guilty."

I almost jumped out of my shorts when my phone rang. It was Jeremy, and he was in a panic.

He said, "Mike, we just intercepted a radio message from Camp Gruber. They just dispatched a helicopter to our location. I don't know what kind, but they do have air-assault helicopters, and they've been ordered to come in over the lake and approach from behind."

I responded, "Well crap. We are sitting ducks here from a rear attack. Tell Brin to take it out if he can't disable it." I kept him on the line, but I told Nancy what they are doing and my instructions.

Nancy said, "Those sneaky bastards. Tell him to take out the last truck in line, also as a show of force." Then she turned back to the FEMA Officer and said, "So, you want to play games do you? If you have anyone in the last truck you better get them out quick."

I'm thinking that this FEMA Officer was understanding that he made a mistake, but he thought he had the upper hand. Still, he quickly yelled back to empty the trucks of personnel. Luckily, there were only drivers and they were quickly coming and armed, but suddenly the last truck disintegrated in an explosion. One second it was there and the next it was a growing cloud of dust. Wow! So that was Brin's "Rail Gun".

The Officer said, "Damn you bitch! You just wait."

Nancy said, "What? Wait for the helicopter? I don't think it is going to make it here."

As if to accent her last statement, an approaching helicopter from behind began spinning in the sky. I was pleased that Brin didn't have to kill anyone, but our, at least my, inexperience almost

327

proved fatal. We turned at the helicopter sound and watched as the helicopter went down in the lake. It feathered down, so it didn't hit hard, but it was definitely out of action. I realized my mistake when I heard a shot ring out. I turned in time to catch two horrifying visions. I saw the angry FEMA Officer firing at Nancy, who was also turned to see the helicopter. I also saw Tom in the process of shoving Nancy out of the way as his head exploded in a cloudy plume of red goo. Robert's pistol reports sounded before the other one stopped ringing in my ear. Robert put three shots and three bloody holes in the FEMA Officer's chest. The officer's look of shock continued as he fell dead. All this happened in a fraction of a second but continued to play back in my mind in slow motion. Immediately all guns on our side took aim at targets, but no one moved on the other side. I think they were in more shock than us.

The apparent ranking US Marshal shot his arms up high in the air in surrender and yelled, "Whoa! Hold your fire! He was not authorized to use lethal force. Just hold on."

While he was talking I ran forward to check on Nancy. She was not hurt, maybe a scrape on her knee, but she was alive, thanks to Tom. I knew he was dead, but I checked anyway. We had all been lucky that Robert and Tom had enough battle savvy not to take their eyes off the enemy. They saved Nancy and probably me. I would have been the next target. I started trying to gather my wits, and looked around. The Army soldiers had not even gone for their guns. I think they really had no idea

328

what was going on. They were just following orders.

Nancy calmed herself enough to assess the situation and said to the Marshal, "Are you in charge now? Your illegal army has fired first and killed one of us. Tell me why we shouldn't finish what you started."

The Marshal registered a look of panic and said, "Wait! Wait! That man was in charge. He organized this, and you were right. He didn't have any orders or authority to do this. He told us a show of force was all he needed to shut you down. We have organized a survivor camp at Camp Gruber and we have been gathering food there. He said you had plenty."

The other FEMA Officer said, "Shut the fuck up you asshole. You aren't in charge now, I am. They killed my partner. Now they are criminals and have no protection under the law. I'm going to call up more helicopters and assault this camp. We'll get their food. We need it you idiot."

All weapons were now focused on this FEMA Officer, which was our second mistake, because the Marshal drew his automatic and shot the dumb SOB right in the face. He immediately dropped his weapon with his hands raised and said, "The dumb bastard was about to get us all killed. The answer to your question is: Yes, I'm in charge... now, and it's over. We just want to leave, if that's OK. I'm really sorry about your man. I didn't know the FEMA Officer was dumb enough to do that. We'll take our dead and won't bother you again."

329

Nancy said, "No. Leave the dead. He was right, the FEMA bodies are evidence of a crime. We will bury them where they will never be found. Without evidence ... no crime. I think they just ran off in a panic, don't you?"

The Marshal actually smiled and said, "Yes Ma'am. We all saw them speed away in their car and leave us. Didn't we?" He looked around at his associates and received nods all around.

As they were about to leave, Robert asked, "Are you staying at Camp Gruber?"

The Marshal said, "Yes, we are staying at Camp Gruber. You do know everything outside is collapsing? It's a war zone out there, and many of our Marshals have been killed already by the rioters. We aren't getting orders anymore. We're kind of on our own, the three of us left."

Robert spoke to one of his officers, who handed him his radio/phone. Robert then said to the Marshal, "I like the way you think. Take this radio/phone. It's encrypted to our base station. It might be helpful if we stay in touch, just ask for Robert. Maybe we can help each other in the future." The Marshal nodded, and they all left, minus one truck and two FEMA Officers and their car.

I called Jeremy to let him know it was all over and told him about Tom. I liked Tom. I liked him even more for saving my Nancy. It was a good thing Nancy recruited him from the Secret Service to protect us. He had done a great job. Now, I dare say, he will be missed. I said to Jeremy, "Can you get a crew out to the gate to get Tom. We will want to bury him with honors. The Secret Service would

330

be proud. Oh, there are also two dead FEMA agents that need to be buried without honors, their car, too. Bury them where no one can ever find them."

In spite of the situation, Jeremy laughed and said, "I'll get right on that. They will become the foundation of our new front gate security building."

Nancy had been incredible. She was smart, strong willed and dominant in the confrontation, but I knew it was just a front. I stood close to her, and as soon as the enemy was out of site she fell sobbing onto my chest. The pressure was more than she could bear, and she had been barely holding on to her resolve. Now she would need a good cry and tension release. On the way back to the Castle we passed a backhoe, trucks and crew headed toward the front gate. Jeremy had wasted no time.

I led Nancy into Bob's Cafe. I needed to get some form of stimulate or depressant into Nancy, at least some nourishment. Bess and Sue came running to meet us, but I held my hand up to slow them down. I said, "Everything worked out well. Nancy did great, but she is still trying to settle down. Can you get us some coffee and something to eat?" They rushed over to pile up some trays with food and coffee. They were back in a rush.

I guess word spreads fast, because Bob came over with a sympathetic look and poured something in our coffee from a flask. He said, "Holler if you need more. It's from my cooking stock."

I gave him a thankful look and helped Nancy take a sip of her coffee. She swallowed then coughed, but it did seem to wake her up from her stupor. Nancy said, "I wasn't so great. I got Tom killed!"

"No!" I said, "You did not get him killed. The FEMA Officer got him killed. He tried to kill you, and Tom saved you. That is what Tom was trained to do, and he would do it again. Tom is a hero and will be honored. Know this, hon, you saved a lot of other people today. You handled the whole situation masterfully. I really mean it."

Nancy looked hopefully at me and asked, "Really?"

I said, "Oh hell yes. I'm so very proud of you, and everyone else will be also when they hear how you handled it. You took charge and won the argument against the bully. That's why the bastard wanted to kill you. I still don't know how you prevented the imminent coming battle, but you did it. I think you even made some friends on the other side."

Nancy embraced me and kissed me and said, "Thanks my love. I needed that."

After she seemed to calm some, I said, "Try to eat something, and do have some more coffee." I winked after I said that and got a half-baked smile in return. I knew she was over the worst, and by now there was a crowd gathered, listening but wanting to know more. I said, "Nancy was fantastic. She shut him down. I don't know anyone that could have done better, or even stood up to his argument."

Brin, Meg and Peg had come up and Brin said, "We all heard the exchange, and you are absolutely correct." When I looked puzzled, Brin continued,

"Yeah, we all heard. Robert had opened his radio so we could follow the conversation."

Brin noticed that things seem to be calming and said, "We need to start thawing out my crew, and we can use some help from your doctors."

I said, "I'll take you up to the Clinic to meet the doctors. Sue, tell Bob there will be more for dinner." I laughed. "You know what to tell him. Also, tell Mary about housing needs for Brin's crew. Thanks"

I took them up to the Clinic and introduced them to Dr. Groom and let them talk about what was needed. Dr. Groom was happy to be asked and joined right in. Dr. Groom called Dr. Norcross to help, and they took off for the Dome. I returned to Bob's Cafe to rejoin Nancy. She was doing much better, but a little weak from the ordeal. Jeremy had returned, congratulating Nancy for a job well done.

When Jeremy saw me he said where only I could hear, "We lay Tom out in the freezer until we are ready for a service." More loudly he continued, "The new guard building is going well. The foundation is already dug, packed, backfilled and will be poured today. Oh, I haven't reported yet, but I dispatched two boats to recover the soldiers from the helicopter crash in the lake. None were hurt, and they have no idea what happened to the helicopter, and we didn't tell them. We dropped them off at the docks by the dam and sent a radio dispatch to Camp Gruber telling them where to pick them up. They consider us friends for helping them. Hell, I'm even sending some divers out to strip the helicopter of usable items."

Robert came up with a food tray and sat down beside me. He said, "I just got a report from my communication monitors, and it's not good. There is no longer any organized law enforcement. They have been either killed, neutralized, or run off by the large forces of rioters and gangs rampaging. Private citizens are fighting back, but they don't have much of a chance against the gangs. Lots of people are being killed. Even Tulsa and Oklahoma City have collapsed. Without police protection the few remaining firefighters refuse to go out. As a result, cities are burning across the country. To put it bluntly, civilization no longer exists. I've put our security on high alert. Anyone trying to get in now will be hostile. I've ordered them to shoot to kill."

I said, "This is sad to hear, but we knew it was inevitable. This is what we prepared for ... survival, and we will survive."

I looked over at Nancy to see how she was doing. She was much calmer, but I could tell she was still greatly stressed inside. The last time I was able to relieve her stress with a massive orgasm. Unfortunately, I was still under orders not to have sex with Nancy. So, I had to come up with something just as good, and my kinky mind was doing just that. I called Sue and Bess to the side and told them what I was thinking and asked them to help organize and supervise it. They were somewhat shocked when I mentioned it but quickly began to smile and giggle, and I knew then that they approved. I insisted that Nancy have a good meal then a nap. She reluctantly agreed and accepted a tray of steak and eggs, cold tea and another shot of whiskey from

Bob. After we finished eating I led Nancy back to our quarters. She still seemed a little dazed, so I stripped her and myself and got into the shower. I set the temperature level on the hot side. I figured the hot water massage would relax her stiff muscles. I enjoyed drying her off ... everywhere. When we got out of the shower Sue and Bess were waiting on us and took a naked Nancy by the hands and led her to our giant bed.

Nancy looked strangely at them and said, "What's going on with you two?"

Bess said, "Just trust us. We will be with you every moment."

I watched as they took Nancy away. They were her sisters, and she must have trusted them completely and went along. Sue put a blindfold on her and laid her out in the middle of the bed. Nancy reached for the blindfold, but Sue slapped her hand away and slipped bindings over her wrist. When Nancy tried to bring her other hand up, Bess did the same on that side. They tightened the binding, extending her arms out to the side. I thought Nancy was becoming concerned, but the girls kept telling her to relax and trust them. Finally she did. The girls moved down to her feet and slipped binding on her ankles and stretched her legs wide. Bess began to massage Nancy and rub baby oil all over her body, especially on her inner thighs and pussy. I could tell Nancy was finally relaxing and submitting to whatever was coming. Nancy started to catch on when the girls lifted her butt and slipped a pillow under her. I had left it up to the girls to organize this, which they seemed to enjoy doing. Like I, they

335

knew Nancy had been excited, really excited, at the few times she had been used for sex by multiple men taking her. It seemed to thrill her to be a little trashy. I hadn't thought about the blindfold, but Sue said it would add to the excitement, not knowing who was using her.

Bess came back in the room leading about five men. She said, "No one say a word. Let her guess who you are. When you finish send another one in."

I knew the five. Robert was the first. He got up on the bed and knee walked between her thighs and plunged his dick deep and started pumping hard. Nancy immediately groaned and fought against her restraints but quickly stopped as he built a fast rhythm. Robert did not try to prolong his orgasm. It was hard and fast, and when he shot his load inside Nancy, he didn't say a word. He just moved out of the way for Al Martinez. Al took over the hard and fast pumping. Nancy was squirming, moaning and starting to scream out her first orgasm. Mark Springer, the new recruit from the Army Corp, replaced Al and continued the relentless pounding. Bob was even there, grinning like an opossum. Jeremy stood behind him. As one would leave another would come in, some I knew, others I didn't. There was no kissing, maybe a little mauling of her breasts, but it mostly consisted of steady and fast pounding of her pussy. Nancy's entire body was shaking and quivering, but she was obviously loving it, judging by her screaming orgasms. She also knew she was safe, because Bess would reassure her that she was there from time to time.

336

As I lay in the other bed and watched I was becoming increasingly aroused. The smell of sex permeated the room, arousing me even further. This is when I noticed JJ slipping into my bed. She must have come with Robert. JJ was already naked. She was so beautiful and sexy, and slid her hot body over mine as our lips met. Those full warm lips stirred my hormones. I was already hard from watching the activity in the other bed, but with JJ's attention I was ready. Still, I remembered how incredibly tight her small pussy was. This was going to hurt, but I didn't care. I pulled her thigh over mine and probed into her. Yep, it was tight. I reached up and held her shoulders and pulled her down hard on my cock. I was surprised that I managed to pull her all the way down on my cock but very pleased to feel the incredible heat of her pussy surround my cock. JJ moaned and started riding me. It felt wonderful. I pulled her down to kiss her and began pumping into her hot, slick pussy. I was so aroused that I quickly exploded inside her. Her pussy shuttered, but she did not stop riding me. I just lay back, closed my eyes and enjoyed it. JJ was riding through one orgasm after another. Her nectar continued to flow, keeping us lubricated. Wow! this girl had learned some things and figured out how to take me. I don't know how, nor did I care. She didn't let me go down. She kept it up, and I felt myself bubbling up another orgasm. When it hit, it was a strong one. I arched my back and drove my cock deep, lifting her up and setting her off screaming. I knew we were both done, but she stayed on my cock and lay over me, kissing me. We watched Nancy's assault.

Eventually, Bess stopped the assault and said, "That's enough. She passed out."

JJ slipped off my cock and said, "I did better this time, huh? I've been practicing. I still want to do it again on occasion."

I smiled and said, "Any time sweetie." With that she took off back to where her clothes were. I watched Bess removed Nancy's blindfold and the restraints, and I slipped in beside her. Bess cradled beside her on the other side. Nancy was coming around. I said, "Hi, hon, are you all right?"

Nancy smiled and said, "I'm more than all right. I'm a little sore, but I've never experienced anything like that before. I do feel like a total slut. I guess I am, but I don't care. Wow! In addition to the slutty turn-on of being gang-banged, there is something about being blindfolded and having no control over the situation that aroused me greatly, and that surprised me. I had so many orgasms I can't believe it. How many men used me anyway?"

Bess laughed and said, "Well, I lined up fifteen, and some of them went twice. I'm not even going to tell you who they were. That should remain a mystery"

Nancy said, "That's probably best, but I do know Jeremy was one of them. I would recognize that rabbit fuck anywhere."

We all laughed hard at that. Yep, That is the way Jeremy always did it, hard and fast like a jackrabbit.

It was still early in the evening, so I suggested that we take another shower and see if there was still some food in the cafe. We all ran to the shower, and it was wonderful to see Nancy in a jovial mood and back to normal. The shower was uneventful, sexually, for all of us, though comforting. We took our time, dried each other off, dressed and moved toward the elevator. There was still a crowd in the cafe, and I saw quickly why. Brin was there with about fifteen of his crew. Bob was catering to them, and they were devouring his fish. If a cook takes pride in the appreciation of his/her cooking, Bob would have to be ecstatic at their reaction. As before with Brin, Meg and Peg, utensils had been discarded and they were feeding themselves with both hands with obvious enjoyment. I asked, "Hey, Bob, do you have more?"

Bob smiled and said, "You bet I do. Take a seat, and I will get you some."

We sat at the table with Brin and his girls and I said, "I see you have some of your crew awake, and I see that they like Bob's fish?

Brin said, "Oh yes. We love the way he cooks the fish. Oh, and yes. This is my first group awakened. Most of these are my leaders. We also woke some of our water friends and fish. Dr. Groom helped me, and we turned them out into the lake."

"What kind of friends?"

Brin said, "You would call them porpoises, but ours are genetically enhanced and more evolved and smarter. We can communicate with them. They will protect our home world fish until they can populate. I bet you didn't know your porpoises were

339

introduced on Earth by our race thousands of years ago."

I said, "No, I didn't know that. I didn't know your race had ever been here."

Brin said, "We have been most everywhere in our ancient past. That is how we knew you lived here."

I was listening and watching also. I was proud of my crew. They weren't at all shy. They were mingling with the blue crew, and they all seemed to be getting along great. The novelty of a blue color was just that ... only a color.

Brin said, "I will watch over my crew for a while and get them in their quarters. But, first I must indoctrinate them in what we have been missing sexually for centuries." He smiled at that, and his eyes glazed over with the memory. "They will be pleasantly surprised, as I was. Afterwards, I'm sure they will want to learn first-hand from many of you humans. Meg and Peg thoroughly enjoyed learning true sex from you. I'm sure they want to be taught more."

Chapter 15
(Attack)

We continued to visit with many in the cafe and had our fill of the fish. When I noticed Nancy begin to nod off, I took the girls back to our quarters. The lingering smile never left Nancy's face. Sue, Bess and I kept kidding her, but nothing seemed to phase her. That made us laugh even more. It was just us. We hadn't been alone in quite some time, and I enjoyed our alone time. Even so, I knew Sue and Bess were still aroused from watching Nancy being chained. I didn't have to wait long. We all undressed each other and put Nancy to bed, cuddled in soft covers. She went to sleep almost immediately, and they then turned to me and sandwiched me between them. I pulled them tight and kissed them. There is something about having warm, soft breast pressed against your chest and warm thighs laying over your legs to stir your blood, but when fingers wrap around your dick, the fire blazes. I was instantly on fire, a fire I needed to quench. I decided, however, that I was not going to just let them satisfy themselves, I was going to take it to them ... both of them. I struggled out of their embrace to my knees behind them and grabbed Sue by the hips and pulled her to her knees. I then did the same to Bess. I gently pushed their heads down on their pillows with those beautiful heart-shaped, brown booties high. What a wonderful sight. Their booties were side by side, and I wrapped my arms around both, pulling

341

them tight together. I sank my face into the pussy of one then the other, letting my tongue wiggle and push deep. Both girls began their screaming ritual as I lapped at their nectar. Both booties shook with orgasmic excitement, but I couldn't wait anymore. I moved behind Sue and rubbed my hard cock up and down her wet slit then pushed deep into that wonderful tunnel. She began another orgasm even before I sank all the way inside her. While she was calming I pulled out and moved behind Bess and pushed deep into her. She screamed into her pillow. I grabbed her hips and drove deep, over and over. I was not gentle but insistent, fast and hard. I was slapping against her butt cheeks, but I was holding her so she couldn't collapse on the bed. Her pussy clamped down on my cock in an enormous orgasm. I had to push against her butt to pull my cock out. When it came free I moved back to Sue and slammed deep into her already quivering pussy. I gave her the same hard fast attention. When she climaxed this time her body slumped down to the bed, but I followed her down and remained inside, absorbing her quivers. I straddled her thighs and continued to pump my cock. As I did so I began rubbing her anus and slipped my thumb inside. I knew she liked that, and she certainly did. Her whole body went into convulsions with another gigantic orgasm. I pulled out and moved to Bess who had fallen to the bed. I straddled her thighs, spread her cheeks and pushed back inside her. She started screaming again as I entered her. I had been holding off my own climax, but I was losing my battle. I held her shoulders as I drove into her. I watched

342

her muscular cheeks take my pounding. This time when she climaxed and clamped down on my cock I was already pumping copious shots of semen deep into her womb. The clamping only accented the strength of my orgasm. I fell over her back trying to calm my own body's quivering but tried to brace my weight on my arms so I wouldn't crush her. After a few moments I was able to pull my cock out and roll between the girls. Both were exhausted, and so was I. I managed to pull the sheets up over us, and I quickly joined the sleeping trio.

As always the alarm seemed to go off way too early, but it is what it is. We all stumbled around and got a quick shower and dressed. Actually, I felt very refreshed by the time we went down in the elevator to Bob's Cafe. I looked forward to breakfast today. As was turning out to be a normal occurrence, we were all hungry, and I got my usual full plate of eggs, bacon, toast, grits and a tall glass of cold milk. Coffee would come later. As we ate I noticed many more of the blue crew in the cafe, mostly females. Brin must have worked late into the night reviving more of his crew. I also noticed that my crew had accepted them totally and were helping them adjust to the new surrounding and different food. Some seemed to really like it, while others were a little more reluctant. As they went through the line Bob was making suggestions to them. It seemed that things were going well.

We finished our breakfast and proceeded through the exit line to dump and deposit our trays. Bob was taking an active interest in any waste of food. Several times he commented to passersby, "If you're not going to eat it, don't take it. We can't be wasting food." He was not bashful, and I liked that. After all, many outside were already starving. We needed to be very respectful of our food, even though it wasn't wasted, it fed the hogs. It was too bad we couldn't help feed some outside, but that would be impossible. It would be suicide for us.

When we went into the conference room many had beaten us there, even Brin and some others of the blue team. By the time I got my coffee the others had arrived. For the first time the room was almost filled. I said, "Good morning, Brin. I see you have had a busy night reviving a lot of your crew. I also see you brought some of them with you and assume these are some of your leaders. Would you like to introduce them?"

Brin stood and said, "Yes, most of you know Meg and Peg. They are my satellite monitors and pilots. Trix here," pointing to a beautiful lady beside him with almost totally orange hair, "Is the head of my security. Flay heads up my engineering, and Blane runs our underwater food production, including fish herding. Tina is in charge of our medical. You would call her a doctor, but her duties extend to biological analysis and genetics."

I said, "Thanks Brin. We welcome you all. Now, does anyone have any problems or situations requiring immediate attention?"

Robert stood and said, "Well, thanks to the 'Blue Team', no offense meant with the name, we have been monitoring the satellite images. It's not of immediate concern to us yet, but I need to report that Oklahoma City, Ft. Smith and Tulsa, our clos-

344

est large cities, are all in flames from the riots and people are pouring out of the cities in alarming numbers. Tens of thousands have already died in the food riots, and outright race wars and fires. Anything that is believed to have any stores of food is already sacked and destroyed. These ravaging gangs have moved into the country and are decimating the farms. Some of the groups are combining and organizing into small armies and attacking any other group competing for food. Unfortunately, the stronger groups are based at or near National Guard facilities or military bases. They can't survive if they share, and they obviously have the armaments to defend themselves and their stores. Hell, they even have tanks, and they are using them."

I asked, "Is the government trying to help in any way?"

Robert said, "Mike, it is like this everywhere. In point of fact, it's worse in most places. It will run its course, like you predicted, and that is likely to take a couple of years. By then 80% or more of the population will likely be dead, and most of those left will be undesirables. The government has gone underground and will most likely stay there until the apocalypse is over."

I said, "What does the rest of the world look like?"

Robert said, "When the dollar collapsed the world economy crashed also. The world economy was extremely fragile to begin with, and it only took a slight push to topple it. So, I guess it is like this everywhere, at least in the developed countries. Many of the 3rd world countries would hardly noticed. They had little anyway. Actually, many could survive."

I said, "OK, we are on our own. Any suggestions or recommendations on what we should or can do?"

Brin stood to get everyone's attention and said, "Wars are won or lost before the first bullet is fired. We can't win by waiting and defending against an attacking army. We attack ... always. Wars are won by planning. Now we plan."

"We know eventually the armies will come here, so we limit their access and try to isolate ourselves. Hordes are coming out of the big cities, and we can't save them. There are simply too many of them. They will die or eventually join the armies we must fight. No, I suggest we try to drive the escaping hordes away from our location. We can do that by destroying key bridges that lead toward us. This won't stop the traffic, but it will sure slow them down and hopefully send them in other directions."

Jeremy said, "That makes a lot of sense, bridges like at Gore, Muskogee, Wagner, Ft. Smith and the bridge on I-40 crossing Lake Eufaula. Will the Rail Gun reach that far?"

Brin said, "All these targets are well within range of the roof mounted Rail Gun. The only limit is line of sight. We may not have line of sight on all those targets, but our fighter saucers also have Rail Guns, and we can make a night attack. I doubt we would be seen, since the Rail Gun has no sound or explosive signature."

346

I said, "Does everyone agree this is the course of action we should take?"

Affirmative nods from all passed around the table, and James said, "Maybe we should expand our reach beyond what we have discussed. I'm thinking that we should also be concerned about influx from the Dallas Ft. Worth metroplexes. These are far larger than the cities here. There aren't too many natural barriers like our rivers to take advantage of, but there are a couple of major highways leading out of that area that cross Lake Texhoma. I'm thinking we should take those out also."

I said, "Good idea. Brin, how can we help you with this plan?"

Brin said, "The Rail Gun uses a massive amount of electrical energy. So, we will need to switch over to our electrical generator for any extended use of the gun. Don't worry Jeremy, we configured it already to be compatible with your power requirements. Other than that, we could use someone to help us identify the targets, both on the roof and in our saucer. We can start as soon as we make the generator switchover."

Jeremy said, "Your generators are already installed and hooked up and ready to switch over and take our power load. Al did that the first day. I can also volunteer Dam Mark (Mark Springer) as the target spotter. When he was with the Army Corp he worked on most of the bridges and should be able to easily spot them, or at least know what to look for."

Brin said, "Excellent. Flay, get with this Al and finalize the connections and transfer of energy. Meg will operate the roof gun, and Peg will pilot our fighter saucer tonight. Find this Dam Mark and make arrangements."

I had to chuckle, along with a few others at the use of Dam Mark, but we all knew that that name would follow him in the community. I said, "Unless there are other pressing issues that can't wait, let's adjourn till tomorrow." None spoke up, so we all left to follow our own schedules. Jeremy introduced himself to Frey and took temporary charge of her. The immediate need was to get her with Al Martinez for the generator transfer, but I'm sure he would want to show her around his operations and get her involved. Robert did likewise with Trix. I also noticed that Bess went directly to Blane. She would be interested in showing him her operation, getting his ideas and learning more about what he planned. The doctors gathered around Tina to absorb medical knowledge from her and show her around the facilities. Plus, they still had many of the Blue Team to awaken. That kind of left us alone with nothing to do.

Nancy and I had, for the most part, completed our jobs in getting it all organized, put together and operational. Sue had paid all the bills, and with the mail and outside businesses totally defunct, she had done her job and more. Millions of dollars remained in now collapsed banks, but she had been buying gold, silver, platinum, and precious stones all along. So, the collapsed banks didn't hurt us as much as I had thought. She had many millions in hard assets in our vault. Once we weathered the storm we would be in great shape when civilization started again.

We went back to the cafe and waited over coffee. After a while we worked our way around the cafe, visiting with many. Suddenly, we heard a blood curdling scream coming from the clinic. We were standing by the stairs, so we rushed up and ran toward the clinic, from which the screams were coming from. When we burst through the doors of Dr. Groom's examining room we immediately all burst out laughing. Dr. Groom's dick was stuck in the pussy of one of the blue females freshly awakened. Obviously, he was up to his old tricks of taking advantage of women on his examining table, but unfortunately this recently awakened blue female had not yet been indoctrinated by Brin. She simply felt a dick in her and milked it of its seed. Dr. Groom had not been told about the blue's method of sex, but he was quickly learning.

Sue said, "Serves him right."

The other doctors had rushed in first and were looking concerned at his situation and puzzled at our laughter. I briefly explained what was happening and that she would release him after she had his semen. Once they understood, they smiled, knowing from experience what Dr. Groom had done.

We left them alone to wrestle Dr. Grooms dick out of his patient. As we were leaving we got word that the alien generators were operational and ready. We rushed to the roof to watch the activities. Dam Mark was already there sighting through the targeting telescope, while Meg sat at the controls of the Rail Gun.

Mark said, "OK, we're sighted in on the bridge crossing the upper Ft. Gibson lake, but let me give you the signal during a lull in the traffic. I hate to kill people just trying to escape. Now!"

Meg fired the Rail Gun.

Immediately Mark said, "Wow! Most of the bridge just disintegrated. Now let me find the Arkansas River crossing east of Muskogee." After a few minutes he said, "Ready. Fire! It's gone. There is a crossing on the lower end of Ft. Gibson lake, but we will have to leave it alone. That crossing is over the dam. We don't want to destroy that one."

It took him a while longer to find the bridge west of Gore crossing the Arkansas River, but he finally did. He was concerned with a direct line of sight. Finally he was satisfied and said, "Ready. Fire now!"

With the destruction of this last bridge we were, more or less, cut off from traffic coming from west of the Arkansas River but not all. The rest would have to be done from the saucer after dark. We were about to leave the roof when Peg came up with a new problem. Flay had just handed her a tablet device showing satellite images.

Flay said, "We were too late on the northern bridges. I'm tracking an army caravan, including tanks, en route toward Camp Gruber. The caravan evidently crossed before we took out the Muskogee bridge, but most disturbing is the makeup of this caravan. It includes many of the Tulsa gangs spawned up during the riots. This caravan doesn't appear military, only military led."

Mike asked, "Does anyone have an idea what their intent is?"

Robert said, "Well, Camp Gruber is the designated FEMA emergency food distribution center. The army would know that, and I think this army is invading to get the food. I believe their intent is totally hostile, but we will know soon."

Brin said, "They could also be trying to combine with Camp Gruber, but either way the army caravan is our enemy. They will come for our food sooner or later. Should they intend to attack Camp Gruber, maybe we should let them fight it out and kill each other. Both are our potential enemies. Remember, this is why we destroyed the bridges ... to keep them out."

I said, "Do we know if Camp Gruber is actually trying to help the local residence?"

Robert said, "There are many cars and trucks there, so I do believe they are trying to help, but we don't know how much food they have stockpiled and how long and how many they can take care of. The FEMA officers were certainly trying to confiscate food from everyone, including us, so they probably do have a major stockpile."

I said, "If they are taking in the locals, this is good for us, because they aren't trying to come here. If the army is trying to invade Camp Gruber, maybe we should help defend them and keep them alive. They could be our first line of defense from the refugees and other gangs."

Brin said, "Looking at it that way, I agree. Let's see what happens when they meet."

Meg's assistant came to the roof and handed Meg a video tablet. Meg took it immediately, took a moment to scan it, then said, "It looks like Camp

351

Gruber is taking up a defensive position, preparing to repel an attack. It also looks like the approaching army is repositioning for an attack. It appears to be an invasion."

I said, "Very well. It's war then, but let's wait until the first shots are fired."

Mark had already gone to the targeting telescope and was viewing the battlefield. He said, "They have five tanks lining up. I'm sighted in on the first tank. Ouch! They fired!"

We huddled around Meg to view Camp Gruber and saw the first explosion. They were targeting the helicopters, and we saw the first one explode. The others were trying to take off.

I said, "Go ahead and take out the tanks." Meg immediately fired and we watched a tank turn instantly to dust. They continued to target and fire until all five tanks no longer existed. Shortly afterwards several helicopters swooped down on the army and fired upon the gathered invading troops. They cut down many until they were met with rockets from hand-held launchers. Two helicopters exploded in mid-air before they could retreat. I said, "Keep taking out trucks and groups of soldiers, anything else you can see." We watched the damage inflicted as truck after truck disappeared, and in some instances, crowded areas of the line sprang into dust. The invading rabble turned and ran, followed closely by the returning helicopters. The helicopters were relentless and pursued the running gangs, killing all they could find. They knew there was no choice, that they would have to continue to deal with any survivors. I'm sure some escaped, but not a lot.

Robert said, "I'm getting a call from that US Marshal I gave the radio to."

We gathered around Robert and heard, "This is Marshal Brady. Is this Robert? Was that you guys?"

Robert said, "Yes, this is Robert, and yes, it was us."

Marshal Brady said, "Thanks. We thought we were goners. Colonel Kline offers his thanks, also. The colonel and I would like to come meet with you."

Robert looked at me for approval, which he got, and said, "Come on over. We'll leave word at the gate to let you in. They will give you directions." He then said to me, "I don't guess it matters now if we let the secret out about the Blue Team."

I just shrugged and said, "Your right. It's not likely to concern anyone at this point."

I didn't believe it would take long for them to get here, so we went to the conference room to wait. Since we intended to let it be known about the Blue Team, at least to our new friends, I motioned for Brin and Meg and Peg to follow us down. We had just gathered and was working on our coffee when the front gate called on the radio to let us know they had passed them. Nancy and I watched at the rail as the two of them came in and went to the security desk. The guards checked them over for weapons and disarmed them before sending them to the elevator. I wanted Nancy there, because the marshal would more easily recognize her. When the elevator doors opened we were waiting and introduced ourselves. We then led them into the conference room. I could tell they were duly impressed with our facilities, but when they saw Brin and his girls they stared in disbelief. Even though they obviously were more than curious about them, I chose to wait and not offer any explanation. I said, "You asked for this meeting, so you have the floor."

Marshal Brady said, "Well, first of all, Colonel Kline and I wanted to thank you in person for saving us. They were about to do some serious damage to us, and there was little we could have done. Of course, we would have fought back, but they had the heavy power and ground to air portable missiles. It was hard to believe that they intended to attack. At first we thought they wanted to merge with us, but that hope vanished fast. When we saw the tanks start to disintegrate I knew it was you. I've seen it before. By the way, I told the colonel everything that happened at the gate and my part in it. I think he suspected, but after society devolved it didn't seem to matter anymore. Those FEMA agents were assholes anyway. They did, however, gather a lot of food stores, which we now have. We can hold out quite a while, even with all the refugees, and there are several hundred of them. I can tell you that we aren't nearly as comfortable as your group though."

Colonel Kline interrupted, "We don't want to compete with you. We hope we can be partners in defense. It happened once, it can happen again."

I said, "We came together as a survival group, and that is what we intend to do ... survive. As

354

long as you don't try to attack us or take our food stores we won't bother you. We helped you because they were our enemy too. I'm glad your group didn't go rogue like many of the others. You are actually trying to do some good. We like that."

Colonel Kline said, "That sounds like a truce to me, which I am happy to honor. Unfortunately, the danger is not over. From what I can tell from our radio communications, what's left of it, and incoming refugees of course, most of the big cities have fallen to gangs, and they are spilling out into the country. That means they will eventually show up here."

I stopped him and explained what we had done with the bridges and those we intended to demolish tonight. He knew as well as I that it wasn't a total isolation but certainly a big help. He actually began to smile.

Colonel Kline got around to the Blue Team and asked, "May I ask," pointing at Brin and the girls, "who these people are?"

I said, "They are half of our survival team. They are new to Earth, but they are human and our brothers and sisters. I guess you could call them illegal immigrants, but they belong here now. Do you have a problem with that?"

A startled colonel said, "No, not at all. I was just curious. I'm also assuming they are the source of the weapons you used against the army, Marshal Brady told me he had seen that weapon's used before. Can I also assume that you downed our helicopter?"

I said, "Yes. You sent it to assist the FEMA agent's attempt to steal our food, but we used a different weapon that only disabled it. We also retrieved your men and called your base to notify you where to pick them up."

"Thank you for that," he said.

"By the way," I said, "Are you set up for long term there? I mean, are you set up to grow crops for food for the future and support life there? If not, we can help with equipment and seed for your own crops. We prepared ourselves here for life after the apocalypse."

The colonel said, "We have food to last us quite a while, even with the many refugees, but little else. For long term recovery we would welcome your help, however, we have few women to begin life again beyond the current generation. Most of our military men were National Guard. We were called up at the start of the collapse, and our families were left behind unprotected. We didn't know it would get this bad this quick, and most of our families were killed in the looting and riots. We saved some of our families but not nearly enough. So, we get our satisfaction by saving others."

I said, "We already knew that you were taking in refugees. Otherwise, we wouldn't have helped you. Nancy, do you think there are any concentration of women we could salvage for them?"

Nancy said, "Wow! That's a tall task, but we can scan the satellite images to see. Actually, the only groups of only women that might have survived would probably be nuns in a convent way off the beaten path. That would pose difficult to per-

356

suade them to break their vows of chastity, however. Meg and I can search around."

Colonel Kline said, "Am I to understand that you have satellite feeds?"

I said, "Yes we do. You can thank my brother Brin and his team for that. They launched them. That's how we knew the army was coming, and we will let you know if something else is coming. Just keep your radio on."

Robert interrupted me saying, "Mike, we have a situation at the front gate. There is a group of herders driving a fairly large number of cattle down the access road."

I said, "OK. We better go check it out. Colonel, we can meet often if you like, but we have to go now."

Colonel Kline said, "Thank you. We have learned that we have friends here. I'm sure we will meet again soon."

With that Nancy, Robert and I followed the colonel and marshal out and to the front gate. Security was holding two people on horseback, a male and female. I said, "What do you want here. This is private property."

The man said, "I'm Tom Johnson and this is my sister, Betty. The five of us are all that remains of our family. We want to live under your protection, and brought thirty-five head of cattle to contribute and several horses. We brought other food too and can live on our own if we have protection." I really didn't know what to say. They asked nicely, and we could use more horses and cattle. I looked to Nancy to see her reaction.

357

Surprising, Nancy came up with the perfect solution when she said, "You know we do have a couple of nice empty ranch houses on the north property we bought ... barns and pastures too. We could let them move in there. It should be safe there."

I said, "Were you attacked? And, who are the other people with you?"

Tom said, "Yes, my father's plan was to round-up our cattle and drive them over here and ask for protection. They were already being rustled and killed by refugees and some roaming gangs, so my father figured this was the only way to save them. He also figured we would come under attack sooner or later also. We knew about you. We live close enough to watch you build this fortress and know you have strong security."

"Anyway, while we were out rounding up the cattle, a small gang attacked and killed our father, mother and our youngest sibling. He was only twelve. We heard the shots and came running, but we were too late to save them. We did manage to kill some of the gang and the others ran off, but we knew they would come back. We continued with our father's plan, and here we are. We offer you our cattle for a secure place to live. There are five of us siblings, two men and three women. Our youngest sister is following us with a tractor pulling a trailer with all our belongings, food and supplies."

I said, "We will give it a try. Drive your cattle straight through. You will find cattle already grazing in the north pasture, so turn them loose there. It's fenced, so don't worry. Pick a ranch house and unload your things there, then put your horses up at

358

the stable. Tell cowboy we said it's all right, and that we asked her to bring you to the Castle when you're done. We'll put you up there tonight and get you checked out by our doctor, while we decide how best to handle you and how you can interface with the group."

Tom said, "Thank you. We welcome the opportunity to join with you in any way we can. We will work hard to earn your trust. I promise you won't regret it."

We left and returned to the Castle, where we were immediately met by a very excited Sue and Meg.

Sue said, "Meg and I researched the convents in the area and focused the satellite images in on them to check on their status. Mike, these dehumanized gangs have no respect for them and almost all have been decimated. We only found one untouched, and it won't last long. We identified a fairly large mob gang moving in that direction. The convent is located a good distance north of Oklahoma City in Piedmont in a rural area, but we only have a few hours at best before it is attacked. Brin suggests that we can take his large craft there and defend them long enough to persuade them to join us, some of them anyway. What do you think?"

I noticed that Brin had come up and was listening. I said, "Brin, do you feel comfortable coming out of hiding with your craft and going there?"

Brin said, "Yes, I do. Your government has gone underground. I don't think they will come to investigate. If they do, we can defend ourselves."

I made a quick decision and said, "Very well, let's do it. Sue, call James to look after the cattle herders I invited here, and call Marshal Brady and ask him to come here as quick as possible and come in full uniform and armed. Also call Robert and have him come in uniform with JJ and a few other security officers. I want us to look as official as possible. Oh, by the way, Nancy. You will be doing the talking for us." Her eyes slightly bulged but she nodded.

Within an hour we were all gathered and descending down the interlock tunnel toward the Dome. Many were seeing the spacecraft for the first time and were wide-eyed but followed Brin down the hatch into the craft. I must admit, I was awed as well, but I tried to act like this was just a normal occurrence. We entered into a large circular open space. The only visible apparatus was a central control panel. Meg and Peg took positions at the controls. An invisible panel lit up in the air like a Christmas tree and a large video display came to life showing a digital outline of the ship, the Dome and surrounding obstacles. I felt a slight vibration and purr of equipment as it started. I then felt the clamps click release from the Dome and a slight floating feeling as we began to move. It was amazing watching the movement of the ship on the digital monitor. The girls steered the ship clear and to the surface. It didn't seem to matter if we were underwater or not, but once we surfaced the display changed to dual images, three actually. The digital layout remained, while the rest of the display converted to visual images forward and below. I took all this in passing, because the ship took off at a fast pace, but we were not tossed around with the acceleration, even though most of us were free standing without any restraints.

Brin noticed my surprise and said, "We have artificial gravity in the ship that overrides outside gravity. We could fly upside down and you would still be standing as you are. Don't worry. You are all safe."

The twins steered the craft away quickly, so we couldn't be tracked easily. Surprisingly, it only took us about ten minutes to approach the coordinates Mark had provided.

Brin said, "We may be too late. It looks like the mob is already here."

I looked at the display of the down view and saw a small caravan moving toward the convent with a few empty pickups already at the convent driveway. As I watched I could see puffs of smoke coming from rifles in the caravan. That's all the excuse I needed and said, "Well, it looks like they declared war against us. I guess we should fire back."

Brin smiled and waved his hand before the display, activating a crosshatch indicator on the image. He then moved his hand along a smaller image, and the crosshatch moved on the display to focus on a target. His thumb flicked and the pickup exploded. He continued to move the crosshatch and flick his thumb all along the caravan until all were disintegrated. Brin pointed down, and the twins landed the spacecraft in the front lawn area. Brin then led us down through the ship to a hatch and out the lower open ramp. The armed security fanned out in front of us as we reached the ground to protect us from any mob attack, but we saw none. We went toward the front door without any encounters, but as we entered the building we heard screaming coming from down the hall. We rushed toward the screaming and burst through a set of double doors. Inside were six men in various degrees of undress. Most had a struggling sister in their arms with obvious intent of rape. Two of the mob were holding the other sisters at gunpoint, with two of the sisters unmoving and bleeding on the floor. Robert, in obvious rage at what he saw, opened fire on the two armed gang members, killing them instantly. The other four released their struggling sisters and scrambled for their guns, but they never reached them. Our security cut them down with a vengeance.

Robert barked, "Are there more of them?"

An elderly sister, assumably in charge, said, "I'm not sure. These men just came busting in, but I don't think there are others. They were evil men. Thank you for saving my sisters."

Robert sent some of our security to look for any others, while instructing others to drag the dead out. No other of the gang were discovered, but they took up guard positions just in case.

Nancy spoke then saying, "You are actually extremely lucky that we came to protect you this time, because most of your other convents haven't been so lucky. They have been looted and destroyed already, and most likely many of the sisters have been raped, like was about to happen here, killed or imprisoned as sex slaves." This brought gasps from the gathered sisters. "This is the fate you will be presented with sooner or later, because we can't come again. We came this once to offer some of you a chance to survive. I'll just put it out to you and let you decide."

"We are representatives from two survival groups in eastern Oklahoma. We have banded together and have defenses against these roaming mobs and gangs, as you put it, 'evil men'. We also have stored food and the ability to survive for several years and begin civilization over again after this evil runs its course. What we don't have are enough childbearing females for the next generations. Simply put, we offer a home and future life for the childbearing age sisters here. I'm sorry we can't take all of you, but our food and facilities are limited. Everything we do is focused on the future and surviving and repopulating."

The sisters gasped again and the elder sister said, "You can't be serious. These sisters have given vows of chastity to God. You are asking them to break their vows. The answer is an emphatic NO!"

Nancy said, "I understand your concern, but I ask you to consider what would have happened to all of you if we had not stopped the mob outside and in here. Most of you would be dead, or even worse, and your order destroyed. At a very minimum, they would steal all your food, which would certainly kill you in the long run. More likely, most of you would be raped, some killed outright, and some would become sex slaves to the mob of evil men.

Think about your vows of chastity in this case. Still, if your answer is no, we will leave."

The sister said, "We must believe God will surely save us."

Nancy said, "God didn't save the other convents and sisters, but just maybe God sent us to save some of you and give you a new purpose. Think about that. The sisters joining us will survive and still have a good life, although a more traditional role. We have been taught that in the beginning God made women to help populate this world, and that basic role hasn't changed. In point of fact, tens of millions of humans have already died in this apocalypse, and many more will die before things begin to get better. The original role of women is now even more necessary for our recovery. Maybe God is saving many of you for this purpose. Discuss it and give us your answer quickly, so we can continue our search if necessary."

The elder sister, whom I assumed to be the Mother Superior, looked thoughtful then said, "Can we have a few moments to discuss this among ourselves before I give you our answer?"

Nancy said, "Of course, but remember time is short for us to be able to save others of your kind, possibly too late."

The sister led the others into the sanctuary for a discussion. I had no idea what they were thinking, but Nancy had done an excellent job of explaining the situation and options. After about thirty minutes some came filing back in. Many had taken off somewhere. I suddenly noticed that none of the younger ones came back in, which made me hopeful.

The sister said, "You have provided a reasonable and convincing argument for us, and we believe you. We have decided that it IS God's will that you came to us. We have decided to accept your offer of physical salvation for our younger sisters. They have been released from their vows and will no longer be sisters and have gone to change into civilian clothing. They will be here shortly. The rest of us believe we will be of little sexual temptation to other gangs that may come, due to our age. Our survival odds here will be better with the younger girls gone, and their odds of survival will be assured. We will hide what food we have. We may be able to survive, and if we do not, that will also be God's will. I do have one request, however. Many of the sisters have experienced sex before they became nuns, but we have five sisters that are vestal virgins. They don't have a clue what they are getting into. These sisters have lived a very sheltered life. They will need special care and treatment in the beginning from someone with the patience to show them the way of life."

I'm sure my eyes bugged out when Nancy said, "Mike here" pointing at me, "is my mate. He will introduce the virgin girls to sex. He is understanding and patient."

The sister looked directly at me, hard, and said, "You be gentle with my girls."

All I could do was nod and say, "Yes Ma'am."

I knew there were quite a few sisters in this convent, but I didn't know the actual count. About

365

25 of the ladies came back in wearing normal clothing. Many were dressed quite fashionable. The sister took the five virgins and brought them to Nancy. Silent looks of appeal and understanding passed between them.

The sisters, now simply young ladies, ranged in age from about 19 to 35; and they were, for the most part, appealing, if not beautiful. But, the five virgins were all young, less than 25, and stunning. Nancy looked at me and gave me a mischievous smile. Well, it was her fault, since she volunteered me.

That left another 25 or so still in habits. Nancy said, "I think you have made a wise decision. They will be safe with us. I wish we could take you all, but what we are building is for the future of our civilization. Can we leave you some guns for your protection?"

The sister said, "No guns, but thanks. We all understand your limitations. We will be fine. It's enough to know our younger sisters will be safe. God knows what he is doing, and we will survive."

Brin interrupted, drawing all eyes toward him, "Mike, we must leave. Another small caravan is approaching, and we must be in the air to take them out."

The elder sister looked hard at Brin, but she said nothing. I personally think she didn't want to know. I welcomed her silence, because I didn't want to take the time to explain him.

I said, "Sister, we will take this approaching mob out before we leave, but do hide your food as soon as you can. If others come tell them your food

366

has already been stolen. Hopefully, they will leave you alone." She nodded, and I continued, "Let's hurry group and load into the craft."

Security led our expanded group quickly out and rushed us into Brin's ship. Shots were already being fired at us as we lifted into the air. Meg and Peg wasted little time getting us high enough for Brin to unleash his rail-gun. The caravan was indeed small, and they disintegrated quickly. We then rushed back toward the Castle and Dome.

Chapter 16
(The Virgin Sacrifices)

The five girls, all of them actually, were wide-eyed from the very first, but the eyes seemed to get wider once we entered the ramp underneath the space saucer, even wider as we traveled back to the Dome. I was afraid all the eyes might pop out when we entered the water and submerged. Their panic seemed to diminish and convert to astonishment as we exited into the crystal Dome. A school of fish swam passed, herded by dolphins and a very fast Blue Team swimmer, which seemed to capture everyone's attention. We then steered the group to the interlocks. The group was so large we had to break them up into two groups. Nancy waited to escort the second group through. Eventually, we made it to the elevators and started ascending in groups in the two elevators. Nancy and the last group finally joined the growing assemble, who by now were drawing stares from everyone in the cafe.

Nancy said, "Mike, I called ahead to have Bob cook enough food for this group. I suggest we eat. I also called Dr. Groom to have his team ready to draw blood samples while they eat."

I said, "Good thinking. That's why I like you." I smiled when I said that, but it didn't stop Nancy from giving me a punch on the arm. "Marshal Brady, do you have a doctor at your camp?"

Marshal Brady said, "Yes, we have doctors and a clinic there. We also have some buses to transport the ladies. I'll call the colonel and let him know the success of our outing so he can prepare for their arrival."

I pulled him to the side so we could speak unheard and said, "I don't think I have to tell you to go slow with these ladies. Give them time to adjust."

Marshal Brady said, "No Sir. We will treat them like the angels they are and let them set the pace. I also want to thank you for your help. We owe you a great deal."

I said, "The five will be staying here for a couple of days. You heard my instructions."

The marshal smiled hugely and said, "Yeah, tough job. Need any help?"

I smiled back and said, "I better not. You heard Nancy and the Mother Superior. I will just have to suffer through it alone." He laughed.

Bob came rushing over and started guiding the ladies toward the buffet. Lots of hungry eyes studied the food he had lined out for them. None of the ex-sisters were plump or even slightly chubby. I'm sure their standard diet was just enough to keep them alive. This would be a major treat for them, especially having been cooked by a master chef like Bob. He only had to invite them once. They piled in with gusto. I also realized I was famished. The cafe was busy, but tables cleared out to make room for the ladies. As I looked around the cafe I was heartened to see Blue Team females dispersed throughout the population, many paired up with men from my team. I also noticed that Nancy, although next to me, had ushered the five virgins next to her or across from her. Sue was at the other end of them. They were like bookends. I knew Nancy took her responsibility seriously and intended to look after them. I didn't know how I was going to service them all but left it to Nancy to work out the details. Hell, I hadn't even been introduced to them yet.

As we ate, the doctors and nurses went through the group taking names and drawing vials of blood. I noticed that Nancy had them start with the five. I guess she wanted to make sure they were healthy. I don't think she was concerned about STDs, since these five were virgins, but she was being careful about something. She spoke to Dr. Groom, and I saw him nod.

Curiosity got the best of me, and I leaned close and whispered, "What are you worried about?"

Nancy smiled and whispered back, "Sisters are famous for taking care of sick people others won't deal with like TB, HIV, serious viral infections, even leprosy. The odds are good these won't have any of those infections, but I think it wise to make sure."

All I could say was, "Oh, okay."

While we continued to eat, a pretty, young girl of maybe 16 came up behind Nancy and tapped her on the shoulder. When Nancy turned, the girl asked if she could speak to her privately for a moment. Nancy got up and they walked over in an open area. I could see them talking back and forth for a while. When they came back Nancy grabbed a vacant chair and slipped it in beside her and the young girl sat down in our group.

370

Nancy leaned toward me and said, "This is the youngest sibling of the family that brought the cattle. She heard we were giving a course in Sex 101 for virgins and wants to join it. I let her." When she saw the shock on my face she added, "Don't worry, I have some Viagra."

Damn, six virgins? I would definitely need some Viagra. I hope Nancy realizes that sex with a virgin is painful for the man too. Now I was starting to get more scared.

Nancy said, "I have a plan. Trust me. When you finish eating, why don't you go on up to our apartment and shower and try to get a nap. Us girls need to talk."

It was after dark, but it was still early in the evening. Still, it was Nancy's show, so I did exactly as she said. I took a shower and settled in for a nap. I must have been tired, because I went to sleep almost immediately. I don't know how long I slept, but it must have been several hours. I woke up to Nancy's scent and warm kisses. My arms wrapped around her in response, and my kisses got more intense.

Nancy said, "Hold on Trigger." You're going to get busy soon. I just want to talk to you first. Sue, Bess and I have been talking with the six young ladies about sex and losing their virginity. I have to admit that we have turned a shy and fearful group of young ladies into an excited and fired up group, anxious to experience sex for the first time. They have all been cleared by Dr. Groom, They have showered, and even let Bess groom their bushes. That was a sight to see. They are ready. Are

371

you ready?" I just nodded. Nancy laughed and said, "I bet you are, but remember there are six of them, so you will have to pace yourselves. I will help by directing some of the activities. Before we get started take this Viagra." I did.

While Nancy talked I noticed she was lying beside me naked. I looked toward the door and saw that Sue and Bess were also naked, and I glimpsed other naked bodies behind them. This was getting exciting already but scary, too.

Nancy said, "Sue and Bess will come in first to set an example for the others. Just spend a few moments with each. I'll direct the girls when the time is right. OK?" I just nodded.

I didn't know what was about to happen, but I was game. Nancy moved to the end of the bed when Sue came in. Although I still had a sheet covering me, Sue lay over me and started kissing me passionately. I responded in kind. Our tongues mingled as her hands held my face. This went on for a few moments then she moved to the other bed when Bess came in and lay over me to continue the kissing, my hands sliding up and down over her back and taunt butt cheeks. After a few minutes Bess also moved to the other bed.

Nancy said to the young ladies standing naked in the door, "Ladies come on in, introduce yourselves and kiss Mike hello."

The first lady came in very naked and very beautiful. She had short black hair and deep black eyes. Her firm breasts and brown, hard nipples pointed up. I could tell she was shy, but at the same time she appeared to be aroused. Nancy was correct, my girls had gotten them excited and ready.

She crawled up on the bed and pressed her warm breast on my chest and said, "Hello Mike, my name is Tina." She then kissed me, softly and tentatively at first, then passionately. My arms wrapped around her, and I felt my cock growing hard. Just as I was beginning to really get into it, Nancy said, "Tina, that's enough for now. Go get on the other bed." When Tina's breasts lifted, my chest longed for the warmth. I sat up and propped pillows behind me so I could enjoy the view better.

The next young lady came in. Her skin was white as alabaster, and she had large breasts for such a small lady. Her bright pink nipples stood out like fingers. I remembered seeing her before, but I didn't remember the bright red hair that seemed to flow around her breasts, accenting them even more. She said, "My name is Kathy. I want to thank you for helping us with this." I thought, *"Are you fucking kidding me? It's my pleasure!"* But, what I said out loud was, "You're welcome, Kathy." I even tried to say it without leering or drooling. She smiled and tossed her leg and thigh over mine and straddled me. I felt the warmth of her breasts before I felt her soft lips kissing me. I wanted to attack her, but I kept remembering the Mother Superior telling me to be gentle with her girls. I restrained myself, but I got passionately into the kiss. I almost lost it when she slipped her sweet tongue deep into my mouth. A mental picture slipped into my mind of Bess teaching them how to kiss. I knew my Bess

373

was deeply involved in their training. Far too soon, Nancy shooed her to the other bed.

Like Kathy, Karrie introduced herself, followed her lead and straddled me. This one was a hot looking blonde, and she was already extremely aroused from watching. She went after me with a hungry thirst. She was ready already. Her hard nipples and soft breast rubbed hard into my chest, and her kisses smothered my face. I could feel her hot pussy rubbing on my cock, even through the sheet. Nancy didn't let this get out of hand and moved her to the other bed fairly quickly.

Tammy was the next girl. She was a petite brunette with small but firm breasts and really shy, but she did like the others. Her blush lit up her pretty face as she slowly straddled me. Even straddling me she couldn't bring herself to initiate the first kiss, so I gently took her face in my hands and kissed her. My kiss broke her shy dam, and she delved into our embrace with gusto, seeking my lips and tongue. Nancy allowed Tammy to work herself into excitement before sending her to the other bed.

Sarah was the fifth, former sister. She was a tall ebony beauty, with short springy curls. Sarah wasted no time at all jumping on me. After her speedy introduction her full, soft lips immediately pressed to mine, caressing and hot. The heat from her obviously steamy pussy radiated through me, as she slowly ground her pussy over my cock. This girl was hot in more ways than one. Nancy allowed her to work off her shyness (Ha) for a few moments, then rushed her away.

I don't know what I really expected from these ex-sisters, maybe extreme shyness, even strong reluctance, but these girls were reacting completely opposite from what I expected. These girls were hungry for sex. I think it helped that they were together in a group for support. I'm sure Nancy and the girls and I would eventually talk about how they had inspired them to this point. Don't get me wrong, I'm glad they did. I just couldn't figure how they did it.

Nancy led the last girl in by the hand and said, "Mike, this is Sissy. She is a little shy, but she wants to join this indoctrination group."

I was shocked with her youth, even though she was abundantly mature in appearance, stunningly mature and abundantly endowed. Sissy was a beautiful natural, platinum blond, which was evident from her manicured platinum blond bush. I couldn't resist asking, "Are you of legal Age?"

Nancy answer, "Mike, she is eighteen, but even so, remember there is no legal age anymore, and Sissy is obviously mature enough and wants this."

Sissy's shyness flashed to instant anger and said, "I know what I want, and I'm old enough!"

I regretted my comment, and even though I still had my doubts, Nancy had said she was 18, and Nancy was right about the law, they didn't exist now. Additionally, my small head reminded me she was indeed beautiful. I said, "Sorry. I'm sorry I said that. You are obviously mature enough, and you are very beautiful." Sissy's anger flashed back to a shy, embarrassed blush at my comment. "I just wanted to make sure this is what you want."

Sissy said, "I want it."

I smiled and held out my hand to her. She took my hand, and I gently guided her on the bed and pulled her muscular leg over me to settle down. My arms wrapped around her and pulled her close to my face. I leaned forward to gently kiss her soft lips. She didn't know how to react but soon began to respond as I nibbled her lips, and she eventually kissed me back. I pulled her against me as we kissed and felt her breast spread out on my chest. I could even feel her nipples getting hard. Sissy's body began to quiver, and our kisses turned more passionate. I felt her hot pussy on my cock begin to slide up and down it. That is as far as we got before Nancy took over.

Nancy told the girls we were moving into phase two and to gather around my bed, which they quickly did. She asked, "How many of you have seen an adult man's cock?" All shook their heads. She then reached up and slowly pulled my sheet down revealing my already hard cock. I heard some gasps and Ohhhs as they all stared intently. They all leaned as close as they could, as Nancy slipped her fingers around my cock and started stroking it. She talked about the physical anatomy of my cock and even cupped my balls. Actually, I was somewhat embarrassed and felt like a lab experiment, but no one was even looking at my reaction. They were all interested in my cock, and I began to appreciate the attention. After all, it was all about them, not me. Nancy said, "I want each of you to hold it and explore it. Get used to it." They all tried to reach for it at once but voluntarily began to share it. Damn, this was so arousing, and I had to think of many other things to keep from climaxing. They explored it thoroughly and even hefted my testicles. They kept talking and asking questions as they held it and stroked it, but I hardly heard a word due to my arousal. After everyone had a turn stroking my cock Nancy said, "Let me show you a way to arouse a man for sex. We won't share him this way right now, because he would probably climax, and we need to keep him hard for additional phases of instruction." With that she scooted up and took my cock in her mouth and took it quickly down her throat. I loved that, but she only did it a couple of times. She knew I would erupt if she did it longer. The girls watched intently to what she was doing.

Nancy told the girls we were moving into phase three and had them lay side by side on the edge of the bed. She went down the line and lifted and spread their legs. She had them lay back and close their eyes. Nancy motioned for me to join her on the side of the bed. What a beautiful view: six sexy pussies stared back at me. I was so hard, but Nancy wouldn't turn me free yet. She pushed me down to my knees and smiled down at me. There was no need to tell me more. I began licking the first pussy I came to. It was Kathy, I could tell from the manicured red bush and pink pussy lips. I tried to go slow, but my excitement pushed me to devour that sweet pussy. Her moans told me all I needed to know. I let my tongue play inside and flick over her little, hard clit. When I began sucking it, she began a long squeal and climax, flooding her nectar over my tongue.

I moved to the next one, which was Sissy. I took special care to bring her along slowly, plus I enjoyed playing with her sweet pussy. Bess had groomed her pussy well, leaving a triangle of platinum blond hair to play with. Her nectar was sweet to taste. Her moans were slow to come, but when they did, they were loud. I rubbed my nose up and down over her nub as my tongue licked the length of her pussy. The quivering started just as she released a strong squirt of fluid. She lay back trying to catch her breath as I moved to the next one.

Tammy was the really shy one, but when my tongue slid through her wet pussy she forgot about being shy. She began humping my tongue and mouth and came almost immediately. The juice flooded my face as she screamed her climax. I heard moans before I got to the next girl and almost laughed out loud when I saw Bess working over Kathy. Her face and tongue were rooted in Kathy's pussy. I bet Bess had been fantasizing about these pussies since she groomed them. Now Bess was getting her satisfaction.

Sarah was easy to identify. She was the only ebony in the group. Bess had left me a surprise. When I spread her thighs I saw Sarah's pussy lips were clean shaven, but Bess had left a heart shaped bush above her pussy. The hair had been left fairly long, and I buried my face in it. It was soft and springy and very erotic. I know she felt my hot breath on her pussy lips and had begun a low guttural moan that grew in intensity as I slid my tongue between her lips to probe inside. Her inner thighs began to quaver, and I knew she was already close.

When I started flicking my tongue on her clit she let loose and clamped her thighs down tight on my head. I really take great satisfaction in pleasing, and I knew she enjoyed this greatly. After she relaxed I moved on to the next young lady.

I remembered Karrie. She was the hot blonde, hot in several ways. Bess had left a small landing strip and arrow of blond hair pointing to her pussy, but I had no trouble finding it. This girl was ready, so I skipped the building up and devoured her pussy. Karrie screamed and kept screaming through two orgasms.

The last girl on the bed was the first girl that came in the room, Tina, the oldest of the group. The olive complexion was appealing to me. I remembered her pitch black eyes and hair, and Bess had left a diamond shape bush for me to play with. I let my tongue play in it for a while before diving in. I'm not sure if moans described what was coming out of her mouth. It sounded more like a modulated hum that grew in pitch as my tongue played between her lips, but it definitely turned into a high squeal as I nibbled and sucked on her clit. Of all six girls, she was the only one that grabbed my head and pulled me deeper into her humping pussy. I loved it. Her squeal lasted all the way through her orgasm. I couldn't resist any longer and stood and guided my steel hard cock between her lips and gently pushed inside. I felt her intact hymen blocking me. I knew the combination of my large size, their extremely tight vaginas, and the existence of a hymen could be painful to both of us, but I figured it would be easier for both of us to just get it done.

That's what I did. I drove in with a single stab and sank deep. I was so hard I think I could have punched a hole in a brick. I kept it inside and deep through her scream, enjoying the heat and snugness. When her scream died out I began pulling it out and slowly back in. Her humming started again, so I began slowly pumping my shaft in and out. When the screaming didn't start again I continued. Her legs flayed out wide, giving me total access. I leaned forward to find her breasts and nipples. When she began hunching me I speeded up. Soon I was pounding hard into her wet pussy. I was getting really aroused and felt my climax building, but she beat me. Her pussy clamped down on my cock so hard I couldn't pull it out. I had to wait for her body and pussy muscles to stop their convulsing. Damn it felt good.

Nancy said, "Mike, don't forget you have five more."

She was right. I let my main head engage and pulled out of the warm pussy I wanted to lose myself in and went down the line. My main head told me to take care of the painful part while my cock remained hard as a metal ramrod. Bess was in the way, so I moved back to the first girl, Kathy. She had recovered and saw me coming and spread her legs wide. I wasted no time, but I didn't want to cause her any unnecessary pain if I could help it. I rubbed the head of my cock up and down between her slick pussy lips. She was so hot. I plunged into her sudden and sank deep. She wasn't able to take it all before I hit bottom, but she certainly took much of my cock. It hurt to tear through her hy-

380

men, but the sheer pleasure dampened the pain. I began slowly pumping in and out, and her moans got louder. I knew she would orgasm quick, like before. By the time I began driving hard and fast into her tight pussy her body shook with a large orgasm. I left it inside for a moment to enjoy her quivers, but quickly moved to the next one.

I saw platinum blond hair and knew it was Sissy, and it excited me greatly. I knew Sissy would get my load. As my cock approached and touched her pussy she pulled me hard into her with her arms and legs. It shocked me as I tore through her hymen and plunged deep. She may have been virgin and young, but her desire was great. Her pussy felt like a raging furnace. I was also amazed that I sank full depth. She took all of me with a groan of ecstasy. I started pumping in and out, slowly at first. Her heels on my butt cheeks and her hands on the small of my back set our pace, and it was fast. I worked within her rhythm and was pounding her hard. She orgasmed with a scream and clamped down on my cock, but she never stopped humping and pulling me. I felt my balls tighten and I gushed my seed deep inside her. Her pussy milked my cock, and it felt fantastic. I lay over her and nursed her nipples, leaving my cock inside being massaged, until the girl next to us began to pull me toward her.

Tammy was the shy one but not anymore. She pulled me between her thighs. I must have shot a cup full of seed in Sissy, but my arousal remained very high and my cock jumped when I saw Tammy's pussy. It was very wet and her lips swollen with excitement. Tammy even grabbed my cock and guided it to her pussy. Ok, she wanted it, I would give it to her. I grabbed her hips and drove my cock in. I didn't feel much of a restriction, only slightly. If I had known that I wouldn't have driven so hard. It didn't seem to bother her, however. Her groans matched my thrusts, and my thrusts were fast and hard. When she climaxed her eyes rolled back in her head and she passed out, falling limp on the bed. Her legs dropped to the floor, and I was still inside her. I knew the Viagra I took would make me last much longer than I could normally. I got mischievous and wondered if she could orgasm again, even passed out. Since I was still in her tight pussy, I kept pumping into her. I lifted her legs over my arms and pounded hard, while I watched her. At first her body continued to feel limp, but the longer I pumped, the more animated her body became. Soon she was awake and screaming and flooded my cock with hot juice. As I pulled out I saw Bess dive in for a feast. Tammy just smiled and lay back to enjoy Bess' attention.

I moved between those beautiful lean, ebony thighs. Her honey hole was already dripping nectar. I thought about tasting it again, but my smaller head was beginning to rule me again. I placed my cock between her puffy lips, slid my hands up to grip her hip and pushed in. I failed to break through, so I gripped harder and drove deep. Sarah squealed in pain, but I held still to let her get used to it inside, which she quickly did. She began pushing against my cock, so I began pumping in and out. Her thighs began to quiver, hell everything began to quiver. My pace was relentless now, pounding hard and fast. I was glad she was slick, because she was tight as a vise. She orgasmed extremely hard and screamed along with it. I was excited with the intensity of her climax, and if I hadn't just climaxed, her orgasm would have set me off again. After she relaxed to recover, I pulled out and moved down the line.

The last remaining virgin was Karrie, the hot one. I knew she would orgasm fast and maybe multiple times. This one had some built up passion inside her wanting to get out. I aimed my cock at her spread pussy lips and drove in. She grunted, but not in pain. It was a welcome grunt of passion. I started pumping fast, like Nancy calls rabbit-fucking. Karrie tried to pull me completely inside her pussy. Her arms and legs flailed about in an instant orgasm that turned into another, then, incredibly, a third and fourth. I think I would have just kept going, but Nancy stopped me.

Nancy grabbed me around the waist and said, "Let her recover stud."

I had worked myself to favor pitch again, but I heard Nancy and pulled out. I hoped it wasn't over. They had all now lost their virginity, but I needed more relief, a lot more.

Nancy said to the girls, "We will try a different position now. Get on your knees at the edge of the bed. This is called the dogie position."

Yes, omg yes. What a beautiful sight to see. I was on fire with desire and plunged my cock into the closest girl. I was beyond worrying about them. I held her hips and drove my cock like a jackhammer into pussy after pussy. I don't know if they had orgasms, but I think they all did. I just kept moving up and down the line multiple times. I felt another orgasm coming and unloaded in one of the tightest and hottest pussy. I'm not sure who it was, nor did it matter at this point. I was tired and headed to the other bed to get my breath. Nancy came to check on me and grabbed my cock.

Nancy smiled and said to the girls, "He is still hard if any of you want to try riding his cock."

Sissy was the first one to jump on the bed. She took hold of my cock and plunged her mouth down on it. She didn't have any technique at all, but she sure had the willingness. She sucked on it for a few strokes then tossed her leg over mine, guided my cock into her pussy and forced herself down on it. She began riding my cock like she was on a horse at full gallop. Sissy kept it up until she had a shuddering orgasm and fell off to the side, leaving my cock pointing straight in the air.

It took only a few second before I felt another hot pussy sinking down on it. I opened my eyes and saw that it was Karrie. She had her eyes shut tight, enjoying my cock inside her. She ground her pussy on my cock and started bouncing up and down on it. Her scream told me she climaxed, but she kept going. She screamed two more times before Nancy made her get off. I was liking this.

They each took a turn riding me, driving me wild, but when Sarah plunged down on me to my base, I was so hot. I started driving hard up into her, bouncing her in the air. My orgasm hit me hard, and I dare say it hit her as well. We exploded together, and my scream joined hers. That Viagra

384

really does work. I don't know how many times I came, but I felt my cock deflating … finally. I think that if I hadn't looked over at the other bed I might have gone right to sleep, but noooo, I had to look. I saw a tangle of beautiful, naked bodies, but what got my attention was Bess. Her legs were spread wide and Sissy was lying flat between them in the process of totally devouring Bess' pussy, and it looked like Sissy was thoroughly enjoying it. The site of their passion and Sissy's muscular butt and legs aimed directly at me made me instantly hard again. I jumped up and straddled Sissy's legs, spread her cheeks and plunged right in. Sissy squealed into Bess' pussy but never pulled away. She continued to ravish Bess' pussy in earnest, while I pistoned into her. I reached under her chest to hold her firm breasts as I pounded against her cheeks. I was driving Sissy's face harder into Bess' pussy, which Bess seemed to love. This was so erotic that I found a final explosion in my balls. There probably wasn't much ejection, but my jerking cock didn't care. This time my cock deflated inside her, and I left them and went back to my bed. I was done for sure. Nancy and Sue slipped in tight beside me and we drifted off to sleep wrapped together.

I didn't bother to set the alarm, and as predicted, I woke up late … really late. I was not alone, however. Nancy and Sue awoke as I started moving. Sue spoke first.

Sue said, "Mike, that was sooooo hot last night. I watched it all, and I think Bess got her fill, finely, and found a girl-friend in the process."

I looked over and saw Bess and Sissy all wrapped up together, their faces pressed into each other's. I laughed and Nancy joined me. I said, "Nancy, last night was fun, but please don't volunteer me to introduce sex to six virgins again, especially with Viagra. My dick is extremely sore, and I won't be able to use it for a while." Nancy and Sue busted out laughing.

Nancy said, "I promise. I got very aroused watching you last night, and wanted sex myself and had to go without. I'll be wanting sex again, too. I don't like going without, so I won't volunteer you … much."

We were already more than late for the morning meeting, so there was no need to hurry. The other girls were all still sacked out, so I settled back to hold my girls close. It was then that Sue shocked the hell out of me.

Sue turned her head and looked at me and said, "You do know that none of these ex-sisters and Sissy, for that matter, are on birth control, and some are most likely pregnant from last night's escapade."

I blurted out, "Crap! I hadn't even thought about that. What should we do?"

Nancy said, "Nothing. I'm sure they thought about it and must not care. I know the Blues want to get pregnant and probably most of the women here. It's what we need to do, propagate for the next generation. Sue and I want your children, too. You may eventually have a bunch of kids running around here … stud."

I didn't know what to think about these new revelations. It certainly was a surprise to me, but I guess Nancy was right. I was still smiling as we headed to the shower. I also noticed that Nancy and Sue seemed content that I didn't freak out.

When we were finished with the shower we started cycling the girls in as well. Nancy, Sue and I kind of gave each other a surprised look when Bess and Sissy went off to the shower hand in hand. I guess they did make a connection.

When everyone was finished and dressed we took off for the cafe. I guess there were no secrets in our compound, because all were staring at our group, and I got quite a few knowing smiles, both men and women. I tried to act nonchalant, but I'm sure my blush gave me away. Still, I was famished and dug into my brunch with a frenzy.

Nancy had called Marshal Brady to come get the girls before we came down, and he joined us. I asked, "How are the sisters errr, I mean ladies? Did you get them all settled in?

Brady said, "Oh, yeah, they stirred up a lot of attention when we brought them in, but the colonel had spoken to soldiers. They will be fine, and they won't have any trouble or lack of attention. Are these girls ready?"

I smiled and said, "These girls are great. Girls, are you ready to go live with the Army?" It surprised me, but they all smiled and looked excited." They all came to me and gave me a big hug and kiss as they filed out behind Marshal Brady. The cafe patrons took it all in, much to my embarrassment.

387

Mary came up to us as they left and said, "I put the Johnson family up with James last night, since the boys seemed to have taken up with the chicken twins and cowboy, and the girls seem to be hitting it off with James and one of his ranchers." I must have had a stupid look on my face to which Mary said, "The Johnson family, siblings of Sissy. She can move in with them, too."

Sissy clung to Bess and said, "I'm not going anywhere. I'm staying with Bess. Is that right, Bess?"

Bess gave us a pleading look and said, "Yes, Sissy. You can stay with us."

I looked at Nancy and Sue and just shrugged my shoulders, as if to say, *"It's OK with me if it's OK with you two."*

Nancy said, "That's fine." She then leaned to me and said, "I didn't tell you but Sissy and at least two of the sisters are in their ovulation cycle. Sissy is probably pregnant with your child already with as much seed as you pumped into her last night. She might as well stay, and Bess seems to want it."

I was a little shaken with that bit of news, but I said, "OK Sissy, but you better go talk to your brothers and sisters and explain what you're doing. I don't want your brothers coming after me for taking advantage of you."

Sissy laughed and said, "I think it is the other way around. I think I took advantage of you, and I will probably do it again. But, I will go talk to them. Want to come along, Bess?"

Bess smiled and quickly got up. They took off together holding hands. Bess seemed to be really smitten with Sissy, and Sissy was evidently feeling the same about Bess. Nancy, Sue and I just looked at each other, no longer surprised at the turn of events.

We had just settled back and was enjoying our second cup of coffee when a smiling Brin bounced into the chair next to me. He was quickly followed by Meg, Peg, Tina, Flay, and the orange haired Trix. I knew something was up, because Brin seldom smiles.

Brin could hardly contain himself and blurted, "Our race has been saved ... partly anyway. Tina ran some test on Meg and Peg, and they are both impregnated!" When I looked confused he continued, "They are going to have a child. Our race can now continue."

I guess I still didn't grasp the meaning, So Sue said, "Duh. Mike, don't you get it? You impregnated them and they are going to have your babies."

I said, "How do you know I impregnated them?"

Tina said, "They are impregnated with your DNA. DNA doesn't lie."

Brin said, "We now know our races can crossbreed, at least with your sperm, anyway. This is very good news for our race. Since it worked with Meg and Peg, Flay, Tina and Trix are most enthusiastic for you to impregnate them also."

I'm not sure what kind of expression I was sporting, maybe shock, maybe fear; but both Nancy and Sue burst out laughing at my apparent stupid look. I didn't know what to say, but I certainly wasn't anxious to enter another sex marathon so soon, certainly after last night. I mean my dick was really sore.

Nancy saw my dilemma and saved me from having to say anything. Nancy said, "Brin, we are happy for your people. We are all glad that it is going to work out well for your race, but Mike will have to wait another day. Bring the girls over tomorrow night and bring Blane with them."

That seemed to satisfy the blue girls and I noticed a gleam in Brin's eyes as well. I know putting it off another day certainly pleased me; even though my small head twitched at the thought of being with these beautiful blue ladies. Brin and the girls thanked us and scurried off, no doubt to brag to others of their team. That could be a really scary thought if the blue girls all wanted me to impregnate them. I'm sure many other men could impregnate them and would love to get the chance. The Blue Team would discover that soon enough.

I suddenly realized what I had thought. I was going to be a father ... evidently a father of several children with many different women. Damn, I was becoming the sire of a clan. But, it got worse or better, depending on how you looked at it.

Nancy and Sue were smiling and staring at me, and Nancy said, "Bess, Sue and I have been talking, and we are going to stop taking our birth control pills. We want to be impregnated, also. We want to bear your children."

It had finally settled into my mind, and I liked the idea. I started laughing and said, "I feel like a racehorse being put out for stud, but I would love to

390

impregnate you three, the ones I care most about in this crazy, topsy-turvy world.

We decided to spend the rest of the day touring all the facilities and operation. We were quite impressed with the efficiency and production output of all department, and everyone was happy to see us and our interest in their departments. We had chosen the members well. I'm glad we took the tour. It gave us confidence in our ultimate survival.

Chapter 17
(A Promising Future)

After a very productive and rewarding tour of the facilities and a restful sleep, we were all up with the alarm and ready. We had some quality cuddling time with no sex. Well, no sex that I was involved in. Bess and Sissy kept us awake with their giggling for quite a while, since they were apparently still on their honeymoon in the other bed, but that activity finally died down to random coos and kisses. We all eventually faded into welcome sleep.

We were anxious for today, because after several days we were finally going to meet for a full review from all departments at the morning meeting. Nancy had even invited Marshal Brady and Colonel Kline to the meeting.

The weather had turned a little on the chilly side during our tour, so I finally graduated from shorts to longer Docker pants, but I refused to give up my polo shirt. I did, however, slip on a light sweater before we headed down to the cafe.

Bob was in his usual jovial mood, and I noticed him patting a smiling blue, female cook on her behind. Yep, something was going on there. We got our breakfast and on the way to a table we noticed a smiling Marshal Brady waving us over to join them. Colonel Kline was also there, but he seemed to be somewhere else mentally. His eyes seemed unfocused and he had a huge shit-eating grin on his face.

I looked at Marshal Brady as if to say, *"What the hell is up with him?"*

Marshal Brady laughed and quietly said, "I don't know what you did to those five sisters, but they are wild. Thank you, whatever you did. As soon as I returned to Camp Gruber with them Kerri and Tammy latched on to Colonel Kline and wouldn't be budged. They let it be known that they intended to live with him. It shocked the hell out of the old man, but as you can see, he must enjoy their attention. He hasn't stopped smiling since."

I said, "What about Tina, Kathy and Sarah?"

Marshal Brady blushed brightly and said, "Well, those three latched on to me. I think I will have to pick only one. They almost killed me last night. I don't know what you did, but they are like nymphs. They can't get enough."

Nancy said, "We just showed them the way and what they were missing."

Brady grinned and said, "Well, you sure did a good job."

We finished our breakfast and headed to the Conference Room, which was filling up fast. For the first time we had to bring additional chairs in to accommodate everyone. When all were settled, I said, "Welcome everyone. It looks like we have a full staff now, and it is time to analyze our status. Who wants to go first?"

Brin stood and said, "I want to thank all members of this community for making us, the Blue Team as you call us, welcome here. Our original purpose in coming here was to insure our survival

393

as a race. This has been realized with the fertilization of some of our females. We will survive."

"All our Blue Team members have been awakened and have joined with the human departments. My team supervisors report that we have all been assimilated into the various departments and production is high. In some cases we have brought new knowledge and departments into operation, like our underwater fish herding and water grown vegetable production. Blane reports our fish stock and water plants we brought are thriving in this lake and many trees and bushes are also thriving in Bess' fantastic Greenhouse. Additionally, our proposes have been successful in herding many of the native fish into traps."

"All in all, we are very pleased to be here and are optimistic about our survival"

"Oh, Peg and Dam Mark were successful in destroying the bridges targeted, and they report that most of the traffic has been diverted in other direction."

Robert stood next and said, "I can confirm that the discussed bridges have been destroyed, and we are monitoring the traffic flow. Taking the bridges out has indeed altered the flow and had, for the most part, the desired effect. We are continuing to monitor the migration activities and will report any problems."

"Trix and her security team are a welcome addition to our security and have reinforced security greatly. They are interfacing well, with the exception of the canine dogs, but once the dogs get used to us it should work well. We have full camera, infrared and motion sensor coverage of our perimeter and bay, roving canine teams patrolling, various sentry towers, and security boats at the ready to divert bay-side intrusions. Our mainline defense remains with the Castle roof-top Rail Gun and EMP Gun."

"We haven't had much trouble. We have had confrontations, but most disperse when we show force. Sadly, however, we have killed some roaming bands that tried to gain entrance. We figure that if they cut fences at night to gain access or fire shots at our security team, they are up to no good and are fair game. We act quickly and decisively."

"Almost all members are cross-trained and have been attending Bess' hand-to-hand combat training classes and JJ's firing range. We now have a current defense force and back-up capable of repelling most any attacks, plus we have the support of Camp Gruber's attack helicopter force and our own attack saucers to launch against any attacks. In short, we can and are defending ourselves."

James stood next and said, "Our farming operation is fully staffed and established. All the allocated farming fields are either already supporting crops or prepared to be planted. We have also already expanded our fencing and irrigation systems and cleared other fields. By next summer we will be fully supporting our required food production needs. We have also began to clear and plow fields at Camp Gruber for their food production. The twins' chicken house is already fully providing our egg requirements and in a few months our chicken needs as well. Hog, cattle and sheep product is on schedule. Bess' greenhouse is already providing an abundant supply of vegetables, and it's just starting. Blane's underwater operation can supply far more fish than we can use. Milk harvest is more than required, and they have begun developing cheese, butter and other dairy products that can be stored. In short, our future supply of food looks fantastic."

Jeremy took the next presentation time. Jeremy stood and said, "All mechanical, electrical, waste handling and water production is going well. Everything is built and operating, and we are mostly on maintenance mode; however, our electricians are modifying the electric grid to power outside our complex. Soon Camp Gruber and any others along the grid will receive power for their complex so they can shut down their generator and save diesel fuel. We are also open to helping out others in need of extra manpower. Just ask."

Mary stood next and said, "You said we are fully staffed, but we have no Chaplin yet. As we all know, our community is not what we would call an overly religious community, but I do get request concerning counseling and spiritual needs. I've also been asked about church services, and it is reasonable to assume many within our group at some point in the future will want to be formally married. I know that the Chaplin scheduled to interview with Nancy didn't show up, and it is probably too late to recruit a Chaplin at this late date; but I wanted the group to know that there still exists a need."

Colonel Kline interrupted saying, "I think this is something we may be able to help with. As an emergency disaster group established by FEMA we were required for our staff to have several Chaplains. We can transfer one to your community if you like."

Nancy said, "That's great Colonel Kline. Please, send him or her over to talk with us."

Colonel Kline said, "Yes. We have several. I will send a couple of them to pick from."

Mary continued, "Well, that problem solved. Now as to the Castle, everything else is going great. We still have quite a few unoccupied rooms. I guess this board will eventually answer this questions. Other than these items mentioned I have no other concerns."

Bob stood next and said, "Our cafeteria is feeding all residents, and most of the food is coming from our own food production. The storerooms are brimming with supplies. I don't think anyone is going without. Still, I have a problem with wasted food. I'm getting pretty vocal about this waste, and I would appreciate all department heads to talk to their people and tell them not to pick up food if they can't eat it. The hogs like the extra food, but we need to conserve. I'm at full staff, and we are handling the load quite well. Soon we will expand our menu to include dishes made and provided by the Blue Team cooks. They like our human food, so maybe we will like theirs."

Colonel Kline waited to see if any others stood, and when no one did he stood and said, "We at Camp Gruber appreciate all you have done to help us. I'm not sure we would or could survive without your help and assistance. Our survival plans, as designed, were only short term plans. I don't think there were any long term plans considered, but with your help, I believe we too will survive. You can count on our help for anything. James has already began building planting fields, and Jeremy has offered assistance in installing security fencing. We will be sending a security team out to obtain material soon."

I waited to see if any others wanted to speak then said, "These reports all sound fantastic. I believe, barring unforeseen circumstances, we will survive. I'm sure we will be forced to deal with many other problems in the future, and we will have to deal with them as they come. I now declare Phase I of our Apocalypse Project a complete success." Cheers rang out in the conference room, but my mind shot forward to a time when I would have so many children running around the complex. I'm sure that would be one or many of the future challenges we would have to face.

The End of Phase I

www.ingramcontent.com/pod-product-compliance
Lightning Source LLC
Chambersburg PA
CBHW011402010726
47495CB00009B/2734